OLD MAN'S WAR

OLD MAN'S
WAR

John Scalzi

A TOM DOHERTY ASSOCIATES BOOK
NEW YORK

OLD MAN'S WAR

Edited by Patrick Nielsen Hayden

A Tor Book
Published by Tom Doherty Associates, LLC
175 Fifth Avenue
New York, NY 10010

www.tor.com

Tor® is a registered trademark of Tom Doherty Associates, LLC.

Library of Congress Cataloging-in-Publication Data

Scalzi, John, 1969-
   Old man's war / John Scalzi.—1st ed.
      p. cm.
   "A Tom Doherty Associates book."
   ISBN 0-765-30940-8 (acid-free paper)
   EAN 978-0765-30940-2
      1. Life on other planets—Fiction.   2. Space colonies—Fiction.   3. Space warfare—
Fiction.   4. Older men—Fiction.   5. Soldiers—Fiction.   I. Title.

PS3619.C256O43 2005
813'.6—dc22

                                                                        2004057953

First Edition: January 2005

Printed in the United States of America

0   9   8   7   6   5   4   3   2   1

To Regan Avery, first reader extraordinaire,
And always to Kristine and Athena.

PART I

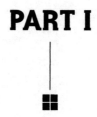

PART 1

ONE I did two things on my seventy-fifth birthday. I visited my wife's grave. Then I joined the army.

Visiting Kathy's grave was the less dramatic of the two. She's buried in Harris Creek Cemetery, not more than a mile down the road from where I live and where we raised our family. Getting her into the cemetery was more difficult than perhaps it should have been; neither of us expected needing the burial, so neither of us made the arrangements. It's somewhat mortifying, to use a rather apt word, to have to argue with a cemetery manager about your wife not having made a reservation to be buried. Eventually my son, Charlie, who happens to be mayor, cracked a few heads and got the plot. Being the father of the mayor has its advantages.

So, the grave. Simple and unremarkable, with one of those small markers instead of a big headstone. As a contrast, Kathy lies next to Sandra Cain, whose rather oversized headstone is polished black granite, with Sandy's high school photo and some maudlin quote from Keats about the death of youth and beauty sand-blasted into the front. That's Sandy all over. It would have amused Kathy to know Sandra was parked next to her with her big dramatic headstone; all their lives Sandy nurtured an entertainingly passive-aggressive competition with her. Kathy would come to the local bake sale with a pie, Sandy would bring three and simmer, not so subtly, if Kathy's pie sold first. Kathy would attempt to solve the problem by preemptively buying one of Sandy's pies. It's hard to say whether this actually made things better or worse, from Sandy's point of view.

I suppose Sandy's headstone could be considered the last word in the matter, a final show-up that could not be rebutted, because, after all, Kathy was already dead. On the other hand, I don't actually recall anyone visiting Sandy. Three months after Sandy passed, Steve Cain sold the house and moved to Arizona with a smile as wide as Interstate 10 plastered on his skull. He sent me a postcard some time later; he was shacking up with a woman down there who had been a porn star fifty years earlier. I felt unclean for a week after getting that bit of information. Sandy's kids and grandkids live one town over, but they might as well be in Arizona for as often as they visit. Sandy's Keats quote probably hadn't been read by anyone since the funeral but me, in passing, as I move the few feet over to my wife.

Kathy's marker has her name (Katherine Rebecca Perry), her dates, and the words: BELOVED WIFE AND MOTHER. I read those words over and over every time I visit. I can't help it; they are four words that so inadequately and so perfectly sum up a life. The phrase tells you nothing about her, about how she met each day or how she worked, about what her interests were or where she liked to travel. You'd never know what her favorite color was, or how she liked to wear her hair, or how she voted, or what her sense of humor was. You'd know nothing about her except that she was loved. And she was. She'd think that was enough.

I hate visiting here. I hate that my wife of forty-two years is dead, that one minute one Saturday morning she was in the kitchen, mixing a bowl of waffle batter and talking to me about the dustup at the library board meeting the night before, and the next minute she was on the floor, twitching as the stroke tore through her brain. I hate that her last words were "Where the hell did I put the vanilla."

I hate that I've become one of those old men who visits a cemetery to be with his dead wife. When I was (much) younger I used to ask Kathy what the point would be. A pile of rotting meat and bones that used to be a person isn't a person anymore; it's just a pile of rotting meat and bones. The person is gone—off to heaven or hell or wherever or nowhere. You might as well visit a side of beef. When you get older you realize this is still the case. You just don't care. It's what you have.

For as much as I hate the cemetery, I've been grateful it's here, too. I miss my wife. It's easier to miss her at a cemetery, where she's never been anything but dead, than to miss her in all the places where she was alive.

I didn't stay long; I never do. Just long enough to feel the stab that's still fresh enough after most of eight years, the one that also serves to remind me that I've got other things to do than to stand around in a cemetery like an old, damned fool. Once I felt it, I turned around and left and didn't bother looking around. This was the last time I would ever visit the cemetery or my wife's grave, but I didn't want to expend too much effort in trying to remember it. As I said, this is the place where she's never been anything but dead. There's not much value in remembering that.

Although come to think of it, signing up for the army wasn't all that dramatic either.

My town was too small for its own recruiting office. I had to drive into Greenville, the county seat, to sign up. The recruiting office was a small storefront in a nondescript strip mall; there was a state liquor authority store on one side of it and a tattoo parlor on the other. Depending on what order you went into each, you could wake up the next morning in some serious trouble.

The inside of the office was even less appealing, if that's possible. It consisted of a desk with a computer and a printer, a human behind that desk, two chairs in front of the desk and six chairs lining a wall. A small table in front of those chairs held recruiting information and some back issues of *Time* and *Newsweek*. Kathy and I had been in here a decade earlier, of course; I suspect nothing had been moved, much less changed, and that included the magazines. The human appeared to be new. At least I don't remember the previous recruiter having that much hair. Or breasts.

The recruiter was busy typing something on the computer and didn't bother to look up as I came in. "Be right with you," she muttered, by way of a more or less Pavlovian response to the door opening.

"Take your time," I said. "I know the place is packed." This attempt at marginally sarcastic humor went ignored and unappreciated, which has been par for the course for the last few years; good to see I had not lost my form. I sat down in front of the desk and waited for the recruiter to finish whatever she was doing.

"You coming or going?" she asked, still without actually looking up at me.

"Pardon me?" I said.

"Coming or going," she repeated. "Coming in to do your Intent to Join sign-up, or going out to start your term?"

"Ah. Going out, please."

This finally got her to look at me, squinting out through a rather severe pair of glasses. "You're John Perry," she said.

"That's me. How did you guess?"

She looked back to her computer. "Most people who want to enlist come in on their birthday, even though they have thirty days afterward to formally enlist. We only have three birthdays today. Mary Valory already called to say she won't be going. And you don't look like you'd be Cynthia Smith."

"I'm gratified to hear that," I said.

"And since you're not coming in for an initial sign-up," she continued, ignoring yet another stab at humor, "it stands to reason you're John Perry."

"I could just be a lonely old man wandering around looking for conversation," I said.

"We don't get many of those around here," she said. "They tend to be scared off by the kids next door with the demon tattoos." She finally pushed her keyboard away and gave me her full attention. "Now, then. Let's see some ID, please."

"But you already know who I am," I reminded her.

"Let's be sure," she said. There was not even the barest hint of a smile when she said this. Dealing with garrulous old farts every day had apparently taken its toll.

I handed over my driver's license, birth certificate and national identity card. She took them, reached into her desk for a handpad, plugged it into the computer and slid it over to me. I placed my hand on it palm down and waited for the scan to finish. She took the pad and slid my ID card down the side to match the print information. "You're John Perry," she said, finally.

"And now we're back where we started," I said.

She ignored me again. "Ten years ago during your Intent to Join orientation session, you were provided information concerning the Colonial Defense Forces, and the obligations and duties you would assume by joining the CDF," she said, in the tone of voice which indicated that she said this at least once a day, every day, most of her working life. "Additionally, in the interim period, you have been sent refresher materials to remind you of the obligations and duties you would be assuming.

"At this point, do you need additional information or a refresher presentation, or do you declare that you fully understand the obligations and duties you are about to assume? Be aware there is no penalty either for asking for refresher materials or opting not to join the CDF at this time."

I recalled the orientation session. The first part consisted of a bunch of senior citizens sitting on folding chairs at the Greenville Community Center, eating donuts and drinking coffee and listening to a CDF apparatchik drone on about the history of human colonies. Then he handed out pamphlets on CDF service life, which appeared to be much like military life anywhere. During the question and answer session we found out he wasn't actually in the CDF; he'd just been hired to provide presentations in the Miami valley area.

The second part of the orientation session was a brief medical exam—a doctor came in and took blood, swabbed the inside of my cheek to dislodge some cells, and gave me a brain scan. Apparently I passed. Since then, the pamphlet I was provided at the orientation session was sent to me once a year through the mail. I started throwing it out after the second year. I hadn't read it since.

"I understand," I said.

She nodded, reached into her desk, pulled out a piece of paper and a pen, and handed both to me. The paper held several paragraphs, each with a space for a signature underneath. I recognized the paper; I had signed another, very similar paper ten years earlier to indicate that I understood what I would be getting into a decade in the future.

"I'm going to read to you each of the following paragraphs," she said. "At the end of each paragraph, if you understand and accept what has been read to you, please sign and date on the line immediately following the paragraph. If you have questions, please ask them at the end of each paragraph reading. If you do not subsequently understand or do not accept what has been read and explained to you, do not sign. Do you understand?"

"I understand," I said.

"Very good," she said. "Paragraph one: I the undersigned acknowledge and understand that I am freely and of my own will and without coercion volunteering to join the Colonial Defense Forces for a term of service of not less than two years in length. I additionally understand that the term of service may be extended unilaterally by the Colonial Defense Forces for up to eight additional years in times of war and duress."

This "ten years total" extension clause was not news to me—I did read the information I was sent, once or twice—although I wondered how many people glossed over it, and of those who didn't, how many people actually thought they'd be stuck in the service ten years. My feeling on it was that the CDF wouldn't ask for ten years if it didn't feel it was going to need them. Because of the Quarantine Laws, we don't hear much about colonial wars. But what we do hear is enough to know it's not peacetime out there in the universe.

I signed.

"Paragraph two: I understand that by volunteering to join the Colonial Defense Forces, I agree to bear arms and to use them against the enemies of the Colonial Union, which may include other human forces. I may not during the term of my service refuse to bear and use arms as ordered or cite religious or moral objections to such actions in order to avoid combat service."

How many people volunteer for an army and then claim conscientious objector status? I signed.

"Paragraph three: I understand and agree that I will faithfully and with all deliberate speed execute orders and directives provided to me by superior officers, as provided for in the Uniform Code of Colonial Defense Forces Conduct."

I signed.

"Paragraph four: I understand that by volunteering for the Colonial Defense Forces, I consent to whatsoever medical, surgical or therapeutic regimens or procedures are deemed necessary by the Colonial Defense Forces to enhance combat readiness."

Here it was: Why I and countless other seventy-five-year-olds signed up every year.

I once told my grandfather that by the time I was his age they'd have figured out a way to dramatically extend the human life span. He laughed at me and told me that's what he had assumed, too, and yet there he was, an old man anyway. And here I am as well. The problem with aging is not that it's one damn thing after another—it's every damn thing, all at once, all the time.

You can't stop aging. Gene therapies and replacement organs and plastic surgery give it a good fight. But it catches up with you anyway. Get a new lung, and your heart blows a valve. Get a new heart, and your liver swells up to the size of an inflatable kiddie pool. Change out your liver, a stroke gives you a whack. That's aging's trump card; they still can't replace brains.

Life expectancy climbed up near the ninety-year mark a while back, and that's where it's been ever since. We eked out almost another score from the "three score and ten" and then God seems to have put his foot down. People can live longer, and do live longer—but they still live those years as an old person. Nothing much has ever changed about that.

Look, you: When you're twenty-five, thirty-five, forty-five or even fifty-five, you can still feel good about your chances to take on the world. When you're sixty-five and your body is looking down the road at imminent physical ruin, these mysterious "medical, surgical and therapeutic regimens and procedures" begin to sound interesting. Then you're seventy-five, friends are dead, and you've replaced at least one major organ; you have to pee four times a night, and you can't go up a flight of stairs without being a little winded—and you're told you're in pretty good shape for your age.

Trading that in for a decade of fresh life in a combat zone begins to look like a hell of a bargain. Especially because if you don't, in a decade you'll be eighty-five, and then the only difference between you and a raisin will be that while you're both wrinkled and without a prostate, the raisin never had a prostate to begin with.

So how does the CDF manage to reverse the flow of aging? No one down here knows. Earthside scientists can't explain how they do it, and can't replicate their successes, though it's not for the lack of trying. The CDF doesn't operate on-planet, so you can't ask a CDF veteran. However, the CDF only recruits on-planet, so the colonists don't know, either, even if you could ask them, which you can't. Whatever therapies the CDF performs are done off-world, in the CDF's own authority zones, away from the purview of global and national governments. So no help from Uncle Sam or anyone else.

Every once in a while, a legislature or president or dictator decides to ban CDF recruiting until it reveals its secrets. The CDF never argues; it packs up and goes. Then all the seventy-five-year-olds in that country take long international vacations from which they never return. The CDF offers no explanations, no rationales, no clues. If you want to find out how they make people young again, you have to sign up.

I signed.

"Paragraph five: I understand that by volunteering for the Colonial Defense Forces, I am terminating my citizenship in my national political entity, in this case the United States of America, and also the Residential Franchise that allows me to reside on the planet Earth. I understand that my citizenship will henceforth be transferred generally to the Colonial Union and specifically to the

Colonial Defense Forces. I further recognize and understand that by terminating my local citizenship and planetary Residential Franchise, I am barred from subsequent return to Earth and, upon completion of my term of service within the Colonial Defense Forces, will be relocated to whatsoever colony I am allotted by the Colonial Union and/or the Colonial Defense Forces."

More simply put: You can't go home again. This is part and parcel of the Quarantine Laws, which were imposed by the Colonial Union and the CDF, officially at least, to protect Earth from any more xenobiological disasters like The Crimp. Folks on the Earth were all for it at the time. Funny how insular a planet will become when a third of its male population permanently loses its fertility within the space of a year. People here are less enthused about it now—they've gotten bored with Earth and want to see the rest of the universe, and they've forgotten all about childless Great Uncle Walt. But the CU and CDF are the only ones with spaceships that have the skip drives that make interstellar travel possible. So there it is.

(This makes the agreement to colonize where the CU tells you to colonize something of a moot point—since they're the only ones with the ships, you go where they take you anyway. It's not as if they're going to let you drive the starship.)

A side effect of the Quarantine Laws and the skip drive monopoly is to make communication between Earth and the colonies (and between the colonies themselves) all but impossible. The only way to get a timely response from a colony is to put a message onto a ship with a skip drive; the CDF will grudgingly carry messages and data for planetary governments this way, but anyone else is out of luck. You could put up a radio dish and wait for communication signals from the colonies to wash by, but Alpha, the closest colony to Earth, is eighty-three light-years away. This makes lively gossip between planets difficult.

I've never asked, but I would imagine that it is this paragraph that causes the most people to turn back. It's one thing to think you want to be young again; it's quite another thing to turn your back on everything you've ever known, everyone you've ever met or loved, and every experience you've ever had over the span of seven and a half decades. It's a hell of a thing to say good-bye to your whole life.

I signed.

"Paragraph six—final paragraph," the recruiter said. "I recognize and understand that as of seventy-two hours of the final signing of this document, or my transport off Earth by the Colonial Defense Forces, whichever comes first, I will be presumed as deceased for the purposes of law in all relevant political entities, in this case the State of Ohio and the United States of America. Any and all assets remaining to me will be dispensed with according to law. All legal obligations or responsibilities that by law terminate at death will be so terminated. All previous legal records, be they meritorious or detrimental, will be hereby stricken, and all debts discharged according to law. I recognize and understand that if I have not yet arranged for the distribution of my assets, that at my request the Colonial Defense Forces will provide me with legal and financial counsel to do so within seventy-two hours."

I signed. I now had seventy-two hours to live. So to speak.

"What happens if I don't leave the planet within seventy-two hours?" I said as I handed the paper back to the recruiter.

"Nothing," she said, taking the form. "Except that since you're legally dead, all your belongings are split up according to your will, your health and life benefits are canceled or disbursed to your heirs and being legally dead, you have no legal right to protection under the law from everything from libel to murder."

"So someone could just come up and kill me, and there would be no legal repercussions?"

"Well, no," she said. "If someone were to murder you while you were legally dead, I believe that here in Ohio they could be tried for 'disturbing a corpse.' "

"Fascinating," I said.

"However," she continued, in her ever-more-distressing matter-of-fact tone, "it usually doesn't get that far. Anytime between now and the end of those seventy-two hours you can simply change your mind about joining. Just call me here. If I'm not here, an automated call responder will take your name. Once we've verified it's actually you requesting cancellation of enlistment, you'll be released from further obligation. Bear in mind that such cancellation permanently bars you from future enlistment. This is a onetime thing."

"Got it," I said. "Do you need to swear me in?"

"Nope," she said. "I just need to process this form and give you your ticket." She turned back to her computer, typed for a few minutes, and then pressed the ENTER key. "The computer is generating your ticket now," she said. "It'll be a minute."

"Okay," I said. "Mind if I ask you a question?"

"I'm married," she said.

"That wasn't what I was going to ask," I said. "Do people really proposition you?"

"All the time," she said. "It's really annoying."

"Sorry about that," I said. She nodded. "What I was going to ask was if you've actually ever met anyone from CDF."

"You mean apart from enlistees?" I nodded. "No. The CDF has a corporation down here that handles recruiting, but none of us are actual CDF. I don't think even the CEO is. We get all our information and materials from the Colonial Union embassy staff and not the CDF directly. I don't think they come Earthside at all."

"Does it bother you to work for an organization you never met?"

"No," she said. "The work is okay and the pay is surprisingly good, considering how little money they've put in to decorate around here. Anyway, you're going to join an organization you've never met. Doesn't that bother you?"

"No," I admitted. "I'm old, my wife is dead and there's not much reason to stay here anymore. Are you going to join when the time comes?"

She shrugged. "I don't mind getting old."

"I didn't mind getting old when I was young, either," I said. "It's the being old now that's getting to me."

Her computer printer made a quiet hum and a business card–like object came out. She took it and handed it to me. "This is your ticket," she said to me. "It identifies you as John Perry and a CDF recruit. Don't lose it. Your shuttle leaves from right in front of this office in three days to go to the Dayton Airport. It departs at 8:30 A.M.; we suggest you get here early. You'll be allowed only one carry-on bag, so please choose carefully among the things you wish to take.

"From Dayton, you'll take the eleven A.M. flight to Chicago and then the two P.M. delta to Nairobi from there. They're nine hours ahead in Nairobi, so you'll arrive there about midnight, local time. You'll be met by a CDF representative, and you'll have the option of either taking the two A.M. beanstalk to Colonial Station or getting some rest and taking the nine A.M. beanstalk. From there, you're in the CDF's hands."

I took the ticket. "What do I do if any of these flights is late or delayed?"

"None of these flights has ever experienced a single delay in the five years I've worked here," she said.

"Wow," I said. "I'll bet the CDF's trains run on time, too."

She looked at me blankly.

"You know," I said, "I've been trying to make jokes to you the entire time I've been here."

"I know," she said. "I'm sorry. My sense of humor was surgically removed as a child."

"Oh," I said.

"That was a joke," she said, and stood up, extending her hand.

"Oh." I stood up and took it.

"Congratulations, recruit," she said. "Good luck to you out there in the stars. I actually mean that," she added.

"Thank you," I said, "I appreciate it." She nodded, sat back down again, and flicked her eyes back to the computer. I was dismissed.

On the way out I saw an older woman walking across the parking lot toward the recruiting office. I walked over to her. "Cynthia Smith?" I asked.

"Yes," she said. "How did you know?"

"I just wanted to say happy birthday," I said, and then pointed upward. "And that maybe I'll see you again up there."

She smiled as she figured it out. Finally, I made someone smile that day. Things were looking up.

TWO Nairobi was launched from underneath us, and dropped away; we walked over to the side as if on a fast elevator (which is of course exactly what the beanstalk is) and watched the Earth begin its slide.

"They look like ants from up here!" Leon Deak cackled as he stood next to me. "Black ants!"

I had the strong urge to crack open a window and hurl Leon out of it. Alas, there was no window to crack; the beanstalk's "window" was the same diamond composite materials as the rest of the platform, made transparent so travelers could sightsee below them. The platform was airtight, which would be a handy thing in just a few minutes, when we were high enough up that cracking a window would lead to explosive decompression, hypoxia and death.

So Leon would not find himself making a sudden and entirely unexpected return to the Earth's embrace. More's the pity. Leon had attached himself to me in Chicago like a fat, brat-and-beer-filled tick; I was amazed that someone whose blood was clearly half pork grease had made it to age seventy-five. I spent part of the flight to Nairobi listening to him fart and expound darkly on his theory of the racial composition of the colonies. The farts were the most pleasant part of that monologue; never had I been so eager to purchase headphones for the in-flight entertainment.

I'd hoped to ditch him by opting to take the first 'stalk out of Nairobi. He seemed like the kind of guy who'd need a rest after busily passing gas all day. No such luck. The idea of spending another six hours with Leon and his farts was more than I could take; if the beanstalk platform *had* windows and I couldn't hurl Leon out of one, I might have jumped myself. Instead, I excused myself from Leon's presence by telling him the only thing that seemed to hold him at bay, which was by saying I had to go relieve myself. Leon grunted his permission. I wandered off counterclockwise, in the general direction of the rest rooms but more specifically to see if I could find a place where Leon might not find me.

This was not going to be easy to do. The 'stalk platform was donut-shaped, with a diameter of about one hundred feet. The "hole" of the donut, where the platform slid up the 'stalk, was about twenty feet wide. The cable's diameter was obviously slightly less than that; perhaps about eighteen feet, which if you thought about it hardly seemed thick enough for a cable several thousand miles long. The rest of the space was filled with comfortable booths and couches where people could sit and chat, and small areas where travelers could watch entertainment, play games or eat. And of course there were lots of window areas to look out of, either down to the Earth, across to other 'stalk cables and platforms, or up toward Colonial Station.

Overall the platform gave the impression of being the lobby of a pleasant economy hotel, suddenly launched toward geostationary orbit. The only problem was that the open design made it difficult to hide. The launch was not heavily subscribed; there weren't enough other passengers to hide by blending in. I finally decided to get something to drink at a kiosk near the center of the platform, roughly opposite of where Leon was standing. Sight lines being what they were, that's where I stood the best chance of avoiding him the longest.

Leaving Earth physically had been an irritating thing, thanks to Leon's obnoxiousness, but leaving it emotionally had been surprisingly easy. I had decided a year before my departure that, yes, I *would* join the CDF; from there it was simply a matter of making arrangements and saying good-byes. When Kathy and I had originally decided to join up a decade earlier, we put the house in our son Charlie's name as well as our own, so that he could take possession of it without having to go through probate. Kathy and I otherwise owned nothing of any real value, just the bric-a-brac that you pile up in a life. Most of the really nice stuff was dispersed to friends and family over the last year; Charlie would deal with the rest of it later.

Leaving people was not that much harder. People reacted to the news with varying levels of surprise and sadness, since everyone knows that once you join the Colonial Defense Forces, you don't come back. But it's not entirely like dying. They know that somewhere out there, you're still alive; heck, maybe after a while, they might even come and join you. It's a little what I imagine people felt hundreds of years ago when someone they knew hitched up a wagon and headed west. They cried, they missed them, they got back to what they were doing.

Anyway, I told people a whole year before I left that I was going. That's a lot of time to say what you have to say, to settle matters and to make your peace with someone. Over the course of the year, I had had a few sit-downs with old friends and family and did a final poking of old wounds and ashes; in nearly every case it ended well. A couple of times I asked forgiveness for things I didn't particularly feel sorry about, and in one case I found myself in bed with someone who otherwise I'd rather I hadn't. But you do what you have to do to give people closure; it makes them feel better and it doesn't cost you much to do it. I'd rather apologize for something I didn't really care about, and leave someone on Earth wishing me well, than to be stubborn and have that someone hoping that some alien would slurp out my brains. Call it karmic insurance.

Charlie had been my major concern. Like many fathers and sons, we'd had our go-rounds; I wasn't the most attentive father, and he wasn't the most self-directed son, wandering through life well into his thirties. When he originally found out that Kathy and I intended to join, he'd exploded at us. He reminded us that we'd protested against the Subcontinental War. He reminded us that we'd always taught him violence wasn't the answer. He reminded us that we'd once grounded him for a month when he'd gone out target shooting with Bill Young, which we both thought was a little odd for a man of thirty-five to bring up.

Kathy's death ended most of our battles, because both he and I realized that most of the things we argued about simply didn't matter; I was a widower and he a bachelor, and for a while he and I were all we had left. Not long thereafter he met and married Lisa, and about a year after that he became a father and was re-elected mayor all in one very hectic night. Charlie had been a late bloomer, but it was a fine bloom. He and I had our own sit-down where I apologized for some things (sincerely), and also told him equally sincerely how proud I was of the man he'd become. Then we sat on the porch with our beers, watched my grandson Adam swat a t-ball in the front yard, and talked about nothing of any importance for a nice long time. When we parted, we parted well and with love, which is what you want between fathers and sons.

I stood there by the kiosk, nursing my Coke and thinking about Charlie and his family, when I heard Leon's voice grumbling, followed by another voice, low, sharp and female, saying something in response. In spite of myself, I peered over past the kiosk. Leon had apparently managed to corner some poor woman and was no doubt sharing whatever dumb-ass theory his beef-witted brain stem was promulgating at the moment. My sense of chivalry overcame my desire to hide; I went to intervene.

"All I'm *saying*," Leon was saying, "is that it's not exactly *fair* that you and I and every American has to wait until we're older than *shit* to get *our* chance to go, while all those little Hindis get carted off to brand-new worlds as fast as they can *breed*. Which is pretty damn quick. That's just not *fair*. Does it seem *fair* to you?"

"No, it doesn't seem particularly fair," the woman said back. "But I suppose they wouldn't see it as *fair* that we wiped New Delhi and Mumbai off the face of the planet, either."

"That's exactly my point!" Leon exclaimed. "We *nuked* the dot heads! We *won* that war! Winning should *count* for something. And now look what happens. They *lost,* but they get to go colonize the universe, and the only way *we* get to go is if we sign up to protect them! Excuse me for saying so, but doesn't the Bible say, 'The meek shall inherit the earth'? I'd say losing a goddamn war makes you pretty damn *meek.*"

"I don't think that phrase means what you think it does, Leon," I said, approaching the two of them.

"John! See, here's a man who knows what I'm talking about," Leon said, grinning my way.

The woman turned to face me. "You know this gentleman?" she asked me, with an undercurrent in her voice that implied that if I did, there was clearly something wrong with me.

"We met on the trip to Nairobi," I said, gently raising an eyebrow to indicate that he wasn't my companion of choice. "I'm John Perry," I said.

"Jesse Gonzales," she said.

"Charmed," I replied, and then turned to Leon. "Leon," I said, "you've got the saying wrong. The actual saying is from the Sermon on the Mount, and it says, '*Blessed* are the meek, for they shall inherit the earth.' Inheriting the earth is meant to be a reward, not a punishment."

Leon blinked, then snorted. "Even so, we *beat* them. We kicked their little brown asses. *We* should be colonizing the universe, not them."

I opened my mouth to respond, but Jesse beat me to the punch. " 'Blessed are they which are persecuted, for theirs is the kingdom of Heaven,' " she said, speaking to Leon but looking sidelong at me.

Leon gaped for a minute at the both of us. "You can't be *serious*," he said, after a minute. "There's nothing in the *Bible* that says *we* should be stuck on Earth while a bunch of *brownies*, which don't even *believe* in Jesus, thank you very much, fill up the galaxy. And it certainly doesn't say anything about us *protecting* the little bastards while they do it. Christ, I had a son in that war. Some dot head shot off one of his balls! His *balls*! They *deserved* what they got, the sons of bitches. Don't ask me to be *happy* that now *I'll* have to save their sorry asses up there in the colonies."

Jesse winked at me. "Would you like to field this one?"

"If you don't mind," I said.

"Oh, not at all," she replied.

" 'But I say unto you, Love your enemies,' " I quoted. " 'Bless them that curse you, do good to them that hate you, and pray for them which despitefully use you, and persecute you; That ye may be the children of your Father who is in Heaven: for he maketh his sun to rise on the evil and on the good, and sendeth rain on the just and on the unjust.' "

Leon turned lobster red. "You're both out of your fucking gourds," he said, and stomped off as fast as his fat would carry him.

"Thank you, Jesus," I said. "And this time I mean it literally."

"You're pretty handy with a Bible quotation," Jesse said. "Were you a minister in your past life?"

"No," I said. "But I lived in a town of two thousand people and fifteen churches. It helped to be able to speak the language. And you don't have to be religious to appreciate the Sermon on the Mount. What's your excuse?"

"Catholic school religion class," she said. "I won a ribbon for memorization in the tenth grade. It's amazing what your brain can keep in storage for sixty years, even if these days I can't remember where I parked when I go to the store."

"Well, in any event, let me apologize for Leon," I said. "I barely know him, but I know enough to know he's an idiot."

" 'Judge not, that ye be not judged,' " Jesse said, and shrugged. "Anyway, he's only saying what a lot of people believe. I think it's stupid and wrong, but that doesn't mean I don't understand it. I wish that there had been a different way for me to see the colonies than to wait an entire life and have to join the military for it. If I could have been a colonist when I was younger, I would have."

"You're not joining for a life of military adventure, then," I said.

"Of course not," Jesse said, a little scornfully. "Did *you* join because you have a great desire to fight a war?"

"No," I said.

She nodded. "Neither did I. Neither did most of us. Your friend Leon certainly didn't join to be in the military—he can't stand the people we will protect. People join because they're not ready to die and they don't want to be old. They join because life on Earth isn't interesting past a certain age. Or they join to see someplace new before they die. That's why I joined, you know. I'm not joining to fight or be young again. I just want to see what it's like to be somewhere *else.*"

She turned to look out the window. "Of course, it's funny to hear me say that. Do you know that until yesterday, I'd never been out of the state of Texas my entire life?"

"Don't feel bad about it," I said. "Texas *is* a big state."

She smiled. "Thank you. I don't really feel bad about it. It's just funny. When I was a child, I used to read all the 'Young Colonist' novels and watch the shows, and dreamed about raising Arcturian cattle and battling vicious land worms on colony Gamma Prime. Then I got older and realized that colonists came from India and Kazakhstan and Norway, where they can't support the population they have, and the fact I was born in America meant that I wouldn't get to go. And that there weren't actually Arcturian cattle or land worms! I was *very* disappointed to learn that when I was twelve."

She shrugged again. "I grew up in San Antonio, went 'away' to college at the University of Texas, and then took a job back in San Antonio. I got married eventually, and we took our vacations on the Gulf Coast. For our thirtieth anniversary, my husband and I planned to go to Italy, but we never went."

"What happened?"

She laughed. "His *secretary* is what happened. *They* ended up going to Italy on their honeymoon. I stayed home. On the other hand, they both ended up getting shellfish poisoning in Venice, so it's just as well I never went. But I didn't worry much about traveling after that. I knew I was going to join up as soon as I could, and I did, and here I am. Although now I wish I *had* traveled more. I took the delta from Dallas to Nairobi. That was *fun*. I wish I had done it more than once in my life. Not to mention *this*"—she waved her hand at the window, toward the beanstalk cables—"which I never thought I would ever want to ride in my life. I mean, what's keeping this cable *up*?"

"Belief," I said. "You believe that it won't fall and it won't. Try not to think about it too much or we're all in trouble."

"What I believe," Jesse said, "is that I want to get something to eat. Care to join me?"

"Belief," Harry Wilson said, and laughed. "Well, maybe belief *is* holding up this cable. Because it sure as hell isn't fundamental physics."

Harry Wilson had joined Jesse and me at a booth where we were eating. "You two look like you know each other, and that's one up on everyone else here," he said to us as he came up. We invited him to join us and he accepted gratefully. He had taught physics at a Bloomington, Indiana, high school for twenty years, he said, and the beanstalk had been intriguing him the entire time we had been riding it.

"What do you mean physics isn't holding it up?" Jesse said. "Believe me, this is not what I want to hear right at this moment."

Harry smiled. "Sorry. Let me rephrase. Physics *is* involved in holding up this beanstalk, certainly. But the physics involved aren't of the garden variety. There's a lot going on here that doesn't make sense on the surface."

"I feel a physics lecture coming on," I said.

"I taught physics to teenagers for years," Harry said, and dug out a small notepad and a pen. "It'll be painless, trust me. Okay, now look." Harry began drawing a circle at the bottom of the page. "This is the Earth. And this"—he drew a smaller circle halfway up the page—"is Colonial Station. It's in geosynchronous orbit, which means it stays put relative to the Earth's rotation. It's always hanging above Nairobi. With me so far?"

We nodded.

"Okay. Now, the idea behind the beanstalk is that you connect Colonial Station with the Earth through a 'beanstalk'—a bunch of cables, like those out the window—and a bunch of elevator platforms, like the one we're on now, that can travel back and forth." Harry drew a line signifying the cable, and a small square, signifying our platform. "The idea here is that elevators on these cables don't have to reach escape velocity to get to Earth orbit, like a rocket payload would. This is good for us, because we don't have to go to Colonial Station feeling like an elephant had its foot on our chests. Simple enough.

"The thing is, this beanstalk doesn't conform to the basic physical requirements of a classic Earth-to-space beanstalk. For one thing"—Harry drew an additional line past Colonial Station to the end of the page—"Colonial Station shouldn't be at the *end* of the beanstalk. For reasons that have to do with mass balance and orbital dynamics, there should be additional cable extending tens of thousands of miles past Colonial Station. Without this counterbalance, any beanstalk should be inherently unstable and dangerous."

"And you're saying this one isn't," I said.

"Not only is *not* unstable, it's probably the safest way to travel that's ever been devised," Harry said. "The beanstalk has been in continuous operation for over a century. It's the only point of departure for colonists. There's never been an accident due to instability or matériel failure, which would be related to instability. There was the famous beanstalk bombing forty years ago, but that was sabotage, unrelated to the physical structure of the beanstalk itself. The beanstalk itself is admirably stable and has been since it was built. But according to basic physics, it shouldn't be."

"So what is keeping it up?" Jesse said.

Harry smiled again. "Well, that's the question, isn't it."

"You mean you don't know?" Jesse asked.

"*I* don't know," Harry admitted. "But that in itself should be no cause for alarm, since I am—or was—merely a high school physics teacher. However, as far as I know, no one *else* has much of a clue how it works, either. On Earth, I mean. Obviously the Colonial Union knows."

"Well, how can that be?" I asked. "It's been here for a century, for God's sake. No one's bothered to figure out how it actually works?"

"I didn't say *that*," Harry said. "Of course they've been trying. And it's not like it's been a secret all these years. When the beanstalk was being built, there were demands by governments and the press to know how it worked. The CU essentially said 'figure it out,' and that was that. In physics circles, people have been trying to solve it ever since. It's called 'The Beanstalk Problem.' "

"Not a very original title," I said.

"Well, physicists save their imagination for other things." Harry chuckled. "The point is, it *hasn't* been solved, primarily for two reasons. The first is that it's incredibly complicated—I've pointed out the mass issues, but then there are other issues like cable strength, beanstalk oscillations brought on by storms and other atmospheric phenomena, and even an issue about how cables are supposed to taper. Any of these is massively difficult to solve in the real world; trying to figure them all out at once is impossible."

"What's the second reason?" Jesse asked.

"The second reason is that there's no reason to. Even if we did figure out how to build one of these things, we couldn't *afford* to build it." Harry leaned back. "Just before I was a teacher, I worked for General Electric's civil engineering department. We were working on the SubAtlantic rail line at the time, and one of my jobs was to go through old projects and project proposals to see if any of the technology or practices had application to the SubAtlantic project. Sort of a hail-Mary attempt to see if we could do anything to bring down costs."

"General Electric bankrupted itself on that, didn't they?" I asked.

"Now you know why they wanted to bring down costs," Harry

said. "And why I became a teacher. General Electric couldn't afford me, or much of anyone else, right after that. Anyway, I'm going through old proposals and reports and I get into some classified stuff, and one of the reports is for a beanstalk. General Electric had been hired by the U.S. Government for a third-party feasibility study on building a beanstalk in the Western Hemisphere; they wanted to clear out a hole in the Amazon the size of Delaware and stick it right on the equator.

"General Electric told them to forget it. The proposal said that even assuming some major technological breakthroughs—most of which *still* haven't happened, and none of which approach the technology that has to be involved with *this* beanstalk—the budget for the beanstalk would be *three times* the annual gross national product of the United States economy. That's assuming that the project did not run over budget, which of course it almost certainly would have. Now, this was twenty years ago, and the report I saw was a decade old even then. But I don't expect that the costs have gone down very much since then. So no new beanstalks—there are cheaper ways of getting people and material into orbit. *Much* cheaper."

Harry leaned forward again. "Which leads to two obvious questions: How did the Colonial Union manage to create *this* technological monstrosity, and why did they bother with it at all?"

"Well, obviously, the Colonial Union is more technologically advanced than we are here on Earth," Jesse said.

"Obviously," Harry said. "But why? Colonists are human, after all. Not only that, but since the colonies specifically recruit from impoverished countries with population problems, colonists tend to be poorly educated. Once they get to their new homes, you have to assume they're spending more time staying alive than they are thinking up creative ways to build beanstalks. And the primary technology that allowed interstellar colonization is the skip drive, which was developed right here on Earth, and which has been substantially unimproved for more than a century. So on the face of it, there's no reason why the colonists should be any more technologically advanced than we are."

Something suddenly clicked in my head. "Unless they cheat," I said.

Harry grinned. "Exactly. That's what I think, too."

Jesse looked at me, and then Harry. "I'm not following you two," she said.

"They cheat," I said. "Look, on Earth, we're bottled up. We only learn from ourselves—we make discoveries and refine technology all the time, but it's slow, because we do all the work ourselves. But up there—"

"Up there humans meet other intelligent species," Harry said. "Some of which almost certainly have technology more advanced than ours. We either take it in trade or reverse engineer it and find out how it works. It's much easier to figure out how something works when you've got something to work from than it is to figure it out on your own."

"That's what makes it cheating," I said. "The CU is reading off someone else's notes."

"Well, why doesn't the Colonial Union share what it's discovered with us?" Jesse asked. "What's the point of keeping it to themselves?"

"Maybe they think that what we don't know can't hurt us," I said.

"Or it's something else entirely," Harry said, and waved toward the window, where the beanstalk cables slid by. "This beanstalk isn't here because it's the easiest way to get people to Colonial Station, you know. It's here because it's one of the most *difficult*— in fact, the *most* expensive, *most* technologically complex and *most* politically intimidating way to do it. Its very presence is a reminder that the CU is literally light-years ahead of anything humans can do here."

"I've never found it intimidating," Jesse said. "I really never thought about it much at all."

"The message isn't aimed at you," Harry said. "If you were President of the United States, however, you'd think of it differently. After all, the CU keeps us all here on Earth. There's no space travel except what the CU allows through colonization or enlistment. Political leaders are always under pressure to buck the CU and get their people to the stars. But the beanstalk is a constant reminder. It says, 'Until you can make one of these, don't even *think* of challenging us.' And the beanstalk is the only technology the CU has decided to show us. Think about what they *haven't* let us know about. I can guarantee you the U.S. President has. And that it keeps him and every other leader on the planet in line."

"None of this is making me feel friendly toward the Colonial Union," Jesse said.

"It doesn't have to be sinister," Harry said. "It could be that the CU is trying to protect Earth. The universe is a big place. Maybe we're not in the best neighborhood."

"Harry, were you always this paranoid," I asked, "or was this something that crept up on you as you got older?"

"How do you think I made it to seventy-five?" Harry said, and grinned. "Anyway, I don't have any problems with the CU being much more technologically advanced. It's about to work to my advantage." He held up an arm. "Look at this thing," he said. "It's flabby and old and not in very good shape. Somehow, the Colonial Defense Forces are going to take this arm—and the rest of me—and whip it into fighting shape. And do you know how?"

"No," I said. Jesse shook her head.

"Neither do I," Harry said, and let his arm down with a *plop* onto the table. "I have *no* idea how they'll make it work. What's more, it's likely that I can't even *imagine* how they'll do it—if we assume that we've been held in a state of technological infancy by the CU, trying to explain it to me now would be like trying to explain this beanstalk platform to someone who's never seen a mode of transportation more complex than a horse and buggy. But they've obviously made it work. Otherwise, why would they recruit seventy-five-year-olds? The universe isn't going to be conquered by legions of geriatrics. No offense," he added quickly.

"None taken," Jesse said, and smiled.

"Lady and gentleman," Harry said, looking at the both of us, "we may think we have some idea of what we're getting into, but I don't think we have the first clue. This beanstalk exists to tell us that much. It's bigger and stranger than we can imagine—and it's just the first part of this journey. What comes next is going to be even bigger and stranger. Prepare yourself as best you can."

"How dramatic," Jesse said dryly. "I don't know how to prepare myself after a statement like that."

"I do," I said, and scooted over to get out of the booth. "I'm going to go pee. If the universe is bigger and stranger than I can imagine, it's best to meet it with an empty bladder."

"Spoken like a true Boy Scout," Harry said.

"A Boy Scout wouldn't need to pee as much as I do," I said.

"Sure he would," Harry said. "Just give him sixty years."

THREE "I don't know about you two," Jesse was saying to me and Harry, "but so far this really isn't what I expected the army to be."

"It's not so bad," I said. "Here, have another donut."

"I don't need another donut," she said, taking the donut anyway. "What I need is some sleep."

I knew what she meant. It had been more than eighteen hours since I left home, nearly all of it consumed with travel. I was ready for a nap. Instead I was sitting in the huge mess hall of an interstellar cruiser, having coffee and donuts with about a thousand other recruits, waiting for someone to come and tell us what we were supposed to do next. *That* part, at least, was pretty much like the military I expected.

The rush and wait began on arrival. As soon as we got off the beanstalk platform, we were greeted by two Colonial Union apparatchiks. They informed us that we were the last recruits expected for a ship that was leaving soon, so could we please follow them quickly so that everything could stay on schedule. Then one took the lead and one went to the rear and they effectively and rather insultingly herded several dozen senior citizens across the entire station to our ship, the CDFS *Henry Hudson*.

Jesse and Harry were clearly disappointed at the rush job, as was I. Colonial Station was huge—over a mile in diameter (1800 meters, actually, and I suspected that after seventy-five years of life, I would finally have to start getting used to the metric system) and served as the sole port of transport for recruits and colonists alike. Being herded across it without being able to stop and take it in was like being five years old and being hustled through a toy store at Christmas time by a harried parent. I felt like plopping down on the floor and having a tantrum until I got my way. I was unfortunately too old (or alternately, not nearly old enough) to get away with that sort of behavior.

What I did see on our speedy trek was a tantalizing appetizer. As our apparatchiks poked and prodded us along, we passed a huge holding bay filled to capacity with what I would guess were Pakistanis or Muslim Indians. Most were waiting patiently to gain entrance to shuttles that would take them to an immense colony transport ship, one of which was visible in the distance, floating outside the window. Others could be seen arguing with CU officials about one thing or another in accented English, comforting children who were clearly bored, or digging through their belongings for something to eat. In one corner, a group of men were kneeling on a carpeted area of the bay and praying. I wondered briefly how they had determined where Mecca was from twenty-three thousand miles up, and then we were pushed forward and I lost sight of them.

Jesse tugged on my sleeve and pointed to our right. In a small mess area, I caught a glimpse of something tentacled and blue, holding a martini. I alerted Harry; he was so intrigued that he went back and looked, much to the consternation of the trailing apparatchik. She shooed Harry back into the herd with a sour look on her face. Harry, on the other hand, was grinning like a fool. "A Gehaar," he said. "It was eating a buffalo wing when I looked in. *Disgusting.*" Then he giggled. The Gehaar were one of the first intelligent aliens humans encountered, in the days before the Colonial Union established its monopoly on space travel. Nice enough people, but they ate by injecting their food with acid from dozens of thin head tentacles and then noisily slurping the resulting goop into an orifice. Messy.

Harry didn't care. He'd spotted his first live alien.

Our meander reached its conclusion as we approached a holding bay with the words *"Henry Hudson/CDF Recruits"* glowing from a flight display. Our group gratefully took seats while our apparatchiks went to talk with some other Colonials waiting by the shuttle gate door. Harry, who was clearly showing a tendency toward curiosity, wandered over to the bay window to look at our ship. Jesse and I wearily got up and followed him. A small informational monitor at the window helped us find it among the other traffic.

The *Henry Hudson* was not actually docked at the gate, of course; it's hard to make a hundred-thousand-metric-ton interstellar spacecraft move daintily in tandem with a revolving space station. As with the colony transports, it maintained a reasonable distance while supplies, passengers and crew were transported back and forth by rather more manageable shuttles and barges. The *Hudson* itself was stationed a few miles out and above the station, not the massive, unesthetically functional spoked-wheel design of the colony transports, but sleeker, flatter and, importantly, not at all cylindrical or wheel-shaped. I mentioned this to Harry, who nodded. "Full-time artificial gravity," he said. "And stable over a large field. Very impressive."

"I thought we were using artificial gravity on the way up," Jesse said.

"We were," Harry said. "The beanstalk platform's gravity generators were increasing their output the higher up we went."

"So what's so different about a spaceship using artificial gravity?" Jesse asked.

"It's just extremely difficult," Harry said. "It takes an enormous amount of energy to create a gravitational field, and the amount of energy you have to put out increases exponentially with the radius of the field. They probably cheated by creating multiple, smaller fields instead of one larger field. But even that way, creating the fields in our beanstalk platform probably took more energy than it took to light your hometown for a month."

"I don't know about that," Jesse said. "I'm from San Antonio."

"Fine. *His* hometown, then," Harry said, jerking a thumb toward me. "Point is, it's an incredibly wasteful use of energy, and in most situations where artificial gravity is required, it's simpler and *much* less expensive just to create a wheel, spin it and let that stick people and things to the inside rim. Once you've spun up, you only need to put minimal additional energy into the system to compensate for friction. As opposed to creating an artificial gravity field, which needs a constant and significant output of energy."

He pointed to the *Henry Hudson*. "Look, there's a shuttle next to the *Hudson*. Using that as a scale, I'm guessing the *Hudson* is 800 feet long, 200 feet wide and about 150 feet deep. Creating a single artificial gravity field around *that* baby would definitely dim the lights in San Antonio. Even multiple fields would be an amazing drain on power. So either they have a power source that can keep the gravity on and still run all the ship's other systems, like propulsion and life support, or they've found a new, low-energy way to create gravity."

"It's probably not cheap," I said, and pointed to a colony transport to the right of the *Henry Hudson*. "Look at the colony ship. It's a wheel. And Colonial Station is spinning, too."

"The colonies are saving their best technology for the military," Jesse said. "And *this* ship is just being used to pick up new recruits. I think you're right, Harry. We have no idea what we've gotten ourselves into."

Harry grinned, and turned back to look at the *Henry Hudson*, lazily circling as Colonial Station turned. "I love it when people come around to my way of thinking."

Our apparatchiks presently herded us up again and got us in line to board the shuttle. We presented our identity cards to the CU official at the shuttle gate, who entered us on a list while a counterpart presented us with a personal data assistant. "Thanks for being on Earth, here's a lovely parting gift," I said to him. He didn't seem to get it.

The shuttles did not come equipped with artificial gravity. Our apparatchiks harnessed us in and warned us that under no circumstances were we to try to unlock ourselves; to make sure that the more claustrophobic of us didn't do just that, the locks on the harnesses would not be under our control during the flight. So that solved that problem. The apparatchiks also passed out plastic hairnets to anyone with hair long enough to warrant them; in free fall, long hair apparently goes everywhere.

If anyone felt nauseated, we were told, they were to use the vomit bags in the side pocket of their seats. Our apparatchiks stressed the importance of not waiting until the last second to use the vomit bags. In weightlessness, vomit would float around and irritate the other passengers, making the original vomiter very unpopular for the rest of the flight and possibly the rest of his or her military career. This was followed by a rustling sound as several of our number readied themselves. The woman next to me clutched her vomit bag tightly. I mentally prepared myself for the worst.

There was no vomit, thankfully, and the ride to the *Henry Hudson* was pretty smooth; after the initial *shit, I'm falling* signal my brain shot out when the gravity gave way, it was more like a gentle, extended roller-coaster ride. We made it to the ship in about five minutes; there was a minute or two of docking negotiations as a shuttle bay door irised open, accepted the shuttle, and closed again. This was followed by another few minutes of waiting as air was pumped back into the bay. Then a slight tingle, and the sudden reappearance of weight; the artificial gravity had kicked in.

The shuttle bay door opened and a wholly new apparatchik appeared. "Welcome to the CDFS *Henry Hudson*," she said. "Please unlatch yourselves, gather your belongings, and follow the lighted path out of the shuttle bay. The air will be pumped out of this bay in precisely seven minutes—to launch this shuttle and allow another shuttle to dock—so please be quick."

We were all surprisingly quick.

We were then led to the massive *Henry Hudson* mess hall, where we were invited to have some coffee and donuts and to relax. An official would be along to explain things. While we were waiting, the mess hall had begun to fill up with other recruits who had presumably boarded before us; after an hour there were hundreds of us milling about. I had never seen so many old people in one place at one time. Neither had Harry. "It's like Wednesday morning at the world's biggest Denny's," he said, and then got himself more coffee.

Just about the time that my bladder was informing me that I had overdone it with the coffee, a distinguished-looking gentleman in Colonial diplomatic blues entered the mess hall and made his way toward the front of the room. The noise level in the room began to subside; you could tell that people were relieved that someone was finally there to tell them what the hell was going on.

The man stood there for a few minutes until the room was silent.

"Greetings," he said, and we all jumped. He must have had a body mike; his voice was coming through speakers in the wall. "I'm Sam Campbell, Colonial Union adjunct for the Colonial Defense Forces. Although technically speaking I am not a member of the Colonial Defense Forces, I have been empowered by the CDF to manage your orientation on its behalf, so for the next few days, you can consider me your superior officer. Now, I know many of you have just arrived on the last shuttle and are anxious to get some rest; others have been on ship for up to a day and are equally anxious to know what comes next. For the sake of both groups, I will be brief.

"In about an hour, the CDFS *Henry Hudson* will break orbit and ready for her initial skip to the Phoenix system, where we stop briefly to pick up additional supplies before we head to Beta Pyxis III, where you will begin your training. Don't worry, I don't expect any of this to mean anything to you now. What you need to know is that it will take us a little more than two days to get to our initial skip point, and during that time, you will be undergoing a series of mental and physical evaluations at the hands of my staff. Your schedule is now being downloaded into your PDA. Please review it at your convenience. Your PDA can also direct you to every place you need to go, so you should never worry about getting lost. Those of you who have just arrived on the *Henry Hudson* will also find your stateroom assignments on your PDA.

"Other than finding your way to your staterooms, nothing is expected of you this evening. Many of you have been traveling for quite a while, and we want you to be rested for tomorrow's evaluations. Speaking of which, now is a good time to get you onto ship's time, which is on Colonial Universal Standard Time. It is now"—he checked his watch—"2138 Colonial. Your PDA is set for ship time. Your day begins tomorrow with breakfast mess from 0600 to 0730, followed by a physical evaluation and enhancement. Breakfast mess is not mandatory—you're not on military schedule yet—but you'll be having a long day tomorrow, so I do strongly suggest you attend.

"If you have any questions, your PDA can port into the *Henry Hudson* information system and use the AI interface to assist you; just use your stylus to write the question or speak it into your PDA's microphone. You will also find Colonial Union staff on each stateroom deck; please don't hesitate to ask them for assistance. Based on your personal information, our medical staff is already aware of any issues or needs you may have, and may have made appointments to see you this evening in your staterooms. Check your PDA. You may also visit sick bay at your convenience. This mess hall will be open all night tonight, but will begin normal operating hours as of tomorrow. Again, check your PDA for times and menus. Finally, as of tomorrow you should all be wearing CDF recruit gear; it is now being delivered to your staterooms."

Campbell stopped for a second and gave us all what I think he thought was a significant stare. "On behalf of the Colonial Union and the Colonial Defense Forces, I welcome you as new citizens and our newest defenders. God bless you all and keep you safe in what's to come.

"Incidentally, if you want to watch while we break orbit, we will be porting the video into our observation deck theater. The theater is quite large and can accommodate all recruits, so don't worry about seating. The *Henry Hudson* makes excellent speed, so by breakfast tomorrow the Earth will be a very small disk, and by dinner, nothing more than a bright point in the sky. This will probably be your last chance to see what was your homeworld. If that means something to you, I suggest you drop by."

"So, how is your new roommate?" Harry asked me, taking the seat next to me in the observation deck theater.

"I really don't want to talk about it," I said. I had used my PDA to navigate to my stateroom, where I found my roommate already stowing his belongings: Leon Deak. He glanced over, said, "Oh, look, it's the Bible freak," and then studiously ignored me, which took some doing in a room that was ten by ten. Leon had already taken the bottom bunk (which, to seventy-five-year-old knees at least, is the desirable bunk); I threw my carry-on onto the top bunk, took my PDA and went to get Jesse, who was on the same deck. Her roommate, a nice lady by the name of Maggie, bowed out of watching the *Henry Hudson* break orbit. I told Jesse who my roommate was; she just laughed.

She laughed again when she related the story to Harry, who sympathetically patted me on the shoulder. "Don't feel too bad. It's only until we get to Beta Pyxis."

"Wherever *that* is," I said. "How is your roommate?"

"I couldn't tell you," Harry said. "He was already asleep when I got there. Took the bottom bunk, too, the bastard."

"My roommate was simply lovely," Jesse said. "She offered me a homemade cookie when I met her. Said her granddaughter had made them as a going-away gift."

"She didn't offer *me* a cookie," I said.

"Well, she doesn't have to live with *you*, now does she."

"How was the cookie?" Harry asked.

"It was like an oatmeal rock," Jesse said. "But that's not the point. The point is, I have the best roommate of us all. I'm special. Look, there's the Earth." She pointed as the theater's tremendous video screen flickered to life. The Earth hung there in astounding fidelity; whoever built the video screen had done a bang-up job.

"I wish I had this screen in my living room," Harry said. "I'd have had the most popular Super Bowl parties on the block."

"Just look at it," I said. "All our lives, it's the only place we've ever been. Everyone we ever knew or loved was there. And now we're leaving it. Doesn't that make you feel something?"

"Excited," Jesse said. "And sad. But not too sad."

"Definitely not too sad," Harry said. "There was nothing left to do there but get older and die."

"You can still die, you know," I said. "You *are* joining the military."

"Yeah, but I'm not going to die *old*," Harry said. "I'm going to have a second chance to die young and leave a beautiful corpse. It makes up for missing out on it the first time."

"You're just a romantic that way," Jesse said, deadpan.

"Damn right," Harry said.

"Listen," I said. "We've begun pulling out."

The speakers of the theater broadcast the chatter between the *Henry Hudson* and Colonial Station as they negotiated the terms of the *Henry Hudson*'s departure. Then came a low thrum and the slightest of vibrations, which we could barely feel through our seats.

"Engines," Harry said. Jesse and I nodded.

And then the Earth slowly began to shrink in the video screen, still massive, and still brilliant blue and white, but clearly, inexorably, beginning to take up a smaller portion of the screen. We silently watched it shrink, all of the several hundred recruits who came to look. I looked over to Harry, who, despite his earlier blustering, was quiet and reflective. Jesse had a tear on her cheek.

"Hey," I said, and gripped her hand. "Not too sad, remember?"

She smiled at me and gripped my hand. "No," she said hoarsely. "Not too sad. But even still. Even still."

We sat there some more and watched everything we ever knew shrink in the viewscreen.

———

I had my PDA set to wake me up at 0600, which it did by gently piping music through its little speakers and gradually increasing the volume until I woke. I turned off the music, quietly lowered myself off the top bunk and then rooted for a towel in the wardrobe, flicking on the small light in the wardrobe to see. In the wardrobe hung my and Leon's recruit suits: two sets each of Colonial light blue sweat tops and bottoms, two light blue T-shirts, two pairs blue chino-style drawstring pants, two pairs white socks and briefs-style underwear, and blue sneakers. Apparently we'd have no need for formal dress between now and Beta Pyxis. I slipped on a pair of sweat bottoms and a T-shirt, grabbed one of the towels that was also hanging in the wardrobe, and padded down the hall for a shower.

When I returned, the lights were glowing on full but Leon was still in his bunk—the lights must have come on automatically. I put a sweat top over my T-shirt and added socks and sneakers to my ensemble; I was ready to jog or, well, whatever else I had to do that day. Now for some breakfast. On the way out, I gave Leon a little nudge. He was a schmuck, but even schmucks might not want to sleep through food. I asked him if he wanted to get some breakfast.

"What?" he said, groggily. "No. Leave me alone."

"You sure, Leon?" I asked. "You know what they say about breakfast. It's the most important meal of the day, and all that. Come on. You need your energy."

Leon actually growled. "My mother's been dead for thirty years and as far I know, she hasn't been brought back in your body. So get the hell out of here and let me sleep."

It was nice to see Leon hadn't gone soft on me. "Fine," I said. "I'll be back after breakfast."

Leon grunted and rolled back over. I went to breakfast.

Breakfast was amazing, and I say that having been married

to a woman who could make a breakfast spread that would have made Gandhi stop a fast. I had two Belgian waffles that were golden, crisp and light, wallowing in powdered sugar and syrup that tasted like real Vermont maple (and if you think you can't tell when you have Vermont maple syrup, you've never had it) and with a scoop of creamery butter that was artfully melting to fill the deep wells of the waffle squares. Add over-easy eggs that were actually over easy, four slices of thick, brown sugar–cured bacon, orange juice from fruit that apparently hadn't realized it had been squeezed, and a mug of coffee that was fresh off the burro.

I thought I had died and gone to heaven. Since I was now officially legally dead on Earth and flying across the solar system in a spaceship, I guess I wasn't too far off.

"Oh my," the fellow I sat next to at breakfast said, as I put down my fully-loaded tray. "Look at all the fats on that tray. You're asking for a coronary. I'm a doctor, I know."

"Uh-huh," I said, and pointed to his tray. "That looks like a four-egg omelet you're working on there. With about a pound each of ham and cheddar."

" 'Do as I say, not as I do.' That was my creed as a practicing physician," he said. "If more patients had listened to me instead of following my sorry example, they'd be alive now. A lesson for us all. Thomas Jane, by the way."

"John Perry," I said, shaking hands.

"Pleased to meet you," he said. "Although I'm sad, too, since if you eat all that you'll be dead of a heart attack within the hour."

"Don't listen to him, John," said the woman across from us, whose own plate was smeared with the remains of pancakes and sausage. "Tom there is just trying to get you to give him some of your food, so he doesn't have to get back in line for more. That's how I lost half of my sausage."

"That accusation is as irrelevant as it is true," Thomas said indignantly. "I admit to coveting his Belgian waffle, yes. I won't deny that. But if sacrificing my own arteries will prolong his life, then it's worth it to me. Consider this the culinary equivalent of falling on a grenade for the sake of my comrade."

"Most grenades aren't soaked in syrup," she said.

"Maybe they should be," Thomas said. "We'd see a lot more selfless acts."

"Here," I said, sawing off half of a waffle. "Throw yourself on this."

"I'll launch myself face first," Thomas promised.

"We're all deeply relieved to hear that," I said.

The woman on the other side of the table introduced herself as Susan Reardon, late of Bellevue, Washington. "What do you think of our little space adventure so far?" she asked me.

"If I had known the cooking was this good, I would have found some way to sign up years ago," I said. "Who knew army food would be like this."

"I don't think we're in the army *quite* yet," Thomas said, around a mouthful of Belgian waffle. "I think this is sort of the Colony Defense Forces waiting room, if you know what I mean. Real army food is going to be a lot more spare. Not to mention I doubt we'll be prancing around in sneakers like we are right now."

"You think they're easing us into things, then," I said.

"I do," Thomas said. "Look, there are a thousand complete strangers on this ship, all of whom are now without home, family, or profession. That's a hell of a mental shock. The least they can do is give us a fabulous meal to take our minds off it all."

"John!" Harry had spied me from the line. I waved him over. He and another man came, bearing trays.

"This is my roommate, Alan Rosenthal," he said, by way of introduction.

"Formerly known as Sleeping Beauty," I said.

"About half of that description is right," Alan said. "I am in fact devastatingly beautiful." I introduced Harry and Alan to Susan and Thomas.

"Tsk, tsk," Thomas said, examining their trays. "Two more plaque attacks waiting to happen."

"Better throw Tom a couple bacon strips, Harry," I said. "Otherwise we'll never hear the end of this."

"I resent the implication that I can be bought off with food," Thomas said.

"It wasn't implied," Susan said. "It was pretty much boldly stated."

"Well, I know your roommate lottery turned out badly," Harry said to me, handing over two bacon strips to Thomas, who accepted them gravely, "but mine turned out all right. Alan here is a theoretical physicist. Smart as a whip."

"And devastatingly beautiful," Susan piped in.

"Thanks for remembering that detail," Alan said.

"This looks like a table of reasonably intelligent adults," Harry said. "So what do you think we're in for today?"

"I have a physical scheduled for 0800," I said. "I think we all do."

"Right," Harry said. "But I'm asking what you all think that *means*. Do you think today is the day we start our rejuvenation therapies? Is today the day we begin to stop being old?"

"We don't know that we stop being *old*," Thomas said. "We've all assumed that, because we think of soldiers as being young. But think about it. None of us has actually seen a Colonial soldier. We've assumed, and our assumptions could be way off."

"What would the value of old soldiers be?" Alan asked. "If they're going to put me in the field as is, I don't know what good I'm going to be to anyone. I have a bad back. Walking from the beanstalk platform to the flight gate yesterday just about killed me.

I can't imagine marching twenty miles with a pack and a firearm."

"I think we're due for some repairs, obviously," Thomas said. "But that's not the same as being made 'young' again. I'm a doctor, and I know a little bit about this. You can make the human body work better and achieve high function at any age, but each age has a certain baseline capability. The body at seventy-five is inherently less fast, less flexible and less easily repaired than at younger ages. It can still do some amazing things, of course. I don't want to brag, but I'll have you know that back on Earth I regularly ran ten K races. I ran one less than a month ago. And I made better time than I would have when I was fifty-five."

"What were you like when you were fifty-five?" I asked.

"Well, that's the thing," Thomas said. "I was a fat slob at fifty-five. It took a heart replacement to get me serious about taking care of myself. My point is that a high-functioning seventy-five-year-old can actually do many things without actually being 'young,' but just by being in excellent shape. Maybe that's all that's required for this army. Maybe all the other intelligent species in the universe are pushovers. Presuming that's the case, it makes a weird sort of sense to have *old* soldiers, because young people are more useful to their community. They have their whole lives ahead of them, while *we* are eminently expendable."

"So maybe we'll still be old, just really, really healthy," Harry said.

"That's what I'm saying," Thomas said.

"Well, stop saying that. You're bringing me down," Harry said.

"I'll shut up if you give me your fruit cup," Thomas said.

"Even if we're turned into high-functioning seventy-five-year-olds, as you say," Susan said, "we'd still be getting older. In five years, we'd just be high-functioning eighty-year-olds. There's an upper limit to our usefulness as soldiers."

Thomas shrugged. "Our terms are for two years. Maybe they

only need to keep us in working order for that long. The difference between seventy-five and seventy-seven isn't as great as between seventy-five and eighty. Or even between seventy-seven and eighty. Hundreds of thousands of us sign up each year. After two years, they just swap us out with a crew of 'fresh' recruits."

"We can be retained for up to ten years," I said. "It's in the fine print. That would seem to argue that they have the technology to keep us working for that period of time."

"And they've got our DNA on file," Harry said. "Maybe they've cloned replacement parts or something like that."

"True," Thomas admitted. "But it's a lot of work to transplant every single organ, bone, muscle and nerve from a cloned body to ours. And they'd still have to contend with our brains, which can't be transplanted."

Thomas looked around and finally realized he was depressing the whole table. "I'm not saying that we *won't* be made young again," he said. "Just what we've seen on this ship convinces me that the Colonial Union has much better technology than we ever had back home. But speaking as a medical doctor, I'm having a hard time seeing how they'll reverse the aging process as dramatically as we all think they will."

"Entropy is a bitch," Alan said. "We've got theories to back *that* one up."

"There is one piece of evidence that suggests that they'll improve us no matter what," I said.

"Tell me quickly," Harry said. "Tom's theory of the galaxy's oldest army is ruining my appetite."

"That's just it," I said. "If they couldn't *fix* our bodies, they wouldn't be giving us food with a fat content that could kill most of us within the month."

"That's very true," Susan said. "You make an excellent point, there, John. I feel better already."

"Thank you," I said. "And based on this evidence, I have such faith in the Colonial Defense Forces to cure me of all my ills, that now I'm going back for seconds."

"Get me some pancakes while you're up," Thomas said.

"Hey, Leon," I said, giving his flabby bulk a push. "Get up. Sleepy time is over. You've got an eight o'clock appointment."

Leon lay on his bed like a lump. I rolled my eyes, sighed and bent down to give him a harder push. And noticed his lips were blue.

Oh, shit, I thought, and shook him. Nothing. I grabbed his torso and pulled him off his bunk to the floor. It was like moving dead weight.

I grabbed my PDA and called for medical help. Then I kneeled over him, blew into his mouth, and pumped on his chest until a pair of Colonial medical staffers arrived and pulled me off of him.

By this time a small crowd had gathered around the open door; I saw Jesse and reached out to bring her in. She saw Leon on the floor and her hand flew to her mouth. I gave her a quick hug.

"How is he?" I asked one of the Colonials, who was consulting his PDA.

"He's dead," he said. "He's been dead for about an hour. Looks like a heart attack." He put the PDA down and stood up, glancing back down at Leon. "Poor bastard. Made it this far just to have his ticker crap out."

"A last-minute volunteer for the Ghost Brigades," the other Colonial said.

I shot a hard stare at him. I thought a joke at this moment was in terribly bad taste.

FOUR

"Okay, let's see," the doctor said, glancing at his rather large PDA as I entered the office. "You're John Perry, correct?"

"That's right," I said.

"I'm Dr. Russell," he said, and then looked me over. "You look like your dog just died," he said.

"Actually," I said, "it was my roommate."

"Oh, yes," he said, glancing down at his PDA again. "Leon Deak. I would have been working on him right after you. Bad timing, that. Well, let's get that off the schedule, then." He tapped the PDA screen for a few seconds, smiled tightly when he was through. Dr. Russell's bedside manner left something to be desired.

"Now," he said, turning his attention back to me, "let's get you looked at."

The office consisted of Dr. Russell, me, a chair for the doctor, a small table and two crèches. The crèches were shaped for human contours, and each had a curving transparent door that arched over the contoured area. At the top of each crèche was an arm apparatus, with a cuplike attachment at the end. The "cup" looked just about large enough to fit on a human head. It was, quite frankly, making me a little nervous.

"Please go ahead and make yourself comfortable, and then

we'll get started," Dr. Russell said, opening the door to the crèche nearest to me.

"Do you need me to take anything off?" I said. As far as I remembered, a physical examination required being looked at physically.

"No," he said. "But if it makes you feel more comfortable, go right ahead."

"Does anyone actually strip if they don't have to?" I asked.

"Actually, yes," he said. "If you've been told to do something one way for so long, it's a hard habit to break."

I kept my togs on. I set my PDA on the table, stepped up to the crèche, turned around, leaned back and settled in. Dr. Russell closed the door and stepped back. "Hold on one second while I adjust the crèche," he said, and tapped his PDA. I felt the human-shaped depression in the crèche shift, and then conform to my dimensions.

"That was creepy," I said.

Dr. Russell smiled. "You're going to notice some vibration here," he said, and he was right.

"Say," I said while the crèche was thrumming gently underneath me, "those other fellows who were in the waiting room with me. Where did they go after they came in here?"

"Through the door over there." He waved a hand behind him without looking up from his PDA. "That's the recovery area."

"*Recovery* area?"

"Don't worry," he said. "I've just made the examination sound much worse than it is. In fact, we're just about done with your scan." He tapped his PDA again and the vibration stopped.

"What do I do now?" I asked.

"Just hold tight," Dr. Russell said. "We've got a little more to do, and we need to go over the results of your examination."

"You mean it's done?" I said.

"Modern medicine is wonderful, isn't it," he said. He showed me the PDA screen, which was downloading a summary of my scan. "You don't even have to say, 'Aaahhhh.'"

"Yeah, but how detailed can it be?"

"Detailed enough," he said. "Mr. Perry, when was your last physical examination?"

"About six months ago," I said.

"What was the prognosis from your physician?"

"He said I was in fine shape, other than my blood pressure being a little higher than normal. Why?"

"Well, he's basically right," said Dr. Russell, "although he seems to have missed the testicular cancer."

"Excuse me?" I said.

Dr. Russell flipped the PDA screen around again; this time it was showing a false-color representation of my genitals. It was the first time I'd ever had my own package waved in front of my face. "Here," he said, pointing to a dark spot on my left testicle. "There's the nodule. Pretty big sucker, too. It's cancer, all right."

I glared at the man. "You know, Dr. Russell, most doctors would have found a more tactful way to break the news."

"I'm sorry, Mr. Perry," Dr. Russell said. "I don't want to seem unconcerned. But it's really not a problem. Even on Earth, testicular cancer is easily treatable, particularly in the early stages, which is the case here. At the very worst, you'd lose the testicle, but that's not a significant setback."

"Unless you happen to own the testicle," I growled.

"That's more of a psychological issue," Dr. Russell said. "In any event, right here and right now, I don't want you to worry about it. In a couple of days you'll be getting a comprehensive physical overhaul, and we'll deal with your testicle then. In the meantime, there should be no problems. The cancer is still local to the testicle. It hasn't spread to the lungs or the lymph nodes. You're fine."

"Am I going to drop the ball?" I said.

Dr. Russell smiled. "I think you can hold on to the ball for now," he said. "Should you ever drop it, I suspect it will be the least of your concerns. Now, other than the cancer, which as I say isn't really problematic, you're in as good a shape as any man of your physical age could be. That's good news; we don't have to do anything else to you at this point."

"What would you do if you'd found something really wrong?" I asked. "I mean, what if the cancer had been terminal?"

"'Terminal' is a pretty imprecise term, Mr. Perry," Dr. Russell said. "In the long run, we're all terminal cases. In the case of this examination, what we're really looking to do is to stabilize any recruits who are in imminent danger, so we know they'll make it through the next few days. The case of your unfortunate roommate Mr. Deak isn't all that unusual. We have a lot of recruits who make it to this point just to die before assessment. That's not good for any of us."

Dr. Russell consulted his PDA. "Now, in the case of Mr. Deak, who died of a heart attack, what we probably would have done would be to remove the plaque buildup from his arteries and provide him with an arterial wall-strengthening compound to prevent ruptures. That's our most common treatment. Most seventy-five-year-old arteries can use some propping up. In your case, if you had had advanced stage cancer, we would have trimmed back the tumors to a point where they didn't pose an imminent threat to your vital functions, and shored up the affected regions to make sure you wouldn't have any problems over the next few days."

"Why wouldn't you cure it?" I asked. "If you can 'shore up' an affected region, it sounds like you could probably fix it completely if you wanted to."

"We can, but it's not necessary," Dr. Russell said. "You'll be getting a more comprehensive overhaul in a couple of days. We just need to keep you going until then."

"What does 'comprehensive overhaul' mean, anyway?" I said.

"It means that when it's done, you'll wonder why you ever worried about a spot of cancer on your testicle," he said. "That's a promise. Now, there's one more thing we need to do here. Bring your head forward, please."

I did. Dr. Russell reached up and brought the feared arm cup down directly on the top of my head. "During the next couple of days, it's going to be important for us to get a good picture of your brain activity," he said, moving back. "So to do this, I'm going to implant a sensor array into your skull." As he said this, he tapped the screen on his PDA, an action I was learning to mistrust. There was a slight sucking noise as the cup adhered to my skull.

"How do you do that?" I asked.

"Well, right now, you can probably feel a little tickle on your scalp and down the back of your neck," Dr. Russell said, and I could. "Those are the injectors positioning themselves. They're like little hypodermic needles that will insert the sensors. The sensors themselves are very small, but there's a lot of them. About twenty thousand, more or less. Don't worry, they're self-sterilizing."

"Is this going to hurt?" I asked.

"Not so much," he said, and tapped his PDA screen. Twenty thousand microsensors *slammed* themselves into my skull like four ax handles simultaneously whacking my skull.

"God *damn* it!" I grabbed my head, banging my hands against the crèche door as I did so. "You son of a bitch," I yelled at Dr. Russell. "You said it wouldn't *hurt!*"

"I said 'not so much,'" Dr. Russell said.

"Not so much as what? Having your head stepped on by an elephant?"

"Not so much as when the sensors connect to each other," Dr. Russell said. "The good news is that as soon as they're connected, the pain stops. Now hold still, this will only take a minute."

He tapped the PDA again. Eighty thousand needles shot out in every direction in my skull.

I have never wanted to punch a doctor so much in my life.

"I don't know," Harry was saying. "I think it's an interesting look." And with this, Harry rubbed his head, which like all our heads was now a dusty speckled gray where twenty thousand subcutaneous sensors sat, measuring brain activity.

The breakfast crew had reconvened again at lunchtime, this time with Jesse and her roommate Maggie joining the crowd. Harry had declared that we now constituted an official clique, branded us the "Old Farts," and demanded we begin a food fight with the next table over. He was voted down, in no small part due to Thomas noting that any food we threw we wouldn't get to eat, and lunch was even better than breakfast, if that was possible.

"And a damned good thing, too," Thomas said. "After this morning's little brain injection, I was almost too pissed off to eat."

"I can't imagine that," Susan said.

"Notice how I said 'almost,'" Thomas said. "But I'll tell you what. I wish I'd had one of those crèches back home. Would have cut my appointment times by eighty percent. More time for golfing."

"Your devotion to your patients is overwhelming," Jesse said.

"Fah," Thomas said. "I played golf with most of them. They would have been all for it. And as much as it pains me to say it, it helped my doctor make a much better assessment than I ever could have. That thing is a diagnostician's dream. It caught a microscopic tumor on my pancreas. There's no way I could have caught that back home until it was a hell of a lot larger or a patient started showing symptoms. Did anyone else have anything surprising?"

"Lung cancer," Harry said. "Little spots."

"Ovarian cysts," Jesse said. Maggie seconded.

"Incipient rheumatoid arthritis," said Alan.

"Testicular cancer," I said.

Every man at the table winced. "Ouch," said Thomas.

"They tell me I'll live," I said.

"You'll just be lopsided when you walk," said Susan.

"That's enough of *that*," I said.

"What I don't understand is why they didn't *fix* the problems," Jesse said. "My doctor showed me a cyst the size of a gumball, but told me not to concern myself with it. I don't think I'm cut out *not* to worry about something like that."

"Thomas, you're alleged to be a doctor," Susan said, and tapped her gray-shaded brow. "What's with these little bastards? Why not just give us a brain scan?"

"If I had to guess, which I do, since I really have no clue," Thomas said, "I'd say that they want to see our brains in action while we go through our training. But they can't do that with us strapped to a machine, so they're strapping the machines to us instead."

"Thanks for the cogent explanation of what I already figured out," Susan said. "What I'm asking is, what purpose does that sort of measurement serve?"

"I dunno," Thomas said. "Maybe they're fitting us for new brains after all. Or maybe they've got some way of adding new brain material, and they need to see what parts of our brains need a boost. I just hope they don't need to put in another set of the damned things. The first set nearly killed me from the pain."

"Speaking of which," Alan said, turning to me, "I hear you lost your roommate this morning. Are you okay?"

"I'm all right," I said. "Though it's depressing. My doctor said that if he had managed to make it to his appointment this morning, they probably could have kept him from dying. Given him a plaque remover or something. I feel like I should have made him get up for breakfast. That might have kept him moving long enough to make it to his appointment."

"Don't kick yourself about it," Thomas said. "There's no way you could have known. People just die."

"Sure, but not days from getting a 'comprehensive overhaul,' as my doctor was putting it."

Harry piped in. "Not to be too crass about this—"

"You just know *this* is going to be bad," Susan said.

"—but when I went to college," Harry continued, throwing a piece of bread at Susan, "if your roommate died, you were usually allowed to skip your finals for that semester. You know, because of the trauma."

"And oddly enough, your roommate got to skip them, too," Susan said. "For much the same reason."

"I never thought of it that way," Harry said. "Anyway, think they might let you sit out the evaluations they have planned for today?"

"I doubt it," I said. "Even if they did, I wouldn't take up the offer. What else would I do, sit in my stateroom all day? Talk about depressing. Someone died there, you know."

"You could always move," Jesse said. "Maybe someone else's roommate died, too."

"There's a morbid thought," I said. "And anyway, I don't want to move. I'm sorry Leon's dead, of course. But now I have a room to myself."

"Looks like the healing process has begun," Alan said.

"I'm just trying to move past the pain," I said.

"You don't talk much, do you," Susan said to Maggie, rather suddenly.

"No," Maggie said.

"Hey, what does everyone have next on their schedule?" Jesse asked.

Everyone reached for their PDA, then stopped, guiltily.

"Let's think about just how high school that last moment really was," Susan said.

"Well, hell," Harry said, and pulled out his PDA anyway. "We've already joined a lunchroom clique. Might as well go all the way."

It turned out Harry and I had our first evaluation session together. We were directed to a conference room where chairs with desks had been set up.

"Holy crap," Harry said as we took our seats. "We really *are* back in high school."

This assessment was reinforced when our Colonial came into the room. "You will now be tested on basic language and mathematic skills," the proctor said. "Your first test is being downloaded into your PDA. It is multiple choice. Please answer as many questions as you can within the thirty-minute time limit. If you finish before your thirty minutes are up, please sit quietly or review your answers. Please do not collaborate with other trainees. Please begin now."

I looked down at my PDA. A word analogy question was on it.

"You have *got* to be kidding," I said. Other people in the room were chuckling as well.

Harry raised his hand. "Ma'am?" he said. "What's the score I need to get into Harvard?"

"I've heard that one before," the Colonial said. "Everyone, please settle down and work on your test."

"I've been waiting sixty years to raise my math score," Harry said. "Let's see how I do now."

Our second assessment was even worse.

"Please follow the white square. Use only your eyes, not your head." The Colonial dimmed the lights in the room. Sixty pairs of eyes focused on a white square on the wall. Slowly, it began to move.

"I can't believe I went into space for this," Harry said.

"Maybe things will pick up," I said. "If we're lucky, we'll get another white square to look at."

A second white square appeared on the wall.

"You've been here before, haven't you?" Harry said.

Later, Harry and I separated, and I had some activities of my own.

The first room I was in featured a Colonial and a pile of blocks.

"Make a house out of these, please," the Colonial said.

"Only if I get an extra juice box," I said.

"I'll see what I can do," the Colonial promised. I made a house out of the blocks and then went into the next room, where the Colonial in there pulled out a sheet of paper and a pen.

"Starting from the middle of the maze, try to see if you can get to the outer edge."

"Jesus Christ," I said, "a drug-addled rat could do this."

"Let's hope so," the Colonial said. "Still, let's see you do it anyway."

I did. In the next room, the Colonial there wanted me to call out the numbers and letters. I learned to stop wondering why and just do what they told me.

A little later in the afternoon, I got pissed off.

"I've been reading your file," said the Colonial, a thin young man who looked like a strong wind would sail him off like a kite.

"Okay," I said.

"It says you were married."

"I was."

"Did you like it? Being married."

"Sure. It beats the alternative."

He smirked. "So what happened? Divorce? Fuck around one time too many?"

Whatever obnoxiously amusing qualities this guy had were fading fast. "She's dead," I said.

"Yeah? How did that happen?"

"She had a stroke."

"Gotta love a stroke," he said. "Bam, your brain's skull pudding, just like that. Good that she didn't survive. She'd be this fat, bedridden turnip, you know. You'd just have to feed her through a straw or something." He made slurping noises.

I didn't say anything. Part of my brain was figuring how quickly I could move to snap his neck, but most of me was just sitting there in blind shock and rage. I simply could not believe what I was hearing.

Down in some deep part of my brain, someone was telling me to start breathing again soon, or I was going to pass out.

The Colonial's PDA suddenly beeped. "Okay," he said, and stood up quickly. "We're done. Mr. Perry, please allow me to apologize for the comments I made regarding your wife's death. My job here is to generate an enraged response from the recruit as quickly as possible. Our psychological models showed that you would respond most negatively to comments like the ones I have just made. Please understand that on a personal level I would never make such comments about your late wife."

I blinked stupidly for a few seconds at the man. Then I roared at him. "What kind of sick, fucked-up test was THAT?!?"

"I agree it is an extremely unpleasant test, and once again I apologize. I am doing my job as ordered, nothing more."

"Holy Christ!" I said. "Do you have any idea how close I came to breaking your fucking neck?"

"In fact, I do," the man said in a calm, controlled voice that indicated that, in fact, he did. "My PDA, which was tracking your mental state, beeped right before you were about to pop. But even if it hadn't I would have known. I do this all the time. I know what to expect."

I was still trying to come down from my rage. "You do this thing with every recruit?" I asked. "How are you even still *alive?*"

"I understand that question," the man said. "I was in fact chosen for this assignment because my small build gives the recruit the impression that he or she can beat the hell out of me. I am a very good 'little twerp.' However, I am capable of restraining a recruit if I have to. Though usually I don't have to. As I said, I do this a lot."

"It's not a very nice job," I said. I had finally managed to get myself back into a rational state of mind.

" 'It's a dirty job, but someone's got to do it,' " the man said. "I find it interesting, in that every recruit has a different thing that causes him or her to explode. But you're right. It's a high-stress assignment. It's not really for everyone."

"I bet you're not very popular in bars," I said.

"Actually, I'm told I'm quite charming. When I'm not intentionally pissing people off, that is. Mr. Perry, we're all finished here. If you'll step through the door to your right, you'll begin your next assessment."

"They're not going to try to piss me off again, are they?"

"You may become pissed off," the man said, "but if you do, it'll be on your own. We only do this test once."

I headed to the door, then stopped. "I know you were doing your job," I said. "But I still want you to know. My wife was a wonderful person. She deserves better than to be used like this."

"I know she does, Mr. Perry," the man said. "I know she does."

I went through the door.

In the next room, a very nice young lady, who happened to be completely naked, wanted me to tell her anything I could possibly remember about my seventh birthday party.

"I can't believe they showed us that film right before dinner," Jesse said.

"It wasn't right before dinner," Thomas said. "The Bugs Bunny cartoon was after that. Anyway, it wasn't so bad."

"Yes, well, maybe you're not utterly disgusted by a film on intestinal surgery, Mister Doctor, but the rest of us found it pretty disturbing," Jesse said.

"Does this mean you don't want your ribs?" Thomas said, pointing to her plate.

"Did anyone else get the naked woman asking about your childhood?" I asked.

"I got a man," Susan said.

"Woman," said Harry.

"Man," said Jesse.

"Woman," said Thomas.

"Man," said Alan.

We all looked at him.

"What?" Alan said. "I'm gay."

"What was the point of that?" I asked. "About the naked person, I mean, not about Alan being gay."

"Thanks," Alan said dryly.

"They're trying to provoke particular responses, that's all," said Harry. "All of today's tests have been of pretty basic intellectual or emotional responses, the foundation of more complex and subtle emotions and intellectual abilities. They're just trying to figure out how we think and react on a primal level. The naked person was obviously trying to get you all worked up sexually."

"But what was that whole thing about asking you about your childhood, is what I'm saying," I said.

Harry shrugged. "What's sex without a little guilt?"

"What pissed me off was the one where they got me all pissed off," Thomas said. "I swear I was going to clobber that guy. He said the Cubs ought to have been demoted to the minor leagues after they went two centuries without a World Series championship."

"That sounds reasonable to me," Susan said.

"Don't *you* start," Thomas said. "Man. Pow. I'm telling you. You don't mess with the Cubs."

If the first day was all about demeaning feats of intellect, the second day was about demeaning feats of strength, or lack thereof.

"Here's a ball," one proctor said to me. "Bounce it." I did. I was told to move on.

I walked around a small athletic track. I was asked to run a small distance. I did some light calisthenics. I played a video game. I was asked to shoot at a target on a wall with a light gun. I swam (I liked that part. I've always liked swimming, so long as my head's above water). For two hours, I was placed in a rec room with several dozen other people and told to do whatever I wanted. I shot some pool. I played a game of Ping-Pong. God help me, I played shuffleboard.

At no point did I even break a sweat.

"What the hell sort of army is this, anyway?" I asked the Old Farts at lunch.

"It makes a little bit of sense," Harry said. "Yesterday we did basic intellect and emotion. Today was basic physical movement. Again, they seem interested in the foundations of high order activity."

"I'm not really aware of Ping-Pong being indicative of higher order physical activity," I said.

"Hand-eye coordination," Harry said. "Timing. Precision."

"And you never know when you're going to have to bat back a grenade," Alan piped in.

"Exactly," Harry said. "Also, what do you want them to do? Have us run a marathon? We'd all drop before the end of the first mile."

"Speak for yourself, flabby," Thomas said.

"I stand corrected," Harry said. "Our friend Thomas would make it to mile six before *his* heart imploded. If he didn't get a food-related cramp first."

"Don't be silly," Thomas said. "Everyone knows you need to power up with carbohydrates before a race. Which is why I'm going back for more fettuccine."

"You're not running a marathon, Thomas," Susan said.

"The day is young," Thomas said.

"Actually," Jesse said, "my schedule is empty. I've got nothing planned for the rest of the day. And tomorrow, the only thing on the schedule is 'Concluding Physical Improvements' from 0600 to 1200 and a general recruit assembly at 2000, after dinner."

"My schedule is finished until tomorrow, too," I said. A quick glance up and down the table showed that everyone else was done for the day as well. "Well, then," I said. "What are we going to do to amuse ourselves?"

"There's always more shuffleboard," Susan said.

"I have a better idea," Harry said. "Anyone have plans at 1500?"

We all shook our heads.

"Swell," Harry said. "Then meet me back here. I have a field trip for the Old Farts."

"Are we even supposed to be here?" Jesse asked.

"Sure," said Harry. "Why not? And even if we're not, what are they going to do? We're not really in the military yet. We can't officially be court-martialed."

"No, but they can probably blow us out an air lock," Jesse said.

"Don't be silly," Harry said. "That would be a waste of perfectly good air."

Harry had led us to an observation deck in the Colonial area of the ship. And indeed, while we recruits had never been specifically told we couldn't go to the Colonial's decks, neither had we been told that we could (or should). Standing as we were in the deserted deck, the seven of us stood out like truant schoolkids at a peep show.

Which, in one sense, was what we were. "During our little exercises today, I struck up a conversation with one of the Colonial folks," Harry said, "and he mentioned that the *Henry Hudson* was going to make its skip today at 1535. And I figure that none of us has actually seen what a skip looks like, so I asked him where one would go to get a good view. And he mentioned here. So here we are, and with"—Harry glanced at his PDA—"four minutes to spare."

"Sorry about that," Thomas said. "I didn't mean to hold everyone up. The fettuccine was excellent, but my lower intestine would apparently beg to differ."

"Please feel free not to share such information in the future, Thomas," Susan said. "We don't know you that well yet."

"Well, how else will you *get* to know me that well?" Thomas said. No one bothered to answer that one.

"Anyone know where we are right now? In space, that is," I asked after a few moments of silence had passed.

"We're still in the solar system," Alan said, and pointed out the window. "You can tell because you can still see the constellations.

See, look, there's Orion. If we'd traveled any significant distance, the stars would have shifted their relative position in the sky. Constellations would have been stretched out or would be entirely unrecognizable."

"Where are we supposed to be skipping to?" Jesse asked.

"The Phoenix system," Alan said. "But that won't tell you anything, because 'Phoenix' is the name of the planet, not of the star. There is a constellation named 'Phoenix,' and in fact, there it is"— he pointed to a collection of stars—"but the planet Phoenix isn't around any of the stars in that constellation. If I remember correctly, it's actually in the constellation Lupus, which is farther north"—he pointed to another, dimmer collection of stars—"but we can't actually see the star from here."

"You sure know your constellations," Jesse said admiringly.

"Thanks," Alan said. "I wanted to be an astronomer when I was younger, but astronomers get paid for shit. So I became a theoretical physicist instead."

"Lots of money in thinking up new subatomic particles?" Thomas asked.

"Well, no," Alan admitted. "But I developed a theory that helped the company I worked for create a new energy containment system for naval vessels. The company's profit-sharing incentive plan gave me one percent for that. Which came to more money than I could spend, and trust me, I made the effort."

"Must be nice to be rich," Susan said.

"It wasn't too bad," Alan admitted. "Of course, I'm not rich anymore. You give it up when you join. And you lose other things, too. I mean, in about a minute, all that time I spent memorizing the constellations will be wasted effort. There's no Orion or Ursa Minor or Cassiopeia where we're going. This might sound stupid, but it's entirely possible I'll miss the constellations more than I miss the money. You can always make more money. But we're not coming back here. It's the last time I'll see these old friends."

Susan went over and put an arm around Alan's shoulder. Harry looked down at his PDA. "Here we go," he said, and began a countdown. When he got to "one," we all looked up and out the window.

It wasn't dramatic. One second we were looking at one star-filled sky. The next, we were looking at another. If you blinked, you would have missed it. And yet, you could tell it was an entirely alien sky. We all may not have had Alan's knowledge of the constellations, but most of us know how to pick out Orion and the Big Dipper from the stellar lineup. They were nowhere to be found, an absence subtle and yet substantial. I glanced over at Alan. He was standing like a pillar, hand in Susan's.

"We're turning," Thomas said. We watched as the stars slid counterclockwise as the *Henry Hudson* changed course. Suddenly the enormous blue arm of the planet Phoenix hovered above us. And above it (or below it, from our orientation) was a space station so large, so massive, and so *busy* that all we could do was bulge our eyes at it.

Finally someone spoke. And to everyone's surprise, it was Maggie. "Would you look at that," she said.

We all turned to look at her. She was visibly annoyed. "I'm not *mute*," she said. "I just don't talk much. *This* deserves comment of some kind."

"No kidding," Thomas said, turning back to look at it. "It makes Colonial Station look like a pile of puke."

"How many ships do you see?" Jesse said to me.

"I don't know," I said. "Dozens. There could be hundreds, for all I know. I didn't even know this many starships *existed*."

"If any of us were still thinking Earth was the center of the human universe," Harry said, "now would be an excellent time to revise that theory," Harry said.

We all stood and looked at the new world out the window.

My PDA chimed me awake at 0545, which was notable in that I had set it to wake me at 0600. The screen was flashing; there was a message labeled URGENT on it. I tapped the message.

NOTICE:

From 0600 to 1200, we will be conducting the final physical improvement regimen for all recruits. To ensure prompt processing, all recruits are required to remain in their staterooms until such time as Colonial officials arrive to escort them to their physical improvement sessions. To aid in the smooth function of this process, stateroom doors will be secured as of 0600. Please take this time to take care of any personal business that requires use of the rest rooms or other areas outside your stateroom. If after 0600 you need to use the rest-room facilities, contact the Colonial staffer on your stateroom deck through your PDA.

You will be notified fifteen minutes prior to your appointment; please be dressed and prepared when Colonial officials arrive at your door. Breakfast will not be served; lunch and dinner will be served at the usual time.

At my age, you don't have to tell me twice to pee; I padded down to the rest room to take care of business and hoped that my appointment was sooner rather than later, as I didn't want to have to get permission to relieve myself.

My appointment was neither sooner nor later; at 0900 my PDA alerted me, and at 0915 there was a sharp rap at my door and a man's voice calling my name. I opened the door to find two Colonials on the other side. I received permission from them to make a quick rest-room stop, and then followed them from my deck, back to the waiting room of Dr. Russell. I waited briefly before I was allowed entrance into his examination room.

"Mr. Perry, good to see you again," he said, extending his hand.

The Colonials who accompanied me left through the far door. "Please step up to the crèche."

"The last time I did, you jackhammered several thousand bits of metal into my head," I said. "Forgive me if I'm not entirely enthusiastic about climbing in again."

"I understand," Dr. Russell said. "However, today is going to be pain-free. And we are under something of a time constraint, so, if you please." He motioned to the crèche.

I reluctantly stepped in. "If I feel so much as a twinge, I'm going to hit you," I warned.

"Fair enough," Dr. Russell said as he closed the crèche door. I noted that unlike the last time, Dr. Russell bolted down the door to the crèche; maybe he was taking the threat seriously. I didn't mind. "Tell me, Mr. Perry," he said as he bolted the door, "what do you think of the last couple of days?"

"They were confusing and irritating," I said. "If I knew I was going to be treated like a preschooler, I probably wouldn't have signed up."

"That's pretty much what everyone says," Dr. Russell said. "So let me explain a little bit about what we've been trying to do. We put in the sensor array for two reasons. First, as you may have guessed, we're monitoring your brain activity while you perform various basic functions and experience certain primal emotions. Every human's brain processes information and experience in more or less the same way, but at the same time each person uses certain pathways and processes unique to them. It's a little like how every human hand has five fingers, but each human being has his own set of fingerprints. What we've been trying to do is isolate your mental 'fingerprint.' Make sense?"

I nodded.

"Good. So now you know why we had you doing ridiculous and stupid things for two days."

"Like talking to a naked woman about my seventh birthday party," I said.

"We get a lot of really useful information from that one," Dr. Russell said.

"I don't see how," I said.

"It's technical," Dr. Russell assured me. "In any event, the last couple days give us a good idea of how your brain uses neural pathways and processes all sorts of stimuli, and that's information we can use as a template."

Before I could ask, *A template for what,* Dr. Russell continued. "Second, the sensor array does more than record what your brain is doing. It can also transmit a real-time representation of the activity in your brain. Or to put it another way, it can broadcast your consciousness. This is important, because unlike specific mental processes, consciousness can't be recorded. It has to be live if it's going to make the transfer."

"The transfer," I said.

"That's right," Dr. Russell said.

"Do you mind if I ask you what the hell you're talking about?" I said.

Dr. Russell smiled. "Mr. Perry, when you signed up to join the army, you thought we'd make you young again, right?"

"Yes," I said. "Everybody does. You can't fight a war with old people, yet you recruit them. You have to have some way to make them young again."

"How do you think we do it?" Dr. Russell asked.

"I don't know," I said. "Gene therapy. Cloned replacement parts. You'd swap out old parts somehow and put in new ones."

"You're half right," Dr. Russell said. "We do use gene therapy and cloned replacements. But we don't 'swap out' anything, except *you.*"

"I don't understand," I said. I felt very cold, like reality was being tugged out from under my feet.

"Your body is *old,* Mr. Perry. It's old and it won't work for much longer. There's no point in trying to save it or upgrade it. It's not something that gains value when it ages or has replaceable parts that keep it running like new. All a human body does when it gets older is get old. So we're going to get rid of it. We're getting rid of it all. The only part of you that we're going to save is the only part of you that *hasn't* decayed—your mind, your consciousness, your sense of self."

Dr. Russell walked over to the far door, where the Colonials had exited, and rapped on it. Then he turned back to me. "Take a good look at your body, Mr. Perry," he said. "Because you're about to say good-bye to it. You're going somewhere else."

"Where am I going, Dr. Russell?" I asked. I could barely make enough spit to talk.

"You're going here," he said, and opened the door.

From the other side, the Colonials came back in. One of them was pushing a wheelchair with someone in it. I craned my head to take a look. And I began to shake.

It was me.

Fifty years ago.

FIVE "Now, I want you to relax," Dr. Russell said to me.

The Colonials had wheeled the younger me to the other crèche and were in the process of placing the body into it. It or he or I or whatever offered no resistance; they might as well have been moving someone in a coma. Or a corpse. I was fascinated. And horrified. A small little voice in my brain told me it was good I had gone to the bathroom before I came in, or otherwise I'd be peeing down my leg.

"How—" I began, and I choked. My mouth was too dry to talk. Dr. Russell spoke to one of the Colonials, who left and returned with a small cup of water. Dr. Russell held the cup as he gave the water to me, which was good, because I don't think I could have managed to grip it. He spoke to me as I drank.

"'How' is usually attached to one of two questions," he said. "The first is, How did you make a younger version of me? The answer to that is that ten years ago we took a genetic sample and used that to make your new body." He took the cup away.

"A clone," I said, finally.

"No," Dr. Russell said. "Not exactly. The DNA has been heavily modified. You can see the most obvious difference—your new body's skin."

I looked back over and realized that in the shock of seeing a younger version of me, I missed a rather obvious and glaring difference.

"He's *green*," I said.

"*You're* green, you mean," Dr. Russell said. "Or will be in about five minutes. So that's one 'how' question. The second one is, How do you get me into there?" He pointed to my green-skinned doppelganger. "And the answer to that is, we're transferring your consciousness."

"How?" I asked.

"We take the representation of brain activity that's tracked by your sensor array and send it—and you—over there," Dr. Russell said. "We've taken the brain pattern information we've collected over the last couple of days and used it to prepare your new brain for your consciousness, so when we send you over, things will look familiar. I'm giving you the simplified version of things, obviously; it's vastly more complicated. But it'll do for right now. Now, let's get you plugged in."

Dr. Russell reached up and began to maneuver the crèche's arm over my head. I started to move my head away, so he stopped. "We're not putting anything in this time, Mr. Perry," he said. "The injector cap has been replaced with a signal amplifier. There's nothing to worry about."

"Sorry," I said, and moved my head back into position.

"Don't be," Dr. Russell said, and fit the cap over my skull. "You're taking this better than most recruits. The guy before you screamed like a pig and fainted. We had to transfer him over unconscious. He's going to wake up young and green and very, very disturbed. Trust me, you're a doll."

I smiled, and glanced over to the body that would soon be me. "Where's his cap?" I asked.

"Doesn't need one," Dr. Russell said, and began tapping his PDA. "Like I said, this body's been heavily modified."

"That sounds ominous," I said.

"You'll feel differently once you're inside." Dr. Russell finished playing with his PDA and turned back to me. "Okay, we're ready. Let me tell you what's going to happen next."

"Please," I said.

He turned the PDA around. "When I press this button"—he indicated a button on the screen—"your sensor array will begin transmitting your brain activity into the amplifier. Once your brain activity is sufficiently mapped, I'll connect this crèche to a specialized computer bank. At the same time, a similar connection will be opened to your new brain over there. When the connections check out, we'll broadcast your consciousness into your new brain. When the brain activity takes hold in your new brain, we'll sever the connection, and there you are, in your new brain and body. Any questions?"

"Does this procedure ever fail?" I asked.

"You *would* ask that question," Dr. Russell said. "The answer is yes. On rare occasions something can go wrong. However, it's extremely rare. I've been doing this for twenty years—thousands of transfers—and I've lost someone only once. The woman had a massive stroke during the transfer process. Her brain patterns became chaotic and consciousness didn't transfer. Everyone else made it through fine."

"So as long as I don't actually die, I'll live," I said.

"An interesting way to put it. But yes, that's about right."

"How do you know when consciousness has transferred?"

"We'll know it through here"—Dr. Russell tapped the side of his PDA—"and we'll know it because you'll tell us. Trust me, you'll know when you've made the transfer."

"How do *you* know?" I asked. "Have you ever done this? Been transferred?"

Dr. Russell smiled. "Actually, yes," he said. "Twice, in fact."

"But you're not green," I said.

"That's the second transfer. You don't have to stay green forever," he said, almost wistfully. Then he blinked and looked at his PDA again. "I'm afraid we have to cut the questions short now, Mr. Perry, since I have several more recruits to transfer after you. Are you ready to begin?"

"Hell no, I'm not ready," I said. "I'm so scared my bowels are about to cut out."

"Then let me rephrase," Dr. Russell said. "Are you ready to get it over with?"

"God, yes," I said.

"Then let's get to it," Dr. Russell said, and tapped the screen of his PDA.

The crèche gave a slight *thunk* as something physically switched on inside it. I glanced over to Dr. Russell. "The amplifier," he said. "This part will take about a minute."

I grunted acknowledgment and looked over to my new me. It was cradled in the crèche, motionless, like a wax figurine that someone had spilled green coloring into during the casting process. It looked like I did so long ago—better than I did, actually. I wasn't the most athletic young adult on the block. This version of me looked like he was muscled like a competitive swimmer. And it had a *great* head of hair.

I couldn't even *imagine* being in that body.

"We're at full resolution," Dr. Russell said. "Opening connection." He tapped his PDA.

There was a slight jolt, and then it suddenly felt like there was a big, echoey room in my brain. "Whoa," I said.

"Echo chamber?" Dr. Russell asked. I nodded. "That's the

computer bank," he said. "Your consciousness is perceiving the small time lag between there and here. It's nothing to worry about. Okay, opening connection between the new body and the computer bank." Another PDA tap.

From across the room, the new me opened his eyes.

"I did that," Dr. Russell said.

"He's got cat's eyes," I said.

"*You've* got cat's eyes," Dr. Russell said. "Both connections are clear and noise-free. I'm going to start the transfer now. You're going to feel a little disoriented." A PDA tap—

—and I fell

waaaaaaaaaaaaaaay down

(and felt like I was being pressed hard through a fine mesh mattress)

and all the memories I ever had hit me in the face like a runaway brick wall

one clear flash of standing at the altar

watching kathy walk down the aisle

seeing her foot catch the front of her gown

a small stutter in her step

then she corrected beautifully

smiled up at me as if to say

*yeah like **that's** going to stop me*

*another flash of kathy *where the hell did i put the vanilla* and then the clatter of the mixing bowl hitting kitchen tile*

(god damn it kathy)

And then I'm *me* again, staring into Dr. Russell's room feeling dizzy and looking straight at Dr. Russell's face and also the back of his head and thinking to myself, *Damn, that's a neat trick,* and it seems like I just had that thought in stereo.

And it hits me. I'm in two places at the same time.

I smile and see the old me and the new me smile simultaneously.

"I'm breaking the laws of physics," I say to Dr. Russell from two mouths.

And he says, "You're in."

And then he taps that goddamned PDA of his.

And there's just one of me again.

The *other* me. I can tell because I'm no longer staring at the new me anymore, I'm looking at the old me.

And it stares at me like it knows something truly strange has just happened.

And then the stare seems to say, *I'm no longer needed.*

And then it closes its eyes.

"Mr. Perry," Dr. Russell said, and then repeated it, and then lightly slapped me on the cheek.

"Yes," I said. "I'm here. Sorry."

"What's your full name, Mr. Perry?"

I thought about it for a second. Then, "John Nicholas Perry."

"What's your birthday?"

"June tenth."

"What was the name of your second-grade teacher?"

I looked directly at Dr. Russell. "Christ, man. I couldn't even remember that when I was in my *old* body."

Dr. Russell smiled. "Welcome to your new life, Mr. Perry. You made it through with flying colors." He unlatched the door to the crèche and opened it wide. "Come out of there, please."

I placed my hands—my green hands—on the side of the crèche and pushed outward. I placed my right foot forward and staggered a little bit. Dr. Russell came up beside me and steadied me. "Careful," he said. "You've been an older man for a while. It's going to take you a little bit of time to remember how to be in a young body."

"What do you mean?" I said.

"Well," he said. "For one thing, you can straighten up."

He was right. I was stooped slightly (kids, drink your milk). I straightened up, and took another step forward. And another. Good news, I remembered how to walk. I cracked a grin like a schoolboy as I paced in the room.

"How do you feel?" Dr. Russell asked.

"I feel *young*," I said, only a little joyously.

"You should," Dr. Russell said. "This body has a biological age of twenty. It's actually younger than that, but we can grow them fast these days."

I jumped experimentally and felt like I bounced halfway back to Earth. "I'm not even old enough to drink anymore," I said.

"You're still seventy-five inside," Dr. Russell said.

At that I stopped my little jumping and walked over to my old body, resting in the crèche. It looked sad and sagged, like an old suitcase. I reached out to touch my old face. It was warm, and I felt breath. I recoiled.

"It's still *alive*," I said, backing away.

"It's brain dead," Dr. Russell said quickly. "All your cognitive functions made the transfer. Once they had, I shut down this brain. It's running on autopilot—breathing and pumping blood, but nothing more and that only provisionally. Left on its own, it'll be dead within a few days."

I crept back to my old body. "What's going to happen to it?" I asked.

"We'll store it in the short term," Dr. Russell said. "Mr. Perry, I hate to rush you, but it's time for you to return to your quarters so I can continue my work with other recruits. We have quite a few to get through before noon."

"I have some questions about this body," I said.

"We have a brochure," Dr. Russell said. "I'll have it downloaded into your PDA."

"Gee, thanks," I said.

"Not at all," Dr. Perry said, and nodded toward the Colonials. "These men will escort you back to your quarters. Congratulations again."

I walked over to the Colonials, and we turned to go. Then I stopped. "Wait," I said. "I forgot something." I walked over to my old body again, still in the crèche. I looked over to Dr. Russell and pointed to the door. "I need to unlock this," I said. Dr. Russell nodded. I unlocked it, opened it, and took my old body's left hand. On the ring finger was a simple gold band. I slipped it off and slipped it on my ring finger. Then I cupped my old face with my new hands.

"Thank you," I said to me. "Thank you for everything."

Then I went out with the Colonials.

THE NEW YOU

An introduction to your new body,
for recruits of the Colonial Defense Forces
From the staff of Colonial Genetics
Two centuries of building better bodies!

[This was the splash page of the brochure waiting for me on my PDA. You'll just have to imagine the illustration, which echoed the famous da Vinci study of the human body, only with a nude green man where the other dude used to be. But let's continue.]

By now, you have received your new body from the Colonial Defense Forces. Congratulations! Your new body is the end result of decades of refinement by the scientists and engineers at Colonial Genetics, and is optimized for the rigorous demands of CDF service. This document will serve to give a brief introduction on the important features and functions of your new body, and provide answers to some of the most common questions recruits have about their new body.

NOT JUST A NEW BODY—A *BETTER* BODY

You've surely noticed the green skin tone of your new body. This isn't merely cosmetic. Your new skin (KloraDerm™) incorporates chlorophyll to provide your body with an extra source of energy and to optimize your body's use of both oxygen and carbon dioxide. The result: You'll feel fresher, longer—and better able to perform your duties as a CDF serviceperson! This is only the beginning of the improvements you'll find in your body. Here are some others:

☐ Your blood tissue has been replaced by SmartBlood™—a revolutionary system that increases oxygen-carrying capacity fourfold while it guards your body against disease, toxins, and death from blood tissue loss!

☐ Our patented CatsEye™ technology gives you sight you have to see to believe! Increased rod and cone counts give you better imaging resolution than can be achieved in most naturally evolved systems, while specially designed light amplifiers allow you to see clearly in extreme low-light situations.

☐ Our UncommonSense™ suite of sense enhancements allows you to touch, smell, hear and taste like you never have before, as our expanded nerve placement and optimized connections expand your perceptual ranges in all sense categories. You'll feel the difference from the first day!

☐ How strong do you want to be? With HardArm™ technologies that boost natural muscle strength and reaction time, you'll be stronger and faster than you ever dreamed possible—so strong and fast, in fact, that by law Colonial Genetics can't sell this technology on the consumer market. That's a real "leg up" for you recruits!

☐ Never be unconnected again! You'll never lose your BrainPal™ computer because it resides in your own brain. Our proprietary Assistive Adaptive Interface works *with* you so you can access your BrainPal™ your way. Your BrainPal™ also serves to coordinate nonorganic technologies in your new body, such as SmartBlood™. CDF servicepeople swear by this amazing piece of technology—and so will you.

BUILDING A BETTER YOU

You'll no doubt be amazed at how much your new body can do. But have you wondered how it was designed? You may be interested to know that your body is just the latest series in a line of advanced, improved bodies designed by Colonial Genetics. Through proprietary technology, we adapt both genetic information from other species and the latest in miniaturized robotic technologies to improve your new body. It's hard work, but you'll be glad we made the effort!

From our first improvements nearly two centuries ago, we've progressively built on our work. To introduce changes and improvements, we rely first on advanced computer modeling techniques to simulate the effects of each proposed improvement on the entire body system. The improvements that make it through this process are then tested on biological models. Then and only then are improvements incorporated into the final body design, integrated with the "starter" DNA you provide. Rest assured that each body improvement is safe and tested, and designed to make a better you!

COMMON QUESTIONS ABOUT YOUR NEW BODY

1. *Does My New Body Have a Brand Name?*

Yes! Your new body is known as the Defender Series XII, "Hercules" model. Technically, it's known as CG/CDF Model 12, Revision 1.2.11. This body model is for use only by the Colonial Defense Forces. Additionally, each body has its own model number for maintenance purposes. You can access your own number through your BrainPal". Don't worry, you can still use your given name for everyday purposes!

2. *Does My New Body Age?*

The Defender Series body is designed to provide the CDF with optimum performance its entire operating life. To do this, advanced regenerative techniques are employed at the genetic level to reduce natural entropic tendencies. With a basic maintenance regimen, your new body will remain in top condition as long as you operate it. You'll also find that injuries and disabilities are corrected quickly—so you can be up and running again in no time flat!

3. Can I Pass These Amazing Improvements to My Children?

No. Your body and its biological and technological systems are patented by Colonial Genetics and may not be passed on without permission. Also, due to the extensive nature of Defender Series improvements, its DNA is no longer genetically compatible with unmodified humans, and lab tests indicate that Defender Series mating creates incompatibilities lethal to the embryo in every case. Additionally, the CDF has determined that the ability to transmit genetic information is nonessential to its servicepeople's mission; therefore, each Defender model ships sterile, although other related functionality remains intact.

4. I'm Worried About the Theological Implications of This New Body. What Should I Do?

While neither Colonial Genetics nor the CDF maintains an official position on the theological or psychological ramifications of the transfer of consciousness from one body to another, we understand that many recruits may have questions or concerns. Each recruit transport comes equipped with clergy representing most of Earth's major religions and an additional complement of psychological therapists. We encourage you to seek them out and discuss your questions with them.

5. How Long Will I Stay in My New Body?

Defender Series bodies are designed for CDF use; so long as you stay in the CDF, you will be able to use and enjoy the technological and biological advancements of this new body. When you leave the CDF, you will be provided with a new, unaltered human body based on your own original DNA.

From all of us here at Colonial Genetics, congratulations on your new body! We know it will serve you well through your service in the Colonial

Defense Forces. Thanks for your service to the colonies—and enjoy...
Your New Body.

I set the PDA down, went over to the stateroom sink, and looked
into the mirror at my new face.

It was impossible to ignore the eyes. My old body had brown
eyes—muddy brown, but with interesting flecks of gold. Kathy
used to tell me that she had read that flecks of color in the
iris were nothing more than additional fatty tissue. So I had fat
eyes.

If those eyes were fat, these were positively obese. They were
gold from the pupil outward toward the rim, where they shaded
toward green. The rim of the iris was a deep emerald; spikes of
that color stabbed toward the pupils. The pupils themselves were
slitted, drawn tight by the light directly above the mirror. I turned
off that light and then turned the primary light off as well; the
only light in the room was a small LED on the PDA. My old eyes
would have never been able to see off of that.

My new eyes took only a moment to adjust. The room was un-
deniably dim, but I could make out every object clearly. I went
back to the mirror and looked in; my eyes were dilated like someone with a belladonna overdose. I flicked the sink light back on
and watched my pupils constrict with impressive speed.

I took off my clothes and took the first real look at my new
body. My earlier impression of my form turned out to be correct;
for lack of a better term, I was totally buffed out. I ran my hand
down my chest and washboard stomach. I had never been this
athletically fit in my life. I had no idea how they managed to make
the new me this fit. I wondered how long it would take me to get
it into the flabby shape I had been in during my real twenties.
Then I wondered, given the amount of fiddling they had done

with this body's DNA, if it was even possible for it to become flabby. I hoped not. I liked the new me.

Oh, and I was entirely hairless from the eyelashes down.

I mean, *hairless*—not a spare hair anywhere. Arms bare, legs bare, back bare (not that it had never *not* been bare before, ahem), private bits bare. I rubbed my chin to feel if there was a hint of stubble there. Smooth as a baby's bottom. Or my bottom, now. I looked down at my package; to be honest, without hair, it looked a little forlorn. The hair on my head was full but nondescript brown. That much hadn't changed from my previous incarnation.

I held my hand in front of my face to get a look at the skin tone. It was a shade of green that was light but not glaring, which was good; I don't think I could have handled being chartreuse. My skin was an even tone across my body, although my nipples and the tip of my penis were slightly darker. Basically, I seemed to have the same color contrast as before, just in a different hue. One thing I did notice, however, my veins were more noticeable, and grayish. I suspect that whatever color SmartBlood™ was (whatever it really was), it wasn't bloodred. I dressed myself again.

My PDA beeped at me. I picked it up. There was a message waiting.

You now have access to your BrainPal™ computer system, it read. Would you like to activate it at this time? There were buttons on the screen for YES and NO. I picked YES.

Suddenly, a deep, rich, soothing voice out of nowhere. I nearly jumped out of my new green skin.

"Hello!" it said. "You are interfacing with your BrainPal internal computer, with the patented Assistive Adaptive Interface! Do not be alarmed! Thanks to the BrainPal integration, the voice you are now hearing is being generated directly to the hearing centers of your brain."

Great, I thought. *There's another voice in my head now.*

"After this brief introductory session, you may turn off the voice at any time. We'll begin with some options you can choose by answering 'yes' or 'no.' At this point, your BrainPal would like you to say 'yes' and 'no' when directed, so that it may learn to recognize this response. So when you are ready, please say the word 'yes.' You may say it at any time."

The voice stopped. I hesitated, a little bit dazed.

"Please say 'yes' now," the voice repeated.

"Yes!" I said, a little jumpy.

"Thank you for saying 'yes.' Now, please say 'no.' "

"No," I said, and for a moment wondered if the BrainPal™ would think I was saying "no" to its request, get huffy and fry my brain in its own juices.

"Thank you for saying 'no,' " the voice said, revealing itself to be something of a literalist. "As we progress together, you will learn in time that you will not need to verbalize these commands in order for your BrainPal to respond to them. However, in the short term, you will probably wish to verbalize while you become comfortable communicating with your BrainPal. At this time, you have the option of continuing with audio, or switching to a text interface. Would you prefer to switch now to a text interface?"

"God, yes," I said.

We will now proceed with a text interface, a line of text read, floating directly in my line of sight. The text was perfectly contrasted against what I was staring at. I moved my head, and the text stayed dead center, the contrast changed to stay perfectly readable at all times. Wild.

It is recommended that during your initial text session, you remain seated to avoid injuring yourself, the BrainPal wrote. Please sit now. I sat.

During your initial sessions with your BrainPal™, you will find it easier to communicate by verbalizing. To aid the BrainPal™ in understanding your questions, we will now teach your BrainPal™ to understand your voice as it speaks. Please speak the following phonemes as you read them. In my field of vision, a list of phonemes unspooled. I read them right to left. The BrainPal then had me speak a number of short sentences. I did.

Thank you, the BrainPal wrote. Your BrainPal™ will now be able to take direction from the sound of your voice. Would you like to personalize your BrainPal™ now?

"Yes," I said.

Many BrainPal™ users find it useful to give their BrainPal a name other than BrainPal™. Would you like to name your BrainPal™ at this time?

"Yes," I said.

Please speak the name you would like to give your BrainPal™.

" 'Asshole,' " I said.

You have selected "Asshole," the BrainPal wrote, and to its credit it spelled the word correctly. Be aware that many recruits have selected this name for their BrainPal™. Would you like to choose a different name?

"No," I said, and was proud that so many of my fellow recruits also felt this way about their BrainPal.

Your BrainPal™ is now Asshole, the BrainPal wrote. You may change this name in the future if you like. Now you must choose an access phrase to activate Asshole. While Asshole is active at all times it will only respond to commands after it has been activated. Please choose a short phrase. Asshole suggests "Activate Asshole" but you may choose another phrase. Please say your activation phrase now.

" 'Hey, Asshole,' " I said.

You have chosen "Hey, Asshole." Please say it again to confirm. I did. Then it asked me to choose a deactivation phrase. I chose (of course) "Go away, Asshole."

Would you like Asshole to refer to itself in the first person?

"Absolutely," I said.

I am Asshole.

"Of course you are."

I await your commands or queries.

"Are you intelligent?" I asked.

I am equipped with a natural language processor and other systems to understand questions and comments and to provide answers, which often gives the appearance of intelligence, especially when connected to larger computer networks. Brain Pal™ systems, however, are not natively intelligent. For example, this is an automated response. This question is asked frequently.

"How do you understand me?"

At this stage I am responding to your voice, Asshole wrote. As you speak I am monitoring your brain and learning how your brain activates when you desire to communicate with me. In time I will be able to understand you without the need for you to speak. And in time, you may also learn to use me without conscious audible or visual cues.

"What do you do?" I asked.

I have a range of abilities. Would you like to see a formatted list?

"Please," I said.

A massive list appeared before my eyes. To see a list of subcategories, please select a top category and say, "Expand [category]." To perform an action, please say, "Open [category]."

I read down the list. Apparently, there was very little Asshole couldn't do. He could send messages to other recruits. He could download reports. He could play music or video. He could play games. He could call up any document on a system. He could store incredible amounts of data. He could perform complex calculations. He could diagnose physical ailments and provide suggestions for cures. He could create a local network among a chosen group of other BrainPal users. He could provide instantaneous translations of hundreds of human and alien languages. He could even provide field of vision information on any other BrainPal user. I turned this option on. I barely recognized myself anymore;

I doubt I'd recognize any of the other Old Farts. Overall, Asshole was a pretty useful thing to have sitting inside one's brain.

I heard an unlatching sound at my door. I looked up. "Hey, Asshole," I said. "What time is it?"

It is now 1200, Asshole wrote. I had spent the better part of ninety minutes fiddling with him. Well, enough of that; I was ready to see some real people.

"Go away, Asshole," I said.

Good-bye, Asshole wrote. The text disappeared as soon as I read it.

There was a knock on the door. I walked over to open it. I figured it was Harry; I wondered what he looked like.

He looked like a knockout brunette with dark (green) olive skin and legs that went all the way up.

"You're not Harry," I said, incredibly stupidly.

The brunette looked at me and looked me up and down. "John?" she finally said.

I stared blankly for a second, and the name hit me—just before the ID floated ghostlike before my eyes. "Jesse," I said.

She nodded. I stared. I opened my mouth to say something. She grabbed my head and kissed me so hard that I was knocked back into my quarters. She managed to kick the door shut on our way down to the floor. I was impressed.

I had forgotten just how easy it was for a young man to get an erection.

SIX

I'd forgotten how many times a young man can *get* an erection, too.

"Don't take this the wrong way," Jesse said, lying on top of me after the third (!) time. "But I'm really not all that attracted to you."

"Thank God," I said. "If you were, I'd be worn down to a nub by now."

"Don't get me wrong," Jesse said. "I'm fond of you. Even before the"—she motioned with her hand here, trying to think of a way to describe a rejuvenating, full-body transplant—"the *change*, you were intelligent and kind and funny. A good friend."

"Uh-huh," I said. "You know, Jesse, usually the 'let's be friends' speech is to *prevent* sex."

"I just don't want you to have illusions about what this is about."

"I was under the impression that it was about magically being transported into a body of a twenty-year-old and being so excited about it that it was imperative to have wild sex with the very first person we saw."

Jesse stared at me for a second, then burst out laughing. "Yes!

That's exactly it. Although in my case, it was the second person. I have a roommate, you know."

"Yeah? How does Maggie clean up?"

"Oh my God," Jesse said. "She makes me look like a beached whale, John."

I ran my hands over her sides. "That's a mighty fine beached whale, Jesse."

"I know!" Jesse said, and suddenly sat up, straddling me. She raised her arms up and crossed them behind her head, perking up her already marvelously firm and full breasts. I felt her inner thighs radiating heat as they wrapped around my midsection. I knew that even though I didn't have an erection at that very moment, one was coming right up. "I mean, look at me," she said, unnecessarily, because I hadn't taken my eyes off her from the moment she sat up. "I look *fabulous*. I don't say that to be vain. It's just I never looked this good in real life. Not even *close*."

"I find that hard to believe," I said.

She grabbed her breasts and pointed the nipples at my face. "See these?" she said, and wiggled the left one. "In real life, *this* one was a cup size smaller than *this* one, and it was still too large. I had a permanent backache from puberty onward. And I think they were this firm for one week when I was thirteen. *Maybe*."

She reached down, grabbed my hands, and placed them on her perfect, flat belly. "I never had one of *these*, either," she said. "I always carried a little pouch down here, even before I had babies. After two kids, well, let's just say that if I had ever wanted a third, it would have had a duplex in there."

I slid my hands behind her and grabbed her ass. "What about this?" I said.

"Wide load," Jesse said, and laughed. "I was a big girl, my friend."

"Being big's not a crime," I said. "Kathy was on the larger side. I liked it just fine."

"I didn't have a problem with it at the time," she said. "Body issues are foolish. On the other hand, I wouldn't trade now." She ran her hands over her body, provocatively. "I'm all *sexy!*" And with that, she did a little giggle and a head flip. I laughed.

Jesse leaned forward and peered into my face. "I'm finding this cat's-eye thing incredibly fascinating," she said. "I wonder if they actually used cat DNA to make them. You know, spliced cat DNA with ours. I wouldn't mind being part cat."

"I don't think it's really cat DNA," I said. "We're not exhibiting other catlike attributes."

Jesse sat back up. "Like what?" she said.

"Well," I said, and let my hands wander up to her breasts, "for one thing, male cats have barbs on their penis."

"Get out," Jesse said.

"No, it's true," I said. "It's the barbs that stimulate the female to ovulate. Look it up. Anyway, no barbs down there. I think you'd've noticed if there were."

"That doesn't prove anything," Jesse said, and suddenly sent her back part back, and her forward part forward, to lie directly on top of me. She grinned salaciously. "It could be that we just haven't been doing it hard enough to make them pop out."

"I'm sensing a challenge," I said.

"I'm sensing something, too," she said, and wiggled.

"What are you thinking about?" Jesse asked me, later.

"I'm thinking about Kathy," I said, "and how often we'd lie around like we're doing now."

"You mean, on the carpet," Jesse said, smiling.

I bopped her gently on the head. "Not that part. Just lying

around after sex, talking and enjoying each other's company. We were doing this the first time we talked about enlisting."

"Why did you bring it up?" Jesse said.

"I didn't," I said. "Kathy did. It was on my sixtieth birthday, and I was depressed about getting older. So she suggested that we sign up when the time came. I was a little surprised. We'd always been antimilitary. We protested the Subcontinential War, you know, when it wasn't exactly popular to do that."

"Lots of people protested that war," Jesse said.

"Yeah, but we *really* protested. Became a little bit of a joke about it in town, actually."

"So how did she rationalize signing up with the Colonial Army?"

"She said she wasn't against war or the military in a general sense, just *that* war and our military. She said that people have the right to defend themselves and that it was probably a nasty universe out there. And she said that beyond those noble reasons, we'd be young again to boot."

"But you wouldn't be able to enlist together," Jesse said. "Unless you were the same age."

"She was a year younger than me," I said. "And I did mention that to her—I said that if I joined the army, I'd be officially dead, we wouldn't be married anymore and who knows if we'd ever see each other again."

"What did she say?"

"She said these were technicalities. She'd find me again and drag me to the altar like she had before. And she would have, you know. She could be a bear about these things."

Jesse propped herself up on her elbow and looked at me. "I'm sorry she's not here with you, John."

I smiled. "It's all right," I said. "I just miss my wife from time to time, that's all."

"I understand," Jesse said. "I miss my husband, too."

I glanced over to her. "I thought he left you for a younger woman and then got food poisoning."

"He did and he did, and he deserved to vomit his guts out," Jesse said. "I don't miss the *man*, really. But I miss having a *husband*. It's nice to have someone you know you're supposed to be with. It's nice to be married."

"It's nice to be married," I agreed.

Jesse snuggled up to me and draped an arm over my chest. "Of course, *this* is nice, too. It's been a while since I've done this."

"Lie on a floor?"

It was her turn to bop me. "No. Well, yes, actually. But more specifically, lie around after sex. Or have sex, for that matter. You don't want to know how long it's been since I've had it."

"Sure I do."

"Bastard. Eight years."

"No wonder you jumped me the minute you saw me," I said.

"You got that right," Jesse said. "You happened to be very conveniently located."

"Location is everything, that's what my mother always told me."

"You had a strange mother," Jesse said. "Yo, bitch, what time is it?"

"What?" I said.

"I'm talking to the voice in my head," she said.

"Nice name you have for it," I said.

"What did you name yours?"

"Asshole."

Jesse nodded. "Sounds about right. Well, the bitch tells me it's just after 1600. We have two hours until dinner. You know what that means?"

"I don't know. I think four times is my limit, even when I'm young and superimproved."

"Calm yourself. It means we have just enough time for a nap."

"Should I grab a blanket?"

"Don't be silly. Just because I had sex on the carpet doesn't mean I want to sleep on it. You've got an extra bunk. I'm going to use it."

"So I'm going to have to nap alone?"

"I'll make it up to you," Jesse said. "Remind me when I wake up."

I did. She did.

"God *damn* it," Thomas said as he sat down at the table, carrying a tray so piled with food that it was a miracle he could even lift it. "Aren't we all just too good-looking for words."

He was right. The Old Farts had cleaned up amazingly well. Thomas and Harry and Alan could all have been male models; of the four of us, I was definitely the ugly duckling, and I looked— well, I looked *good*. As for the women, Jesse was stunning, Susan was even more so, and Maggie frankly looked like a goddess. It actually hurt to look at her.

It hurt to look at all of us. In that good, dizzying sort of way. We all spent a few minutes just staring at each other. And it wasn't just us. As I scanned through the room, I couldn't find a single ugly human in it. It was pleasingly disturbing.

"It's impossible," Harry said, suddenly, to me. I looked over at him. "I looked around, too," he said. "There's no way in hell all the people in this room all looked as good as they do now when they were originally this age."

"Speak for yourself, Harry," Thomas said. "If anything, I do believe I am a shade less attractive than in my salad days."

"You're the same color as a salad these days," Harry said. "And even if we excuse Doubtful Thomas over here—"

"I'm going to cry all the way to a mirror," Thomas said.

"—it's well nigh impossible that everyone is in the same basket. I guarantee you I did not look this good when I was twenty. I was fat. I had massive acne. I was already balding."

"Stop it," Susan said. "I'm getting aroused."

"And I'm trying to eat," said Thomas.

"I can laugh about it now, because I look like *this*," Harry said, running his hand down his body, as if to present this year's model. "But the new me has very little to do with the old me, I'll tell you that."

"You sound as if it bothers you," Alan said.

"It does, a little," Harry admitted. "I mean, I'll *take* it. But when someone gives me a gift horse, I look it in the mouth. Why are we so good-looking?"

"Good genes," Alan said.

"Sure," Harry said. "But whose? Ours? Or something that they spliced out of a lab somewhere?"

"We're just all in excellent shape now," Jesse said. "I was telling John that this body is in far better shape than my real one ever was."

Maggie suddenly spoke up. "I say that, too," she said. "I say 'my real body' when I mean 'my old body.' It's as if this body isn't real to me yet."

"It's real enough, sister," Susan said. "You still have to pee with it. I know."

"This from the woman who criticized *me* for oversharing," Thomas said.

"My point, because I did have one," Jesse said, "is that while they were toning up our bodies, they took some time to tone up the rest of us as well."

"Agreed," Harry said. "But that's not telling us *why* they did it."

"It's so we bond," Maggie said.

Everyone stared. "Well, look who's coming out of her shell."

"Bite me, Susan." Maggie said. Susan grinned. "Look, it's basic human psychology that we're inclined to like people who we find attractive. Moreover, everyone in this room, even us, are basically strangers to each other, and have few if any ties to bring us together in a short time. Making us all look good to each other is a way to promote bonding, or will be, once we start training."

"I don't see how it's going to help the army if we're all too busy ogling each other to fight," Thomas said.

"It's not about that," Maggie said. "Sexual attraction is just a side issue here. It's a matter of quickly instilling trust and devotion. People instinctively trust and want to help people they find attractive, regardless of sexual desire. It's why newscasters are always attractive. It's why attractive people don't have to work as hard in school."

"But we're all attractive now," I said. "In the land of the incredibly attractive, the merely good-looking could be in trouble."

"And even now, some of us look better than others," Thomas said. "Every time I look at Maggie, I feel like the oxygen is being sucked from the room. No offense, Maggie."

"None taken," Maggie said. "The baseline here isn't each other as we are now, anyway. It's how we all appeared before. In the short term, that's reflexively the baseline we'll use, and a short-term advantage is all they'd be looking for anyway."

"So you're saying that you don't feel oxygen-deprived when you look at me," Susan said to Thomas.

"It's not meant to be an insult," Thomas said.

"I'll remember that when I'm strangling you," Susan said. "Speaking of oxygen-deprived."

"Stop flirting, you two," Alan said, and turned his attention to Maggie. "I think you're right about the attraction thing, but I think you're forgetting the one person we're supposed to be the most attracted to: ourselves. For better or worse, these bodies we're in are still alien to us. I mean, between the fact that I'm green and I've got a computer named 'Dipshit' in my head—" He stopped, and looked at us all. "What did you all name your BrainPals?"

"Asshole," I said.

"Bitch," Jesse said.

"Dickward," said Thomas.

"Fuckhead," said Harry.

"Satan," said Maggie.

"Sweetie," said Susan. "Apparently, I'm the only one who likes my BrainPal."

"More like you were the only one who wasn't disturbed by having a voice suddenly appear in your skull," Alan said. "But this is my point. Suddenly becoming young and having massive physical and mechanical changes takes a toll on one's psyche. Even if we're glad to be young again—and I know I am—we're still going to be alienated from our new selves. Making us look good to ourselves is one way to help us get 'settled in.'"

"These are crafty people we're dealing with," Harry said with ominous finality.

"Oh, lighten up, Harry," Jesse said, and gave him a little nudge. "You're the only person I know who would turn being young and sexy into a dark conspiracy."

"You think I'm sexy?" Harry said.

"You're dreamy, sweetheart," Jesse said, and batted her eyes dramatically at him.

Harry cracked a goofy grin. "That's the first time this century anyone's said *that* to me. Okay, I'm sold."

The man who stood in front of the theater full of recruits was a battle-tested veteran. Our BrainPals informed us that he'd been in the Colonial Defense Forces for fourteen years and had participated in several battles, the names of which meant nothing to us now, but no doubt would at some point in the future. This man had gone to new places, met new races and exterminated them on sight. He looked all of twenty-three years old.

"Good evening, recruits," he began after we had all settled down. "I am Lieutenant Colonel Bryan Higgee, and for the remainder of your journey, I will be your commanding officer. As a practical matter, this means very little—between now and our arrival at Beta Pyxis III, one week from now, you will have only one command objective. However, it will serve to remind you that from this point forward, you are subject to Colonial Defense Forces rules and regulations. You have your new bodies now, and with those new bodies will come new responsibilities.

"You may be wondering about your new bodies, as to what they can do, what stresses they can endure and how you can use them in the service of the Colonial Defense Forces. All these questions will be answered soon, as you begin your training on Beta Pyxis III. Right now, however, our main goal is simply for you to become comfortable in your new skins.

"And so, for the remainder of your trip, here are your orders: Have fun."

That brought up a murmur and some scattered laughter in the ranks. The idea of having fun being an order was amusingly counterintuitive. Lieutenant Colonel Higgee showed a mirthless grin.

"I understand this appears to be an unusual order. Be that as it may, having fun with your new body is going to be the best way for you to get used to the new abilities you have. When you begin your training, top performance will be required of you from the very start. There will be no 'ramp-up'—there's no time for that. The universe is a dangerous place. Your training will be short and difficult. We can't afford to have you uncomfortable with your body.

"Recruits, consider this next week as a bridge between your old lives and your new ones. In this time, which you will ultimately find all too brief, you can use these new bodies, designed for military use, to enjoy the pleasures you enjoyed as a civilian. You'll find the *Henry Hudson* is filled with recreations and activities you've loved on Earth. Use them. Enjoy them. Get used to working with your new bodies. Learn a little about their potential and see if you can divine their limits.

"Ladies and gentlemen, we will meet again for a final briefing before you begin your training. Until then, have fun. I do not exaggerate when I say that while life in the Colonial Defense Forces has its rewards, this may be the last time you will be entirely carefree in your new bodies. I suggest you use this time wisely. I suggest you have fun. That is all; you're dismissed."

We all went *insane.*

Let's start, of course, with the sex. Everyone was doing it with everybody else, in more places on the ship than it is probably sensible to discuss. After the first day, in which it became clear that any semisecluded place was going to be used for enthusiastic humping, it became courteous to make a lot of noise as one moved about, to alert the conjugal that you were on your way in. Sometime during the second day it became general knowledge that I had a room to myself; I was besieged with pleas for access. They were summarily denied. I'd never operated a house of ill repute, and I wasn't about to start now. The only people who were going to fuck around in my room were me and any invited guests.

There was only one of those. And it wasn't Jesse; it was Maggie, who, as it turned out, had had a thing for me even when I was wrinkled. After our briefing with Higgee, she more or less ambushed me at my door, which made me wonder if this was somehow standard operating procedure for post-change women. Regardless, she was great fun and, in private at least, not in the least retiring. It turned out that she had been a professor at Oberlin College. She taught philosophy of Eastern religions. She wrote six books on the subject. The things you learn about people.

The other Old Farts also stuck to their own. Jesse paired up with Harry after our initial fling, while Alan, Tom and Susan worked out some arrangement with Tom in the center. It was good that Tom liked to eat a lot; he needed his strength.

The ferocity at which the recruits went for sex undoubtedly appears unseemly from the outside, but it made perfect sense from where we stood (or lay, or were bent over upon). Take a group of people who generally have had little sex, due to lack of partners or declining health and libido, stuff them into brand-new young, attractive and highly functional bodies and then hurl them into space far away from anything they ever knew and everyone they ever loved. The combination of the three was a recipe for sex. We did it because we could, and because it beats being lonely.

It's not the only thing we did, of course. Using these gorgeous new bodies only for sex would be like singing only one note. Our bodies were claimed to be new and improved, and we found it to be true in simple and surprising ways. Harry and I had to call off a Ping-Pong game when it became clear neither of us was going to win—not because we were both incompetent, but because our reflexes and hand-eye coordination made it damn near impossible to get the ball past the other guy. We volleyed for thirty minutes and would have gone longer if the Ping-Pong ball we were using hadn't cracked from the force of being hit at such tremendously high speeds. It was ridiculous. It was marvelous.

Other recruits found out the same thing we did in other ways. On the third day, I was in a crowd that watched two recruits engage in what was possibly the most thrilling martial arts battle ever; they did things with their bodies that simply shouldn't have been possible assuming normal human flexibility and standard gravity. At one point, one of the men placed a kick that launched the other halfway across the room; instead of collapsing in a pile of broken bones, as I'm sure I would have, the other guy did a backflip *midflight,* righted himself, and launched himself back at his opponent. It looked like a special effect. In a way it was.

After the battle, both men breathed deeply and bowed to his opponent. And then both of them collapsed onto each other, simultaneously laughing and sobbing hysterically. It's a weird, wonderful and yet troubling thing to be as good at something as you ever wanted to be, and then to be even better than that.

People went too far, of course. I personally saw one recruit leap off a high landing, either under the assumption that she could fly or, barring that, at least land without injury. My understanding is that she shattered her right leg, right arm, jaw, and cracked her skull. However, she was still alive after the leap, a state of affairs that probably wouldn't have existed back on Earth. More impressively, however, she was back in action two days later, which obviously spoke more to the Colonial medical technology than this silly woman's recuperative powers. I hope someone told her not to do such a stupid move in the future.

When people weren't playing with their bodies, they were playing with their minds, or with their BrainPals, which was close enough. As I would walk about the ship, I would frequently see recruits simply sitting around, eyes closed, slowly nodding their heads. They were listening to music or watching a movie or something similar, the piece of work called up in their brain for them alone. I'd done it myself; while searching the ship's system, I had come across a compilation of every Looney Tunes cartoon created, both during their classic Warner days and then after the characters were put into the public domain. I spent hours one night watching

Wile E. Coyote get smashed and blown up; I finally stopped when Maggie demanded I choose between her and Road Runner. I chose her. I could pick Road Runner anytime, after all. I had downloaded all the cartoons into Asshole.

"Choosing friends" was something I did a lot of. All of the Old Farts knew that our group was temporary at best; we were simply seven people thrown together at random, in a situation that had no hope for permanence. But we became friends, and close friends at that, in the short period of time we had together. It's no exaggeration to say that I became as close to Thomas, Susan, Alan, Harry, Jesse and Maggie as I had to anyone in the last half of my "normal" life. We became a band, and a family, down to the petty digs and squabbles. We gave one another someone to care about, which was something we needed in a universe that didn't know or cared that we existed.

We bonded. And we did it even before we were biologically prodded to do so by the colonies' scientists. And as the *Henry Hudson* drew closer to our final destination, I knew I was going to miss them.

"In this room right now are 1,022 recruits," Lieutenant Colonel Higgee said. "Two years from today, 400 of you will be dead."

Higgee stood in the front of the theater, again. This time, he had a backdrop: Beta Pyxis III floated behind him, a massive marble streaked with blue, white, green and brown. We were all ignoring it and focusing on Lieutenant Colonel Higgee. His statistic had gotten everyone's attention, a feat considering the time (0600 hours) and the fact that most of us were still staggering from the last night of freedom we assumed we would have.

"In the third year," he continued, "another 100 of you will die. Another 150 in years four and five. After ten years—and yes, recruits, you *will* most likely be required to serve a full ten years—750 of you will have been killed in the line of duty. Three-quarters of you, gone. These have been the survival statistics—not just for the last ten or twenty years, but for the over two hundred years the Colonial Defense Forces have been active."

There was dead silence.

"I know what you're thinking right now, because I was thinking it when I was in your place," Lieutenant Colonel Higgee said. "You're thinking—what the hell am I doing here? This guy is telling me I'm going to be dead in ten years! But remember that back home, you most likely would have been dead in ten years, too—frail and old, dying a useless death. You may die in the Colonial Defense Forces. You probably *will* die in the Colonial Defense Forces. But your death will not be a useless one. You'll have died to keep humanity alive in our universe."

The screen behind Higgee blanked out, to be replaced with a three-dimensional star field. "Let me explain our position," he said, and as he did, several dozen of the stars burned bright green, randomly distributed across the field. "Here are the systems where humans have colonized—gained a foothold in the galaxy. And these are where alien races of comparable technology and survival requirements are known to exist." This time hundreds of stars blazed up, redly. The human points of light were utterly surrounded. Gasps were heard in the theater.

"Humanity has two problems," Lieutenant Colonel Higgee said. "The first is that it is in a race with other sentient and similar species to colonize. Colonization is the key to our race's survival. It's as simple as that. We must colonize or be closed off and contained by other races. This competition is fierce. Humanity has few allies among the sentient races. Very few races are allies with anyone, a situation that existed long before humanity stepped into the stars.

"Whatever your feelings about the possibility for diplomacy in the long run, the reality is that on the ground, we are in fierce and furious competition. We cannot hold back our expansion and hope that we can achieve a peaceful solution that allows for colonization by all races. To do so would be to condemn humanity. So we fight to colonize.

"Our second problem is that when we do find planets suitable for colonization, they are often inhabited by intelligent life. When we can, we live with native population and work to achieve harmony. Unfortunately, much of the time, we are not welcome. It is regrettable when this happens, but the needs of humanity are and must be our priority. And so the Civil Defense Forces become an invading force."

The background switched back to Beta Pyxis III. "In a perfect universe, we would not need the Colonial Defense Forces," Higgee said. "But this is not that perfect universe. And so, the Colonial Defense Forces have three mandates. The first is to protect existing human colonies and protect them from attack and invasion. The second is to locate new planets suitable for colonization, and hold them against predation, colonization and invasion from competing races. The third is to prepare planets with native populations for human colonization.

"As Colonial Defense Forces soldiers, you will be required to uphold all three mandates. This is not easy work, nor is it simple work, nor is it clean work, in any number of ways. But it must be done. The survival of humanity demands it—and we will demand it of you.

"Three-quarters of you will die in ten years. Despite improvements to soldiers' bodies, weapons and technology, this is a constant. But in your wake, you leave the universe as a place where your children, their children, and all the children of humanity can grow and thrive. It's a high cost, and one worth paying.

"Some of you may wonder what you'll get personally from

your service. What you'll get after your term of service is another new life. You will be able to colonize and to start again, on a new world. The Colonial Defense Forces will back your claim and provide you with everything you'll need. We can't promise you success in your new life—that's up to you. But you'll have an excellent start, and you'll have the gratitude of your fellow colonists for your time of service to them and theirs. Or you can do as I have, and reenlist. You might be surprised at how many do."

Beta Pyxis III flickered momentarily and then disappeared, leaving Higgee as the sole focus of attention. "I hope you all took my advice to have fun in this last week," he said. "Now your work begins. In one hour, you will be transported off the *Henry Hudson* to begin your training. There are several training bases here; your assignments are being transmitted to your BrainPals. You may return to your rooms to pack your personal belongings; don't bother with clothing, it will be provided on base. Your BrainPal will inform you where to assemble for transport.

"Good luck, recruits. May God protect you, and may you serve humanity with distinction, and with pride."

And then Lieutenant Colonel Higgee saluted us. I didn't know what to do. Neither did anyone else.

"You have your orders," Lieutenant Colonel Higgee said. "You are dismissed."

The seven of us stood together, crowding around the seats in which we just sat.

"They certainly don't leave much time for good-byes," Jesse said.

"Check your computers," Harry said. "Maybe some of us are going to the same bases."

We checked. Harry and Susan were reporting to Alpha Base;

Jesse to Beta. Maggie and Thomas were Gamma; Alan and I were Delta.

"They're breaking up the Old Farts," Thomas said.

"Don't get all misty," Susan said. "You knew it was coming."

"I'll get misty if I want," Thomas said. "I don't know anyone else. I'll even miss you, you old bag."

"We're forgetting something," Harry said. "We may not be together, but we can still keep in touch. We have our BrainPals. All we have to do is create a mailbox for each other. The 'Old Farts' clubhouse."

"That works here," Jesse said. "But I don't know about when we're in active duty. We could be on the other side of the galaxy from each other."

"The ships still communicate with each other through Phoenix," Alan said. "Each ship has skip drones that go to Phoenix to pick up orders and to communicate ship status. They carry mail, too. It might take a while for our news to reach each other, but it'll still reach us."

"Like sending messages in bottles," Maggie said. "Bottles with superior firepower."

"Let's do it," Harry said. "Let's be our own little family. Let's look out for each other, no matter where we are."

"Now you're getting misty, too," Susan said.

"I'm not worried about missing *you*, Susan," Harry said. "I'm taking you with me. It's the rest of these guys I'll miss."

"A pact, then," I said. "To stay the Old Farts, through thick and thin. Look out, universe." I held out my hand. One by one, each of the Old Farts put their hand on mine.

"Christ," Susan said as she put her hand on the pile. "Now *I'm* misty."

"It'll pass," Alan said. Susan hit him lightly with her other hand.

We stayed that way as long as we could.

PART II

SEVEN On a far plain on Beta Pyxis III, Beta Pyxis, the local sun, was just beginning its eastward journey up the sky; the composition of the atmosphere gave the sky an aqua tint, greener than Earth's but still nominally blue. On the rolling plain, grasses waved purple and orange in the morning breeze; birdlike animals with two sets of wings could be seen playing the sky, testing out the currents and eddies with wild, chaotic swoops and dives. This was our first morning on a new world, the first I or any of my former shipmates had ever set upon. It was beautiful. If there hadn't been a large, angry master sergeant on it, bellowing in my ear, it would have been just about perfect.

Alas, there was.

"Christ on a Popsicle stick," Master Sergeant Antonio Ruiz declared after he had glared at the sixty of us in his recruit platoon, standing (we hoped) more or less at attention on the tarmac of Delta Base's shuttleport. "We have clearly just lost the battle for the goddamn universe. I look at you people and the words 'tremendously fucked' leap right out of my goddamned skull. If you're the best that the Earth has got to offer, it's time we bend over and get a tentacle right up the ass."

This got an involuntary chuckle from several recruits. Master Sergeant Antonio Ruiz could have come from central casting. He was exactly what you expected from a drill instructor—large, angry and colorfully abusive right from the get-go. No doubt in the next few seconds, he would get into one of the amused recruit's faces, hurl obscenities and demand one hundred push-ups. This is what you get from watching seventy-five years' worth of war dramas.

"Ha, ha, ha," Master Sergeant Antonio Ruiz said, back at us. "Don't think I don't know what you're thinking, you dumb shits. I know you're enjoying my performance at the moment. How delightful! I'm just like all those drill instructors you've seen in the movies! Aren't I just the fucking quaint one!"

The amused chuckles had come to a stop. That last bit was not in the script.

"You don't *understand*," Master Sergeant Antonio Ruiz said. "You're under the impression that I'm talking like this because this is just something drill instructors are *supposed* to do. You're under the impression that after a few weeks of training, my gruff but fair façade will begin to slip and I will show some inkling of being impressed with the lot of you, and that at the end of your training, you'll have earned my grudging respect. You're under the impression I'll think fondly of you while you're off making the universe safe for humanity, secure in the knowledge I've made you better fighting men and women. Your *impression*, ladies and gentlemen, is completely and irrevocably fucked."

Master Sergeant Antonio Ruiz stepped forward and paced down the line. "Your impression is fucked, because unlike you, I have actually been out in the universe. I have seen what we're up against. I have seen men and women that I knew personally turned into hot fucking chunks of meat that could still manage to scream. On my first tour of duty, my commanding officer was turned into a goddamn alien lunch buffet. I watched as the fuckers grabbed him, pinned him to the ground, sliced out his internal organs, passed them out and gobbled them down—and slid back under the ground before any of us could do a goddamned thing."

A stifled giggle from somewhere behind me. Master Sergeant Antonio Ruiz stopped and cocked his head. "Oh. One of you thinks I'm *kidding*. One of you dumb motherfuckers always does. That's why I keep *this* around. Activate now," he said, and suddenly in front of each of us a video screen appeared; it took me a disorienting second before I realized Ruiz had somehow managed to activate my BrainPal remotely, switching on a video feed. The feed appeared to be taken from a small helmet camera. We saw several soldiers hunkered down in a foxhole, discussing plans for the next day's travel. Then one of the soldiers stopped talking for a second and slammed a palm down onto the dirt. He glanced up fearfully and yelled "incoming" a split second before the ground erupted beneath him.

What happened next happened so quickly that not even the instinctive, panicked turn of the camera's owner was fast enough to miss it all. It was not pleasant. In the real world, someone was vomiting, ironically matching the action of the camera's owner. Blessedly, the video feed switched off right after that.

"I'm not so funny now, am I?" Master Sergeant Antonio Ruiz said, mockingly. "I'm not that happy fucking stereotypical drill instructor anymore, am I? You're not in a military comedy anymore, are you? Welcome to the fucking universe! The universe is a fucked-up place, my friends. And I'm not talking to you like this because I'm putting on some amusing little drill instructor routine. That man who was sliced and diced was among the best fighting men I have ever had the privilege of knowing. None of you are his equal. And yet you see what happened to *him*. Think what will happen to *you*. I'm talking to you like this because I sincerely believe, from the bottom of my heart, that if you're the best humanity can do, we are magnificently and totally fucked. Do you believe me?"

Some of our number managed to mumble a "Yes, sir" or something close to it. The rest of us were still replaying the evisceration in our heads, without the benefit of the BrainPal.

"Sir? Sir?!? I am a fucking master sergeant, you shitheads. I work for a living! You will answer with 'Yes, Master Sergeant' when you need to answer in the affirmative, and 'No, Master Sergeant' when you answer in the negative. Do you understand?"

"Yes, Master Sergeant!" we replied.

"You can do better than that! Say it again!"

"Yes, Master Sergeant!" we screamed. Some of us were clearly on the verge of tears by the sound of that last bellow.

"For the next twelve weeks, my job is to attempt to train you to be soldiers, and by God, I am going to do it, and I'm going to do it despite the fact that I can already tell that none of you mother-fuckers is up to the challenge. I want each of you to think about what I'm saying here. This isn't the old-time Earth military, where drill sergeants had to tone up the fat, bulk up the weak, or educate the stupid—each of you comes with a lifetime of experience and a new body that is in peak physical condition. You would think that would make my job easier. It. Does. Not.

"Each of you has seventy-five years of bad habits and personal feelings of entitlement that I have to purge in three goddamn months. And each of you thinks your new body is some kind of shiny new toy. Yeah, I know what you've been doing for the last week. You've been fucking like rabid monkeys. Guess what? Play-time is *over*. For the next twelve weeks, you'll be lucky if you have time to jerk off in the shower. Your shiny new toy is going to be put to work, my pretties. Because I have to make you into soldiers. And *that* is going to be a full-time job."

Ruiz resumed his pacing in front of the recruits. "I want to make one thing clear. I do not like, nor will I ever like, any one of you. Why? Because I know that despite the fine work of myself and my staff, you will inevitably make all of us look bad. It *pains* me. It keeps me awake at night knowing that no matter how much I teach you, you will inevitably fail those who fight with you. The best I can do is make sure that when you go, you don't take your whole fucking platoon down with you. That's right—if you only get *yourself* killed, I count that as a success!

"Now, you may think that this is some sort of generalized hatred that I will carry for the lot of you. Let me assure you that this is not the case. Each of you will fail, but you will fail in your own unique way, and therefore I will dislike each of you on an individual basis. Why, even now, each of you has qualities that irritate the living fuck out of me. Do you believe me?"

"Yes, Master Sergeant!"

"Bullshit! Some of you are still thinking that I'm just going to hate the other guy." Ruiz shot out an arm and pointed out toward the plain and the rising sun. "Use your pretty new eyes to focus on that transmission tower out there; you can just barely see it. It is ten klicks away, ladies and gentlemen. I'm going to find something about each of you that will piss me off, and when I do, you will *sprint* to that fucking tower. If you are not back in an hour, this entire platoon will run it again tomorrow morning. Do you understand?"

"Yes, Master Sergeant!" I could see people trying to do the math in their heads; he was telling us to run five-minute miles all the way there and all the way back. I strongly suspected we'd be running it again tomorrow.

"Which of you was in the military back on Earth? Step up, now," Ruiz asked. Seven recruits stepped forward.

"God *damn* it," Ruiz said. "There is nothing I hate more in the entire fucking universe than a veteran recruit. We have to spend extra time and effort on you bastards, making you unlearn every single fucking thing you learned back home. All you sons of bitches had to do was fight humans! And even that you did badly! Oh, yes, we *saw* that whole Subcontinental War of yours. Shit. Six fucking years to beat an enemy that barely had firearms, and you had to cheat to win. Nukes are for pussies. *Pussies.* If the CDF fought like the U.S. forces fought, you know where humanity would be today? On an asteroid, scraping algae off the fucking tunnel *walls*. And which ones of you assholes are Marines?"

Two recruits stepped forward. "You fuckers are the *worst*," Ruiz said, getting right in their faces. "You smug bastards have killed more CDF soldiers than any alien species—doing things that Marine fucking way instead of the way they're *supposed* to be done. You probably had 'Semper Fi' tattoos somewhere on your old body, didn't you? Didn't you?"

"Yes, Master Sergeant!" they both replied.

"You are so fucking lucky they were left behind, because I *swear* I would have held you down and sliced them off myself. Oh, and you don't think I wouldn't? Well, unlike your precious fucking Marines, or any other military branch down there, up here the drill instructor *is* God. I could turn your fucking intestines into a sausage pie and all that would happen to me is they'd tell me to get one of the other recruits to mop up the mess." Ruiz stepped back to glare at all the veteran recruits. "This is the *real* military, ladies and gentlemen. You're not in the army, navy, air force, or Marines now. You're one of us. And every time you forget it, I'm going to be there to step on your fucking head. Now start running!"

They ran.

"Who's homosexual?" Ruiz said. Four recruits stepped forward, including Alan, who was standing next to me. I saw his eyebrows arch as he stepped up.

"Some of the finest soldiers in history were homosexual," Ruiz said. "Alexander the Great. Richard the Lionhearted. The Spartans had a special platoon of soldiers who were gay lovers, on the idea that a man would fight harder to protect his lover than he would for just another soldier. Some of the best fighters I ever knew personally were as queer as a three-dollar bill. Damn fine soldiers, all of them.

"But I will tell you the one thing that pisses me off about you all: You pick the wrong fucking moments to get confessional. *Three separate times* I've been fighting alongside a gay man when things have gone sour, and each fucking time he chooses *that* moment to tell me how he's always loved me. God*damn,* that's inappropriate. Some alien is trying to suck out my fucking brains, and my squadmate wants to talk about our relationship! As if I wasn't already *busy.* Do your squadmates a fucking favor. You got the hots, deal with it on leave, not when some creature is trying to rip out your goddamn heart. Now run!" Off they went.

"Who's a minority?" Ten recruits stepped forward. "Bullshit. Look around you, you assholes. Up here, everyone is green. There are no minorities. You want to be in a fucking minority? Fine. There are twenty billion humans in the universe. There are four *trillion* members of other sentient species, and they *all* want to turn you into a midday snack. And those are only the ones we know about! The first one of you who bitches about being a minority up here will get my green Latino foot squarely up your whiny ass. Move!" They heaved out toward the plain.

On it went. Ruiz had specific complaints against Christians, Jews, Muslims and atheists, government workers, doctors, lawyers, teachers, blue-collar joes, pet owners, gun owners, practitioners of martial arts, wrestling fans and, weirdly (both for the fact it bothered him and the fact that there was someone in the platoon who fit the category), clog dancers. In groups, pairs, and singly, recruits were peeled off and forced to run.

Eventually, I became aware that Ruiz was looking directly at me. I remained at attention.

"I will be goddamned," Ruiz said. "One of you shitheads is left!"

"Yes, Master Sergeant!" I yelled as loudly as I could.

"I find it somewhat difficult to believe that you do not fit into any of the categories I have railed against!" Ruiz said. "I suspect that you are attempting to avoid a pleasant morning jog!"

"No, Master Sergeant!" I bellowed.

"I simply refuse to acknowledge that there is not something about you I despise," Ruiz said. "Where are you from?"

"Ohio, Master Sergeant!"

Ruiz grimaced. Nothing there. Ohio's utter inoffensiveness had finally worked to my advantage. "What did you do for a living, recruit?"

"I was self-employed, Master Sergeant!"

"As what?"

"I was a writer, Master Sergeant!"

Ruiz's feral grin was back; obviously he had it in for those who worked with words. "Tell me you wrote fiction, recruit," he said. "I have a bone to pick with novelists."

"No, Master Sergeant!"

"Christ, man! What did you write?"

"I wrote advertising copy, Master Sergeant!"

"Advertising! What sort of dumbass things did you advertise?"

"My most famous advertising work involved Willie Wheelie, Master Sergeant!" Willie Wheelie had been the mascot for Nirvana Tires, who made tires for specialty vehicles. I'd developed the basic idea and his tagline; the company's graphic artists took it from there. Willie Wheelie's arrival coincided with the revival of motorcycles; the fad lasted for several years and Willie made a fair amount of money for Nirvana, both as an advertising mascot and through licensing for plush toys, T-shirts, shot glasses and so on. A children's entertainment show was planned but nothing came of it. It was a silly thing, but on the other hand Willie's success meant I never ran out of clients. It worked out pretty well. Until this very moment, it seemed.

Ruiz suddenly lunged forward, directly into my face, and bellowed. "*You* are the mastermind behind Willie Wheelie, recruit?"

"Yes, Master Sergeant!" There was a perverse pleasure in screaming at someone whose face was just millimeters away from your own.

Ruiz hovered in my face for a few seconds, scanning it with his eyes, daring me to flinch. He actually snarled. Then he stepped back and began to unbutton his shirt. I remained at attention but suddenly I was very, very scared. He whipped off his shirt, turned his right shoulder to me, and stepped forward again. "Recruit, tell me what you see on my shoulder!"

I glanced down, and thought, *No fucking way.* "It is a tattoo of Willie Wheelie, Master Sergeant!"

"Goddamn right," snapped Ruiz. "I'm going to tell you a story, recruit. Back on Earth, I was married to an evil, vicious woman. A veritable pit viper. Such was her hold on me that even though being married to her was a slow death by paper cuts, I still felt suicidal when she demanded a divorce. At my lowest moment, I stood at a bus stand, contemplating hurling myself in front of the next bus that came along. Then I looked over and saw an advertisement with Willie Wheelie in it. And do you know what it said?"

" 'Sometimes You Just Gotta Hit the Road,' Master Sergeant!" That tagline had taken me all of fifteen seconds to write. What a world.

"Exactly," he said. "And as I stared at that ad, I had what some would call a Moment of Clarity—I knew that what I needed was to just hit the fucking road. I divorced the evil slug of a wife, sang a song of thanks, packed my belongings into a saddlebag and lit out. Ever since that blessed day, Willie Wheelie has been my avatar, the symbol of my desire for personal freedom and expression. He saved my life, recruit, and I am forever grateful."

"You're welcome, Master Sergeant!" I bellowed.

"Recruit, I am honored that I have had a chance to meet you; you are additionally the first recruit in the history of my tenure that I have not found immediate grounds to despise. I cannot tell you how much that disturbs and unnerves me. However, I bask in the almost certain knowledge that soon—possibly within the next few hours—you will undoubtedly do something to piss me off. To assure that you do, in fact, I assign to you the role of platoon leader. It is a thankless fucking job that has no upside, since you have to ride these sad-ass recruits twice as hard as I do, because for every one of the numerous fuckups that they perform, you will also share the blame. They will hate you, despise you, plot your downfall, and I will be there to give you an extra ration of shit when they succeed. What do you think about that, recruit? Speak freely!"

"It sounds like I'm pretty fucked, Master Sergeant!" I yelled.

"That you are, recruit," Ruiz said. "But you were fucked the moment you landed in my platoon. Now get running. Can't have the leader not run with his 'toon. Move!"

"I don't know whether to congratulate you or be scared for you," Alan said to me as we headed toward the mess hall for breakfast.

"You can do both," I said. "Although it probably makes more sense to be scared. I am. Ah, there they are." I pointed to a group of five recruits, three men, two women, who were milling about in front of the mess hall.

Earlier in the day, as I was heading toward the communication tower on my run, my BrainPal almost caused me to collide with a tree by flashing a text message directly into my field of view. I managed to swerve, merely clipping a shoulder, and told Asshole to switch to voice navigation before I got myself killed. Asshole complied and started the message over.

"Master Sergeant Antonio Ruiz's appointment of John Perry as leader of the 63rd Training Platoon has been processed. Congratulations on your advancement. You now have access to personnel files and Brain-Pal information relating to recruits within the 63rd Training Platoon. Be aware that this information is for official use only; access for nonmilitary use is cause for immediate termination of platoon leader position and a court-martial trial at the base commander's discretion."

"Swell," I said, leaping a small gully.

"You will need to present Master Sergeant Ruiz with your selections for squad leaders by the end of your platoon's breakfast period," Asshole continued. *"Would you like to review your platoon files to aid in your selection process?"*

I would. I did. Asshole spewed out details at high speed on each recruit as I ran. By the time I made it to the comm tower, I had narrowed the list to twenty candidates; by the time I was nearing the base, I'd parceled out the entire platoon among squad leaders and sent mail to each of the five new squad leaders to meet me at the mess hall. That BrainPal was certainly beginning to come in handy.

I also noted that I managed to make it back to base in fifty-five minutes, and I hadn't passed any other recruits on the way back. I consulted Asshole and discovered that the slowest of the recruits (one of the former Marines, ironically) had clocked in at fifty-eight minutes thirteen seconds. We wouldn't be running to the comm tower tomorrow, or at least not because we were slow. I didn't doubt Sergeant Ruiz's ability to find another excuse, however. I was just hoping not to be the one to give it to him.

The five recruits saw me and Alan coming and snapped, more or less, to attention. Three of them saluted immediately, followed somewhat sheepishly by the other two. I saluted back and smiled. "Don't fret it," I said to the two who lagged. "This is new to me, too. Come on, let's get in line and talk while we eat."

"Do you want me to light out?" Alan asked me while we were in line. "You've probably got a lot to cover with these guys."

"No," I said. "I'd like you there. I want your opinion on these guys. Also, I have news for you, you're my second in command in our own squad. And since I've got a whole platoon to babysit, that means you're really going to be in charge of it. Hope you don't mind."

"I can handle it," Alan said, smiling. "Thanks for putting me in your squad."

"Hey," I said. "What's the point of being in charge if you can't indulge in pointless favoritism. Besides, when I go down, you'll be there to cushion my fall."

"That's me," Alan said. "Your military career air bag."

The mess hall was packed but the seven of us managed to commandeer a table. "Introductions," I said. "Let's know each other's names. I'm John Perry, and for the moment at least I'm platoon leader. This is my squad's second in command, Alan Rosenthal."

"Angela Merchant," said the woman immediately across from me. "Of Trenton, New Jersey."

"Terry Duncan," said the fellow next to her. "Missoula, Montana."

"Mark Jackson. St. Louis."

"Sarah O'Connell. Boston."

"Martin Garabedian. Sunny Fresno, California."

"Well, aren't we geographically diverse," I said. That got a chuckle, which was good. "I'll be quick about this, since if I spend any amount of time on this it'll be clear that I have no idea what the hell I'm doing. Basically, you five got chosen because there's something in your history that suggests that you'd be able to handle being a squad leader. I chose Angela because she was a CEO. Terry ran a cattle ranch. Mark was a colonel in the army, and with all respect to Sergeant Ruiz, I actually do think that's an advantage."

"That's nice to hear," Mark said.

"Martin was on the Fresno city council. And Sarah here taught kindergarten for thirty years, which automatically makes her the most qualified of all of us." Another laugh. Man, I was on a roll.

"I'm going to be honest," I said. "I'm not planning to be a hard-ass on you. Sergeant Ruiz has got that job covered, and I'd just be a pale imitation. It's not my style. I don't know what your command style will be, but I want you to do what you need to do to keep on top of your recruits and to get them through the next three months. I don't really care about being platoon leader, but I think I care very much about making sure every recruit in this platoon has the skills and training they're going to need to survive out there. Ruiz's little home movie got my attention and I hope it got yours."

"Christ, did it ever," Terry said. "They dressed that poor bastard out like he was beef."

"I wish they had shown us that before we signed up," Angela said. "I might have decided to stay old."

"It's war," Mark said. "It's what happens."

"Let's just do what we can to make sure our guys make it through things like that," I said. "Now, I've cut the platoon into six squads of ten. I'm top of A squad; Angela, you have B; Terry, C; Mark, D; Sarah, E; and Martin, F. I've given you permission to examine your recruit files with your BrainPal; choose your second in command and send me the details by lunch today. Between the two of you, keep discipline and training going smoothly; from my point of view, my whole reason for selecting you folks is so I don't have anything to do."

"Except run your own squad," Martin said.

"That's where I come in," Alan said.

"Let's meet every day at lunch," I said. "We'll take other meals with our squads. If you have something that needs my attention, of course contact me immediately. But I *do* expect you to attempt to solve as many problems as you can by yourself. Like I said, I'm not planning on having a hard-ass style, but for better or worse, I am the platoon leader, so what I say goes. If I feel you're not measuring up, I'm going to let you know first, and then if that doesn't work I'm going to replace you. It's not personal, it's making sure we all get the training we need to live out here. Everyone good with that?" Nods all around.

"Excellent," I said, and held up my tumbler. "Then let's toast to the 63rd Training Platoon. Here's to making it through in one piece." We clunked our tumblers together and then got to eating and chatting. Things were looking up, I thought.

It didn't take long to change *that* opinion.

EIGHT

The day on Beta Pyxis is twenty-two hours thirteen minutes twenty-four seconds long. We got two of those hours to sleep.

I discovered this charming fact on our first night, when Asshole blasted me with a piercing siren that jolted me awake so quickly I fell out of my bunk, which was, of course, the top bunk. After checking to make sure my nose wasn't broken, I read the text floating in my skull.

Platoon Leader Perry, this is to inform you that you have—and here there was a number, at that second being one minute and forty-eight seconds and counting down—until Master Sergeant Ruiz and his assistants enter your barracks. You are expected to have your platoon awake and at attention when they enter. Any recruits not at attention will be disciplined and noted against your record.

I immediately forwarded the message to my squad leaders through the communication grouping I had created for them the day before, sent a general alarm signal to the platoon's BrainPals, and hit the barrack lights. There were a few amusing seconds as every recruit in the platoon jerked awake to a blast of noise that only he or she could hear. Most leaped out of bed, deeply disoriented; I and the squad leaders grabbed the ones still lying down and yanked them out onto the floor. Within a minute we had everyone up and at attention, and the remaining few seconds were spent convincing a few particularly slow recruits that now was not the time to pee or dress or do anything but stand there and not piss off Ruiz when he came through the door.

Not that it mattered. "For fuck's sake," Ruiz declared. "Perry!"

"Yes, Master Sergeant!"

"What the hell were you doing for your two-minute warning? Jerking off? Your platoon is unready! They are not dressed for the exertions to which they will soon be tasked! What is your excuse?"

"Master Sergeant, the message stated that the platoon was required to be at attention when you and your staff arrived! It did not specify the need to dress!"

"Christ, Perry! Don't you assume that being dressed is part of being at attention?"

"I would not presume to assume, Master Sergeant!"

" 'Presume to assume'? Are you being a smartass, Perry?"

"No, Master Sergeant!"

"Well, presume to get your platoon out to the parade ground, Perry. You have forty-five seconds. Move!"

"A squad!" I bellowed and ran at the same time, hoping to God my squad was following directly behind me. As I went through the door, I heard Angela hollering at B squad to follow her; I had chosen her well. We made it to the parade grounds, my squad forming in a line directly behind me. Angela formed her line directly to my right, with Terry and the rest forming subsequently. The last man of F squad formed up at the forty-four-second mark. Amazing. Around the parade grounds, other recruit platoons were also forming up, also in the same state of undress as the 63rd. I felt briefly relieved.

Ruiz strolled up momentarily, trailed by his two assistants. "Perry! What is the time!"

I accessed my BrainPal. "Oh one hundred local time, Master Sergeant!"

"Outstanding, Perry. You can tell time. What time was lights out?"

"Twenty-one hundred, Master Sergeant!"

"Correct again! Now some of you may be wondering why we're getting you up and running on two hours of sleep. Are we cruel? Sadistic? Trying to break you down? Yes we *are*. But these are *not* the reasons we have awakened you. The reason is simply this— *you don't need any more sleep.* Thanks to these pretty new bodies of yours, you get all the sleep you need in two hours! You've been sleeping eight hours a night because that's what you're used to. No longer, ladies and gentlemen. All that sleep is wasting *my* time. Two hours is all you need, so from now on, two hours is all you will *get*.

"Now, then. Who can tell me why I had you run those twenty klicks in an hour yesterday?"

One recruit raised his hand. "Yes, Thompson?" Ruiz said. Either he had memorized the names of every platoon recruit, or he had his BrainPal on, providing him the information. I wouldn't hazard a guess as to which it was.

"Master Sergeant, you had us run because you hate each of us on an individual basis!"

"Excellent response, Thompson. However, you are only partially correct. I had you run twenty klicks in an hour because you *can*. Even the slowest of you finished the run two minutes under the cutoff time. That means that without training, without even a hint of *real* effort, every single one of you bastards can keep pace with Olympic gold medalists back on Earth.

"And do you know why that is? Do you? It's because *none of you is human anymore.* You're *better*. You just don't know it yet. Shit, you spent a week bouncing off the walls of a spaceship like little wind-up toys and you probably still don't understand what you're made of. Well, ladies and gentlemen, that is going to change. The first week of your training is all about making you believe. And you *will* believe. You're not going to have a *choice*."

And then we ran 25 kilometers in our underwear.

Twenty-five-klick runs. Seven-second hundred-meter sprints. Six-foot vertical jumps. Leaping across ten-meter holes in the ground. Lifting two hundred kilos of free weights. Hundreds upon hundreds of sit-ups, chin-ups, push-ups. As Ruiz said, the hard part was not doing these things—the hard part was believing they could be done. Recruits were falling and failing at every step of the way for what's best described as a lack of nerve. Ruiz and his assistants would fall on these recruits and scare them into performing (and then have me do push-ups because I or my squad leaders clearly hadn't scared them enough).

Every recruit—*every* recruit—had his or her moment of doubt. Mine came on the fourth day, when the 63rd Platoon arrayed itself around the base swimming pool, each recruit holding a twenty-five-kilo sack of sand in his or her arms.

"What is the weak point of the human body?" Ruiz asked as he circled around our platoon. "It's not the heart, or the brain, or the feet, or anywhere you think it is. I'll tell you what it is. It's the blood, and that's bad news because your blood is everywhere in your body. It carries oxygen, but it also carries disease. When you're wounded, blood clots, but often not fast enough to keep you from dying of blood loss. Although when it comes down to it, what everyone *really* dies of is oxygen deprivation—from blood being unavailable because it's spewed out on the fucking ground where it doesn't do you a goddamned bit of good.

"The Colonial Defense Forces, in their divine wisdom, have

given human blood the boot. It's been replaced by SmartBlood. SmartBlood is made up of billions of nano-sized 'bots that do everything that blood did but better. It's not organic, so it's not vulnerable to biological threats. It speaks to your BrainPal to clot in milliseconds—you could lose a fucking leg and you wouldn't bleed out. Most importantly to you right now, each 'cell' of Smart-Blood has four times the oxygen-carrying capacity of your natural red blood cells."

Ruiz stopped walking. "This is important to each of you right now because you're all about to jump into the pool with your sacks of sand. You will sink to the bottom. And you will *stay* there for no less than six minutes. Six minutes is enough to kill your average human, but each of *you* can stay down for that long and not lose a single brain cell. To give you incentive to stay down, the first of you that comes up gets latrine duty for a week. And if that recruit comes up before the six minutes are up, well, let's just say that each of you is going to develop a close-up and personal relationship with a shit hole somewhere on this base. Got it? Then in you go!"

We dove, and as promised, sank straight down to the bottom, three meters down. I began to freak out almost immediately. When I was a child, I fell into a covered pool, tore through the cover and spent several disoriented and terrified minutes trying to break through to the surface. It wasn't long enough for me to actually begin to drown; it was just long enough for me to develop a life-long aversion to having my head completely enveloped by water. After about thirty seconds, I began to feel like I needed a big, fresh gulp of air. There was no way I was going to last a minute, much less six.

I felt a tug. I turned a little wildly, and saw that Alan, who had dived in next to me, had reached over. Through the murk, I could see him tap his head and then point to mine. At that second, Asshole notified me that Alan was asking for a link. I subvocalized acceptance. I heard an emotionless simulacrum of Alan's voice in my head.

Something wrong — Alan asked.

Phobia — I subvocalized.

Don't panic — Alan responded. *Forget you're underwater* —

Not fucking likely — I replied.

Then fake it — Alan responded. *Check on your squads to see if anyone else is having trouble and help them* —

The eerie calm of Alan's simulated voice helped. I opened a channel to my squad leaders to check on them and ordered them to do the same with their squads. Each of them had one or two recruits on the edge of panic and worked to talk them down. Next to me, I could see Alan make an accounting of our own squad.

Three minutes, then four. In Martin's group, one of the recruits began to thrash, jerking his body back and forth as the bag of sand in his hand acted as an anchor. Martin dropped his own bag and swam over to his recruit, grabbing him roughly by the shoulders, and then bringing his recruit's attention to his face. I tapped into Martin's BrainPal and heard him say — *Focus on me on my eyes* — to his recruit. It seemed to help; the recruit stopped his thrashing and began to relax.

Five minutes, and it was clear that extended oxygen supply or not, everyone was beginning to feel the pinch. People began shifting from one foot to the other, or hopping in place, or waving their bags. Over in a corner, I could see one recruit slamming her head into her sandbag. Part of me laughed; part of me thought about doing it myself.

Five minutes forty-three seconds, and one of the recruits in Mark's squad dropped his bag and began heading for the surface. Mark dropped his bag and silently lunged, snagging the recruit by the ankle and using his own weight to drag him back down.

I was thinking Mark's second in command should probably help his squad leader with the recruit; a quick BrainPal check informed me that the recruit *was* his second in command.

Six minutes. Forty recruits dropped their bags and punched to the surface. Mark let go of his second in command's ankle and then pushed him from underneath to make sure he would break the surface first, and get the latrine duty he was willing to get for his whole platoon. I prepared to drop my sandbag when I caught Alan shaking his head.

Platoon leader — he sent. *Should stick it out*—

Blow me — I sent.

Sorry, not my type — he replied.

I made it through seven minutes and thirty-one seconds before I went up, convinced my lungs were going to explode. But I had made it through my moment of doubt. I believed. I was something more than human.

In the second week, we were introduced to our weapon.

"This is the CDF standard-issue MP-35 Infantry Rifle," Ruiz said, holding out his while ours sat where they had been placed, still within protective wrapping, in the parade-ground dirt at our feet. "The 'MP' stands for 'Multi-Purpose.' Depending on your need, it can create and fire on the fly six different projectiles or beams. These include rifle bullets and shot of both explosive and nonexplosive varieties, which can be fired semiautomatically or automatically, low-yield grenades, low-yield guided rockets, high-pressure flammable liquid, and microwave energy beams. This is possible through the use of high-density nano-robotic ammunition"—Ruiz held up a dully gleaming block of what appeared to be metal; a similar block was located next to the rifle at my feet—"that self-assembles immediately prior to firing. This allows for a weapon with maximum flexibility with minimum training, a fact that you sad lumps of ambulatory meat will no doubt appreciate.

"Those of you who have military experience will remember how you were required to frequently assemble and disassemble your weapon. *You will not do this with your MP-35.* The MP-35 is an extremely complex piece of machinery and you cannot be trusted to fuck with it! It carries onboard self-diagnostic and repair capabilities. It can also patch into your BrainPal to alert you of problems, if any, which there will be none, since in thirty years of service there has yet to be an MP-35 that has malfunctioned. This is because, unlike your dipshit military scientists on Earth, *we* can build a weapon that works! Your job is not to fuck with your weapon; your job is to *fire* your weapon. Trust your weapon, it is almost certainly smarter than you are. Remember this and you may yet live.

"You will activate your MP-35 momentarily by taking it out of its protective wrapping, and accessing it with your BrainPal. Once you do this, your MP-35 will truly be yours. While you are on this base, only you will be able to fire your MP-35, and then only when you are given clearance from your platoon leader or your squad leaders, who must in turn get clearance from their drill instructors. In actual combat situations, only CDF soldiers with CDF-issued BrainPals will be able to fire your MP-35. So long as you don't piss off your own squadmates, you will never have to fear your own weapon being used against you.

"From this point forward you will take your MP-35 with you everywhere you go. You will take it with you when you take a shit. You will take it with you when you shower—don't worry about getting it wet, it will spit out anything it regards as foreign. You will take it to meals. You will sleep with it. If you somehow manage to find time to fuck, your MP-35 damn well better have a fine view.

"You will learn how to use this weapon. It will save your life. The U.S. Marines are fucking chumps, but the one thing they got right was their Marine Rifle Creed. It reads, in part, 'This is my rifle. There are many like it, but this one is mine. My rifle is my best friend. It is my life. I must master it as I must master my life. My rifle, without me, is useless. Without my rifle, I am useless. I must fire my rifle true. I must shoot straighter than my enemy who is trying to kill me. I must shoot him before he shoots me. And I will.'

"Ladies and gentlemen, take this creed to heart. This is your rifle. Pick it up and activate it."

I knelt down and removed the rifle from its plastic wrap. Notwithstanding everything Ruiz described about the rifle, the MP-35 did not appear especially impressive. It had heft but was not unwieldy, was well balanced and well sized for maneuverability. On the side of the rifle stock was a sticker. "TO ACTIVATE WITH BRAINPAL: Initialize BrainPal and say *Activate MP-35, serial number ASD-324-DDD-4E3C1.*"

"Hey, Asshole," I said. "Activate MP-35, serial number ASD-324-DDD-4E3C1."

MP-35 ASD-324-DDD-4E3C1 is now activated for CDF Recruit John Perry, Asshole responded. **Please load ammunition now.** A small graphic display hovered in the corner of my field of vision, showing me how to load my rifle. I reached back down and picked up the rectangular block that was my ammunition—and nearly lost my balance trying to pick it up. It was impressively heavy; they weren't kidding about the "high density" part. I jammed it into my rifle where instructed. As I did so, the graphic showing me how to load my rifle disappeared and a counter sprang up in its place, which read:

Firing Options Available
Note: Using One Type of Round Decreases Availability of
Other Types

Rifle Rounds: 200
Shot Rounds: 80
Grenade Rounds: 40
Missile Rounds: 35
Fire Rounds: 10 Minutes
Microwave: 10 Minutes
Rifle Rounds Currently Selected.

"Select shot rounds," I said.

Shot rounds selected, Asshole replied.

"Select missile rounds," I said.

Missile rounds selected, Asshole replied. Please select target. Suddenly every member of the platoon had a tight green targeting outline; glancing directly at one would cause an overlay to flash. What the hell, I thought, and selected one, a recruit in Martin's squad named Toshima.

Target selected. Asshole confirmed. You may fire, cancel, or select a second target.

"Whoa," I said, canceled the target, and stared down at my MP-35. I turned to Alan, who was holding his weapon next to me. "I'm scared of my weapon," I said.

"No shit," Alan said. "I just nearly blew you up two seconds ago with a grenade."

My response to this shocking admission was cut short when, on the other side of the platoon, Ruiz suddenly wheeled into a recruit's face. "What did you just say, recruit?" Ruiz demanded. Everybody fell silent as we turned to see who had incurred Ruiz's wrath.

The recruit was Sam McCain; in one of our lunch sessions I recalled Sarah O'Connell describing him as more mouth than brain. Unsurprisingly, he'd been in sales most of his life. Even with Ruiz hovering a millimeter from his nose, McCain projected smarminess; a mildly surprised smarminess, but smarminess all the same.

He clearly didn't know what got Ruiz so worked up, but whatever it was, he expected to walk away from this encounter unscathed.

"I was just admiring my weapon, Master Sergeant," McCain said, holding up his rifle. "And I was telling recruit Flores here how it almost made me feel sorry for the poor bastards we're going up against out—"

The rest of McCain's comment was lost to time when Ruiz grabbed McCain's rifle from the surprised recruit and with one supremely relaxed spin clocked McCain in the temple with the flat side of the rifle butt. McCain crumpled like laundry; Ruiz calmly extended a leg and jammed a boot into McCain's throat. Then he flipped the rifle around; McCain stared up, horrified, into the barrel of his own rifle.

"Not so smug now, are you, you little shit?" Ruiz said. "Imagine I'm your enemy. Do you almost feel sorry for me now? I just disarmed you in less time than it takes to fucking *breathe*. Out there, those *poor bastards* move faster than you would ever believe. They are going to spread your fucking liver on crackers and eat it up while you're still trying to get them in your sights. So don't you ever feel *almost sorry* for the poor bastards. They don't need your pity. Are you going to remember this, recruit?"

"Yes, Master Sergeant!" McCain rasped, over the boot. He was very nearly sobbing.

"Let's make sure," Ruiz said, pressed the barrel into the space between McCain's eyes, and pulled the trigger with a dry *click*. Every member of the platoon flinched; McCain wet himself.

"Dumb," Ruiz said after McCain realized he wasn't, in fact, dead. "You weren't listening earlier. The MP-35 can only be fired by its owner while it's on base. That's *you*, asshole." He straightened up and contemptuously flung the rifle at McCain, then turned to face the platoon at large.

"You recruits are even stupider than I have imagined," Ruiz

declared. "Listen to me now: There has *never* been a military in the entire history of the human race that has gone to war equipped with more than the *least* that it needs to fight its enemy. War is expensive. It costs money and it costs lives and no civilization has an infinite amount of either. So when you fight, you conserve. You use and equip only as much as you have to, never more.

He stared at us grimly. "Is *any* of this getting through? Do any of you *understand* what I'm trying to tell you? You don't have these shiny new bodies and pretty new weapons because we want to give you an unfair advantage. You have these bodies and weapons because they are the *absolute minimum* that will allow you to fight and survive out there. We didn't *want* to give you these bodies, you dipshits. It's just that if we didn't, the human race would already be *extinct*.

"Do you understand now? Do you *finally* have an idea of what you're up against? Do you?"

But it wasn't all fresh air, exercise, and learning to kill for humanity. Sometimes, we took classes.

"During your physical training, you've been learning to overcome your assumptions and inhibitions regarding your new body's abilities," Lieutenant Oglethorpe said to a lecture hall filled with training battalions 60th through 63rd. "Now we need to do this with your mind. It's time to flush out some deeply held preconceptions and prejudices, some of which you probably aren't even aware you have."

Lieutenant Oglethorpe pressed a button on the podium where he stood. Behind him, two display boards shimmered to life. In the one to the audience's left a nightmare popped up—something black and gnarled, with serrated lobster claws that nestled pornographically inside an orifice so dank you could very nearly smell the stench. Above the shapeless pile of a body, three eyestalks or antennae or whatever perched. Ochre dripped from them. H. P. Lovecraft would have run screaming.

To the right was a vaguely deerlike creature with cunning, almost human hands, and a quizzical face that seemed to speak of peace and wisdom. If you couldn't pet this guy, you could at least learn something about the nature of the universe from him.

Lieutenant Oglethorpe took a pointer and waved it in the direction of the nightmare. "This guy is a member of the Bathunga race. The Bathunga are a deeply pacifistic people; they have a culture that reaches back hundreds of thousands of years, and features an understanding of mathematics that makes our own look like simple addition. They live in the oceans, filtering plankton, and enthusiastically coexist with humans on several worlds. These are good guys, and this guy"—he tapped the board—"is unusually handsome for his species."

He whacked the second board, which held the friendly deer man. "Now, this little fucker is a Salong. Our first official encounter with the Salong happened after we tracked down a rogue colony of humans. People aren't supposed to freelance colonize, and the reason why becomes pretty obvious here. The colonists landed on a planet that was also a colonization target for the Salong; somewhere along the way the Salong decided that humans were good eatin', so they attacked the humans and set up a human meat farm. All the adult human males but a handful were killed, and those that were kept were 'milked' for their sperm. The women were artificially inseminated and their newborns taken, penned and fattened like veal.

"It was years before we found the place. When we did so, the CDF troops razed the Salong colony to the ground and barbecued the Salong colony leader in a cookout. Needless to say we've been fighting the baby-eating sons of bitches ever since.

"You can see where I'm going with this," Oglethorpe said. "Assuming you know the good guys from the bad guys will get you killed. You can't afford anthropomorphic biases when some of the aliens most like us would rather make human hamburgers than peace."

Another time Oglethorpe asked us to guess what the one advantage was that Earth-based soldiers had over CDF soldiers. "It's certainly not physical conditioning or weaponry," he said, "since we're clearly ahead on both those counts. No, the advantage soldiers have on Earth is that they know who their opponents are going to be, and also, within a certain range, how the battle will be conducted—with what sort of troops, types of weapons, and range of goals. Because of this, battle experience in one war or engagement can be directly applicable to another, even if the causes for the war or the goals for the battle are entirely different.

"The CDF has no such advantage. For example, take a recent battle with the Efg." Oglethorpe tapped on one of the displays to reveal a whalelike creature with massive side tentacles that branched into rudimentary hands. "The guys are up to forty meters long and have a technology that allows them to polymerize water. We'd lose water ships when the water around them turned into a quicksand-like sludge that pulled them down, taking their crews with them. How does the experience of fighting one of these guys translate into experience that can be applied to, say, the Finwe,"—the other screen flipped on, revealing a reptilian charmer—"who are small desert dwellers who prefer long-distance biological attacks?

"The answer is that it really can't. And yet CDF soldiers go from one sort of battle to the other all the time. This is one reason why the mortality rate in the CDF is so high—every battle is new, and every combat situation, in the experience of the individual soldier at least, is unique. If there's one thing you bring out of these little chats of ours, it's this: Any ideas you have about how war is waged had better be thrown out the window. Your training here will open your eyes to some of what you'll encounter out there, but remember that as infantry, you'll often be the first point of contact with new hostile races, whose methods and motives are unknown and sometimes unknowable. You have to think fast, and not assume what's worked before will work now. That's a quick way to be dead."

One time, a recruit asked Oglethorpe why CDF soldiers should even care about the colonists or the colonies. "We're having it drilled into our heads that we're not even really human any-more," she said. "And if that's the case, why should we feel any attachment to the colonists? They're only human, after all. Why not breed CDF soldiers as the next step in human evolution and give ourselves a leg up?"

"Don't think you're the first one to ask that question," Ogle-thorpe said, and this got a general chuckle. "The short answer is that we can't. All the genetic and mechanical fiddling that gets done to CDF soldiers renders them genetically sterile. Because of common genetic material used in the template of each of you, there are far too many lethal recessives to allow any fertilization process to get very far. And there's too much nonhuman material to allow successful crossbreeding with normal humans. CDF sol-diers are an amazing bit of engineering, but as an evolutionary path, they're a dead end. This is one reason why none of you should be too smug. You can run a mile in three minutes, but you can't make a baby.

"In a larger sense, however, there's no need. The next step of evolution is already happening. Just like the Earth, most of the colonies are isolated from each other. Nearly all people born on a colony stay there their entire lives. Humans also adapt to their new homes; it's already beginning culturally. Some of the oldest of the colony planets are beginning to show linguistic and cultural drift from their cultures and languages back on Earth. In ten thousand years there will be genetic drift as well. Given enough time, there will be as many different human species as there are colony planets. Diversity is the key to survival.

"Metaphysically, maybe you should feel attached to the colonies because, having been changed yourself, you appreciate the human potential to become something that will survive in the universe. More directly, you should care because the colonies represent the future of the human race, and changed or not, you're still far closer to human than any other intelligent species out there.

"But ultimately, you should care because you're old enough to know that you should. That's one of the reasons the CDF selects old people to become soldiers, you know—it's not just because you're all retired and a drag on the economy. It's also because you've lived long enough to know that there's more to life than your own life. Most of you have raised families and have children and grandchildren and understand the value of doing something beyond your own selfish goals. Even if you never become colonists yourselves, you still recognize that human colonies are good for the human race, and worth fighting for. It's hard to drill that concept into the brain of a nineteen-year-old. But you know from experience. In this universe, experience counts."

We drilled. We shot. We learned. We kept going. We didn't sleep much.

In week six, I replaced Sarah O'Connell as squad leader. E squad consistently fell behind in team exercises and that was costing the 63rd Platoon in intra-platoon competitions. Every time a trophy went to another platoon, Ruiz would grind his teeth and take it out on me. Sarah accepted it with good grace. "It's not exactly like herding kindergarteners, unfortunately," is what she had to say. Alan took her place and whipped the squad into shape. Week seven found the 63rd shooting a trophy right out from under the 58th; ironically, it was Sarah, who turned out to be a hell of a shot, who took us over the top.

In week eight, I stopped talking to my BrainPal. Asshole had studied me long enough to understand my brain patterns and began seemingly anticipating my needs. I first noticed it during a simulated live-fire exercise, when my MP-35 switched from rifle rounds to guided missile rounds, tracked, fired and hit two long-range targets, and then switched again to a flamethrower just in time to fry a nasty six-foot bug that popped out of some nearby rocks. When I realized I hadn't vocalized any of the commands, I felt a creepy vibe wash over me. After another few days, I noticed I became annoyed whenever I would actually have to ask Asshole for something. How quickly the creepy becomes commonplace.

In week nine, I, Alan and Martin Garabedian had to provide a little administrative discipline to one of Martin's recruits, who had decided that he wanted Martin's squad leader job and was not above attempting a little sabotage to get it. The recruit had been a moderately famous pop star in his past life and was used to getting his way through whatever means necessary. He was crafty enough to enlist some squadmates into the conspiracy, but unfortunately for him, was not smart enough to realize that as his squad leader, Martin had access to the notes he was passing. Martin came to me; I suggested that there was no reason to involve Ruiz or the other instructors in what could easily be resolved by ourselves.

If anyone noticed a base hovercraft briefly going AWOL later that night, they didn't say anything. Likewise if anyone saw a recruit dangling from it upside down as it passed dangerously close to some trees, the recruit held to the hovercraft only by a pair of hands on each ankle. Certainly no one claimed to hear either the recruit's desperate screaming, or Martin's critical and none-too-favorable examination of the former pop star's most famous album. Master Sergeant Ruiz did note to me at breakfast the next morning that I was looking a little windblown; I replied that it may have been the brisk thirty-klick jog he had us run prior to the meal.

In week eleven, the 63rd and several other platoons dropped into the mountains north of the base. The objective was simple; find and wipe out every other platoon and then have the survivors make it back to base, all within four days. To make things interesting, each recruit was fitted with a device that registered shots taken at them; if one connected, the recruit would feel paralyzing pain and then collapse (and then be retrieved, eventually, by drill instructors watching nearby). I knew this because I had been the test case back on base, when Ruiz wanted to show an example. I stressed to my platoon that they did *not* want to feel what I felt.

The first attack came almost as soon as we hit the ground. Four of my recruits went down before I spotted the shooters and called them to the attention of the platoon. We got two; two got away. Sporadic attacks over the next few hours made it clear that most of the other platoons had broken into squads of three or four and were hunting for other squads.

I had another idea. Our BrainPals made it possible for us to maintain constant, silent contact with each other regardless of whether we were standing close to one another or not. Other platoons seemed to be missing the implications of this fact, but that was too bad for them. I had every member of the platoon open a secure BrainPal communication line with every other member, and then I had each platoon member head off individually, charting terrain and noting the location of enemy squads they spotted. This way, we would all have an ever-widening map of the ground and the positions of the enemy. Even if one of our recruits got picked off, the information they provided would help another platoon member avenge his or her death (or at least keep from getting killed right away). One soldier could move quickly and silently and harass the other platoon's squads, and still work in tandem with other soldiers when the opportunity arose.

It worked. Our recruits took shots when they could, laid low and passed on information when they couldn't, and worked together when opportunities presented themselves. On the second day, I and a recruit named Riley picked off two squads from opposing platoons; they were so busy shooting at each other that they didn't notice Riley and me sniping them from a distance. He got two, I got three and the other three apparently got each other. It was pretty sweet. After we were done, we didn't say anything to each other, just faded back into the forest and kept tracking and sharing terrain information.

Eventually the other platoons figured out what we were doing and tried to do the same, but by that time, there were too many of the 63rd, and not enough of them. We mopped them up, getting the last of them by noon, and then started our jog into base, some eighty klicks away. The last of us made it in by 1800. In the end, we lost nineteen members of the platoon, including the four at the beginning. But we were responsible for just over half of the total kills across seven other platoons, while losing less than a third of our own people. Even Master Sergeant Ruiz couldn't complain about that. When the base commander awarded him the War Games trophy, he even cracked a smile. I can't even imagine how much it hurt him to do that.

"Our luck will never cease," the newly minted Private Alan Rosenthal said as he came up to me at the shuttle boarding area. "You and I got assigned to the same ship."   .

Indeed we had. A quick jaunt back to Phoenix on the troop ship *Francis Drake,* and then leave until the CDFS *Modesto* came to call. Then we'd hook up with the 2nd Platoon, Company D, of the 233rd CDF Infantry Battalion. One battalion per ship—roughly a thousand soldiers. Easy to get lost. I'd be glad to have Alan with me once again.

I glanced over to Alan and admired his clean, new Colonial blue dress uniform—in no small part because I was wearing one just like it. "Damn, Alan," I said. "We sure look good."

"I've always loved a man in uniform," Alan said to me. "And now that I'm the man in the uniform, I love him even more."

"Uh-oh," I said. "Here comes Master Sergeant Ruiz."

Ruiz had spotted me waiting to board my shuttle; as he approached I put down the duffel bag that contained my everyday uniform and few remaining personal belongings, and presented him with a smart salute.

"At ease, Private," Ruiz said, returning the salute. "Where are you headed?"

"The *Modesto,* Master Sergeant," I said. "Private Rosenthal and I both."

"You're shitting me," Ruiz declared. "The 233rd? Which company?"

"D, Master Sergeant. Second Platoon."

"Out-fucking-standing, Private," Ruiz said. "You will have the pleasure in serving in the platoon of Lieutenant Arthur Keyes, if that dumb son of a bitch hasn't managed to have his ass chewed on by now by some alien or another. When you see him, extend to him my compliments, if you would. You may additionally tell him that Master Sergeant Antonio Ruiz has declared that you are not nearly the dipshit that most of your fellow recruits have turned out to be."

"Thank you, Master Sergeant."

"Don't let it go to your head, Private. You are still a dipshit. Just not a very big one."

"Of course, Master Sergeant."

"Good. And now, if you will excuse me. Sometimes you just gotta hit the road." Master Sergeant Ruiz saluted. Alan and I saluted back. Ruiz glanced at us both, offered a tight, tight smile, and then walked away without looking back.

"That man scares the shit out of me," Alan said.

"I don't know. I kind of like him."

"Of course you do. He thinks you're almost not a dipshit. That's a compliment in his world."

"Don't think I don't know it," I said. "Now all I have to do is live up to it."

"You'll manage," Alan said. "After all, you *do* still get to be a dipshit."

"That's comforting," I said. "At least I'll have company."

Alan grinned. The shuttle doors opened. We grabbed our stuff and went inside.

NINE

"I can take a shot," Watson said, sighting over his boulder. "Let me drill one of those things."

"No," said Viveros, our corporal. "Their shield is still up. You'd just be wasting ammo."

"This is bullshit," Watson said. "We've been here for hours. We're sitting here. They're sitting there. When their shield goes down, we're supposed to do what, walk over and start blasting at them? This isn't the fucking fourteenth century. We shouldn't make an *appointment* to start killing the other guy."

Viveros looked irritated. "Watson, you're not paid to think. So shut the fuck up and get ready. It's not going to be long now, anyway. There's only one thing left in their ritual before we get at it."

"Yeah? What's that?" Watson said.

"They're going to sing," Viveros said.

Watson smirked. "What are they going to sing? Show tunes?"

"No," Viveros said. "They're going to sing our deaths."

As if on cue, the massive, hemispherical shield enclosing the Consu encampment shimmered at the base. I adjusted my eyesight and focused down the several hundred meters across the field as a single Consu stepped through, the shield lightly sticking to its massive carapace until it moved far enough away for the electrostatic filaments to collapse back into the shield.

He was the third and final Consu who would emerge out of the shield before the battle. The first had appeared nearly twelve hours ago; a low-ranking grunt whose bellowing challenge served to formally signal the Consu's intent to battle. The low rank of the messenger was meant to convey the minimal regard in which our troops were held by the Consu, the idea being that if we had been really important, they would have sent a higher-up. None of our troops took offense; the messenger was always of low rank, regardless of opponent, and anyway, unless you are extraordinarily sensitive to Consu pheromones, they pretty much all look alike.

The second Consu emerged from behind the shield several hours later, bellowed like a herd of cows caught in a thresher, and then promptly exploded, pinkish blood and bits of his organs and carapace momentarily splashing against the Consu shield and sizzling lightly as they drizzled down to the ground. Apparently the Consu believed that if a single soldier was ritually prepared beforehand, its soul can be persuaded to reconnoiter the enemy for a set amount of time before moving on to wherever it is Consu souls go. Or something along that line. This is a signal honor, not lightly given. This seemed to me to be a fine way to lose your best soldiers in a hurry, but given that I was one of the enemy, it was hard to see the downside for us in the practice.

This third Consu was a member of the highest caste, and his role was simply to tell us the reasons for our death and the manner by which we would all die. After which point, we could actually get to the killing and dying. Any attempt to hasten things along by preemptively taking a shot at the shield would be useless; short of dropping it into a stellar core, there was very little that could ding a Consu shield. Killing a messenger would accomplish nothing other than causing the opening rituals to be restarted, delaying the fighting and killing even more.

Besides, the Consu weren't *hiding* behind the shield. They just had a lot of prebattle rituals to take care of, and they preferred that they were not interrupted by the inconvenient appearance of bullets, particle beams or explosives. Truth was, there was nothing the Consu liked better than a good fight. They thought nothing of the idea of tromping off to some planet, setting themselves down, and daring the natives to pry them off in battle.

Which was the case here. The Consu were entirely disinterested in colonizing this planet. They had merely blasted a human colony here into bits as a way of letting the CDF know they were in the neighborhood and looking for some action. Ignoring the Consu wasn't a possibility, as they'd simply keep killing off colonists until someone came to fight them on a formal basis. You never knew what they'd consider enough for a formal challenge, either. You just kept adding troops until a Consu messenger came out and announced the battle.

Aside from their impressive, impenetrable shields, the Consu's battle technology was of a similar level as the CDF's. This was not as encouraging as you might think, as what reports filtered back from Consu battles with other species indicated that the Consu's weaponry and technology were always more or less matched with that of their opponent. This added to the idea that what the Consu were engaging in was not war but sports. Not unlike a football game, except with slaughtered colonists in the place of proper spectators.

Striking first against Consu was not an option. Their entire inner home system was shielded. The energy to generate the shield came from the white dwarf companion of the Consu sun. It had been completely encased with some sort of harvesting mechanism, so that all the energy coming off it would fuel the shield. Realistically speaking, you just don't fuck with people who can do that. But the Consu had a weird honor system; clean them off a planet in battle, and they didn't come back. It was like the battle was the vaccination, and we were the antiviral.

All of this information was provided by our mission database, which our commanding officer Lieutenant Keyes had directed us to access and read before the battle. The fact that Watson didn't seem to know any of this meant he hadn't accessed the report. This was not entirely surprising, since from the first moment I met Watson it was clear that he was the sort of cocky, willfully ignorant son of a bitch who would get himself or his squadmates killed. My problem was I was his squadmate.

The Consu unfolded its slashing arms—specialized at some point in their evolution to deal with some unimaginably horrifying creature on their homeworld, most likely—and underneath, its more recognizably armlike forelimbs raised to the sky. "It's starting," Viveros said.

"I could pop him so easy," Watson said.

"Do it and I'll shoot you myself," Viveros said.

The sky cracked with a sound like God's own rifle shot, followed by what sounded like a chain saw ripping through a tin roof. The Consu was singing. I accessed Asshole and had it translate from the beginning.

> *Behold, honored adversaries,*
> *We are the instruments of your joyful death.*
> *In our ways we have blessed you*
> *The spirit of the best among us has sanctified our battle.*
> *We will praise you as we move among you*
> *And sing your souls, saved, to their rewards.*
> *It is not your fortune to have been born among The People*
> *So we set you upon the path that leads to redemption.*
> *Be brave and fight with fierceness*
> *That you may come into our fold at your rebirth.*

This blessed battle hallows the ground
And all who die and are born here henceforth are delivered.

"Damn, that's loud," Watson said, sticking a finger in his left ear and twisting. I doubted he had bothered to get a translation.

"This isn't a war or a football game, for Christ's sake," I said to Viveros. "This is a baptism."

Viveros shrugged. "CDF doesn't think so. This is how they start every battle. They think it's their equivalent of the National Anthem. It's just ritual. Look, the shield's coming down." She motioned toward the shield, which was now flickering and failing across its entire length.

"About fucking time," Watson said. "I was about to take a nap."

"Listen to me, both of you," Viveros said. "Stay calm, stay focused and keep your ass down. We've got a good position here, and the lieutenant wants us to snipe these bastards as they come down. Nothing flashy—just shoot them in the thorax. That's where their brains are. Every one we get means one less for the rest of them to worry about. Rifle shots only, anything else is just going to give us away faster. Cut the chatter, BrainPals only from here on out. You get me?"

"We get you," I said.

"Fucking A," Watson said.

"Excellent," Viveros said. The shield finally failed, and the field separating human and Consu was instantly streaked with the trails of rockets that had been sighted and readied for hours. The concussive burps of their explosions were immediately followed by human screams and the metallic chirps of Consu. For a few seconds there was nothing but smoke and silence; then a long, serrated cry as the Consu surged forward to engage the humans, who in turn kept their positions and tried to cut down as many Consu as they could before their two fronts collided.

"Let's get to it," Viveros said. And with that she raised her Empee, sighted it on some far-distant Consu, and began to fire. We quickly followed.

How to prepare for battle.

First, systems check your MP-35 Infantry Rifle. This is the easy part; MP-35s are self-monitoring and self-repairing, and can, in a pinch, use material from an ammunition block as raw material to fix a malfunction. Just about the only way you can permanently ruin an Empee is to place it in the path of a firing maneuvering thruster. Inasmuch as you're likely to be attached to your weapon at the time, if this is the case, you have other problems to worry about.

Second, put on your war suit. This is the standard self-sealing body-length unitard that covers everything but the face. The unitard is designed to let you forget about your body for the length of the battle. The "fabric" of organized nanobots lets in light for photosynthesis and regulates heat; stand on an arctic floe or a Saharan sand dune and the only difference your body notes is the visual change in scenery. If you somehow manage to sweat, your unitard wicks it away, filters it and stores the water until you can transfer it to a canteen. You can deal with urine this way, too. Defecating in your unitard is generally not recommended.

Get a bullet in your gut (or anywhere else), and the unitard stiffens at the point of impact and transfers the energy across the surface of the suit, rather than allowing the bullet to burrow through. This is massively painful but better than letting a bullet ricochet merrily through your intestines. This only works up to a point, alas, so avoiding enemy fire is still the order of the day.

Add your belt, which includes your combat knife, your multipurpose tool, which is what a Swiss army knife wants to be when it grows up, an impressively collapsible personal shelter, your canteen, a week's worth of energy wafers and three slots for ammo blocks. Smear your face with a nanobot-laden cream that interfaces with your unitard to share environmental information. Switch on your camouflage. Try to find yourself in the mirror.

Third, open a BrainPal channel to the rest of your squad and leave it open until you return to the ship or you die. I thought I was pretty smart to think of this in boot camp, but it turns out to be one of the holiest of unofficial rules during the heat of battle. BrainPal communication means no unclear commands or signals—and no speaking to give away your position. If you hear a CDF soldier during the heat of battle, it's because he is either stupid or screaming because he's been shot.

The only drawback to BrainPal communication is that your BrainPal can also send emotional information if you're not paying attention. This can be distracting if you suddenly feel like you're going to piss yourself in fright, only to realize it's not you who's about to cut loose on the bladder, but your squadmate. It's also something none of your squadmates will ever let you live down.

Link *only* to your squadmates—try to keep a channel open to your entire platoon and suddenly sixty people are cursing, fighting and dying inside your head. You do not need this.

Finally, forget everything except to follow orders, kill anything that's not human and stay alive. The CDF makes it simple to do this; for the first two years of service, every soldier is infantry, no matter if you were a janitor or surgeon, senator or street bum in your previous life. If you make it through the first two years, then you get the chance to specialize, to earn a permanent Colonial billet instead of wandering from battle to battle, and to fill in the niche and support roles every military body has. But for two years, all you have to do is go where they tell you, stay behind your rifle, and kill and not be killed. It's simple, but simple isn't the same as easy.

It took two shots to bring down a Consu soldier. This was new—none of the intelligence on them mentioned personal shielding. But something was allowing them to take the first hit; it sprawled them on whatever you might consider to be their ass, but they were up again in a matter of seconds. So two shots; one to take them down, and one to keep them down.

Two shots in sequence on the same moving target is not easily accomplished when you're firing across a few hundred meters of very busy battleground. After figuring this one out, I had Asshole create a specialized firing routine that shot two bullets on one trigger pull, the first a hollow tip, and the second with an explosive charge. The specification was relayed to my Empee between shots; one second I was squeezing off single standard-issue rifle ammo, the next I was shooting my Consu killer special.

I loved my rifle.

I forwarded the firing specification to Watson and Viveros; Viveros forwarded it up the chain of command. Within about a minute, the battlefield was peppered with the sound of rapid double shots, followed by dozens of Consu puffing out as the explosive charges strained their internal organs against the insides of their carapaces. It sounded like popcorn popping. I glanced over at Viveros. She was emotionlessly sighting and shooting. Watson was firing and grinning like a boy who just won a stuffed animal at the state farm BB shoot.

Uh oh—sent Viveros. *We're spotted get down*—

"What?" Watson said, and poked his head up. I grabbed him and pulled him down as the rockets slammed into the boulders we'd been using for cover. We were pelted with newly formed gravel. I looked up just in time to see a chunk of boulder the size of a bowling ball twirling madly down toward my skull. I swatted at it without thinking; the suit went hard down the length of my arm and the chunk flew off like a lazy softball. My arm ached; in my other life I'd be the proud owner of three new, short, likely terribly misaligned arm bones. I wouldn't be doing that again.

"Holy shit, that was close," said Watson.

"Shut up," I said, and sent to Viveros. *What now?*—

Hold tight—she sent and took her multipurpose tool off her belt. She ordered it into a mirror, then used it to peek over the edge of her boulder. *Six no seven on their way up*—

There was a sudden *krump* close by. *Make that five*—she corrected, and closed up her tool. *Set for grenades then follow up then we move*—

I nodded, Watson grinned, and when Viveros sent *Go*—we all pumped grenades over the boulders. I counted three each; after nine explosions I exhaled, prayed, popped up and saw the remains of one Consu, another dragging itself dazedly away from our position, and two scrambling for cover. Viveros got the wounded one; Watson and I each plugged one of the other two.

"Welcome to the party, you shitheads!" Watson whooped, and then bobbled up exultantly over his boulder just in time to get it in the face from the fifth Consu, who had gotten ahead of the grenades and had stayed low while we mopped up its friends. The Consu leveled a barrel at Watson's nose and fired; Watson's face cratered inward and then outward as a geyser of SmartBlood and tissue that used to be Watson's head sprayed over the Consu. Watson's unitard, designed to stiffen when hit by projectiles, did just that when the shot hit the back of his hood, pressuring the shot, the SmartBlood, and bits of skull, brain and BrainPal back out the only readily available opening.

Watson didn't know what hit him. The last thing he sent through his BrainPal channel was a wash of emotion that could best be described as disoriented puzzlement, the mild surprise of someone who knows he's seeing something he wasn't expecting but hasn't figured out what it is. Then his connection was cut off, like a data feed suddenly unexpectedly shut down.

The Consu who shot Watson sang as it blew his face apart. I had left my translation circuit on, and so I saw Watson's death subtitled, the word "Redeemed" repeated over and over while bits of his head formed weeping droplets on the Consu's thorax. I screamed and fired. The Consu slammed backward and then its body exploded as bullet after bullet dug under its thoracic plate and detonated. I figured I wasted thirty rounds on an already dead Consu before I stopped.

"Perry," Viveros said, switching back to her voice to snap me out of whatever I was in. "More on the way. Time to move. Let's go."

"What about Watson?" I asked.

"Leave him," Viveros said. "He's dead and you're not and there's no one to mourn him out here anyway. We'll come for the body later. Let's go. Let's stay alive."

We won. The double-bullet rifle technique thinned out the Consu herd by a substantial amount before they got wise and moved to switch tactics, falling back to launch rocket attacks rather than to make another frontal assault. After several hours of this the Consu fell back completely and fired up their shield, leaving behind a squad to ritually commit suicide, signaling the Consu's acceptance of their loss. After they had plunged their ceremonial knives into their brain cavity, all that was left was to collect our dead and what wounded had been left in the field.

For the day, 2nd Platoon came through pretty well; two dead, including Watson, and four wounded, only one seriously. She'd be spending the next month growing back her lower intestine, while the other three would be up and back on duty in a matter of days. All things considered, things could have been worse. A Consu armored hovercraft had rammed its way toward 4th Platoon, Company C's position and detonated, taking sixteen of them with it, including the platoon commander and two squad leaders, and wounding much of the rest of the platoon. If 4th Platoon's lieutenant weren't already dead, I'd suspect he'd be wishing he were after a clusterfuck like that.

After we received an all clear from Lieutenant Keyes, I went back to get Watson. A group of eight-legged scavengers was already at him; I shot one and that encouraged the rest to disperse. They had made impressive progress on him in a short amount of time; I was sort of darkly surprised at how much less someone weighed after you subtracted his head and much of his soft tissues. I put what was left of him in a fireman's carry and started on the couple of klicks to the temporary morgue. I had to stop and vomit only once.

Alan spied me on the way in. "Need any help?" he said, coming up alongside me.

"I'm fine," I said. "He's not very heavy anymore."

"Who is it?" Alan said.

"Watson," I said.

"Oh, *him*," Alan said, and grimaced. "Well, I'm sure someone somewhere will miss him."

"Try not to get all weepy on me," I said. "How did you do today?"

"Not bad," Alan said. "I kept my head down most of the time, poked my rifle up every now and then and shot a few rounds in the general direction of the enemy. I may have hit something. I don't know."

"Did you listen to the death chant before the battle?"

"Of course I did," Alan said. "It sounded like two freight trains mating. It's not something you can choose *not* to hear."

"No," I said. "I mean, did you get a translation? Did you listen to what it was saying?"

"Yeah," Alan said. "I'm not sure I like their plan for converting us to their religion, seeing as it involves dying and all."

"The CDF seems to think it's just ritual. Like it's a prayer they recite because it's something they've always done," I said.

"What do you think?" Alan asked.

I jerked my head back to indicate Watson. "The Consu who killed him was screaming, 'Redeemed, redeemed,' as loud as he could, and I'm sure he'd have done the same while he was gutting me. I'm thinking the CDF is underestimating what's going on here. I think the reason the Consu don't come back after one of these battles isn't because they think they've lost. I don't think this battle is really about winning or losing. By their lights, this planet is now consecrated by blood. I think they think they *own* it now."

"Then why don't they occupy it?"

"Maybe it's not time," I said. "Maybe they have to wait until some sort of Armageddon. But my point is, I don't think the CDF knows whether the Consu consider this their property now or not. I think somewhere down the line, they're going to be mightily surprised."

"Okay, I'll buy that," Alan said. "Every military I've ever heard of has a history of smugness. But what do you propose to do about it?"

"Shit, Alan, I haven't the slightest idea," I said. "Other than to try to be long dead when it happens."

"On an entirely different, less depressing subject," Alan said, "good job thinking up the firing solution for the battle. Some of us were really getting pissed off that we'd shoot those bastards and they'd just get up and keep coming. You're going to get your drinks bought for you for the next couple of weeks."

"We don't pay for drinks," I said. "This is an all-expenses-paid tour of hell, if you'll recall."

"Well, if we did, you would," Alan said.

"I'm sure it's not that big of a deal," I said, and then noticed that Alan had stopped and was standing at attention. I looked up and saw Viveros, Lieutenant Keyes, and some officer I didn't recognize striding toward me. I stopped and waited for them to reach me.

"Perry," Lieutenant Keyes said.

"Lieutenant," I said. "Please forgive the lack of salute, sir. I'm carrying a dead body to the morgue."

"That's where they go," Keyes said, and motioned at the corpse. "Who is that?"

"Watson, sir."

"Oh, *him*," Keyes said. "That didn't take very long, did it."

"He was excitable, sir," I said.

"I suppose he was," Keyes said. "Well, anyway. Perry, this is Lieutenant Colonel Rybicki, the 233rd's commander."

"Sir," I said. "Sorry about not saluting."

"Yes, dead body, I know," said Rybicki. "Son, I just wanted to congratulate you on your firing solution today. You saved a lot of time and lives. Those Consu bastards keep switching things up on us. Those personal shields were a new touch and they were giving us a hell of a lot of trouble there. I'm putting you in for a commendation, Private. What do you think about that?"

"Thank you, sir," I said. "But I'm sure someone else would have figured it out eventually."

"Probably, but you figured it out first, and that counts for something."

"Yes, sir."

"When we get back to the *Modesto*, I hope you'll let an old infantryman buy you a drink, son."

"I'd like that, sir," I said. I saw Alan smirk in the background.

"Well, then. Congratulations again." Rybicki motioned at Watson. "And sorry about your friend."

"Thank you, sir." Alan saluted for the both of us. Rybicki saluted back, and wheeled off, followed by Keyes. Viveros turned back to me and Alan.

"You seem amused," Viveros said to me.

"I was just thinking that it's been about fifty years since anyone called me 'son,' " I said.

Viveros smiled, and indicated Watson. "You know where you're taking him?" she asked.

"Morgue's just over that ridge," I said. "I'm going to drop off Watson and then I'd like to catch the first transport back to the *Modesto,* if that's okay."

"Shit, Perry," Viveros said. "You're the hero of the day. You can do anything you want." She turned to go.

"Hey, Viveros," I said. "Is it always like this?"

She turned back. "Is what always like this?"

"This," I said. "War. Battles. Fighting."

"What?" Viveros said, and then snorted. "Hell, no, Perry. Today was a cakewalk. This is as easy as it gets." And then she trotted off, highly amused.

That was how my first battle went. My era of war had begun.

TEN

Maggie was the first of the Old Farts to die.

She died in the upper atmosphere of a colony named Temperance, an irony because like most colonies with a heavy mining industry, it was sprinkled liberally with bars and brothels. Temperance's metal-laden crust had made it a hard colony to get and a difficult one for humans to keep—the permanent CDF presence there was three times the usual Colonial complement, and they were always sending additional troops to back them up. Maggie's ship, the *Dayton,* caught one of these assignments when Ohu forces dropped into Temperance space and salted an army's worth of drone warriors onto the surface of the planet.

Maggie's platoon was supposed to be part of the effort to take back an aluminum mine one hundred klicks out of Murphy, Temperance's main port. They never made it to the ground. On the way down, her troop transport hull was struck by an Ohu missile. It tore open the hull and sucked several soldiers into space, including Maggie. Most of these soldiers died instantly from the force of the impact or by chunks of the hull tearing into their bodies.

Maggie wasn't one of them. She was sucked out into the space above Temperance fully conscious, her combat unitard automatically closing around her face to keep the air from vomiting out of her lungs. Maggie immediately messaged to her squad and platoon leader. What was left of her squad leader was flapping about in his descent harness. Her platoon leader wasn't much more help, but he wasn't to blame. The troopship was not equipped for space rescue and was in any event gravely damaged and limping, under fire, toward the closest CDF ship to discharge its surviving passengers.

A message to the *Dayton* itself was likewise fruitless; the *Dayton* was exchanging fire with several Ohu ships and could not dispatch rescue. Nor could any other ship. In nonbattle situations she was already too small a target, too far down Temperance's gravity well and too close to Temperance's atmosphere for anything but the most heroic retrieval attempts. In a pitched battle situation, she was already dead.

And so Maggie, whose SmartBlood was by now reaching its oxygen-carrying limit and whose body was undoubtedly beginning to scream for oxygen, took her Empee, aimed it at the nearest Ohu ship, computed a trajectory, and unloaded rocket after rocket. Each rocket burst provided an equal and opposite burst of thrust to Maggie, speeding her toward Temperance's darkened, nighttime sky. Battle data would later show that her rockets, propellant long spent, did indeed impact against the Ohu ship, dealing some minor damage.

Then Maggie turned, faced the planet that would kill her, and like the good professor of Eastern religions that she used to be, she composed *jisei*, the death poem, in the haiku form.

> *Do not mourn me, friends*
> *I fall as a shooting star*
> *Into the next life*

She sent it and the last moments of her life to the rest of us, and then she died, hurtling brightly across the Temperance night sky.

She was my friend. Briefly, she was my lover. She was braver than I ever would have been in the moment of death. And I bet she was a hell of a shooting star.

"The problem with the Colonial Defense Forces is not that they aren't an excellent fighting force. It's that they're far too easy to use."

Thus spoke Thaddeus Bender, two-time Democratic senator from Massachusetts; former ambassador (at various times) to France, Japan and the United Nations; Secretary of State in the otherwise disastrous Crowe administration; author, lecturer, and finally, the latest addition to Platoon D. Since the latest of these had the most relevance to the rest of us, we had all decided that Private Senator Ambassador Secretary Bender was well and truly full of crap.

It's amazing how quickly one goes from being fresh meat to being an old hand. On our first arrival to the *Modesto*, Alan and I received our billets, were greeted cordially if perfunctorily by Lieutenant Keyes (who raised an eyebrow when we passed along Sergeant Ruiz's compliments), and were treated with benign neglect by the rest of the platoon. Our squad leaders addressed us when we needed to be addressed, and our squadmates passed on information we needed to know. Otherwise, we were out of the loop.

It wasn't personal. The three other new guys, Watson, Gaiman and McKean, all got the same treatment, which centered on two facts. The first was that when new guys come in, it was because some old guy has gone—and typically "gone" meant "dead." Institutionally, soldiers can be replaced like cogs. On the platoon and squad level, however, you're replacing a friend, a squadmate, someone who had fought and won and died. The idea that you, whoever you are, could be a replacement or a substitute for that dead friend and teammate is mildly offensive to those who knew him or her.

Secondly, of course, you simply haven't fought yet. And until you do, you're not one of them. You can't be. It's not your fault, and in any event, it will be quickly corrected. But until you're in the field, you're just some guy taking up space where a better man or woman used to be.

I noticed the difference immediately after our battle with the Consu. I was greeted by name, invited to share mess-hall tables, asked to play pool or dragged into conversations. Viveros, my squad leader, started asking my opinion about things instead of telling me how things would be. Lieutenant Keyes told me a story about Sergeant Ruiz, involving a hovercraft and a Colonial's daughter, that I simply did not believe. In short, I'd become one of them—one of *us*. The Consu firing solution and the subsequent commendation helped, but Alan, Gaiman and McKean were also welcomed into the fold, and they didn't do anything but fight and not get killed. It was enough.

Now, three months in, we'd had a few more rounds of fresh meat come through the platoon, and seen them replace people we'd befriended—we knew how the platoon felt when we came to take someone else's place. We had the same reaction: Until you fight, you're just taking up space. Most fresh meat clued in, understood, and toughed out the first few days until we saw some action.

Private Senator Ambassador Secretary Bender, however, was having none of this. From the moment he showed up, he had been ingratiating himself to the platoon, visiting each member personally and attempting to establish a deep, personal relationship. It was annoying. "It's like he's campaigning for something," Alan complained, and this was not far off. A lifetime of running for office will do that to you. You just don't know when to shut it off.

Private Senator Ambassador Secretary Bender also had a lifetime of assuming people were passionately interested in what it was he had to say, which is why he wouldn't ever shut up, even when no one appeared to be listening. So when he was opining wildly on the CDF's problems in mess hall, he was essentially talking to himself. Be that as it may, his statement was provocative enough to get a rise out of Viveros, with whom I was lunching.

"Excuse me?" she said. "Would you mind repeating that last bit?"

"I said, I think the problem with the CDF is not that it's not a good fighting force, but that it's too easy to use," Bender repeated.

"Really," Viveros said. "This I have to hear."

"It's simple, really," Bender said, and shifted into a position that I immediately recognized from pictures of him back on Earth—hands out and slightly curved inward, as if to grasp the concept he was illuminating, in order to give it to others. Now that I was on the receiving end of the movement, I realized how condescending it was. "There's no doubt the Colonial Defense Forces are an extremely capable fighting force. But in a very real sense, that's not the issue. The issue is—what are we doing to *avoid* its use? Are there times when the CDF has been deployed where intensive diplomatic efforts might not have yielded better results?"

"You must have missed the speech I got," I said. "You know, the one about it not being a perfect universe and competition for real estate in the universe being fast and furious."

"Oh, I *heard* it," Bender said. "I just don't know that I *believe* it. There are how many stars in this galaxy? A hundred billion or so? Most of which have a system of planets of some sort. The real estate is functionally infinite. No, I think the real issue here may be that the *reason* we use force when we deal with other intelligent alien species is that force is the easiest thing to use. It's fast, it's straightforward, and compared to the complexities of diplomacy, it's simple. You either hold a piece of land or you don't. As opposed to diplomacy, which is intellectually a much more difficult enterprise."

Viveros glanced over to me, and then back to Bender. "You think what we're doing is *simple*?"

"No, no." Bender smiled and held up a hand placatingly. "I said simple *relative* to diplomacy. If I give you a gun and tell you to take a hill from its inhabitants, the situation is relatively simple. But if I tell you to go to the inhabitants and negotiate a settlement that allows you to acquire that hill, there's a lot going on—what do you do with the current inhabitants, how are they compensated, what rights do they continue to have regarding the hill, and so on."

"Assuming the hill people don't just shoot you as you drop by, diplomatic pouch in hand," I said.

Bender smiled at me and pointed vigorously. "See, that's *exactly* it. We assume that our opposite numbers have the same warlike perspective as we do. But what if—*what if*—the door was opened to diplomacy, even just a crack? Would not any intelligent, sentient species choose to walk through that door? Let's take, for example, the Whaid people. We're about to war on them, aren't we?"

Indeed we were. The Whaidians and humans had been circling each other for more than a decade, fighting over the Earnhardt system, which featured three planets habitable to both our people. Systems with multiple inhabitable planets were fairly rare. The Whaidians were tenacious but also relatively weak; their network of planets was small and most of their industry was still concentrated on their home world. Since the Whaid would not take the hint and stay out of the Earnhardt system, the plan was to skip to Whaid space, smash their spaceport and major industrial zones, and set their expansionary capabilities back a couple of decades or so. The 233rd would be part of the task force that was set to land in their capital city and tear the place up a bit; we were to avoid killing civilians when we could, but otherwise knock a few holes in their parliament houses and religious gathering centers and so on. There was no industrial advantage to doing this, but it sends the message that we can mess with them anytime, just because we feel like it. It shakes them up.

"What about them?" Viveros asked.

"Well, I've done a little research into these people," Bender said. "They've got a remarkable culture, you know. Their highest art form is a form of mass chant that's like a Gregorian round—they'll get an entire city full of Whaidians and start chanting. It's said you can hear the chant for dozens of klicks, and the chants can go on for hours."

"So?"

"*So,* this is a culture we should be celebrating and exploring, not bottling up on its planet simply because they're in our way. Have the Colonials even attempted to reach a peace with these people? I see no record of an attempt. I think we should *make* an attempt. Maybe an attempt could be made by *us.*"

Viveros snorted. "Negotiating a treaty is a little beyond our orders, Bender."

"In my first term as senator, I went to Northern Ireland as part of a trade junket and ended up extracting a peace treaty from the Catholics and the Protestants. I didn't have the authority to make an agreement, and it caused a huge controversy back in the States. But when an opportunity for peace arises, we must take it," Bender said.

"I remember that," I said. "That was right before the bloodiest marching season in two centuries. Not a very successful peace agreement."

"That wasn't the fault of the *agreement*," Bender said, somewhat defensively. "Some drugged-out Catholic kid threw a grenade into an Orangemen's march, and it was all over after that."

"Damn real live people, getting in the way of your peaceful ideals," I said.

"Look, I already said diplomacy wasn't easy," Bender said. "But I think that ultimately we have more to gain by trying to work with these people than we have by trying to wipe them out. It's an option that should at least be on the table."

"Thanks for the seminar, Bender," Viveros said. "Now if you'll yield the floor, I have two points to make here. The first is that until you fight, what you know or what you think you know out here means shit to me and to everyone else. This isn't Northern Ireland, it's not Washington, DC, and it's not planet Earth. When you joined up, you joined up as a soldier, and you better remember that. Second, no matter what you think, *Private*, your responsibility right now isn't to the universe or to humanity at large—it's to me, your squadmates, your platoon and to the CDF. When you're given an order, you'll follow it. If you go beyond the scope of your orders, you're going to have to answer to me. Do you get me?"

Bender regarded Viveros somewhat coolly. "Much evil has been done under the guise of 'just following orders,'" he said. "I hope we never have to find ourselves using the same excuse."

Viveros narrowed her eyes. "I'm done eating," she said, and got up, taking her tray with her.

Bender arched his eyebrows as she left. "I didn't mean to offend her," he said to me.

I regarded Bender carefully. "Do you recognize the name 'Viveros' at all, Bender?" I asked.

He frowned a bit. "It's not familiar," he said.

"Think way back," I said. "We would have been about five or six or so."

A light went on in his head. "There was a Peruvian president named Viveros. He was assassinated, I think."

"Pedro Viveros, that's right," I said. "And not just him—his wife, his brother, his brother's wife and most of their families were murdered in the military coup. Only one of Pedro's daughters survived. Her nanny stuffed her down a laundry chute while the soldiers went through the presidential palace, looking for family members. The nanny was raped before they slit her throat, incidentally."

Bender turned a greenish shade of gray. "She can't be the daughter," he said.

"She is," I said. "And you know what, when the coup was put down and the soldiers who killed her family were put on trial, their excuse was that they were just following orders. So regardless of whether your *point* there was well made or not, you made it to just about the last person in the universe to whom you ought to lecture on the banality of evil. She knows *all* about it. It slaughtered her family while she lay in a basement laundry cart, bleeding and trying not to cry."

"God, I'm sorry, of course," Bender said. "I wouldn't have said anything. But I didn't know."

"Of course you didn't, Bender," I said. "And that was Viveros' point. Out here, you *don't* know. You don't know anything."

"Listen up," Viveros said on the way down to the surface. "Our job is strictly to smash and dash. We're landing near the center of their government operations—blast buildings and structures but avoid shooting live targets unless CDF soldiers are targeted first. We've already kicked these people in the balls, now we're just pissing on them while they're down. Be fast, do damage and get back. Are we clear?"

The operation had been a cakewalk up to that point; the Whaidians had been utterly unprepared for the sudden and instantaneous arrival of two dozen CDF battleships in their home space. The CDF had opened up a diversionary offensive in the Earnhardt system several days before to lure Whaidian ships there to support the battle, so there was almost nobody to defend the home fort, and those that were, were blasted out of the sky in short, surprised order.

Our destroyers also made quick work of the Whaidians' major spaceport, shattering the kilometers-long structure at critical junctures, which allowed the port's own centripetal forces to tear it apart (no need to waste more ammo than necessary). No skip pods were detected as launched to alert Whaidian forces in the Earnhardt system to our attack, so they wouldn't know they were duped until it was too late. If any of the Whaidian forces survived the battle there, they would return home to find nowhere to dock or repair. Our forces would be long gone when they arrived.

With the local space cleared of threats, the CDF leisurely targeted industrial centers, military bases, mines, refineries, desalination plants, dams, solar arrays, harbors, space launch facilities, major highways and any other target that would require the Whaidians to rebuild it before rebuilding their interstellar capabilities. After six hours of solid, unremitting pummeling, the Whaidians had been effectively pushed back to the days of internal combustion engines, and would be likely to stay there for a while.

The CDF avoided a wide-scale random bombing of major cities, since wanton civilian death was not the goal. CDF intelligence suspected major casualties downstream of the destroyed dams, but that really couldn't be helped. There would have been no way for the Whaidians to stop the CDF from cratering the major cities, but the thinking was the Whaidians would have enough problems with the disease, famine and the political and social unrest that inevitably comes as a result of having your industrial and technological base yanked out from under you. Therefore, actively going after the civilian population was seen as inhumane and (equally as important to the CDF brass) an inefficient use of resources. Aside from the capital city, which was targeted strictly as an exercise in psychological warfare, no ground attacks were even considered.

Not that the Whaidians in the capital seemed to appreciate that. Projectiles and beams were bouncing off our troop transports even as we landed. It sounded like hail and frying eggs on the hull.

"Two by two," Viveros said, pairing up the squad. "No one goes off on their own. Refer to your maps and don't get trapped. Perry, you got Bender watch. Try to keep him from signing any peace treaties, if you please. And as an added bonus, you two are first out the door. Get high and deal with snipers."

"Bender." I motioned him over. "Set your Empee for rockets and follow me. Camo on. BrainPal chatter only." The transport ramp went down and Bender and I sprinted out the door. Directly in front of me at forty meters was an abstract sculpture of some description; I nailed it as Bender and I ran. Never much liked abstract art.

I was heading for a large building northwest of our landing position; behind the glass in its lobby I could see several Whaidians with long objects in their paws. I launched a couple of missiles in their direction. The missiles would impact on the glass; they probably wouldn't kill the Whaidians inside, but they'd distract them long enough for Bender and I to disappear. I messaged Bender to blow out a window on the building's second floor; he did, and we launched ourselves at it, landing in what looked like a suite of office cubicles. Hey, even aliens have got to work. No live Whaidians to speak of, however. I imagine most of them had stayed home from work that day. Well, who could blame them.

Bender and I found a rampway that spiraled upward. No

Whaidians followed us up from the lobby. I suspected they were so busy with other CDF soldiers that they forgot all about us. The rampway terminated at the roof; I stopped Bender just before we rose into view and crept up slowly to see three Whaidians sniping down the side of the building. I plugged two and Bender got the other one.

What now — sent Bender.

Come with me — I sent.

Your average Whaidian looks rather like a cross between a black bear and a large, angry flying squirrel; the Whaidians we shot looked like large angry flying bear-squirrels with rifles and the backs of their heads blown out. We crab-walked as quickly as possible to the edge of the roof. I motioned to Bender to go to one of the dead snipers; I took the one next to him.

Get under it — I sent.

What? — Bender sent back.

I motioned to other roofs. *Other Whaidians on other roofs* — I sent. *Camouflage while I take them out* —

What do I do? — Bender sent.

Watch the roof entrance and don't let them do to us what we did to them — I sent.

Bender grimaced and got under his dead Whaidian. I did the same and immediately regretted it. I don't know what a live Whaidian smells like but a dead one smells positively fucking rank. Bender shifted and aimed at the door; I sent to Viveros, gave her an overhead view through the BrainPal, and then started doing damage to other rooftop snipers.

I got six on four different roofs before they began to figure out what was going on. Finally I saw one train its weapon onto my roof; I gave it a love tap in the brain with my rifle and sent to Bender to ditch his corpse and clear the roof. We made it off a few seconds before the rockets hit.

On the way down we ran into the Whaidians I was expecting on our way up. The question of who was more surprised, us or them, was answered when Bender and I opened fire first and wheeled back to the closest building level. I pumped a few grenades down the ramp to give the Whaidians something to think about while Bender and I ran.

"What the hell do we do now?" Bender yelled at me as we ran through the building level.

BrainPal, you asshole — I sent, and turned a corner. *You'll give us away* — I went to a glass wall and looked out. We were at least thirty meters up, too far to jump even with our enhanced bodies.

Here they come — Bender sent. From behind us came the sound of what I suspected were some very angry Whaidians.

Hide — I sent to Bender, trained my Empee at the glass wall closest to me, and fired. The glass shattered but didn't break. I grabbed what I would guess was a Whaidian chair and threw it out the window. Then I ducked into the cubicle next to Bender.

What the hell — Bender sent. *Now they're coming right for us—*

Wait — I sent. *Stay down. Be ready to fire when I tell you. Automatic—*

Four Whaidians turned the corner and carefully made their way toward the shattered wall pane. I heard them gargling to each other; I turned on the translation circuit.

"—went out the hole in the wall," one was saying to another as they approached the wall.

"Impossible," another said. "It is too far down. They would die."

"I have seen them leap great distances," the first said. "Perhaps they would survive."

"Even those [untranslatable] cannot fall 130 deg [unit of measurement] and live," said the third, coming up on the first two. "Those [untranslatable] eaters of [untranslatable] are still here somewhere."

"Did you see [untranslatable—probability personal name] on the ramp? Those [untranslatable] tore [it] apart with their grenades," said the fourth.

"We came up the same ramp as you," said the third. "Of course we saw [it]. Now quiet yourselves and search this area. If they are here, we will exact revenge on the [untranslatable] and celebrate it in service." The fourth closed the gap between him and the third Whaidian, and reached out a great paw to it, as if in commiseration. All four were now conveniently standing in front of the gaping hole in the wall.

Now — I sent to Bender and opened fire. The Whaidians jerked like marionettes for a few seconds and then fell as the force of the bullet impacts pushed them back into the wall that wasn't there anymore. Bender and I waited a few seconds, then snuck back to the ramp. It was unoccupied except for the remains of [untranslatable—probability personal name], which smelled even worse than his dead sniper compatriots up on the roof. So far, the entire experience of the Whaid homeworld had been a real nasal treat, I had to say. We headed back down to the second floor and headed out the same way we had come in, passing by the four Whaidians whom we had helped out the window.

"This isn't really what I expected," Bender said, gawking at the remains of the Whaidians as he passed.

"What did you expect?" I asked.

"I don't rightly know," he replied.

"Well, then, how can it not be what you expected," I said, and switched my BrainPal to speak to Viveros. *We're down* — I sent.

Come over here — Viveros sent and sent her location information. *And bring Bender. You're not going to believe this—* And as she said it, I heard it over the random fire and grenade booms: a low, guttural chant, echoing through the buildings of the government center.

"This is what I told you about," Bender declared, almost joyously, as we cleared the final corner and began our descent into the natural amphitheater. In it, hundreds of Whaidians had assembled, chanting and swaying and waving clubs. Around it, dozens of CDF troops had staked out positions. If they opened fire, it would be a turkey shoot. I switched on my translation circuit again but came up with nothing; either the chants meant nothing or they were using a dialect of Whaidian speech that Colonial linguists hadn't figured out.

I spotted Viveros and went to her. "What's going on?" I shouted to her, over the din.

"You tell me, Perry," she shouted back. "I'm just a spectator here." She nodded over to her left, where Lieutenant Keyes was conferring with other officers. "They're trying to figure out what we should do."

"Why hasn't anyone fired?" Bender asked.

"Because they haven't fired on us," Viveros said. "Our orders were not to fire on civilians unless necessary. They appear to be civilians. They're all carrying clubs but they haven't threatened us with them; they just wave them around while they chant. Therefore, it's not necessary to kill them. I'd think you'd be happy with that, Bender."

"I *am* happy about that," Bender said, and pointed, clearly entranced. "Look, the one that's leading the congregation. He's the Feuy, a religious leader. He's a Whaidian of great stature. He probably wrote the chant they're singing right now. Does anyone have a translation?"

"No," Viveros said. "They're not using a language we know. We have no idea what they're saying."

Bender stepped forward. "It's a prayer for peace," he said. "It has to be. They must know what we've done to their planet. They can see what we're doing to their city. Any people to whom this has been done must be crying for it to cease."

"Oh, you are so full of shit," Viveros snapped. "You have no fucking clue what they're chanting about. They could be chanting about how they're going to rip off our heads and piss down our necks. They could be chanting for their dead. They could be singing their goddamn grocery list. *We* don't know. *You* don't know."

"You're wrong," Bender said. "For five decades I was on the front lines of the battle for peace on Earth. I *know* when a people are ready for peace. I know when they're reaching out." He pointed to the chanting Whaidians. "These people are ready, Viveros. I can *feel* it. And I'm going to prove it to you." Bender set down his Empee and started toward the amphitheater.

"God damn it, Bender!" Viveros yelled. "Get back here now! That's an order!"

"I'm not 'just following orders' anymore, Corporal!" Bender yelled back, and then started to sprint.

"Shit!" Viveros screamed, and started after him. I grabbed for her and missed.

By now Lieutenant Keyes and the other officers looked up and saw Bender racing toward the Whaidians, Viveros chasing behind. I saw Keyes yell something and Viveros pull up suddenly; Keyes must have sent his order over the BrainPal as well. If he had ordered Bender to stop, Bender ignored the command and continued his race to the Whaidians.

Bender finally stopped at the lip of the amphitheater, and stood there silently. Eventually the Feuy, the one leading the chant, noticed the sole human standing at the edge of his congregation and stopped his chanting. The congregation, confused, lost the chant and spent a minute or so muttering before noticing Bender as well, and turned to face him.

This was the moment Bender was waiting for. Bender must

have spent the few moments while the Whaidians noticed his presence composing what he was going to say and translating it into Whaidian, because when he spoke, he attempted their language, and by all professional accounts, did a reasonable job of it.

"My friends, my fellow searchers for peace," he began, reaching out to them with his hands curved in.

Data culled from the event would eventually show that no fewer than forty thousand tiny needlelike projectiles that Whaidians call *avdgur* struck Bender's body in the space of less than one second, shot from clubs that were not clubs at all, but traditional projectile weapons in the shape of a tree branch sacred to the Whaidian people. Bender literally melted as each *avdgur* sliver penetrated his unitard and his body, slicing away at the solidity of his form. Everyone agreed later that it was one of the most interesting deaths any of us had ever seen in person.

Bender's body fell apart in a misty splash and the CDF soldiers opened fire into the amphitheater. It was indeed a turkey shoot; not a single Whaidian made it out of the amphitheater or managed to kill or wound another CDF soldier other than Bender. It was over in less than a minute.

Viveros waited for the cease-fire order, walked over to the puddle that was what was left of Bender, and started stamping in it furiously. "How do you like your peace now, motherfucker?" she cried as Bender's liquefied organs stained the lower half of her legs.

"Bender was right, you know," Viveros said to me on the way back to the *Modesto.*

"About what?" I asked.

"About the CDF being used too fast and too much," Viveros said. "About it being easier to fight than to negotiate." She waved in the general direction of the Whaidian home planet, which was receding behind us. "We didn't *have* to do this, you know. Knock these poor sons of bitches out of space and make it so they spend the next couple of decades starving and dying and killing each other. We didn't murder civilians today—well, other than the ones that got Bender. But they'll spend a nice long time dying from disease and murdering each other because they can't do much of anything else. It's no less of a genocide. We just feel better about it because we'll be gone when it happens."

"You never agreed with Bender before," I said.

"That's not true," Viveros said. "I said that he didn't know shit, and that his duty was to us. But I didn't say he was wrong. He should have listened to me. If he'd have followed his fucking orders, he'd be alive now. Instead I'm scraping him off the bottom of my foot."

"He'd probably say he died for what he believed in," I said.

Viveros snorted. "Please," she said. "Bender died for Bender. Shit. Walking up to a bunch of people whose planet we just destroyed and acting like he was their *friend*. What an asshole. If I were one of them, I'd have shot him, too."

"Damn real live people, getting in the way of peaceful ideals," I said.

Viveros smiled. "If Bender were *really* interested in peace instead of his own ego, he'd have done what I'm doing, and what you should do, Perry," she said. "Follow orders. Stay alive. Make it through our term of infantry service. Join officer training and work our way up. Become the people who are giving the orders, not just following them. That's how we'll make peace when we can. And that's how I can live with 'just following orders.' Because I know that one day, I'll make those orders change." She leaned back, closed her eyes and slept the rest of the way back to our ship.

Luisa Viveros died two months later on a shithole ball of mud called Deep Water. Our squad walked into a trap set in the natural catacombs below the Hann'i colony that we'd been ordered to clear out. In battle we'd been herded into a cave chamber that had four additional tunnels feeding into it, all ringed with Hann'i infantry. Viveros ordered us back into our tunnel and began firing at its mouth, collapsing the tunnel and sealing it off from the chamber. BrainPal data shows she then turned and began taking out the Hann'i. She didn't last long. The rest of the squad fought our way back to the surface; not an easy thing to do, considering how we'd been herded in the first place, but better than dying in an ambush.

Viveros got a medal posthumously for bravery; I was promoted to corporal and given the squad. Viveros' cot and locker were given to a new guy named Whitford, who was decent enough, as far as it went.

The institution had replaced a cog. And I missed her.

ELEVEN

Thomas died because of something he ate.

What he ingested was so new the CDF didn't have a name for it yet, on a colony so new it also didn't have a name, merely an official designation: Colony 622, 47 Ursae Majoris. (The CDF continued to use Earth-based stellar designations for the same reason they continued to use a twenty-four-hour clock and a 365-day year: Because it was easiest to do it that way.) As a matter of standard operating procedure, new colonies transmit a daily compilation of all colony data into a skip drone, which then skips back to Phoenix so that the Colonial government can keep tabs on colony matters.

Colony 622 had sent drones since its landing six months earlier; aside from the usual arguments, snafus and scuffles that accompany any new colony founding, nothing of any note was reported, except for the fact that a local slime mold was gunking up damn near everything, popping up in machinery, computers, animal pens and even colony living quarters. A genetic analysis of the material was sent back to Phoenix with the request that someone create a fungicide that would get the mold literally out of the colonist's hair. Blank skip drones started arriving immediately after that, with no information uploaded from the colony.

Thomas and Susan were stationed on the *Tucson,* which was dispatched to investigate. The *Tucson* attempted to raise the colony from orbit; no luck. Visual targeting of the colony buildings showed no movement between buildings—no people, no animals, no nothing. The buildings themselves, however, didn't seem to be damaged. Thomas' platoon got the call for recon.

The colony was covered with goo, a coating of slime mold several centimeters thick in some places. It dripped off power lines and was all over the communication equipment. This was good news—there was now a possibility that the mold had simply overwhelmed the equipment's transmission ability. This momentary burst of optimism was brought to an abrupt halt when Thomas' squad got to the animal pens to find all of the livestock dead and deeply decomposed thanks to the industrious work of the mold. They found the colonists shortly thereafter, in much the same state. Nearly all of them (or what was left of them) were in or near their beds; the exceptions being families, who were often found in children's rooms or the hallways leading to them, and the members of the colony working the graveyard shift, who were found at or near their posts. Whatever hit, hit late and so fast that colonists simply didn't have time to react.

Thomas suggested taking one of the corpses to the colony's medical quarters; he could perform a quick autopsy that might give some insight into what had killed the colonists. His squad leader gave assent, and Thomas and a squadmate hunkered over one of the more intact bodies. Thomas grabbed under the arms and the squadmate took the legs. Thomas told his squadmate to lift on the count of three; he got to two when the slime mold rose up from the body and slapped him wetly on the face. He gasped in surprise; the slime mold slid into his mouth and down his throat.

The rest of Thomas' squad immediately cued their suits to provide faceplates, and not a moment too soon, since in a matter of seconds, slime mold leaped from every crack and crevice to attack. All over the colony, similar attacks were made nearly simultaneously. Six of Thomas' platoon mates also found themselves with a mouthful of slime mold.

Thomas tried to pull the slime mold out of his mouth, but it slid farther into his throat, blocking his airway, pushing into his lungs and down his esophagus into his stomach. Thomas sent via his BrainPal that his squadmates should take him to the medical quarters, where they might be able to suction enough of the mold out of his body to allow him to breathe again; the SmartBlood meant they would have almost fifteen minutes before Thomas began to suffer permanent brain damage. It was an excellent idea and probably would have worked, had not the slime mold begun to excrete concentrated digestive acids into Thomas' lungs, eating him from the inside while he was still alive. Thomas' lungs began to dissolve immediately; he was dead from shock and asphyxiation minutes later. The six other platoon mates joined in his fate, the fate that had, everyone later agreed, also befallen the colonists.

Thomas' platoon leader gave orders to leave Thomas and the other victims behind; the platoon retreated to the transport and made its way back to the *Tucson*. The transport was denied permission to dock. The platoon was led in, one by one, in hard vacuum to kill whatever mold was still lingering on their suits, and then subjected to an intense external and internal decontamination process that was every bit as painful as it sounds.

Subsequent unmanned probes showed no survivors of Colony 622 anywhere, and that the slime mold, beyond possessing enough intelligence to mount two separate coordinated attacks, was nearly impervious to traditional weaponry. Bullets, grenades and rockets affected only small portions while leaving other portions unharmed; flamethrowers fried up a top layer of slime mold, leaving layers underneath untouched; beam weaponry slashed through the mold but did minimal overall damage. Research on the fungicide the colonists had requested had begun but was halted when it was determined that the slime mold was present almost everywhere on the planet. The amount of effort to locate another inhabitable planet was deemed less expensive than eradicating the slime mold on a global scale.

Thomas' death was a reminder that not only don't we know what we're up against out here, sometimes we simply can't *imagine* what we're up against. Thomas made the mistake of assuming the enemy would be more like us than not. He was wrong. He died because of it.

Conquering the universe was beginning to get to me.

The unsettled feeling had begun at Gindal, where we ambushed Gindalian soldiers as they returned to their aeries, slashing their huge wings with beams and rockets that sent them tumbling and screeching down sheer two-thousand-meter cliff faces. It had really started to affect me above Udaspri, as we donned inertia-dampening power packs to provide better control as we leaped from rock fragment to rock fragment in Udaspri's rings, playing hide-and-seek with the spiderlike Vindi who had taken to hurling bits of the ring down to the planet below, plotting delicate decaying orbits that aimed the falling debris directly on top of the human colony of Halford. By the time we arrived at Cova Banda, I was ready to snap.

It might have been because of the Covandu themselves, who in many respects were clones of the human race itself: bipedal, mammalian, extraordinarily gifted in artistic matters, particularly poetry and drama, fast breeding and unusually aggressive when it came to the universe and their place in it. Humans and the Covandu frequently found themselves fighting for the same undeveloped real estate. Cova Banda, in fact, had been a human colony before it had been a Covandu one, abandoned after a native virus had caused the settlers to grow unsightly additional limbs and homicidal additional personalities. The virus didn't give the Covandu even a headache; they moved right in. Sixty-three years later, the Colonials finally developed a vaccine and wanted the planet back. Unfortunately, the Covandu, again all too much like humans, weren't very much into the whole sharing thing. So in we went, to do battle against the Covandu.

The tallest of whom is no more than one inch tall.

The Covandu are not so stupid as to launch their tiny little armies against humans sixty or seventy times their size, of course. First they hit us with aircraft, long-range mortars, tanks and other military equipment that might actually do some damage—and did; it's not easy to take out a twenty-centimeter-long aircraft flying at several hundred klicks an hour. But you do what you can to make it difficult to use these options (we did this by landing in Cova Banda's main city's park, so any artillery that missed us hit their own people) and anyway, eventually you'll dispose of most of these annoyances. Our people used more care destroying Covandu forces than they typically might, not only because they're smaller and require more attention to hit. There's also the matter that no one wants to have been killed by a one-inch opponent.

Eventually, however, you shoot down all the aircraft and take out all the tanks, and then you have to deal with the individual Covandu themselves. So here's how you fight one: You step on him. You just bring your foot down, apply pressure and it's done. As you're doing this, the Covandu is firing his weapon at you and screaming at the top of his tiny little lungs, a squeak that you may just be able to hear. But it's useless. Your suit, designed to apply brakes on a human-scale high-powered projectile, barely registers the bits of matter flung at your toes by a Covandu; you barely register the crunch of the little being you've stomped. You spot another one, you do it again.

We did this for hours as we waded through Cova Banda's main city, stopping every now and then to sight a rocket on a skyscraper five or six meters high and take it down with a single shot. Some of our platoon would spray a shotgun blast into a building instead, letting the individual shot, each big enough to take a Covandu's head clean off, rattle through the building like mad pachinko balls. But mostly, it was about the stomping. Godzilla, the famous Japanese monster, who had been undergoing his umpteenth revival as I left the Earth, would have felt right at home.

I don't remember exactly when it was I began to cry and kick skyscrapers, but I had done it long enough and hard enough that when Alan was finally called over to retrieve me, Asshole was informing me that I had managed to break three toes. Alan walked me back to the city park we'd landed in and had me sit down; as soon as I did, some Covandu emerged from behind a boulder and aimed his weapon at my face. It felt like tiny grains of sand were plunking into my cheek.

"God *damn* it," I said, grabbed the Covandu like a ball bearing, and angrily flung him into a nearby skyscraper. He zoomed off, spinning in a flat arc, decelerated with a tinny *thunk* when he hit the building, and fell the two remaining meters to the ground. Any other Covandu in the area apparently decided against assassination attempts.

I turned to Alan. "Don't you have a squad to pay attention to?" I asked. He'd been promoted after his squad leader had had his face torn off by an angry Gindalian.

"I could ask you the same question," he said, and then shrugged. "They're fine. They have their orders and there's no real opposition anymore. It's clean and sweep, and Tipton can handle the squad for that. Keyes told me to come hose you down and find out what the hell is wrong with you. So what the hell *is* wrong with you?"

"Christ, Alan," I said. "I've just spent three hours stepping on intelligent beings like they were fucking bugs, that's what's wrong with me. I'm stomping people to death with my fucking *feet*. This"—I swept out an arm—"it's just totally fucking ridiculous, Alan. These people are *one inch tall*. It's like Gulliver beating the shit out of the Lilliputians."

"We don't get to choose our battles, John," Alan said.

"How does this battle make you feel?" I asked.

"It bothers me a little," Alan said. "It's not a stand-up fight at all; we're just blowing these people to hell. On the other hand, the worst casualty I have in my squad is a burst eardrum. That's a miracle for you right there. So overall I feel pretty good about it. And the Covandu aren't entirely helpless. The overall scoreboard between us and them is pretty much tied."

This was surprisingly true. The Covandu's size worked to their advantage in space battles; their ships are hard for ours to track and their tiny fighter craft do little damage individually but an immense amount in aggregate. It was only when it came to ground fights that we had the overwhelming advantage. Cova Banda had a relatively small space fleet protecting it; it was one of the reasons the CDF decided to try to take it back.

"I'm not talking about who's ahead in the overall tally, Alan," I said. "I'm talking about the fact that our opponents are one fucking inch tall. Before this, we were fighting spiders. Before *that*, we were fighting goddamned pterodactyls. It's all messing with my sense of scale. It's messing with my sense of me. I don't feel human anymore, Alan."

"Technically speaking, you're *not* human anymore," Alan said. It was an attempt to lighten my mood.

It didn't work. "Well, then, I don't feel connected with what it *was* to be human anymore," I said. "Our job is to go meet strange new people and cultures, and kill the sons of bitches as quickly as we possibly can. We know only what we need to know about these people in order to fight with them. They don't exist to be anything other than an enemy, as far as we know. Except for the fact that they're smart about fighting back, we might as well be fighting animals."

"That makes it easier for most of us," Alan said. "If you don't identify with a spider, you don't feel as bad about killing one, even a big, smart one. Maybe especially a big, smart one."

"Maybe that's what's bothering me," I said. "There's no sense of consequence. I just took a living, thinking thing and hurled it into the side of a building. Doing it didn't bother me at all. The fact that it didn't *does* bother me, Alan. There ought to be consequences to our actions. We have to acknowledge at least some of the horror of what we do, whether we're doing it for good reasons or not. I have no horror about what I'm doing. I'm scared of that. I'm scared of what it means. I'm stomping around this city like a goddamned monster. And I'm beginning to think that's exactly what I am. What I've become. I'm a monster. You're a monster. We're *all* fucking inhuman monsters, and we don't see a damned thing wrong with it."

Alan didn't have anything to say to that. So instead we watched our soldiers, stomping Covandu to death, until finally there weren't really any left to stomp.

"So what the hell is wrong with him?" Lieutenant Keyes asked Alan, about me, at the end of our post-battle briefing with the other squad leaders.

"He thinks we're all inhuman monsters," Alan said.

"Oh, *that*," Lieutenant Keyes said, and turned to me. "How long have you been in, Perry?"

"Almost a year," I said.

Lieutenant Keyes nodded. "You're right on schedule, then, Perry. It takes about a year for most people to figure out they've turned into some soulless killing machine with no conscience or morals. Some sooner, some later. Jensen here"—he indicated one of the other squadron leaders—"got to about the fifteen-month point before he cracked. Tell him what you did, Jensen."

"I took a shot at Keyes," Ron Jensen said. "Seeing as he was the personification of the evil system that turned me into a killing machine."

"Nearly took off my head, too," Keyes said.

"It was a lucky shot," Jensen allowed.

"Yeah, lucky that you missed. Otherwise I'd be dead and you'd be a brain floating in a tank, going insane from the lack of outside stimuli. Look, Perry, it happens to everyone. You'll shake it off when you realize you're not actually an inhuman monster, you're just trying to wrap your brain around a totally fucked-up situation. For seventy-five years you lead the sort of life where the most exciting thing that happens is you get laid from time to time, and the next thing you know you're trying to blast space octopi with an Empee before they kill you first. Christ. It's the ones that don't eventually lose it that I don't trust."

"Alan hasn't lost it," I said. "And he's been in as long as I have."

"That's true," Keyes said. "What's your answer to that, Rosenthal?"

"I'm a seething cauldron of disconnected rage on the inside, Lieutenant."

"Ah, repression," Keyes said. "Excellent. Try to avoid taking a potshot at me when you finally blow, please."

"I can't promise anything, sir," Alan said.

"You know what worked for me," said Aimee Weber, another squad leader. "I made a list of the things that I missed about

Earth. It was sort of depressing, but on the other hand, it reminded me that I wasn't totally out of it. If you miss things, you're
still connected."

"So what did you miss?" I asked.

"Shakespeare in the Park, for one," she said. "My last night on
Earth, I saw a production of *Macbeth* that was just perfection. God,
that was great. And it's not like we're getting any good live theater
around these here parts."

"I miss my daughter's chocolate chip cookies," said Jensen.

"You can get chocolate chip cookies on the *Modesto*," Keyes
said. "Damn fine ones."

"They're not as good as my daughter's. The secret is molasses."

"That sounds disgusting," Keyes said. "I hate molasses."

"Good thing I didn't know that when I shot at you," Jensen
said. "I wouldn't have missed."

"I miss swimming," said Greg Ridley. "I used to swim in the
river next to my property in Tennessee. Cold as hell most of the
time, but I liked it that way."

"Roller coasters," said Keyes. "Big ones that made you feel like
your intestines would drop out through your shoes."

"Books," said Alan. "A big fat hardcover on a Sunday morning."

"Well, Perry?" Weber said. "Anything you're missing right
about now?"

I shrugged. "Only one thing," I said.

"It can't be any stupider than missing roller coasters," Keyes
said. "Out with it. That's an order."

"The only thing I really miss is being married," I said. "I miss
sitting around with my wife, just talking or reading together or
whatever."

This got utter silence. "That's a new one on me," Ridley said.

"Shit, I don't miss that," Jensen said. "The last twenty years of
my marriage were nothing to write home about."

I looked around. "Don't any of you have spouses who joined up? Don't you keep in touch with them?"

"My husband signed up before I did," Weber said. "He was already dead by the time I got my first posting."

"My wife is stationed on the *Boise*," Keyes said. "She drops me a note occasionally. I don't really get the feeling she's missing me terribly. I guess thirty-eight years of me was enough."

"People get out here and they don't really want to be in their old lives anymore," Jensen said. "Sure, we miss the little things— like Aimee says, that's one of the ways you keep yourself from going nuts. But it's like being taken back in time, to just before you made all the choices that gave you the life you had. If you could go back, why would you make the same choices? You already lived that life. My last comment aside, I don't regret the choices I made. But I'm not in a rush to make those same choices again. My wife's out here, sure. But she's happy to live her new life without me. And, I must say, I'm not in a hurry to sign up on that tour of duty again, either."

"This isn't cheering me up, people," I said.

"What is it about being married you miss?" Alan asked.

"Well, I miss my wife, you know," I said. "But I also miss the feeling of, I don't know, comfort. The sense you're where you're supposed to be, with someone you're supposed to be with. I sure as hell don't feel that out here. We go places that we have to fight for, with people who might be dead the next day or the day after that. No offense."

"None taken," Keyes said.

"There's no stable ground out here," I said. "There's nothing out here I feel really safe about. My marriage had its ups and downs like anyone's, but when it came down to it, I knew it was solid. I miss that sort of security, and that sort of connection with someone. Part of what makes us human is what we mean to other people, and what people mean to us. I miss meaning something to someone, having that part of being human. That's what I miss about marriage."

More silence. "Well, hell, Perry," Ridley finally said. "When you put it that way, I miss being married, too."

Jensen snorted. "I don't. You keep missing being married, Perry. I'll keep missing my daughter's cookies."

"Molasses," Keyes said. "Disgusting."

"Don't start that again, sir," Jensen said. "I may have to go get my Empee."

Susan's death was very nearly the flip side of Thomas'. A drillers' strike on Elysium had severely reduced the amount of petroleum being refined. The *Tucson* was assigned to transport scab drillers and protect them while they got several of the shut-down drilling platforms back online. Susan was on one of the platforms when the striking drillers attacked with improvised artillery; the explosion knocked Susan and two other soldiers off the platform and down several dozen meters to the sea. The other two soldiers were already dead when they hit the water but Susan, severely burned and barely conscious, was still alive.

Susan was fished out of the sea by the striking drillers who had launched the attack; they decided to make an example of her. The Elysium seas feature a large scavenger called a gaper, whose hinged jaw is easily capable of taking up a person in a single swallow. Gapers frequent the drilling platforms because they feed off the trash the platforms shed into the sea. The drillers propped Susan up, slapped her into consciousness, and then reeled off a hurried manifesto in her general direction, relying on her BrainPal connection to carry their words to the CDF. They then found Susan guilty of collaborating with the enemy, sentenced her to death, and pushed her back into the sea directly below the platform's trash chute.

A gaper was not long in coming; one swallow and Susan was in. At this point Susan was still alive and struggling to exit the gaper from the same orifice from which she entered. Before she could manage this, however, one of the striking drillers shot the gaper directly below the dorsal fin, where the animal's brain was located. The gaper was killed instantly and sank, taking Susan with it. Susan was killed, not from being eaten and not even from drowning, but from the pressure of the water as she and the fish that had swallowed her sank into the abyss.

Any celebration by the striking drillers over this blow to the oppressor was short-lived. Fresh forces from the *Tucson* swept through the drillers' camps, rounded up several dozen ringleaders, shot them and fed them all to the gapers. Except for the ones who killed Susan, who were fed to gapers without the intermediary step of being shot first. The strike ended shortly thereafter.

Susan's death was clarifying to me, a reminder that humans can be as inhuman as any alien species. If I had been on the *Tucson*, I could see myself feeding one of the bastards who killed Susan to the gapers, and not feeling in the least bit bad about it. I don't know if this made me better or worse than what I had feared I was becoming when we battled the Covandu. But I no longer worried about it making me any less human than I was before.

TWELVE

Those of us who were at the Battle for Coral remember where we were when we first heard the planet had been taken. I was listening to Alan explain how the universe I thought I knew was long gone.

"We left it the first time we skipped," he said. "Just went up and out into the universe next door. That's how skipping works."

This got a nice, long mute reaction from me and Ed McGuire, who were sitting with Alan in the battalion's "At Ease" lounge. Finally Ed, who had taken over Aimee Weber's squad, piped up. "I'm not following you, Alan. I thought that the skip drive just took us up past the speed of light or something like that. That's how it works."

"Nope," Alan said. "Einstein's still right—the speed of light is as fast as you can go. Besides which, you wouldn't want to start flying around the universe at any real fraction of the speed of light, anyway. You hit even a little chunk of dirt while you're going a couple hundred thousand klicks a second and you're going to put a pretty good hole in your spaceship. It's just a speedy way to get killed."

Ed blinked and then swept his hand over his head. "Whoosh," he said. "You lost me."

"All right, look," Alan said. "You asked me how the skip drive works. And like I said, it's simple: It takes an object from one universe, like the *Modesto,* and pops it into another universe. The problem is that we refer to it as a 'drive.' It's not really a drive at all, because acceleration is not a factor; the only factor is location within the multiverse."

"Alan," I said. "You're doing another flyby."

"Sorry," Alan said, and looked thoughtful for a second. "How much math do you guys have?" he asked.

"I vaguely recall calculus," I said. Ed McGuire nodded in agreement.

"Oy," Alan said. "Fine. I'm going to use small words here. Please don't be offended."

"We'll try not to," Ed said.

"Okay. First off, the universe you're in—the universe we're in right at this moment—is only one of an infinite number of possible universes whose existence is allowed for within quantum physics. Every time we spot an electron in a particular position, for example, our universe is functionally defined by that electron's position, while in the alternate universe, that electron's position is entirely different. You following me?"

"Not at all," said Ed.

"You nonscientists. Well, just trust me on it, then. The point is: multiple universes. The multiverse. What the skip drive does is open a door to another one of those universes."

"How does it do that?" I asked.

"You don't have the math for me to explain it to you," Alan said.

"So it's magic," I said.

"From your point of view, yes," Alan said. "But it's well allowed in physics."

"I don't get it," Ed said. "We've been through multiple universes then, yet every universe we've been in has been exactly like ours. Every 'alternate universe' I ever read about in science fiction has major differences. That's how you know you're in an alternate universe."

"There's actually an interesting answer to that question," Alan said. "Let us take as a given that moving an object from one universe to another is a fundamentally unlikely event."

"I can accept that," I said.

"In terms of physics, this is allowable, since at its most basic level, this is a quantum physics universe and pretty much anything *can* happen, even if as a practical matter it doesn't. However, all other things being equal, each universe prefers to keep unlikely events to a bare minimum, especially above the subatomic level."

"How does a universe 'prefer' anything?" Ed asked.

"You don't have the math," Alan said.

"Of course not," Ed said, rolling his eyes.

"But the universe does prefer some things over others. It prefers to move toward a state of entropy, for example. It prefers to have the speed of light as a constant. You can modify or mess with these things to some extent, but they take work. Same thing here. In this case, moving an object from one universe to another is so unlikely that typically the universe to which you move the object is otherwise exactly like the one you left—a conservation of unlikeliness, you might say."

"But how do you explain us moving from one place to another?" I asked. "How do we get from one point in space in one universe, to an entirely different point in space in another?"

"Well, think about it," Alan said. "Moving an entire ship into another universe is the incredibly unlikely part. From the universe's point of view, *where* in that new universe it appears is really very trivial. That's why I said that the word 'drive' is a misnomer. We don't really *go* anywhere. We simply *arrive*."

"And what happens in the universe that you just left?" asked Ed.

"Another version of the *Modesto* from another universe pops right in, with alternate versions of us in it," Alan said. "Probably. There's an infinitesimally small chance against it, but as a general rule, that's what happens."

"So do we ever get to go back?" I asked.

"Back where?" Alan said.

"Back to the universes where we started from," I said.

"No," Alan said. "Well, again, it's theoretically possible you *could*, but it's extremely unlikely. Universes are continually being created from branching possibilities, and the universes we go to are generally created almost instantly before we skip into them— it's one of the reasons why we *can* skip to them, because they are so very close to our own in composition. The longer in time you're separated from a particular universe, the more time it has to become divergent, and the less likely you are to go back to it. Even going back to a universe you left a second before is phenomenally unlikely. Going back to the one we left over a year ago, when we first skipped to Phoenix from Earth, is really out of the question."

"I'm depressed," Ed said. "I liked my universe."

"Well, get this, Ed," Alan said. "You don't even come from the same original universe as John and I, since you didn't make that first skip when we did. What's more, even the people who *did* make that same first skip with us aren't in the same universe as us now, since they've since skipped into different universes because they're on different ships—any versions of our old friends that we meet up with will be alternate versions. Of course, they will look and act the same, because except for the occasional electron placement here and there, they *are* the same. But our originating universes are completely different."

"So you and I are all that's left of our universe," I said.

"It's a pretty good bet that universe continues to exist," Alan said. "But we are almost certainly the only two people from it in *this* universe."

"I don't know what to think about that," I said.

"Try not to let it worry you too much," Alan said. "From a day-to-day point of view, all this universe hopping doesn't matter. Functionally speaking, everything is pretty much the same no matter what universe you're in."

"So why do we need starships at all?" Ed asked.

"Quite obviously, to get where you're going once you're in your new universe," Alan said.

"No, no," Ed said. "I mean, if you can just pop from one universe to another, why not just do it planet to planet, instead of using spaceships at all? Just skip people directly to a planet surface. It'd save us from getting shot up in space, that's for sure."

"The universe prefers to have skipping done away from large gravity wells, like planets and stars," Alan said. "Particularly when skipping to another universe. You can skip very close *to* a gravity well, which is why we enter new universes near our destinations, but skipping out is much easier the farther away you are from one, which is why we always travel a bit before we skip. There's actually an exponential relationship that I could show you, but—"

"Yeah, yeah, I know, I don't have the math," Ed said.

Alan was about to provide a placating response when all of our BrainPals flicked on. The *Modesto* had just received news of the Coral Massacre. And in whatever universe you were in, it was horrifying stuff.

Coral was the fifth planet humans settled, and the first one that was indisputably better acclimated for humans than even Earth itself. It was geologically stable, with weather systems that spread a temperate growing zone across most of its generous landmasses, and laden with native plant and animal species genetically similar enough to Earth's that they fulfilled human nutritional and esthetic needs. Early on, there was talk of naming the colony Eden, but it was suggested that such a name was karmically tantamount to asking for trouble.

Coral was chosen instead, for the corallike creatures that created gloriously diverse island archipelagos and undersea reefs around the planet's equatorial tropical zone. Human expansion on Coral was uncharacteristically kept to a minimum, and those humans who did live there largely chose to live in a simple, almost pre-industrial way. It was one of the few places in the universe where humans attempted to adapt to the existing ecosystem rather than plow it over and introduce, say, corn and cattle. And it worked; the human presence, small and accommodating, dovetailed into Coral's biosphere and thrived in a modest and controlled way.

It was therefore entirely unprepared for the arrival of the Rraey invasion force, which carried in its numbers a one-to-one ratio of soldiers to colonists. The garrison of CDF troops stationed above and on Coral put up a brief but valiant fight before being over-whelmed; the colonists likewise made the Rraey pay for their attack. In short order, however, the colony was laid waste and the surviving colonists literally butchered, as the Rraey had long ago developed a taste for human meat when they could get it.

One of the snippets broadcast to us via BrainPal was a segment of an intercepted food program, in which one of the Rraey's most famous celebrity chefs discussed the best way to carve up a human for multiple food uses, neck bones being particularly prized for soups and consommés. In addition to sickening us, the video was anecdotal proof that the Coral Massacre was planned in enough detail that they brought along even second-rate Rraey celebrities to take part in the festivities. Clearly, the Rraey were planning to stay.

The Rraey wasted no time toward their primary goal for the

invasion. After all the colonists had been killed, the Rraey transported down platforms to begin strip-mining Coral's islands. The Rraey had previously tried to negotiate with the Colonial government to mine the islands; corallike reefs had been extensive on the Rraey homeworld until a combination of industrial pollution and commercial mining had destroyed them. The Colonial government refused permission for mining, both because of Coral's colonists' wishes to keep the planet whole, and because the Rraey's anthropophagous tendencies were well known. No one wanted the Rraey overflying the colonies, looking for unsuspecting humans to turn into jerky.

The Colonial government's failing was in not recognizing what a priority the Rraey had made coral mining—beyond its commerce, there was a religious aspect involved that Colonial diplomats grossly misinterpreted—or the lengths that the Rraey were willing to go to undertake the operation. The Rraey and the Colonial government had mixed it up a few times; relations were never good (how comfortable can you really be with a race that sees you as a nutritious part of a complete breakfast). By and large, however, they kept to their knitting and we to ours. It was only now, as the last of the Rraey's native coral reefs choked toward extinction, that the extent of their desire for Coral's resources came to slug us in the face. Coral was theirs, and we'd have to hit them harder than they had hit us to get it back.

"It's pretty fucking grim," Lieutenant Keyes was telling the squad leaders, "and it's going to be grimmer by the time we get there."

We were in the platoon ready room, cups of coffee growing cold as we accessed page upon page of atrocity reports and surveillance information from the Coral system. What skip drones weren't blasted from the sky by the Rraey reported back a continuing stream of inbound Rraey ships, both for battle and for hauling coral. In less than two days after the Coral Massacre, almost a thousand Rraey ships hovered in the space above the planet, waiting to begin their predation in earnest.

"Here's what we know," Keyes said, and popped up a graphic of the Coral system in our BrainPals. "We estimate that the largest portion of Rraey ship activity in the Coral system is commercial and industrial; from what we know of their ship design, about a quarter of the ships, three hundred or so, have military-grade offensive and defensive capabilities, and many of those are troop transports, with minimal shielding and firepower. But the ones that are battleship class are both larger and tougher than our equivalent ships. We also estimate up to one hundred thousand Rraey forces on the surface, and they've begun to entrench for invasion.

"They're expecting us to fight for Coral, but our best intelligence suggests they expect us to launch an attack in four to six days—the amount of time it will take us to maneuver enough of our big ships into skip position. They know CDF prefers to make overwhelming displays of force, and that is going to take us some time."

"So when are we going to attack?" Alan asked.

"About eleven hours from now," Keyes said. We all shifted uncomfortably in our chairs.

"How can that work, sir?" Ron Jensen asked. "The only ships we'll have available are those that are already at skip distance, or those that will be in the next few hours. How many of those can there be?"

"Sixty-two, counting the *Modesto*," Keyes said, and our BrainPals downloaded the list of available ships. I briefly noted the presence of the *Hampton Roads* in the list; that was the ship to which Harry and Jesse were posted. "Six more ships are increasing speed to reach skip distance, but we can't count on them to be there when we strike."

"Christ, Keyes," said Ed McGuire. "That's five to one on the ships, and two to one on ground forces, assuming we can land them all. I think I like our tradition of overwhelming force better."

"By the time we have enough big ships in line to slug it out, they'll be ready for us," Keyes said. "We're better off sending in a smaller force while they're unprepared and doing as much damage as possible right now. There will be a larger force in four days: two hundred ships, packing heat. If we do our job right, they'll have short work of whatever remains of the Rraey forces."

Ed snorted. "Not that we'll be around to appreciate it."

Keyes smiled tightly. "Such lack of faith. Look, people, I know this isn't a happy hike on the moon. But we're not going to be stupid about this. We're not going to slug it out toe to toe. We're going to come in with targeted goals. We're going to hit troop transports on the way in to keep them from bringing in additional ground troops. We're going to land troops to disrupt mining operations before they get going and make it hard for the Rraey to target us without hitting their own troops and equipment. We'll hit commercial and industrial craft as opportunities present themselves, and we'll attempt to draw the big guns out of Coral orbit, so when our reinforcements arrive, we'll be in front and behind them."

"I'd like to go back to the part about the ground troops," Alan said. "We're landing troops and then our ships are going to try to draw Rraey ships *away*? Does that mean for us ground troops what I think it does?"

Keyes nodded. "We'll be cut off for at least three or four days."

"Swell," Jensen said.

"It's war, you jackasses," Keyes snapped. "I'm sorry it's not terribly convenient or comfortable for you."

"What happens if the plan doesn't work and our ships are shot out of the sky?" I asked.

"Well, then I suppose we're fucked, Perry," Keyes said. "But let's not go in with that assumption. We're professionals, we have a job to do. This is what we're trained for. The plan has risks, but they're not stupid risks, and if it works, we'll have the planet back and have done serious damage to the Rraey. Let's all go on the assumption we're going to make a difference, what do you say? It's a nutty idea but it just might work. And if you get behind it, the chances of it working are that much better. All right?"

More shifting in chairs. We weren't entirely convinced, but there was little to be done. We were going in whether we liked it or not.

"Those six ships that might make it to the party," Jensen said, "who are they?"

Keyes took a second to access the information. "The *Little Rock*, the *Mobile*, the *Waco*, the *Muncie*, the *Burlington* and the *Sparrowhawk*," he said.

"The *Sparrowhawk*?" Jensen said. "No shit."

"What about the *Sparrowhawk*?" I asked. The name was unusual; battalion-strength spaceships were traditionally named after mid-size cities.

"Ghost Brigades, Perry," Jensen said. "CDF Special Forces. Industrial-strength motherfuckers."

"I've never heard of them before," I said. Actually I thought I had, at some point, but the when and where escaped me.

"The CDF saves them for special occasions," Jensen said. "They don't play nice with others. It'd be nice to have them there when we got onto the planet, though. Save us the trouble of dying."

"It'd be nice, but it's probably not going to happen," Keyes said. "This is our show, boys and girls. For better or worse."

The *Modesto* skipped into Coral orbital space ten hours later and in its first few seconds of arrival was struck by six missiles fired at close range by a Rraey battle cruiser. The *Modesto*'s aft starboard engine array shattered, sending the ship wildly tumbling ass over head. My squad and Alan's were packed into a transport shuttle when the missiles hit; the force of the blast's sudden inertial shift slammed several of our soldiers into the sides of the transport. In the shuttle bay, loose equipment and material were flung across the bay, striking one of the other transports but missing ours. The shuttles, locked down by electromagnets, thankfully stayed put.

I activated Asshole to check the ship's status. The *Modesto* was severely damaged and active scanning by the Rraey ship indicated it was lining up for another series of missiles.

"It's time to go," I yelled to Fiona Eaton, our pilot.

"I don't have clearance from Control," she said.

"In about ten seconds we're going to get hit by another volley of missiles," I said. "There's your fucking clearance." Fiona growled.

Alan, who was also plugged into the *Modesto* mainframe, yelled from the back. "Missiles away," he said. "Twenty-six seconds to impact."

"Is that enough time to get out?" I asked Fiona.

"We'll see," she said, and opened a channel to the other shuttles. "This is Fiona Eaton, piloting Transport Six. Be advised I will perform emergency bay door procedure in three seconds. Good luck." She turned to me. "Strap in now," she said, and punched a red button.

The bay doors were outlined with a sharp shock of light; the crack of the doors blasting away was lost in the roar of escaping air as the doors tumbled out. Everything not strapped down launched out the hole; beyond the debris, the star field lurched sickeningly as the *Modesto* spun. Fiona fed thrust to the engines and waited just long enough for the debris to clear the bay door before cutting the electromagnetic tethers and launching the shuttle out the door. Fiona compensated for the *Modesto*'s spin as she exited, but just barely; we scraped the roof going out.

I accessed the launch bay's video feed. Other shuttles were blasting out of the bay doors by twos and threes. Five made it out before the second volley of missiles crashed into the ship, abruptly changing the trajectory of the *Modesto*'s spin and smashing several shuttles already hovering into the shuttle bay floor. At least one exploded; debris struck the camera and knocked it out.

"Cut your BrainPal feed to the *Modesto*," Fiona said. "They can use it to track us. Tell your squads. Verbally." I did.

Alan came forward. "We've got a couple of minor wounds back there," he said, motioning to our soldiers, "but nothing too serious. What's the plan?"

"I've got us headed toward Coral and I've cut the engines," Fiona said. "They're probably looking for thrust signatures and BrainPal transmissions to lock missiles on, so as long as we look dead, they might leave us alone long enough for us to get into the atmosphere."

"Might?" Alan said.

"If you've got a better plan, I'm all ears," Fiona said.

"I have no idea what's going on," Alan said, "so I'm happy to go with your plan."

"What the hell happened back there anyway?" Fiona said. "They hit us as we came out of skip drive. There's no way they could have known where we would be."

"Maybe we were just in the wrong place at the wrong time," Alan said.

"I don't think so," I said, and pointed out the window. "Look."

I pointed to a Rraey battle cruiser to port that was sparkling as missiles thrust away from the cruiser. At extreme starboard, a CDF cruiser popped into existence. A few seconds later the missiles connected, hitting the CDF cruiser broadside.

"No fucking way," Fiona said.

"They know exactly where our ships are coming out," Alan said. "It's an ambush."

"How the fuck are they doing that?" Fiona demanded. "What the *fuck* is going on?"

"Alan?" I said. "You're the physicist."

Alan stared at the damaged CDF cruiser, now listing and struck again by another volley. "No ideas, John. This is all new to me."

"This sucks," Fiona said.

"Keep it together," I said. "We're in trouble and losing it is not going to help."

"If you've got a better plan, I'm all ears," Fiona said again.

"Is it okay to access my BrainPal if I'm not trying to reach the *Modesto*?" I asked.

"Sure," Fiona said. "As long as no transmissions leave the shuttle, we're fine."

I accessed Asshole and pulled up a geographic map of Coral. "Well," I said, "I think we can pretty much say the attack on the coral-mining facility is canceled for today. Not enough of us made it off the *Modesto* for a realistic assault, and I don't think all of us are going to make it to the planet surface in one piece. Not every pilot's going to be as quick on her feet as you are, Fiona."

Fiona nodded, and I could tell she relaxed a little. Praise is always a good thing, especially in a crisis.

"Okay, here's the new plan," I said, and transmitted the map to Fiona and Alan. "Rraey forces are concentrated on the coral reefs and in the Colonial cities, here on this coast. So we go *here*"—I pointed to the big fat middle of Coral's largest continent—"hide in this mountain range and wait for the second wave."

"*If* they come," Alan said. "A skip drone is bound to get back to Phoenix. They'll know that the Rraey know they're coming. If they know that, they might not come at all."

"Oh, they'll come," I said. "They might not come when we want them to, is all. We have to be ready to wait for them. The good news here is Coral is human friendly. We can eat off the land for as long as we need to."

"I'm not in the mood to colonize," Alan said.

"It's not permanent," I said. "And it's better than the alternative."

"Good point," Alan said.

I turned to Fiona. "What do you need to do to get us to where we're going in one piece?"

"A prayer," she said. "We're in good shape now because we look like floating junk, but anything that hits the atmosphere that's larger than a human body is going to be tracked by Rraey forces. As soon as we start maneuvering, they're going to notice us."

"How long can we stay up here?" I asked.

"Not that long," Fiona said. "No food, no water, and even with our new, improved bodies, there's a couple dozen of us in here and we're going to run out of fresh air pretty fast."

"How long after we hit the atmosphere are you going to have to start driving?" I asked.

"Soon," she said. "If we start tumbling, I'll never get control of it again. We'll just fall down until we die."

"Do what you can," I said. She nodded. "All right, Alan," I said. "Time to alert the troops about the change in plan."

"Here we go," Fiona said, and hit the thrusters. The force of the acceleration pinned me back into the copilot's seat. No longer falling to the surface of Coral, we were aiming ourselves directly at it.

"Chop coming," Fiona said as we plunged into the atmosphere. The shuttle rattled like a maraca.

The instrumentation board let out a ping. "Active scanning," I said. "We're being tracked."

"Got it," Fiona said, banking. "We have some high clouds

coming up in a few seconds," she said. "They might help to confuse them."

"Do they usually?" I asked.

"No," she said, and flew into them anyway.

We came out several klicks east and were pinged again. "Still tracking," I said. "Aircraft 350 klicks out and closing."

"Going to get as close to the ground as I can before they get on top of us," she said. "We can't outrace them or outshoot them. The best we can hope is to get near the ground and hope some of their missiles hit the treetops and not us."

"That's not very encouraging," I said.

"I'm not in the encouragement business today," Fiona said. "Hold on." We dove sickeningly.

The Rraey aircraft were on us presently. "Missiles," I said. Fiona lurched left and tumbled us toward the ground. One missile overflew and trailed away; the other slammed into a hilltop as we crested.

"Nice," I said, and then nearly bit off my tongue as a third missile detonated directly behind us, knocking the shuttle out of control. A fourth missile concussed and shrapnel tore into the side of the shuttle; in the roaring of the air I could hear some of my men screaming.

"Going down," Fiona said, and struggled to right the shuttle. She was headed toward a small lake at an incredibly high speed. "We're going to hit the water and crash," she said. "Sorry."

"You did good," I said, and then the nose of the shuttle hit the surface of the lake.

Wrenching, tearing sounds as the nose of the shuttle ripped downward, shearing off the pilot's compartment from the rest of the shuttle. A brief register of my squad and Alan's as their compartment flies spinning away—a still shot with mouths open, screams silent in all the other noise, the roar as it flies over the shuttle nose that is already fraying apart as it whirls over the water. The tight, impossible spins as the nose sheds metal and instrumentation. The sharp pain of something striking my jaw and taking it away with it. Gurgling as I try to scream, gray Smart-Blood flung from the wound by centrifugal force. An unintentional glance at Fiona, whose head and right arm are somewhere behind us.

A *tang* of metal as my seat breaks off from the rest of the pilot's compartment and I am skipping on my back toward an outcropping of rock, my chair lazily spinning me in counterclockwise direction as my chair back bounces, bounces, bounces toward the stone. A quick and dizzying change in momentum as my right leg strikes the outcropping followed by a yellow-white burst of two-hundred-proof pain as the femur snaps like a pretzel stick. My foot swings directly up where my jaw used to be and I become perhaps the first person in the history of man to kick himself in his own uvula. I arc over dry land and come to ground somewhere where branches are still falling because the passenger compartment of the shuttle has just crashed through. One of the branches comes down heavily across my chest and breaks at least three of my ribs. After kicking myself in my own uvula, this is strangely anticlimactic.

I look up (I have no choice) and see Alan above me, hanging upside down, the splintered end of a tree branch supporting his torso by wedging itself into the space where his liver should be. SmartBlood is dripping off his forehead onto my neck. I see his eyes twitch, registering me. Then I get a message on my BrainPal.

You look terrible — he sends.

I can't respond. I can only stare.

I hope I can see the constellations where I'm going — he sends. He sends it again. He sends it again. He doesn't send it after that.

———

Chittering. Rough pads gripping my arm. Asshole recognizes the chittering and beams me a translation.

—*This one yet lives.*

—*Leave it. It will die soon. And the green ones aren't good eating. They're not ripe yet.*

Snorting, which Asshole translates as [laughter].

"Holy fuck, would you look at this," someone says. "This son of a bitch is alive."

Another voice. Familiar. "Let me see."

Silence. The familiar voice again. "Get this log off him. We're taking him back."

"Jesus Christ, boss," the first voice says. "Look at him. You ought to just put a fucking bullet in his brain. It'd be the merciful thing to do."

"We were told to bring back survivors," the familiar voice says. "Guess what, he survived. He's the *only* one that survived."

"If you think this qualifies as surviving."

"Are you done?"

"Yes, ma'am."

"Good. Now move the goddamn branch. The Rraey are going to be on our ass real soon."

Opening my eyes is like trying to lift metal doors. What allows me to do it is the blasting pain I feel as the branch is moved off my torso. My eyes fly open and I aspirate in the jawless equivalent of a scream.

"Christ!" the first voice says, and I see it's a man, blond, flinging away the massive branch. "He's awake!"

A warm hand on the side of what's left of my face. "Hey," the familiar voice says. "Hey. You're all right now. It's okay. You're safe now. We're taking you back. It's okay. You're okay."

Her face comes into view. I know the face. I was married to it. Kathy has come for me.

I weep. I know I'm dead. I don't mind.

I begin to slide away.

"You ever see this guy before?" I hear the blond guy ask.

"Don't be stupid," I hear Kathy say. "Of course not."

I'm gone.

Into another universe.

PART III

"Oh, you're awake," someone said to me as I opened my eyes. "Listen, don't try to speak. You're immersed in solution. You've got a breathing tube in your neck. And you don't have a jaw."

I glanced around. I was floating in a bath of liquid, thick, warm and translucent; beyond the tub I could see objects but couldn't focus on any of them. As promised, a breathing tube snaked from a panel at the side of the bath toward my neck; I tried to follow it all the way to my body, but my field of vision was blocked by an apparatus surrounding the lower half of my head. I tried to touch it, but I couldn't move my arms. That worried me.

"Don't worry about that," the voice said. "We've turned off your ability to move. Once you're out of the tub, we'll switch you back on again. Another couple of days. You still have access to your BrainPal, by the way. If you want to communicate, use that. That's how we're talking to you right now."

Where the fuck am I — I sent. *And what happened to me—*

"You're at the Brenneman Medical Facility, above Phoenix," the voice said. "Best care anywhere. You're in intensive care. I'm Dr. Fiorina, and I've been taking care of you since you got here. As for what happened to you, well, let's see. First off, you're in good shape now. So don't worry. Having said that, you lost your jaw, your tongue, most of your right cheek and ear. Your right leg was snapped off halfway down your femur; your left one suffered multiple fractures and your left foot was missing three toes and the heel—we think those were gnawed off. The good news there was that your spinal cord was severed below the rib cage, so you probably didn't feel much of that. Speaking of ribs, six were broken, one of which punctured your gallbladder, and you suffered general internal bleeding. Not to mention sepsis and a host of other general and specific infections brought on by having open wounds for days."

I thought I was dead — I sent. *Dying, anyway—*

"Since you're no longer in real danger of dying, I think I can tell that by all rights, you really *should* be dead," Dr. Fiorina said. "If you were an unmodified human, you *would* be dead. Thank your SmartBlood for keeping you alive; it clotted up before you could bleed out and kept your infections in check. It was a close thing, though. If you hadn't been found when you were, you probably would have been dead shortly after that. As it was, when they got you back to the *Sparrowhawk* they shoved you into a stasis tube to get you here. They couldn't do much for you on the ship. You needed specialized care."

I saw my wife — I sent. *She was the one who rescued me—*

"Is your wife a soldier?"

She's been dead for years—

"Oh," said Dr. Fiorina. Then, "Well, you were pretty far gone. Hallucinations aren't that unusual at that point. The bright tunnel and dead relatives and all of that. Listen, Corporal, your body still needs a lot of work, and it's easier for it to get done while you're asleep. There's nothing for you to do in there but float. I'm going to put you into sleep mode again for a while. The next time you wake up, you'll be out of the tub, and enough of your jaw will have grown back for you to have a real conversation. All right?"

What happened to my squad — I sent. *We were in a crash—*

"Sleep now," Dr. Fiorina said. "We can talk more when you're out of the tub."

I started to craft a truly irritated response but was hit by a wave of fatigue. I was out before I could think about how quickly I was going out.

"Hey, look who's back," this new voice said. "The man too dumb to die."

This time I wasn't floating in a vat of goo. I glanced over and made out where the voice was coming from.

"Harry," I said, as well as I could through an immobile jaw.

"The same," he said, bowing slightly

"Sorry I can't get up," I mumbled. "I'm a little banged up."

"'A little banged up,' he says," Harry said, rolling his eyes. "Christ on a pony. There was more of you missing than was there, John. I know. I saw them haul your carcass back up off of Coral. When they said you were still alive my jaw dropped to the floor."

"Funny," I said.

"Sorry," Harry said. "No pun intended. But you were almost unrecognizable, John. A mess of parts. Don't take this the wrong way, but I prayed you would die. I couldn't imagine they could piece you back together like this."

"Glad to disappoint you," I said.

"Glad to be disappointed," he said, and then someone else entered the room.

"Jesse," I said.

Jesse came around the bed and gave me a peck on the cheek. "Welcome back to the land of the living, John," she said, and then stepped back. "Look at us, together again. The three musketeers."

"Two and a half musketeers, anyway," I said.

"Don't be morbid," Jesse said. "Dr. Fiorina says you're going to make a full recovery. Your jaw should be completely grown by tomorrow, and the leg will be another couple days after that. You'll be skipping around in no time."

I reached down and felt my right leg. It was all there, or at least felt all there. I pulled back the bedcovers to get a better look, and there it was: my leg. Sort of. Right below the knee, there was a verdant welt. Above the welt my leg looked like my leg; below it, it looked like a prosthesis.

I knew what was going on. One of my squad had her leg blown off in battle and had it re-created in the same way. They attached a nutrient-rich fake limb at the point of amputation, and then injected a stream of nanobots into the merge area. Using your own DNA as a guide, the nanobots then convert the nutrients and raw materials of the fake limb into flesh and bone, connecting to already-existing muscles, nerves, blood vessels and so on. The ring of nanobots slowly moved down the fake limb until it had been converted into bone and muscle tissue; once they were done, they migrated through the bloodstream to the intestines and you shat them out.

Not very delicate, but a good solution—there was no surgery, no wait to create cloned parts, no clumsy artificial parts attached to your body. And it took only a couple of weeks, depending on the size of your amputation, to get the limb back. It was how they got back my jaw and, presumably, the heels and toes of my left foot, which were now all present and accounted for.

"How long have I been here?" I asked.

"You've been in this room for about a day," Jesse said. "You were in the tub for about a week before that."

"It took us four days to get here, during which time you were in stasis—did you know about that?" Harry asked. I nodded. "And it was a couple of days before they found you on Coral. So you've been out of it more or less for two weeks."

I looked at both of them. "I'm glad to see both of you," I said. "Don't get me wrong. But why are you here? Why aren't you on the *Hampton Roads*?"

"The *Hampton Roads* was destroyed, John," Jesse said. "They hit us right as we were coming in from our skip. Our shuttle barely got out of the bay and damaged its engines on the way out. We were the only ones. We drifted for almost a day and a half before the *Sparrowhawk* found us. Came real close to asphyxiation."

I recalled watching as a Rraey ship slugged a cruiser on its way in; I wondered if it had been the *Hampton Roads*. "What happened to the *Modesto*?" I asked. "Do you know?"

Jesse and Harry looked at each other. "The *Modesto* went down, too," Harry said, finally. "John, they *all* went down. It was a massacre."

"They can't *all* have gone down," I said. "You said you were picked up by the *Sparrowhawk*. And they came to get me, too."

"The *Sparrowhawk* came later, after the first wave," Harry said. "It skipped in far away from the planet. Whatever the Rraey used to detect our ships missed it, although they caught on after the *Sparrowhawk* parked itself above where you went down. That was a close thing."

"How many survivors?" I asked.

"You were the only one off the *Modesto*," Jesse said.

"Other shuttles got away," I said.

"They were shot down," Jesse said. "The Rraey shot down everything bigger than a bread box. The only reason our shuttle survived was that our engines were already dead. They probably didn't want to waste the missile."

"How many survivors, total?" I said. "It can't just be me and your shuttle."

Jesse and Harry stood mute.

"No fucking *way*," I said.

"It was an ambush, John," Harry said. "Every ship that skipped in was hit almost as soon as it arrived in Coral space. We don't know how they did it, but they did it, and they followed through by mopping up every shuttle they could find. That's why the *Sparrowhawk* risked us all to find you—because besides us, you're the *only* survivor. Your shuttle is the only one that made it to the planet. They found you by following the shuttle beacon. Your pilot flipped it on before you crashed."

I remembered Fiona. And Alan. "How many were lost?" I asked.

"Sixty-two battalion-strength cruisers with full crews," Jesse said. "Ninety-five thousand people. More or less."

"I feel sick," I said.

"This was what you'd call a good, old-fashioned clusterfuck," Harry said. "There's no doubt about that at all. So that's why we're still here. There's nowhere else for us to go."

"Well, that and they keep interrogating us," Jesse said. "As if we knew anything. We were already in our shuttle when we were hit."

"They've been dying for you to recover enough to talk to," Harry said to me. "You'll be getting a visit from the CDF investigators very soon, I suspect."

"What are they like?" I asked.

"Humorless," Harry said.

"You'll forgive us if we're not in the mood for jokes, Corporal Perry," Lieutenant Colonel Newman said. "When you lose sixty ships and one hundred thousand men, it pretty much leaves you in a serious state of mind."

All I had said was "broken up," when Newman asked how I was doing. I thought a slightly wry recognition of my physical condition was not entirely out of place. I guess I was wrong.

"I'm sorry," I said. "Although I wasn't really joking. As you may know, I left a rather significant portion of my body on Coral."

"How did you get to be on Coral, anyway?" asked Major Javna, who was my other interviewer.

"I seem to remember taking the shuttle," I said, "although the last part I did on my own."

Javna glanced over to Newman, as if to say, *Again with the jokes.* "Corporal, in your report on the incident, you mention you gave your shuttle pilot permission to blow the *Modesto* shuttle bay doors."

"That's right," I said. I had filed the report the night before, shortly after my visit from Harry and Jesse.

"On whose authority did you give that command?"

"On my own," I said. "The *Modesto* was getting hammered with missiles. I figured that a little individual initiative at that point in time would not be such a bad thing."

"Are you aware how many shuttles were launched across the entire fleet at Coral?"

"No," I said. "Although it seems to have been very few."

"Less than a hundred, including the seven from the *Modesto*," Newman said.

"And do you know how many made it to the Coral surface?" Javna said.

"My understanding is that only mine made it that far," I said.

"That's right," Javna said.

"So?" I said.

"So," Newman said, "that seems to have been pretty lucky for you that you ordered the doors blown just in time to get your shuttle out just in time to make it to the surface alive."

I stared blankly at Newman. "Do you *suspect* me of something, sir?" I said.

"You have to admit it's an interesting string of coincidences," Javna said.

"The hell I do," I said. "I gave the order *after* the *Modesto* was hit. My pilot had the training and the presence of mind to get us to Coral and close enough to the ground that I was able to survive. And if you recall, I only barely did so—most of my body was scraped over an area the size of Rhode Island. The only *lucky* thing was that I was found before I died. Everything else was skill or intelligence, either mine or my pilot's. Excuse me if we were trained well, *sir*."

Javna and Newman glanced at each other. "We're only following every line of inquiry," Newman said mildly.

"Christ," I said. "Think about it. If I really planned to betray the CDF and survive it, chances are I'd try to do it in a manner that didn't involve removing my own fucking jaw." I figured that in my condition, I just might be able to snarl at a superior officer and get away with it.

I was right. "Let's move on," Newman said.

"By all means, let's," I said.

"You mentioned you saw a Rraey battle cruiser firing on a CDF cruiser as it skipped into Coral space."

"That's correct," I said.

"Interesting you managed to see that," Javna said.

I sighed. "Are you going to do this all through the interview?" I said. "Things will move along a lot quicker if you're not always trying to get me to admit I'm a spy."

"Corporal, the missile attack," Newman said. "Do you remember whether the missiles were launched before or after the CDF ship skipped into Coral space?"

"My guess is that they were launched just before," I said. "At least it seemed that way to me. They knew when and where that ship was going to pop out."

"How do you think that's possible?" Javna asked.

"I don't know," I said. "I didn't even know how skip drives worked until a day before the attack. Knowing what I know, it doesn't seem like there should be any way to know a ship is coming."

"What do you mean, 'knowing what you know'?" Newman said.

"Alan, another squad leader"—I didn't want to say he was a friend, because I suspected they'd think that was suspicious— "said that skip drives work by transferring a ship into another universe just like the one it left, and that both its appearance and disappearance are phenomenally unlikely. If that's the case, it doesn't seem like you should be able to know when and where a ship will appear. It just does."

"What do you think happened here, then?" asked Javna.

"What do you mean?" I asked.

"As you say, there shouldn't be any way to know that a ship is skipping," Javna said. "The only way we can figure this ambush occurred is if someone tipped off the Rraey."

"Back to this," I said. "Look, even if we supposed the existence of a traitor, how did he do it? Even if he somehow managed to get word to the Rraey that a fleet was coming, there's no possible way he could have known where every ship was going to appear in Coral space—the Rraey were waiting for us, remember. They hit us while we were skipping into Coral space."

"So, again," Javna said. "What do you think happened here?"

I shrugged. "Maybe skipping isn't as unlikely as we thought it was," I said.

"Don't get too worked up over the interrogations," Harry said, handing me a cup of fruit juice he'd gotten for me at the medical center's commissary. "They gave us the same 'it's suspicious you survived' bit."

"How did you react?" I asked.

"Hell," Harry said. "I agreed with them. It's *damn* suspicious. Funny thing is, I don't think they liked that response any better. But ultimately, you can't blame them. The colonies have just gotten the rug pulled out from under us. If we don't figure out what happened at Coral, we're in trouble."

"Well, and there's an interesting point," I said. "What do you think happened?"

"I don't know," Harry said. "Maybe skipping isn't as unlikely as we thought." He sipped his own juice.

"Funny, that's what I said."

"Yeah, but I *mean* it," Harry said. "I don't have the theoretical physics background of Alan, God rest his soul, but the entire theoretical model on which we understand skipping has to be wrong somehow. Obviously, the Rraey have some way to predict, with a high degree of accuracy, where our ships are going to skip. How do they do that?"

"I don't think you're supposed to be able to," I said.

"That's exactly right. But they do anyway. So, quite obviously, our model of how skipping works is wrong. Theory gets thrown out the window when observation proves it isn't so. The question now is what is *really* going on."

"Any thoughts on it?" I said.

"A couple, although it's not really my field," Harry said. "I don't really have the math for it."

I laughed. "You know, Alan said something very much like that to me, not too long ago."

Harry smiled, and raised his cup. "To Alan," he said.

"To Alan," I said. "And all our absent friends."

"Amen," Harry said, and we drank.

"Harry, you said you were there when they brought me on board the *Sparrowhawk*," I said.

"I was," he said. "You were a mess. No offense."

"None taken," I said. "Do you remember anything about the squad that brought me in?"

"A little," Harry said. "But not too much. They kept us isolated away from the rest of the ship for most of the trip. I saw you in the sick bay when they brought you in. They were examining us."

"Was there a woman in my rescue party?"

"Yes," Harry said. "Tall. Brown hair. That's all I remember right off the top of my head. To be honest, I was paying more attention to you than who was bringing you in. I knew you. I didn't know them. Why?"

"Harry, one of the people who rescued me was my wife. I'd swear on it."

"I thought your wife is dead," Harry said.

"My wife *is* dead," I said. "But this was her. It wasn't Kathy as she was back when we were married. She was a CDF soldier, green skin and all."

Harry looked doubtful. "You were probably hallucinating, John."

"Yeah, but if I was hallucinating, why would I hallucinate Kathy as a CDF soldier? Wouldn't I just remember her as she was?"

"I don't know," Harry said. "Hallucinations, by definition, aren't real. It's not as if they follow rules. There's no reason you couldn't have hallucinated your dead wife as CDF."

"Harry, I know I sound a little nuts, but *I saw my wife*," I said. "I may have been chopped up, but my brain was working fine. I know what I saw."

Harry sat there for a moment. "My squad had a few days on the *Sparrowhawk* to stew, you know," he said. "We were crammed into a rec room with nowhere to go and nothing to do—they wouldn't even allow us access to the ship's entertainment servers. We had to be escorted to the head. So we talked about the crew of the ship, and about the Special Forces soldiers. And here's an interesting thing: None of us knew anyone who had ever entered the Special Forces from the general ranks. By itself, it doesn't mean anything. Most of us are still in our first couple of years of service. But it's interesting."

"Maybe you have to be in the service a long time," I said.

"Maybe," Harry said. "But maybe it's something else. They call them 'Ghost Brigades,' after all." He took another sip of his juice and then set it down on my bedside table. "I think I'm going to go do some digging. If I don't come back, avenge my death."

"I'll do as best as I can under the circumstances," I said.

"Do that," Harry said, grinning. "And see what you can find out, too. You have at least another couple of interrogation sessions coming up. Try a little interrogating of your own."

"What about the *Sparrowhawk*?" Major Javna said at our next interview session.

"I'd like to send a message to it," I said. "I want to thank them for saving my life."

"It's not necessary," Lieutenant Colonel Newman said.

"I know, but it's the polite thing to do," I said. "When someone keeps you from being eaten toe by toe by woodland animals, the least you can do is send a little note. In fact, I'd like to send the note directly to the guys who found me. How do I do that?"

"You can't," Javna said.

"Why not?" I asked, innocently.

"The *Sparrowhawk* is a Special Forces ship," Newman said. "They run silent. Communication between Special Forces ships and the rest of the fleet is limited."

"Well, that doesn't seem very fair," I said. "I've been in the service for over a year, and I never had a problem getting mail to my friends on other ships. You would think even Special Forces soldiers would want to hear from their friends in the outside universe."

Newman and Javna glanced at each other. "We're getting off track," Newman said.

"All I want to do is send a note," I said.

"We'll look into it," Javna said, in a tone that said, *No we won't.*

I sighed and then told them, for probably the twentieth time, about why I gave permission to blow the *Modesto*'s shuttle bay doors.

"How's your jaw?" Dr. Fiorina asked.

"Fully functional and ready to chew on something," I said. "Not that I don't like soup through a straw, but it gets monotonous after a while."

"I sympathize," Fiorina said. "Now let's look at the leg." I pulled down the covers and let him take a look—the ring was now halfway down the calf. "Excellent," he said. "I want you to start walking on that. The unprocessed portion will support your weight, and it'll be good to give the leg a little exercise. I'll give you a cane to use for the next couple of days. I notice you have some friends who come to visit you. Why don't you have them take you to lunch or something."

"You don't have to tell me twice," I said, and flexed the new leg a little. "Good as new," I said.

"Better," Fiorina said. "We've made a few improvements to the CDF body structure since you were enlisted. They've been incorporated into the leg, and the rest of your body will feel the benefit, too."

"Makes you wonder why the CDF just doesn't go all the way," I said. "Replace the body with something designed totally for war."

Fiorina looked up from his data pad. "You have green skin, cat's eyes, and a computer in your skull," he said. "How much *less* human do you want to be?"

"That's a good point," I said.

"Indeed," Fiorina said. "I'll have an orderly bring in that cane." He tapped his data pad to send the order.

"Hey, doc," I said. "Did you treat anybody else who came off the *Sparrowhawk*?"

"No," he said. "Really, Corporal, you were challenge enough."

"So none of the *Sparrowhawk* crew?"

Fiorina smirked. "Oh, no. They're Special Forces."

"So?"

"Let's just say they have special needs," Fiorina said, and then the orderly came in with my cane.

"You know what you can find out about the Ghost Brigades? Officially, I mean," Harry said.

"I'm guessing not a lot," I said.

"Not a lot is an overstatement," Harry said. "You can't find out a damn thing."

Harry, Jesse and I were lunching at one of Phoenix station's commissaries. For my first trip out, I suggested we go as far away from Brenneman as we could. This particular commissary was on the other side of the station. The view was nothing special—it overlooked a small shipyard—but was known stationwide for its burgers, and the reputation was justified; the cook, in his past life, had begun a chain of specialty hamburger restaurants. For a literal hole in the wall, it was constantly packed. But my and Harry's burgers were growing cold as we talked about the Ghost Brigades.

"I asked Javna and Newman about getting a note to the *Sparrowhawk* and got stonewalled," I said.

"Not surprised," Harry said. "Officially, the *Sparrowhawk* exists, but that's all you can find out. You can't find out anything about its crew, its size, its armament or its location. All the information isn't there. Do a more general search on Special Forces or 'Ghost Brigades' in the CDF database and you likewise get nothing."

"So you guys have nothing at all," Jesse said.

"Oh, I didn't say *that*," Harry said, and smiled. "You can't find out anything officially, but unofficially there's lots to know."

"And how do you manage to find information unofficially?" Jesse said.

"Well, you know," Harry said. "My sparkling personality does wonders."

"Please," Jesse said. "I'm eating here. Which is more than you two can say."

"So what did you find out?" I asked, and took a bite of my burger. It was fabulous.

"Understand that this is all rumor and innuendo," Harry said.

"Which means that it's probably more accurate than what we'd get officially," I said.

"Possibly," Harry granted. "The big news is that there is indeed a reason why they're called 'Ghost Brigades.' It's not an official designation, you know. It's a nickname. The rumor, which I've heard from more than one place, is that Special Forces members are dead people."

"Excuse me?" I said. Jesse looked up from her burger.

"Not real dead people, per se," Harry said. "They're not zombies. But there are a lot of people who sign up to join the CDF who die before their seventy-fifth birthday. When that happens, apparently the CDF doesn't just throw out your DNA. They use it to make Special Forces members."

Something hit me. "Jesse, you remember when Leon Deak died? What the medical technician said? 'A last-minute volunteer for the Ghost Brigades.' I thought it was just some kind of sick joke."

"How can they do that?" Jesse asked. "That's not ethical at all."

"Isn't it?" Harry said. "When you give your intent to sign up, you give the CDF the right to use whatever procedures necessary to enhance your combat readiness, and you can't be combat ready if you're dead. It's in the contract. If it's not ethical, it's at least legal."

"Yeah, but there's a difference between using my DNA to create a new body for me to use, and using the new body without *me* in it," Jesse said.

"Details, details," Harry said.

"I don't like the idea of my body running around on its own," Jesse said. "I don't think it's right for the CDF to do that."

"Well, that's not all they do," Harry said. "You know that these new bodies we have are deeply genetically modified. Well, apparently Special Forces bodies are even more modified than ours. The Special Forces soldiers are guinea pigs for new enhancements and abilities before they're introduced into the general population. And there are rumors that some of the modifications are truly radical— bodies modified to the point of not looking human anymore."

"My doctor said something about Special Forces soldiers having special needs," I said. "But even allowing for hallucinations, the people who rescued me looked human enough."

"And we didn't see any mutants or freaks on the *Sparrowhawk*," Jesse said.

"We weren't allowed full run of the ship, either," Harry pointed out. "They kept us in one area and kept us disconnected from everything else. We saw the sick bay and we saw the rec area, and that was it."

"People see Special Forces in battle and walking around all the time," Jesse said.

"Sure they do," Harry said. "But that's not saying that they see *all* of them."

"Your paranoia is acting up again, sweetie," Jesse said, and fed Harry a french fry.

"Thank you, precious," Harry said, accepting it. "But even throwing out the rumor about supermodified Special Forces, there's still enough there to account for John seeing his wife. It's not really Kathy, though. Just someone using her body."

"Who?" I said.

"Well, that's the question, isn't it," Harry said. "Your wife is dead, so they couldn't put her personality into the body. Either they have some sort of preformatted personality they put into Special Forces soldiers—"

"—or someone else went from an old body into her new one," I said.

Jesse shivered. "I'm sorry, John. But that's just creepy."

"John? You okay?" Harry said.

"What? Yeah, I'm fine," I said. "It's just a lot to deal with at one time. The idea that my wife could be alive—but not really—and that someone who *isn't* her is walking around in her skin. I think I almost preferred it when there was a possibility that I hallucinated her."

I looked over to Harry and Jesse. Both of them were frozen and staring.

"Guys?" I said.

"Speak of the devil," said Harry.

"What?" I said.

"John," Jesse said. "She's in line for a burger."

I spun around, knocking over my plate as I did so. Then I felt like I got dunked directly into a vat of ice.

"Holy shit," I said.

It was her. No doubt about it.

FOURTEEN

I started to get up. Harry grabbed my hand.

"What are you doing?" he asked.

"I'm going to go talk to her," I said.

"You sure you want to do that?" he asked.

"What are you talking about?" I asked. "Of course I'm sure."

"What I'm saying is that maybe you'd want Jesse or me to talk to her first," Harry said. "To see if she wants to meet you."

"Jesus, Harry," I said. "This isn't the sixth fucking grade. That's my wife."

"No it's *not*, John," Harry said. "It's someone entirely different. You don't know if she will even want to speak to you."

"John, even if she does speak to you, you're going to be two total strangers," Jesse said. "Whatever you're expecting out of this encounter, you're not going to get it."

"I'm not expecting anything," I said.

"We just don't want you to be hurt," Jesse said.

"I'll be fine," I said, and looked at them both. "Please. Let me go, Harry. I'll be fine."

Harry and Jesse looked at each other. Harry let go of my hand.

"Thank you," I said.

"What are you going to say to her?" Harry wanted to know.

"I'm going to tell her thanks for saving my life," I said, and got up.

By this time, she and two companions had got their orders and had made their way to a small table farther back in the commissary. I threaded my way to the table. The three of them were talking, but stopped as I approached. She had her back to me as I approached, and turned as her companions glanced up at me. I stopped as I got a look at her face.

It was different, of course. Beyond the obvious skin and eyes, she was so much younger than Kathy had been—a face that was as Kathy was half a century before. Even then, it was different; leaner than Kathy's had ever been, keeping with the CDF genetically-installed predisposition for fitness. Kathy's hair had always been a nearly uncontrolled mane, even as she aged and most other women switched to more matronly cuts; the woman in front of me kept her hair close on her head and off her collar.

It was the hair that was the most jarring. It'd been so long since I'd seen a person without green skin that it didn't register with me anymore. But the hair was nothing that I remembered.

"It's not nice to stare," the woman said, using Kathy's voice. "And before you ask, you're not my type."

Yes I am, a part of my brain said.

"I'm sorry, I don't really mean to intrude," I said. "I was just wondering if you might recognize me."

She flicked her eyes up and down on me. "I really don't," she said. "And trust me, we weren't in basic training together."

"You rescued me," I said. "On Coral."

She perked up a little at this. "No shit," she said. "No wonder I didn't recognize you. The last time I saw you, you were missing the lower half of your head. No offense. And no offense to this, either, but I'm amazed you're still alive. I wouldn't have bet on you to make it."

"I had something to live for," I said.

"Apparently," she said.

"I'm John Perry," I said, and held out my hand. "I'm afraid I don't know your name."

"Jane Sagan," she said, taking it. I held it a little longer than I should have. She had a slightly puzzled expression when I finally let go.

"Corporal Perry," one of her companions began; he had taken the opportunity to access information about me from his Brain-Pal, "we're kind of in a rush to eat here; we have to be back to our ship in a half hour, so if you don't mind—"

"Do you recognize me from anywhere else?" I asked Jane, cutting him off.

"No," she said, slightly frosty now. "Thanks for coming over, but now I'd really like to eat."

"Let me send you something," I said. "A picture. Through your BrainPal."

"That's really not necessary," Jane said.

"One picture," I said. "Then I'll go. Humor me."

"Fine," she said. "Hurry it up."

Among the few possessions that I had taken with me when I left Earth was a digital photo album of family, friends and places that I had loved. When my BrainPal activated, I had uploaded the photos into its onboard memory, a smart move in retrospect since my photo album and all my other Earthly possessions but one went down with the *Modesto*. I accessed one particular photo from the album and sent it to her. I watched as she accessed her BrainPal, and then turned again to look at me.

"Do you recognize me now?" I asked.

She moved fast, faster than even normal CDF, grabbed me, and slammed me against a nearby bulkhead. I was pretty sure I felt one of my newly repaired ribs crack. From across the commissary Harry and Jesse leaped up and moved in; Jane's companions moved to intercept. I tried to breathe.

"Who the fuck are you," Jane hissed at me, "and what are you trying to pull?"

"I'm John Perry," I wheezed. "I'm not trying to pull anything."

"Bullshit. Where did you get that picture?" she said, close up, low. "Who made it for you?"

"No one made it for me," I said, equally low. "I got that picture at my wedding. It's . . . my wedding photo." I almost said *our wedding photo,* but caught myself just in time. "The woman in the picture is my wife, Kathy. She died before she could enlist. They took her DNA and used it to make you. Part of her is in you. Part of you is in that picture. Part of what you are gave me this." I held up my left hand and showed her my wedding ring—my only remaining Earthly possession.

Jane snarled, picked me up and hurled me hard across the room. I skipped over a couple of tabletops, knocking away hamburgers, condiment packages and napkin holders before coming to rest on the ground. Along the way I clocked my head on a metal corner; there was the briefest of oozes coming from my temple. Harry and Jesse disengaged from their wary dance with Jane's companions and headed over to me. Jane stalked toward me but was stopped by her friends halfway across.

"Listen to me, Perry," she said. "You stay the fuck away from me from now on. The next time I see you you're going to wish I'd left you for dead." She stalked off. One of her companions followed after her; the other, who had spoken to me earlier, came over to us. Jesse and Harry got up to engage him, but he put his hands out in a sign of truce.

"Perry," he said. "What was that all about? What did you send her?"

"Ask her yourself, pal," I said.

"That's *Lieutenant* Tagore to you, Corporal." Tagore looked at Harry and Jesse. "I know you two," he said. "You were on the *Hampton Roads*."

"Yes, sir," Harry said.

"Listen to me, all of you," he said. "I don't know what the hell that was about, but I want to be very clear about this. Whatever it was, we weren't part of it. Tell whatever story you want, but if the words 'Special Forces' are anywhere in it, I'm going to make it my personal mission to ensure that the rest of your military career is short and painful. I'm not kidding. I *will* fuck your skull. Are we clear?"

"Yes, sir," Jesse said. Harry nodded. I wheezed.

"Get your friend looked after," Tagore said to Jesse. "He looks like he just got the shit kicked out of him." He walked out.

"Christ, John," Jesse said, taking a napkin and cleaning off my head wound. "What did you do?"

"I sent her a wedding photo," I said.

"That's subtle," Harry said, and looked around. "Where's your cane?"

"I think it's over by the wall she slammed me into," I said. Harry left to go get it.

"Are you okay?" Jesse said to me.

"I think I busted a rib," I said.

"That's not what I meant," she said.

"I know what you meant," I said. "And as far as that goes, I think something else is busted, too."

Jesse cupped my face with her hand. Harry came back with my cane. We limped back to the hospital. Dr. Fiorina was extremely displeased with me.

Someone nudged me awake. When I saw who it was, I tried to speak. She clapped a hand over my mouth.

"Quiet," Jane said. "I'm not supposed to be here."

I nodded. She took her hand away. "Talk low," she said.

"We could use BrainPals," I said.

"No," she said. "I want to hear your voice. Just keep it down."

"Okay," I said.

"I'm sorry about today," she said. "It was just unexpected. I don't know how to react to something like that."

"It's all right," I said. "I shouldn't have broken it to you that way."

"Are you hurt?" she asked.

"You cracked a rib," I said.

"Sorry about that," she said.

"Already healed," I said.

She studied my face, eyes flicking back and forth. "Look, I'm not your wife," she said suddenly. "I don't know who you think I am or what I am, but I was never your wife. I didn't know she existed until you showed me the picture today."

"You had to know about where you came from," I said.

"Why?" she said hotly. "We know we've been made from someone else's genes, but they don't tell us who they were. What would be the point? That person's not us. We're not even clones—I've got things in my DNA that aren't even from Earth. We're the CDF guinea pigs, haven't you heard?"

"I heard," I said.

"So I'm not your wife. That's what I've come here to say. I'm sorry, but I'm not."

"All right," I said.

"Okay," she said. "Good. I'm going now. Sorry about throwing you across the room."

"How old are you?" I asked.

"What? Why?" she asked.

"I'm just curious," I said. "And I don't want you to go yet."

"I don't know what my age has got to do with anything," she said.

"Kathy's been dead for nine years now," I said. "I want to know how long they bothered to wait before mining her genes to make you."

"I'm six years old," she said.

"I hope you don't mind if I say you don't look like most six-year-olds that I've met," I said.

"I'm advanced for my age," she said. Then, "That was a joke."

"I know," I said.

"People don't get that sometimes," she said. "It's because most of the people I know are around the same age."

"How does it work?" I said. "I mean, what's it like? Being six. Not having a past."

Jane shrugged. "I woke up one day and I didn't know where I was or what was going on. But I was already in this body, and I already knew things. How to speak. How to move. How to think and fight. I was told I was in Special Forces, and that it was time to start training, and my name was Jane Sagan."

"Nice name," I said.

"It was randomly selected," she said. "Our first names are common names, our last names are mostly from scientists and philosophers. There's a Ted Einstein and a Julie Pasteur in my squad. At first you don't know that, of course. About the names. Later you learn a little bit about how you were made, after they've let you develop your own sense of who you are. No one you know has many memories. It's not until you meet realborn that you know that anything's really different about you. And we don't meet them very often. We don't really mix."

" 'Realborn'?" I asked.

"It's what we call the rest of you," she said.

"If you don't mix, what were you doing at the commissary?" I said.

"I wanted a burger," she said. "It's not that we can't, mostly. It's that we don't."

"Did you ever wonder about who you were made from?" I asked.

"Sometimes," Jane said. "But we can't know. They don't tell us about our progies—the people we're made from. Some of us are made from more than one, you know. But they're all dead anyway. Have to be or they wouldn't use them to make us. And we don't know who knew them, and if the people who knew them get in the service, it's not like they'd find us most of the time. And you realborn die pretty damn fast out here. I don't know anyone else who's ever met a progie's relative. Or a husband."

"Did you show your lieutenant the picture?" I asked.

"No," she said. "He asked about it. I told him you sent me a picture of yourself, and that I trashed it. And I did, so the action would register if he looked. I haven't told anyone about what we said. Can I have it again? The picture?"

"Of course," I said. "I have others, too, if you want them. If you want to know about Kathy, I can tell you about her as well."

Jane stared at me in the dim room; in the low light she looked more like Kathy than ever. I ached just a little to look at her. "I don't know," she said, finally. "I don't know what I want to know.

Let me think about it. Give me that one picture for now. Please."

"I'm sending it now," I said.

"I have to go," she said. "Listen, I wasn't here. And if you see me anywhere else, don't let on that we've met."

"Why not?" I asked.

"It's important for now," she said.

"All right," I said.

"Let me see your wedding ring," Jane asked.

"Sure," I said, and slipped it off to let her look at it. She held it gingerly, and peered through it.

"It says something," she said.

" 'My Love is Eternal—Kathy,' " I said. "She had it inscribed before she gave it to me."

"How long were you married?" she asked.

"Forty-two years," I said.

"How much did you love her?" Jane asked. "Your wife. Kathy. When people are married for a long time, maybe they stay together out of habit."

"Sometimes they do," I said. "But I loved her very much. All the time we were married. I love her now."

Jane stood up, looked at me again, gave me back my ring, and left without saying good-bye.

"Tachyons," said Harry as he approached my and Jesse's breakfast table.

"Bless you," said Jesse.

"Very funny," he said, sitting down. "Tachyons may be the answer to how the Rraey knew we were coming."

"That's great," I said. "Now if only Jesse and I knew what tachyons were, we'd be a lot more excited about them."

"They're exotic subatomic particles," Harry said. "They travel faster than light and backward through time. So far they've just been a theory, because after all it's difficult to track something that is both faster than light and going backward in time. But the physics of skip drive theory allows for the presence of tachyons at any skip—just as our matter and energy translates into a different universe, tachyons from the destination universe travel back into the universe being left behind. There's a specific tachyon pattern a skip drive makes at a translation event. If you can spot tachyons forming that pattern, you'd know a ship with a skip drive was coming in—and when."

"Where do you hear this stuff?" I said.

"Unlike the two of you, I don't spend my days lounging about," Harry said. "I've made friends in interesting places."

"If we knew about this tachyon pattern or whatever it is, why didn't we do something about it before?" Jesse asked. "What you're saying is that we've been vulnerable all this time, and just been lucky so far."

"Well, remember what I said about tachyons being theoretical to this point," Harry said. "That's sort of an understatement. They're less than real—they're mathematical abstractions at best. They have no relation to the real universes in which we exist and move. No race of intelligence that we know of has ever used them for anything. They have no practical application."

"Or so we thought," I said.

Harry gave a hand motion of assent. "If this guess is correct, then it means that the Rraey have a technology that's well beyond what we have the capability to create ourselves. We're behind them in this technology race."

"So how do we catch up?" Jesse said.

Harry smiled. "Well, who said anything about catching up? Remember when we first met, on the beanstalk, and we talked about the colonies' superior technology? You remember how I suggested they got it?"

"Through encounters with aliens," Jesse said.

"Right," Harry said. "We either trade for it or take it in battle. Now, if there really is a way to track tachyons from one universe to another, we could probably develop the technology ourselves to do it. But that's going to take time and resources we don't have. Far more practical to simply take it from the Rraey."

"You're saying the CDF is planning to go back to Coral," I said.

"Of course we are," Harry said. "But the goal now isn't just to take the planet back. It's not even going to be the primary goal. Now, our primary goal is to get our hands on their tachyon detection technology and find a way to defeat it or use it against them."

"The last time we went to Coral we got our asses kicked," Jesse said.

"We're not going to have a choice, Jesse," Harry said gently. "We have to get this technology. If the technology spreads, every race out there will be able to track Colonial movement. In a very real sense, they'll know we're coming before we do."

"It's going to be a massacre again," Jesse said.

"I suspect they'll use a lot more of the Special Forces this time around," Harry said.

"Speaking of which," I said, and then told Harry of my encounter with Jane the night before, which I had been recounting to Jesse as Harry walked up.

"It looks like she's not planning to kill you after all," Harry said after I was finished.

"It must have been so strange to talk to her," Jesse said. "Even though you know she's not really your wife."

"Not to mention being just six years old. Man, that's odd," Harry said.

"It shows, too," I said. "The being six part. She doesn't have much emotional maturity. She doesn't seem to know what to do with emotions when she has them. She threw me across the room because she didn't know how else to deal with what she was feeling."

"Well, all she knows is fighting and killing," Harry said. "We have a life of memories and experiences to stabilize us. Even younger soldiers in traditional armies have twenty years of experiences. In a real sense, these Special Forces troops are children warriors. It's ethically borderline."

"I don't want to open any old wounds," Jesse said. "But do you see any of Kathy in her?"

I thought about it a moment. "She looks like Kathy, obviously," I said. "And I think I saw a little of Kathy's sense of humor in her, and a little of her temperament. Kathy could be impulsive."

"Did she ever throw you across the room?" Harry asked, smiling.

I grinned back. "There were a couple of times that if she could have, she would have," I said.

"Score one for genetics," Harry said.

Asshole suddenly clicked to life. Corporal Perry, the message read. Your presence is required at a briefing with General Keegan at 1000 hrs at Operational HQ in the Eisenhower Module of Phoenix Station. Be prompt. I acknowledged the message and told Harry and Jesse.

"And I thought I had friends in interesting places," Harry said. "You've been holding out on us, John."

"I have no idea what this is about," I said. "I've never met Keegan before."

"He's only the commander of the CDF Second Army," Harry said. "I'm sure it's nothing important."

"Funny," I said.

"It's 0915 now, John," Jesse said. "You'd better get moving. You want us to walk with you?"

"No, please finish breakfast," I said. "It'll be good for me to have the walk. The Eisenhower Module is only a couple of klicks around the station. I can make it in time." I got up, grabbed a donut to eat on the way, gave Jesse a friendly peck on the cheek and headed off.

In fact, the Eisenhower Module was more than a couple of klicks away, but my leg had finally grown in, and I wanted the exercise. Dr. Fiorina was right—the new leg did feel better than new, and overall I felt as if I had more energy. Of course, I had just recovered from injuries so grave it was a miracle that I lived. Anyone would feel like they had more energy after that.

"Don't turn around," Jane said, into my ear, from directly behind me.

I nearly choked on a bite of donut. "I wish you wouldn't keep sneaking up on me," I finally said, not turning around.

"Sorry," she said. "I'm not intentionally trying to annoy you. But I shouldn't be talking to you. Listen, this briefing you're about to go to."

"How do you know about that?" I said.

"It doesn't matter. What matters is that you agree to what they ask of you. Do it. It's the way you're going to be safe for what's coming up. As safe as can be."

"What's coming up?" I asked.

"You'll find out soon enough," she said.

"What about my friends," I said. "Harry and Jesse. Are they in trouble?"

"We're all in trouble," Jane said. "I can't do anything for them. I worked to sell you as it is. Do this. It's important." There was a quick touch of a hand on my arm, and then I could tell she was gone again.

"Corporal Perry," General Keegan said, returning my salute. "At ease."

I had been escorted into a conference room with more brass in it than an eighteenth-century schooner. I was easily the lowest-ranking person in the room; the next lowest rank, as far as I could tell, as a lieutenant colonel, was Newman, my esteemed questioner. I felt a little queasy.

"You look a little lost, son," General Keegan said to me. He looked, as did everyone in the room, and every soldier in the CDF, no more than in his late twenties.

"I feel a little lost, sir," I said.

"Well, that's understandable," Keegan said. "Please, sit down." He motioned to an empty chair at the table; I took it and sat down. "I've heard a lot about you, Perry."

"Yes, sir," I said, trying not to glance over at Newman.

"You don't sound excited about that, Corporal," he said.

"I'm not trying to be noticed, sir," I said. "Just trying to do my part."

"Be that as it may, you have been noticed," Keegan said. "A hundred shuttles managed to get launched over Coral, but yours was the only one to make it to the surface, in great part due to your orders to pop the shuttle bay doors and get the hell out of there." He jerked a thumb to Newman. "Newman here's been telling me all about it. He thinks we should give you a medal for it."

Keegan could have said, *Newman thinks you should star in the army's annual performance of* Swan Lake, and I would not have been as surprised as I was. Keegan noticed the expression on my face and grinned. "Yes, I know what you were thinking. Newman has the best straight face in the business, which is why he has the job he does. Well, what about it, Corporal? Think you deserve that medal?"

"Respectfully, sir, no," I said. "We crashed and there were no survivors other than myself. It's hardly meritorious service.

Beyond that, any praise in making it to the surface of Coral belongs to my pilot, Fiona Eaton."

"Pilot Eaton has already been decorated posthumously, Corporal," General Keegan said. "Small consolation to her, being dead as she is, but it's important to the CDF that such actions are noted somewhere by us. And despite your modesty, Corporal, you will be decorated as well. Others survived the Battle of Coral, but that was by luck. You took initiative and showed leadership in an adverse situation. And you've shown your capacity to think on your feet before. That firing solution against the Consu. Your leadership in your training platoon. Master Sergeant Ruiz made special note of your use of the BrainPal in the final training war game. I served with that son of a bitch, Corporal. Ruiz wouldn't compliment his mother for giving birth to him, if you know what I mean."

"I think I do, sir," I said.

"That's what I thought. So a Bronze Star for you, son. Congratulations."

"Yes, sir," I said. "Thank you, sir."

"But I didn't ask you here for that purpose," General Keegan said, and then motioned down the table. "I don't believe you've met General Szilard, who heads our Special Forces. At ease, no need to salute."

"Sir," I said, nodding in his direction, at least.

"Corporal," Szilard said. "Tell me, what have you heard about the situation over Coral?"

"Not very much, sir," I said. "Just conversations with friends."

"Really," Szilard said, dryly. "I would think your friend Private Wilson would have given you a comprehensive briefing by now."

I was beginning to realize that my poker face, never very good, was even less so these days. "Yes, of course we know about Private Wilson," Szilard said. "You might want to tell him that his snooping around is not nearly as subtle as he thinks it is."

"Harry will be surprised to hear it," I said.

"No doubt," Szilard said. "I also have no doubt he's also appraised you on the nature of the Special Forces soldiers. It's not a state secret, incidentally, although we don't put information on the Special Forces in the general database. Most of our time is spent on missions that require strict secrecy and confidentiality. We have very few opportunities to spend much time with the rest of you. Not much inclination either."

"General Szilard and Special Forces are taking the lead on our counterattack on the Rraey at Coral," General Keegan said. "While we intend to take the planet, our immediate concern is to isolate their tachyon detection apparatus, disable it without destroying it if we can, but destroy it if we must. Colonel Golden here"—Keegan motioned to a somber-looking man next to Newman—"believes we know where it is. Colonel."

"Very briefly, Corporal," Golden said. "Our surveillance before the first attack on Coral showed the Rraey deploying a series of small satellites in orbits around Coral. At first we thought them to be spy satellites to help the Rraey identify Colonial and troop movement on the planet, but now we think it's an array designed to spot tachyon patterns. We believe the tracking station, which compiles the data from the satellites, is on the planet itself, landed there during the first wave of the attack."

"We think it's on the planet because they figure it's safest there," General Szilard said. "If it were on a ship, there's a chance an attacking CDF ship might hit it, if only by sheer luck. And as you know, no ship but your shuttle got anywhere close to the Coral surface. It's a good bet it's there."

I turned to Keegan. "May I ask a question, sir."

"Go ahead," Keegan said.

"Why are you telling me this?" I asked. "I'm a corporal with no squad, platoon or battalion. I can't see why I should need to know this."

"You need to know this because you're one of the few survivors of the Battle of Coral, and the only one that survived by something more than chance," Keegan said. "General Szilard and his people believe, and I agree, that their counterattack has a better chance of succeeding if someone who was there in the first attack advises and observes the second. That means you."

"With all due respect, sir," I said. "My participation was minimal and disastrous."

"Less disastrous than almost everyone else's," Keegan said. "Corporal, I won't lie to you—I'd prefer we'd have someone else in this role. However, as it stands, we do not. Even if the amount of advice and service you can give is minimal, it is better than nothing at all. Besides, you've shown the ability to improvise and act quickly in combat situations. You will be of use."

"What would I do?" I asked. Keegan glanced over to Szilard.

"You'd be stationed on the *Sparrowhawk*," Szilard said. "They represent the Special Forces with the most experience in this particular situation. Your job would be to advise the *Sparrowhawk* senior staff on your experience at Coral, observe, and act as liaison between CDF regular forces and Special Forces if one is required."

"Would I fight?" I asked.

"You're a supernumerary," Szilard said. "You would most likely not be required to participate in the actual engagement."

"You understand that this assignment is highly unusual," Keegan said. "As a practical matter, due to differences in mission and in personnel, regular CDF and Special Forces are almost never mixed. Even in battles in which the two forces are engaged against a single enemy, both tend to perform separate and mutually exclusive roles."

"I understand," I said. I understood more than they knew. Jane was stationed on the *Sparrowhawk*.

As if following my train of thought, Szilard spoke up. "Corporal, I do understand that you had an incident with one of my people—one stationed on the *Sparrowhawk*. I need to know that there will be no other incidents like that one."

"Yes, sir," I said. "The incident was over a misunderstanding. A case of mistaken identity. It won't happen again."

Szilard nodded to Keegan. "Very well," Keegan said. "Corporal, given your new role, I think your rank is deficit to the task. You are hereby promoted to lieutenant, effective immediately, and will present yourself to Major Crick, CO of the *Sparrowhawk*, at 1500. That should give you enough time to get your things in order and say your good-byes. Any questions?"

"No, sir," I said. "But I have one request."

"Not the usual thing," Keegan said, after I had finished. "And in other circumstances—in both cases—I would say no."

"I understand, sir," I said.

"However, it will be arranged. And some good might come out of it. Very well, Lieutenant. You're dismissed."

Harry and Jesse met me as soon as they could after I messaged them. I told them of my assignment and promotion.

"You think Jane engineered this," Harry said.

"I know she did," I said. "She told me she had. As it happens, I may actually turn out to be useful in some way. But I'm sure she planted a bug in someone's ear. I'm on my way in just a few hours."

"We're being broken up again," Jesse said. "And what's left of Harry's and my platoon is being split up, too. Our platoon mates are getting assignments to other ships. We're waiting to hear our own assignments."

"Who knows, John," Harry said. "We'll probably be back at Coral with you."

"No, you won't," I said. "I asked General Keegan to advance you both out of general infantry and he agreed. Your first term of service is done. You've both been reassigned."

"What are you talking about?" Harry said.

"You've been reassigned to CDF's Military Research arm," I said. "Harry, they knew about you snooping around. I convinced them you'd do less harm to yourself and others this way. You're going to work on whatever we bring back from Coral."

"I can't do that," Harry said. "I don't have the math for it."

"I'm sure you won't let that stop you," I said. "Jesse, you're going to MR, too, on the support staff. It's all I could get you on short notice. It's not going be very interesting, but you can train for other roles while you're there. And you'll both be out of the line of fire."

"This isn't right, John," Jesse said. "We haven't served our time. Our platoon mates are going back out to fight while we'll be sitting here for something we didn't do. *You're* going back out there. I don't want this. I should serve my time." Harry nodded.

"Jesse, Harry, please," I said. "Look. Alan is dead. Susan and Thomas are dead. Maggie is dead. My squad and my platoon are all gone. Everyone I've ever cared about out here is gone but you two. I had a chance to keep you two alive and I took it. I couldn't do anything for anyone else. I can do something for you. I need you to be alive. You're all I have out here."

"You have Jane," Jesse said.

"I don't know what Jane is to me yet," I said. "But I know what you are to me. You're my family now. Jesse, Harry. You're my family. Don't be angry with me for wanting to keep you safe. Just *be* safe. For me. Please."

FIFTEEN

Sparrowhawk was a quiet ship. Your average troopship is filled with the sounds of people talking, laughing, yelling and going through the verbal motions of their lives. Special Forces soldiers don't do any of that crap.

As was explained to me by the *Sparrowhawk*'s CO when I came on board. "Don't expect people to talk to you," Major Crick said as I presented myself.

"Sir?" I said.

"The Special Forces soldiers," he said. "It's not anything personal, it's just we're not much for talking. When we're by ourselves, we communicate almost exclusively by BrainPal. It's faster, and we don't have a bias toward talking, like you do. We're born with BrainPals. The first time anyone ever talks to us, it's with one of them. So it's the way we talk most of the time. Don't be offended. Anyway, I've ordered the troops to speak to you if they have something they need to get across."

"That's not necessary, sir," I said. "I can use my BrainPal."

"You wouldn't be able to keep up," Major Crick said. "Your brain is set to communicate at one speed, and ours at another. Talking to realborn is like talking at half speed. If you've talked to any of us for a great deal of time, you might notice we seem abrupt and curt. It's a side effect of feeling like you're talking to a slow child. No offense."

"None taken, sir," I said. "You seem to communicate well."

"Well, as a CO, I spend a lot of time with non-Special Forces," Crick said. "Also, I'm older than most of my troops. I've picked up a few social graces."

"How old are you, sir?" I asked.

"I'll be fourteen next week," he said. "Now, I'll be having a staff meeting tomorrow at 0600. Until then, get yourself set up and comfortable, have some chow, and get a little rest. We'll talk more in the morning." He saluted and I was dismissed.

Jane was waiting in my quarters.

"You again," I said, smiling.

"Me again," she said, simply. "I wanted to know how you're getting along."

"Fine," I said. "Considering I've been on the ship for fifteen minutes."

"We're all talking about you," Jane said.

"Yes, I can tell by the endless chatter," I said. Jane opened her mouth to speak, but I held up my hand. "That was a joke," I said. "Major Crick told me about the BrainPal thing."

"It's why I like talking to you like this," Jane said. "It's not like talking to anyone else."

"I seem to remember you talking when you rescued me," I said.

"We were worried about being tracked then," Jane said. "Speaking was more secure. We also speak when we're out in public. We don't like to draw attention to ourselves when we don't have to."

"Why did you arrange this?" I asked her. "Getting me stationed here on the *Sparrowhawk*."

"You're useful to us," Jane said. "You have experience that may be useful, both on Coral and for another element of our preparation."

"What does that mean?" I asked.

"Major Crick will talk about it tomorrow at the briefing," Jane said. "I'll be there, too. I command a platoon and do intelligence work."

"Is that the only reason?" I asked. "That I'm useful?"

"No," Jane said, "but it's the reason that got you onto the ship. Listen, I won't be spending too much time with you. I have too many things to do preparing for our mission. But I want to know about her. About Kathy. Who she was. What she was like. I want you to tell me."

"I'll tell you about her," I said. "On one condition."

"What?" Jane asked.

"You have to tell me about you," I said.

"Why?"

"Because for nine years I've been living with the fact my wife is dead, and now you're here and it's messing me up inside," I said. "The more I know about you, the more I can get used to the idea that you're not her."

"I'm not that interesting," Jane said. "And I'm only six. That's hardly any time to have done anything."

"I've done more things in the last year than I did in all the years leading up to it," I said. "Trust me. Six years is enough."

"Sir, want company?" the nice young (probably four-year-old) Special Forces soldier said as he and four of his buddies held their meal trays at attention.

"The table's empty," I said.

"Some people prefer to eat alone," the soldier said.

"I'm not one of them," I said. "Please, sit, all of you."

"Thank you, sir," the soldier said, putting his tray on the table.

"I'm Corporal Sam Mendel. These are Privates George Linnaeus, Will Hegel, Jim Bohr, and Jan Fermi."

"Lieutenant John Perry," I said.

"So, what do you think of the *Sparrowhawk,* sir?" Mendel asked.

"It's nice and quiet," I said.

"That it is, sir," Mendel said. "I was just mentioning to Linnaeus that I don't think I've spoken more than ten words in about a month."

"You've just broken your record, then," I said.

"Would you mind settling a bet for us, sir?" Mendel said.

"Does it involve me doing anything strenuous?" I asked.

"No, sir," Mendel said. "We just want to know how old you are. You see, Hegel here is betting your age is older than twice the combined ages of our entire squad."

"How old are you all?" I asked.

"The squad has ten soldiers in it including myself," Mendel said, "and I'm the oldest. I'm five and a half. The rest are between two and five years old. Total age is thirty-seven years and about two months."

"I'm seventy-six," I said. "So he's right. Although any CDF recruit would have let him win his bet. We don't even enlist until we're seventy-five. And let me just say, there's something profoundly disturbing about being twice as old as your entire squad, combined."

"Yes, sir," Mendel said. "But on the other hand, we've all been in *this* life at least twice as long as you. So it comes out about even."

"I suppose it does at that," I said.

"It must be interesting, sir," Bohr said, a little down the table. "You had an entire life before this one. What was it like?"

"What was what like?" I said. "My life, or just having a life before this one?"

"Either," Bohr said.

I suddenly realized that none of the five other members of the table had even picked up their forks to eat. The rest of the mess hall, which had been alive with the telegraph-tapping sounds of utensils hitting trays, had also gone largely quiet. I recalled Jane's comment about everyone being interested in me. Apparently, she was right.

"I liked *my* life," I said. "I don't know that it was exciting or even interesting to anyone who didn't live it. But for me, it was a good life. As for the idea of having a life before this one, I didn't really think about it at the time. I never really thought about what this life would be like before I was in it."

"Why did you choose it, then?" Bohr asked. "You had to have some idea of what it was like."

"No, I didn't," I said. "I don't think any of us did. Most of us had never been in a war or in the military. None of us knew that they would take who we were and put it into a new body that was only partially what we were before."

"That seems kind of stupid, sir," Bohr said, and I was reminded that being two or whatever age he was, was not conducive to tact. "I don't know why anyone would choose to sign up for something when he really had no idea of what he was getting into."

"Well," I said, "you've also never been old. An unmodified person at seventy-five is a lot more willing to take a leap of faith than you might be."

"How different can it be?" Bohr asked.

"Spoken like a two-year-old who will never age," I said.

"I'm three," Bohr said, a little defensively.

I held up my hand. "Look," I said. "Let's turn this around for a minute. I'm seventy-six, and I did make a leap of faith when I joined the CDF. On the other hand, it *was* my choice. I didn't have to go. If you have a hard time imagining what it must be like for me, think about it on my end." I pointed to Mendel. "When I was five, I hardly knew how to tie my own shoes. If you can't imagine what it's like to be *my* age and joining up, imagine how hard it is for me to imagine being an adult at five years of age and knowing nothing *but* war. If nothing else, I have an idea of what life is like outside the CDF. What is it like for you?"

Mendel looked at his companions, who looked back at him. "It's not anything we usually think about, sir," Mendel said. "We don't know that there's anything unusual about it at first. Everyone we know was 'born' the same way. It's you who are the unusual ones, from our perspective. Having a childhood and living an entire other life before you get into this one. It just seems like an inefficient way to do things."

"Don't you ever wonder about what it would be like not to be in the Special Forces?" I asked.

"I can't imagine it," Bohr said, and the others nodded. "We're all soldiers together. It's what we do. It's who we *are*."

"That's why we find you so interesting," Mendel said. "This idea that this life would be a choice. The idea that there's another way to live. It's alien."

"What did you do, sir?" asked Bohr. "In your other life?"

"I was a writer," I said. They all looked at each other. "What?" I asked.

"Strange way to live, sir," Mendel said. "To get paid for stringing words together."

"There were worse jobs," I said.

"We don't mean to offend you, sir," Bohr said.

"I'm not offended," I said. "You just have a different perspective on things. But it does make me wonder why you do it."

"Do what?" Bohr said.

"Fight," I said. "You know, most people in the CDF are like me. And most people in the colonies are even more different from you than I am. Why would you fight for them? And with us?"

"We're *human,* sir," Mendel said. "No less than you are."

"Given the current state of my DNA, that's not saying much," I said.

"You know you're human, sir," Mendel said. "And so do we. You and we are closer than you think. We know about how the CDF picks its recruits. You're fighting for colonists you've never met—colonists who were your country's enemy at one point. Why do you fight for *them?"*

"Because they're human and because I said I would," I said. "At least, that's why I did at the start. Now I don't fight for the colonists. I mean, I do, but when it comes down to it, I fight—or did fight—for my platoon and my squad. I looked out for them, and they looked out for me. I fought because doing any less would have been letting them down."

Mendel nodded. "That's why we fight, too, sir," he said. "So that's one thing makes us all human together. That's good to know."

"It is," I agreed. Mendel grinned and picked up his fork to eat, and as he did, the room came alive with the clattering utensils. I looked up at the noise, and from a far corner saw Jane staring back at me.

Major Crick got right to the point at the morning briefing. "CDF intelligence believes the Rraey are frauds," he said. "And the first part of our mission is to find out if they're right. We're going to be paying a little visit to the Consu."

That woke me right up. Apparently I wasn't the only one. "What the hell do the Consu have to do with any of this?" asked Lieutenant Tagore, who sat directly to my left.

Crick nodded to Jane, who was sitting near him. "At the request of Major Crick and others, I did some research into some of the other CDF encounters with the Rraey to see if there's been any indication of technological evolution," Jane said. "Over the last hundred years, we've had twelve significant military encounters with the Rraey and several dozen smaller engagements, including one major encounter and six smaller engagements over the last five years. During this entire time, the Rraey technological curve has been substantially behind our own. This is due to a number of factors, including their own cultural biases against systematic technological advancement and their lack of positive engagement with more technologically advanced races."

"In other words, they're backward and bigoted," Major Crick said.

"In the case of skip drive technology, this is especially the case," Jane said. "Up until the Battle of Coral, Rraey skip technology was far behind ours—in fact, their current understanding of skip physics is directly based on information provided by the CDF a little over a century ago, during an aborted trade mission to the Rraey."

"Why was it aborted?" asked Captain Jung, from across the table.

"The Rraey ate about a third of the trade delegates," Jane said.

"Ouch," said Captain Jung.

"The point here is that given who the Rraey are and what their level of tech is, it's impossible that they could have gone from being so far behind us to so far ahead of us in one leap," Major Crick said. "The best guess is that they didn't—they simply got the tech for skip drive prediction from some other culture. We know everyone the Rraey know, and there's only one culture that we estimate has the technological ability for something like this."

"The Consu," said Tagore.

"The Consu indeed," agreed Crick. "Those bastards have a white dwarf yoked to the wheel. It's not unreasonable to assume they might have skip drive prediction licked as well."

"But why would they have anything to do with the Rraey?" asked Lieutenant Dalton, down near the end of the table. "The only time they deal with *us* is when they want a little exercise, and we're far more technologically advanced than the Rraey are."

"The thinking is that the Consu aren't motivated by technology like we are," Jane said. "Our tech is valueless to them much in the same way the secrets of a steam engine might be valueless to us. We think they're motivated by other factors."

"Religion," I said. All eyes shifted to me, and I suddenly felt like a choirboy who has just farted during a chapel service. "What I mean is, when my platoon was fighting the Consu, they started with a prayer that consecrated the battle. I said to a friend at the time that I thought the Consu thought they were baptizing the planet with the battle." More stares. "Of course, I could be wrong."

"You're not wrong," Crick said. "There's been some debate in the CDF about why the Consu fight at all, since it's clear that with their technology they could wipe out every other space-faring culture in the region without much of a second thought. The prevailing thought is that they do it for entertainment, like we play baseball or football."

"*We* never play football or baseball," said Tagore.

"Other humans do, jackass," Crick said with a grin, then sobered up again. "However, a significant minority of CDF's intelligence division believes that their battles have ritual significance, just as Lieutenant Perry has suggested. The Rraey may not be able to trade tech with the Consu on an equal basis, but they might have something else the Consu want. They might be able to give them their souls."

"But the Rraey are zealots themselves," Dalton said. "That's why they attacked Coral in the first place."

"They have several colonies, some less desirable than others,"

Jane said. "Zealots or not, they might see trading one of their less successful colonies for Coral as a good trade."

"Not so good for the Rraey on the traded colony," Dalton said.

"Really, ask me if I care about *them*," Crick said.

"The Consu have given the Rraey technology that puts them far ahead of the rest of the cultures in this part of space," Jung said. "Even for the mighty Consu, tipping the balance of power in the region has to have repercussions."

"Unless the Consu shortchanged the Rraey," I said.

"What do you mean?" Jung said.

"We're assuming that the Consu gave the Rraey the technological expertise to create the skip drive detection system," I said. "But it's possible that they simply gave a single machine to the Rraey, with an owner's manual or something like that so they could operate it. That way, the Rraey get what they want, which is a way to defend Coral from us, while the Consu avoid substantially disrupting the balance of power in the area."

"Until the Rraey figure out how the damn thing works," Jung said.

"Given their native state of technology, that could take years," I said. "Enough time for us to kick their ass and take that technology away from them. *If* the Consu did actually give them the technology. *If* the Consu only gave them a single machine. *If* the Consu actually give a shit about the balance of power in the region. A lot of 'ifs.'"

"And it is to find out the answer to those 'ifs' that we're going to drop in on the Consu," Crick said. "We've already sent a skip drone to let them know we're coming. We'll see what we can get out of them."

"What colony are we going to offer them?" Dalton asked. It was difficult to tell if he was joking.

"No colonies," Crick said. "But we have something that might induce them to give us an audience."

"What do we have?" Dalton asked.

"We have him," Crick said, and pointed at me.

"Him?" Dalton said.

"Me?" I said.

"You," Jane said.

"I'm suddenly confused and terrified," I said.

"Your two-shot firing solution allowed CDF forces to rapidly kill thousands of Consu," Jane said. "In the past, the Consu have been receptive to embassies from the colonies when they have included a CDF soldier who has killed a large number of Consu in battle. Since it was your firing solution specifically that allowed the quick end of those Consu fighters, their deaths accrue to you."

"You've got the blood of 8,433 Consu on your hands," Crick said.

"Great," I said.

"It *is* great," Crick said. "Your presence is going to get us in the door."

"What's going to happen to me *after* we get through the door?" I asked. "Imagine what we would do to a Consu who'd killed eight thousand of us."

"They don't think the same way we do about that," Jane said. "You should be safe."

"*Should* be," I said.

"The alternative is being blasted out of the sky when we show up in Consu space," Crick said.

"I understand," I said. "I just wish I'd been given a little more lead time to get used to the idea."

"It was a rapidly evolving situation," Jane said nonchalantly. And suddenly I got a BrainPal message. *Trust me*—it said. I looked back at Jane, who was looking placidly at me. I nodded, acknowledging one message while appearing to acknowledge the other.

"What do we do after they're done admiring Lieutenant Perry?" asked Tagore.

"If everything goes according to past encounters, we'll have the opportunity to ask up to five questions of the Consu," Jane said. "The actual number of questions will be determined by a contest involving combat between five of us and five of them. The combat is one on one. The Consu fight unarmed, but our fighters will be allowed knives to compensate for our lack of slashing arms. The one thing to be especially aware of is that in previous cases where we've had this ritual, the Consu we've fought were disgraced soldiers or criminals for whom this battle can restore honor. So needless to say, they're very determined. We get to ask as many questions as the number of contests we win."

"How do you win the contest?" Tagore asked.

"You kill the Consu, or it kills you," Jane said.

"Fascinating," Tagore said.

"One other detail," Jane said. "The Consu pick the combatants from those we bring with us, so protocol requires at least three times the number of selectable combatants. The only exempted member of the delegation is its leader, who is, by courtesy, the one human assumed to be above fighting with Consu criminals and failures."

"Perry, you get to be leader of the delegation," Crick said. "Since you're the one who killed eight thousand of the buggers, by their lights you'd be the natural leader. Also, you're the sole non-Special Forces soldier here, and you lack certain speed and strength modifications the rest of us have. If you were to get picked, you might actually get killed."

"I'm touched you care," I said.

"It's not that," Crick said. "If our star attraction was killed by a lowly criminal, it could jeopardize the chances of getting the Consu to cooperate."

"Okay," I said. "For a second there, I thought you were going soft."

"No chance of that," Crick said. "Now, then. We have forty-three hours until we reach skip distance. There will be forty of us in the delegation, including all platoon and squad leaders. I'll choose the rest from the ranks. That means that each of you will drill your soldiers in hand-to-hand combat between now and then. Perry, I've downloaded the delegation protocols to you; study them and don't screw up. Just after we skip, you and I will meet so I can give you the questions we want to ask, in the order we want to ask them. If we're good, we'll have five questions, but we have to be ready if we need to ask fewer. Let's get to it, people. You're dismissed."

During those forty-three hours, Jane learned about Kathy. Jane would pop into where I was, ask, listen and disappear, off to tend to her duties. It was a strange way to share a life.

"Tell me about her," she asked as I studied the protocol information in a forward lounge.

"I met her when she was in the first grade," I said, and then had to explain what first grade was. Then I told her the first memory I had of Kathy, which was of sharing paste for a construction paper project during the art period the first and second grades shared. How she caught me eating a little of the paste and told me I was gross. How I hit her for saying that, and she decked me in the eye. She got suspended for a day. We didn't speak again until junior high.

"How old are you in the first grade?" she asked.

"Six years old," I said. "As old as you are now."

"Tell me about her," she asked again, a few hours later, in a different place.

"Kathy almost divorced me once," I said. "We had been married for ten years and I had an affair with another woman. When Kathy found out she was furious."

"Why would she care that you had sex with someone else?" Jane asked.

"It wasn't really about the sex," I said. "It was that I lied to her about it. Having sex with someone else only counted as a hormonal weakness in her book. Lying counted as disrespect, and she didn't want to be married to someone who had no respect for her."

"Why didn't you divorce?" Jane asked.

"Because despite the affair, I loved her and she loved me," I said. "We worked it out because we wanted to be together. And anyway, she had an affair a few years later, so I guess you could say we evened up. We actually got along better after that."

"Tell me about her," Jane asked, later.

"Kathy made pies like you wouldn't believe," I told her. "She had this recipe for strawberry rhubarb pie that would knock you on your ass. There was one year where Kathy entered her pie in a state fair contest, and the governor of Ohio was the judge. First prize was a new oven from Sears."

"Did she win?" Jane asked.

"No, she got second, which was a hundred-dollar gift certificate to a bed and bath store. But about a week later she got a phone call from the governor's office. His aide explained to Kathy that for political reasons, he gave the first place award to the wife of an important contributor's best friend, but that ever since the governor had a slice of her pie, he couldn't stop talking about how great it was, so would she please bake another pie for him so he would shut up about the damn pie for once?"

"Tell me about her," Jane asked.

"The first time I knew I was in love with her was my junior year in high school," I said. "Our school was doing a performance of *Romeo and Juliet,* and she was selected as Juliet. I was the play's assistant director, which most of the time meant I was building sets or getting coffee for Mrs. Amos, the teacher who was directing. But when Kathy started having a little trouble with her lines, Mrs. Amos assigned me to go over them with her. So for two weeks after rehearsals, Kathy and I would go over to her house and work on her lines, although mostly we just talked about other things, like teenagers do. It was all very innocent at the time. Then the play went into dress rehearsal and I heard Kathy speaking all those lines to Jeff Greene, who was playing Romeo. And I got jealous. She was supposed to be speaking those words to *me.*"

"What did you do?" Jane asked.

"I moped around through the entire run of the play, which was four performances between Friday night and Sunday afternoon, and avoided Kathy as much as possible. Then at the cast party on Sunday night Judy Jones, who had played Juliet's nurse, found me and told me that Kathy was sitting on the cafeteria loading dock, crying her eyes out. She thought I hated her because I'd been ignoring her for the last four days and she didn't know why. Judy then added if I didn't go out there and tell Kathy I was in love with her, she'd find a shovel and beat me to death with it."

"How did she know you were in love?" Jane asked.

"When you're a teenager and you're in love, it's obvious to everyone but you and the person you're in love with," I said. "Don't ask me why. It just works that way. So I went out to the loading dock, and saw Kathy sitting there, alone, dangling her feet off the edge of the dock. It was a full moon and the light came down on her face, and I don't think I'd ever seen her more beautiful than she was right then. And my heart was bursting because I knew, I *really* knew, that I was so in love with her that I could never tell her how much I wanted her."

"What did you do?" Jane asked.

"I cheated," I said. "Because, you know, I *had* just happened to memorize large chunks of *Romeo and Juliet*. So, as I walked toward her on the loading dock, I spoke most of Act II, Scene II to her. 'But soft, what light through yonder window breaks? It is the east, and Juliet is the sun. Arise fair sun . . .' and so on. I knew the words before; it's just this time I actually *meant* them. And after I was done saying them, I went to her and I kissed her for the first time. She was fifteen and I was sixteen, and I knew I was going to marry her and spend my life with her."

"Tell me about how she died," Jane asked, just before the skip to Consu space.

"She was making waffles on a Sunday morning, and she had a stroke while she was looking for the vanilla," I said. "I was in the living room at the time. I remember her asking herself where she had put the vanilla and then a second later I heard a crash and a thump. I ran into the kitchen and she was lying on the floor, shaking and bleeding from where her head had connected with the edge of the counter. I called emergency services as I held her. I tried to stop the bleeding from the cut, and I told her I loved her and kept on telling her that until the paramedics arrived and pulled her away from me, although they let me hold her hand on the ambulance ride to the hospital. I was holding her hand when she died in the ambulance. I saw the light go out in her eyes, but I kept telling her how much I loved her until they took her away from me at the hospital."

"Why did you do that?" Jane asked.

"I needed to be sure that the last thing she heard was me telling her how much I loved her," I said.

"What is it like when you lose someone you love?" Jane asked.

"You die, too," I said. "And you wait around for your body to catch up."

"Is that what you're doing now?" Jane said. "Waiting for your body to catch up, I mean."

"No, not anymore," I said. "You eventually get to live again. You just live a different life, is all."

"So you're on your third life now," Jane said.

"I guess I am," I said.

"How do you like this life?" Jane asked.

"I like it," I said. "I like the people in it."

Out the window, the stars rearranged themselves. We were in Consu space. We sat there quietly, fading in with the silence of the rest of the ship.

SIXTEEN

"You may refer to me as Ambassador, unworthy though I am of the title," the Consu said. "I am a criminal, having disgraced myself in battle on Pahnshu, and therefore am made to speak to you in your tongue. For this shame I crave death and a term of just punishment before my rebirth. It is my hope that as a result of these proceedings I will be viewed as somewhat less unworthy, and will thus be released to death. It is why I soil myself by speaking to you."

"It's nice to meet you, too," I said.

We stood in the center of a football field–size dome that the Consu had constructed not an hour before. Of course, we humans could not be allowed to touch Consu ground, or be anywhere a Consu might again tread; upon our arrival, automated machines created the dome in a region of Consu space long quarantined to serve as a receiving area for unwelcome visitors such as ourselves. After our negotiations were completed, the dome would be imploded and launched toward the nearest black hole, so that none of its atoms would ever contaminate this particular universe again. I thought that last part was overkill.

"We understand you have questions you wish to ask concerning the Rraey," the ambassador said, "and that you wish to invoke our rites to earn the honor of speaking these questions to us."

"We do," I said. Fifteen meters behind me thirty-nine Special Forces soldiers stood at attention, all dressed for battle. Our information told us that the Consu would not consider this a meeting of equals, so there was little need for diplomatic niceties; also, inasmuch as any of our people could be selected to fight, they needed to be prepared for battle. I was dressed up a bit, although that was my choice; if I was going to pretend to be the leader of this little delegation, then by God I was at least going to look the part.

At an equal distance behind the Consu were five other Consu, each holding two long and scary-looking knives. I didn't have to ask what they were doing there.

"My great people acknowledge that you have correctly requested our rites and that you have presented yourselves in accordance to our requirements," said the ambassador. "Yet we would have still dismissed your request as unworthy, had you not also brought the one who so honorably dispatched our warriors to the cycle of rebirth. Is that one you?"

"I am he," I said.

The Consu paused and seemed to consider me. "Strange that a great warrior would appear so," the ambassador said.

"I feel that way, too," I said. Our information told us that once the request had been accepted, the Consu would honor it no matter how we comported ourselves at the negotiations, so long as we fought in the accepted fashion. So I felt comfortable being a little flip. The thinking on the matter, in fact, suggested the Consu preferred us that way; it helped reinforce their feelings of superiority. Whatever worked.

"Five criminals have been selected to compete with your soldiers," the ambassador said. "As humans lack the physical attributes of Consu, we have provided knives for your soldiers to use, if they so choose. Our participants have them, and by providing them to one of your soldiers they will choose who they will fight."

"I understand," I said.

"Should your soldier survive, it may keep the knives as a token of its victory," the ambassador said.

"Thanks," I said.

"We would not wish to have them back. They would be unclean," the ambassador said.

"Got it," I said.

"We will answer whatever questions you have earned after the contests," the ambassador said. "We will select opponents now." The ambassador grunted a shriek that would have shaved pavement off a road, and the five Consu behind him stepped forward, past it and me, and toward our soldiers, knives drawn. Not one flinched. That's discipline.

The Consu didn't spend much time selecting. They went in straight lines and handed the knives to whoever was directly in front of them. To them, one of us was as good as another. Knives were handed to Corporal Mendel, whom I had lunched with, Privates Joe Goodall and Jennifer Aquinas, Sergeant Fred Hawking and Lieutenant Jane Sagan. Wordlessly, each accepted their knives. The Consu retreated behind the ambassador, while the rest of our soldiers stepped back several meters from those who had been selected.

"You will begin each contest," the ambassador said, and then stepped back behind its fighters. Now there was nothing left but me and two lines of fighters fifteen meters from me on either side, patiently waiting to kill each other. I stepped to the side, still between the two rows, and pointed to the soldier and Consu closest to me.

"Begin," I said.

The Consu unfolded its slashing arms, revealing the flattened, razor-sharp blades of modified carapace and freeing again the smaller, almost human secondary arms and hands. It pierced the dome with a screech and stepped forward. Corporal Mendel dropped one of his knives, took the other in his left hand, and started straight at the Consu. When they got within three meters of each other, everything became a blur. Ten seconds after it started, Corporal Mendel had a slash across the length of his rib cage that went down to the bone, and the Consu had a knife jammed deeply into the soft part where its head melded with its carapace. Mendel had gotten his wound as he snuggled into the Consu's grasp, taking the cut for a clear shot at the Consu's most obvious weak spot. The Consu twitched as Mendel tugged the blade around, slicing the creature's nerve cord with a jerk, severing the secondary nerve bundle in the head from the primary brain in the thorax, as well as several major blood vessels. It collapsed. Mendel retrieved his knife and walked back to the rest of the Special Forces, keeping his right arm in to hold his side together.

I signaled Goodall and his Consu. Goodall grinned and danced out, holding his knives low with both hands, blades behind him. His Consu bellowed and charged, head first, slashing arms extended. Goodall returned the charge and then at the last second slid like a base runner on a close play. The Consu slashed down as Goodall slid under it, shaving the skin and ear from the left side of Goodall's head. Goodall lopped off one of the Consu's chitinous legs with a fast upward thrust; it cracked like a lobster claw and skitted off perpendicular to the direction of Goodall's movement. The Consu listed and toppled.

Goodall rotated on his ass, flipped his knives up, did a backward somersault and landed on his feet in time to catch his knives before they came down. The left side of his head was one big gray clot, but Goodall was still smiling as he lunged at his Consu, which was desperately trying to right itself. It flailed at Goodall with its arms too slow as Goodall pirouetted and drove the first knife like a spike into its dorsal carapace with a backward thrust, then reached around and with another backward thrust did the same to the Consu's thoracic carapace. Goodall spun 180 degrees so that he faced toward the Consu, gripped both blade handles and then violently cranked them in a rotating motion. The Consu jerked as the sliced contents of its body fell out in front and behind and then collapsed for a final time. Goodall grinned all the way back to his side, dancing a jig as he went. He'd clearly had fun.

Private Aquinas didn't dance, and she didn't look as if she was having any fun. She and her Consu circled each other warily for a good twenty seconds before the Consu finally lunged, bringing its slashing arm up, as if to hook Aquinas through her gut. Aquinas fell back and lost her balance, fumbling over backward. The Consu jumped her, pinned her left arm by spearing it in the soft gap between the radius and the ulna with its left slashing arm, and brought its other slashing arm up to her neck. The Consu moved its hind legs, positioning itself to provide leverage for a decapitating slash, then moved its right slashing arm slightly to the left, to give itself some momentum.

As the Consu slashed to remove her head, Aquinas grunted mightily and heaved her body in the direction of the cut; her left arm and hand shredded as soft tissues and sinews gave way to the force of her push, and then the Consu rolled as she added her momentum to its. Inside the grip of the Consu, Aquinas rotated and proceeded to stab hard through the Consu's carapace with her right hand and blade. The Consu tried to push her away; Aquinas wrapped her legs around the creature's midsection and hung in. The Consu got in a few stabs at Aquinas' back before it died, but the slashing arms weren't very effective close in to the Consu's own body. Aquinas dragged herself off the Consu's body and made it halfway toward the other soldiers before she collapsed and had to be carried away.

I now understood why I had been exempted from fighting. It wasn't just a matter of speed and strength, although clearly the Special Forces soldiers outpaced me in both. They employed strategies that came from a different understanding of what was an acceptable loss. A normal soldier would not sacrifice a limb like Aquinas just had; seven decades of the knowledge that limbs were irreplaceable, and that the loss of one could lead to death, worked against it. This wasn't a problem with Special Forces soldiers, who never could not have a limb grown back, and who knew their body's tolerance for damage was so much higher than a normal soldier could appreciate. It's not as if Special Forces soldiers didn't have fear. It just kicked in at a far later time.

I signaled Sergeant Hawking and his Consu to begin. For once, a Consu did not open its slashing arms; this one merely walked forward to the center of the dome and awaited its opponent. Hawking, meanwhile, hunched low and moved forward carefully, a foot at a time, judging the right moment to strike: forward, stop, side-step, stop, forward, stop and forward again. It was one of those cautious, well-considered tiny forward steps that the Consu lashed out like an exploding bug and impaled Hawking with both slashing arms, hefting him and hurling him into the air. On the downside of his arc, the Consu slashed viciously into him, severing his head and cutting him through the midsection. The torso and legs went in separate directions; the head dropped directly in front of ·

the Consu. The Consu considered it for a moment, then spiked it at the tip of its slashing arm and flung it hard in the direction of the humans. It bounced wetly as it struck the ground and then twirled over their heads, spraying brains and SmartBlood as it went.

During the previous four bouts, Jane had been standing impatiently at the line, flipping her knives in a sort of nervous twitch. Now she stepped forward, ready to begin, as did her opponent, the final Consu. I signaled for the two to start. The Consu took an aggressive step forward, flung its slashing arms wide, and screamed a battle cry that seemed loud enough to shatter the dome and suck us all into space, opening its mandibles extrawide to do so. Thirty meters away, Jane blinked and then flung one of her knives full force into the open jaw, putting enough force into the throw that the blade went all the way through the back of the Consu's head, the hilt jamming into the far side of the skull carapace. Its dome-shattering battle cry was suddenly and unexpectedly replaced by the sound of a big fat bug choking on blood and a skewer of metal. The thing reached in to dislodge the knife but died before it finished the motion, toppling forward and expiring with a final, wet swallow.

I walked over to Jane. "I don't think you were supposed to use the knives that way," I said.

She shrugged and flipped her remaining knife in her hands. "No one ever said I *couldn't*," she said.

The Consu ambassador glided forward to me, sidestepping the fallen Consu. "You have won the right to four questions," it said. "You may ask them now."

Four questions were more than we had expected. We had hoped for three, and planned for two; we had expected the Consu to be more of a challenge. Not that one dead soldier and several lopped-off body parts constituted a total victory by any means. Still, you take what you can get. Four questions would be just fine.

"Did the Consu provide the Rraey with the technology to detect skip drives?" I asked.

"Yes," the ambassador said, without elaborating further. Which was fine; we didn't expect the Consu to tell us any more than they had obligated themselves to. But the ambassador's answer gave us information on a number of other questions. Since the Rraey received the technology from the Consu, it was highly unlikely that they knew how it worked on a fundamental level; we didn't have to worry about them expanding their use of it or trading the technology to other races.

"How many skip drive detection units do the Rraey have?" We had originally thought to ask how many of these the Consu provided the Rraey, but on the off chance they made more, we figured it'd be best to be general.

"One," said the ambassador.

"How many other races that humans know of have the ability to detect skip drives?" Our third major question. We assumed that the Consu knew of more races than we did, so asking a more general question of how many races had the technology would be of no use to us; likewise asking them who else they had given the technology to, since some other race could have come up with the technology on its own. Not every piece of tech in the universe is a hand-me-down from some more advanced race. Occasionally people think these things up on their own.

"None," the ambassador said. Another lucky break for us. If nothing else, it gave us some time to figure out how to get around it.

"You still have one more question," Jane said, and pointed me back in the direction of the ambassador, who stood, waiting for my last query. So, I figured, what the hell.

"The Consu can wipe out most of the races in this area of space," I said. "Why don't you?"

"Because we love you," the ambassador said.

"Excuse me?" I said. Technically, this could have qualified as a fifth question, one the Consu was not required to answer. But it did anyway.

"We cherish all life that has the potential for *Ungkat*"—that last part was pronounced like a fender scraping a brick wall—"which is participation in the great cycle of rebirth," the ambassador said. "We tend to you, to all you lesser races, consecrating your planets so that all who dwell there may be reborn into the cycle. We sense our duty to participate in your growth. The Rraey believe we provided them with the technology you question after because they offered up one of their planets to us, but that is not so. We saw the chance to move both of your races closer to perfection, and joyfully we have done so."

The ambassador opened its slashing arms, and we saw its secondary arms, hands open, almost imploring. "The time in which your people will be worthy to join us will be that much closer now. Today you are unclean and must be reviled even as you are loved. But content yourself in the knowledge that deliverance will one day be at hand. I myself go now to my death, unclean in that I have spoken to you in your tongue, but assured again a place in the cycle because I have moved your people toward their place in the great wheel. I despise you and I love you, you who are my damnation and salvation both. Leave now, so that we may destroy this place, and celebrate your progression. Go."

"I don't like it," Lieutenant Tagore said at our next briefing, after the others and I recounted our experiences. "I don't like it at all. The Consu gave the Rraey that technology specifically so they could fuck with us. That damn bug said so itself. They've got us dancing like puppets on strings. They could be telling the Rraey right now that we're on our way."

"That would be redundant," Captain Jung said, "considering the skip drive detection technology."

"You know what I mean," Tagore shot back. "The Consu aren't going to do us any favors, since they clearly want us and the Rraey to fight, in order to 'progress' to another cosmic level, whatever the fuck *that* means."

"The Consu weren't going to do us any favors anyway, so enough about them," Major Crick said. "We may be moving according to their plans, but remember that their plans happen to coincide with our own up to a point. And I don't think the Consu give a shit whether we or the Rraey come out on top. So let's concentrate on what we're doing instead of what the Consu are doing."

My BrainPal clicked on; Crick sent a graphic of Coral, and another planet, the Rraey homeworld. "The fact that the Rraey are using borrowed technology means we have a chance to act, to hit them fast and hard, both on Coral and at their homeworld," he said. "While we have been chatting up the Consu, the CDF has been moving ships to skip distance. We have six hundred ships—nearly a third of our forces—in position and ready to skip. Upon hearing from us, the CDF will start the clock on simultaneous attacks on Coral and the Rraey homeworld. The idea is both to take back Coral and to pin down potential Rraey reinforcements. Hitting their homeworld will incapacitate the ships there and force Rraey ships in other parts of space to prioritize between assisting Coral or the Rraey homeworld.

"Both attacks are contingent on one thing: knocking out their ability to know we're coming in. That means taking their tracking station and knocking it offline—but *not* destroying it. The technology in that tracking station is technology the CDF can use. Maybe the Rraey can't figure it out, but we're farther along the technological curve. We blow the station only if there's absolutely no other choice. We're going to take the station and hold it until we can get reinforcements down to the surface."

"How long is that going to take?" asked Jung.

"The simultaneous assaults will be coordinated to begin four hours after we enter Coral space," Crick said. "Depending on the intensity of the ship-to-ship battles, we can expect additional troops to reinforce us sometime after the first couple of hours."

"Four hours after we *enter* Coral space?" Jung asked. "Not after we've taken the tracking station?"

"That's right," Crick said. "So we damn well better take the station, people."

"Excuse me," I said. "I'm troubled by a small detail."

"Yes, Lieutenant Perry," Crick said.

"The success of the offensive attack is predicated on our taking out the tracking station that keeps tabs on our ships coming in," I said.

"Right," said Crick.

"This would be the same tracking station that's going to be tracking *us* when we skip to Coral space," I said.

"Right," said Crick.

"I was on a ship that was tracked as it entered Coral space, if you'll recall," I said. "It was ripped apart and every single person who was on it but me died. Aren't you a little concerned that something very similar will happen to *this* ship?"

"We slid into Coral space undetected before," Tagore said.

"I'm aware of that, since the *Sparrowhawk* was the ship that rescued me," I said. "And believe me, I am grateful. However, that strikes me as the sort of trick you get away with once. And even if we skip into the Coral system far enough away from the planet to avoid detection, it would take us several hours to reach Coral. The timing is way off for that. If this is going to work, the *Sparrowhawk* has to skip in close to the planet. So I want to know how we're going to do that and still expect the ship to stay in one piece."

"The answer to that is really quite simple," Major Crick said. "We *don't* expect the ship to stay in one piece. We expect it to be blasted right out of the sky. In fact, we're counting on it."

"Pardon me?" I said. I looked around the table, expecting to see looks of confusion similar to the one I was wearing. Instead, everyone was looking somewhat thoughtful. I found this entirely too disturbing.

"High-orbit insertion, then, is it?" asked Lieutenant Dalton.

"Yes," Crick said. "Modified, obviously."

I gaped. "You've done this *before?*" I said.

"Not this exactly, Lieutenant Perry," Jane said, drawing my attention to her. "But yes, on occasion we've inserted Special Forces directly from spacecraft—usually when the use of shuttles is not an option, as it would be here. We have special dropsuits to insulate ourselves from the heat of entering the atmosphere; beyond that it's like any normal airdrop."

"Except that in this case, your ship is being shot out from under you," I said.

"That is the new wrinkle here," Jane admitted.

"You people are absolutely insane," I said.

"It makes for an excellent tactic," Major Crick said. "If the ship is torn apart, bodies are an expected part of the debris. The CDF just dropped a skip drone to us with fresh information on the tracking station's location, so we can skip above the planet in a good position to drop our people. The Rraey will think they've destroyed our assault before it happened. They won't even know we're there until we hit them. And then it will be too late."

"Assuming any of you survive the initial strike," I said.

Crick looked over to Jane and nodded. "The CDF has bought us a little wiggle room," Jane said to the group. "They've begun placing skip drives onto shielded missile clusters and tossing them into Coral space. When their shields are struck they launch the missiles, which are very hard for the Rraey to hit. We've gotten several Rraey ships over the last two days this way—now they're waiting a few seconds before they fire in order to accurately track anything that's been thrown at them. We should have anywhere from ten to thirty seconds before the *Sparrowhawk* is hit. That's not enough time for a ship that's not expecting the hits to do anything, but for us it's enough time to get our people off the ship. It's also maybe enough time for the bridge crew to launch a distracting offensive attack as well."

"The bridge crew is going to stay on the ship for this?" I asked.

"We'll be suited up with the others and operating the ship via BrainPal," Major Crick said. "But we'll be on the ship at least until our first missile volley is away. We don't want to operate Brain-Pals once we leave the ship until we're deep in Coral's atmosphere; it would give away the fact we're alive to any Rraey that might be monitoring. There's some risk involved, but there are risks for everyone who is on this ship. Which brings us, incidentally, to you, Lieutenant Perry."

"Me," I said.

"Quite obviously, you're not going to want to be on the ship when it gets hit," Crick said. "At the same time, you haven't trained for this sort of mission, and we also promised you would be here in an advisory capacity. We can't in good conscience ask for you to participate. After this briefing you'll be provided with a shuttle, and a skip drone will be dispatched back to Phoenix with your shuttle's coordinates and a request for retrieval. Phoenix keeps retrieval ships permanently stationed at skip distance; you should be picked up within a day. We'll leave you a month's worth of supplies, however. And the shuttle is equipped with its own emergency skip drones if it comes to that."

"So you're ditching me," I said.

"It's nothing personal," Crick said. "General Keegan will want to have a briefing on the situation and the negotiations with the Consu, and as our liaison with conventional CDF, you're the best person to do both."

"Sir, with your permission, I'd like to remain," I said.

"We really have no place for you, Lieutenant," Crick said. "You'd serve this mission better back on Phoenix."

"Sir, with all due respect, you have at least one hole in your ranks," I said. "Sergeant Hawking died during our negotiations with the Consu; Private Aquinas is missing half her arm. You won't be able to reinforce your ranks prior to your mission. Now, I'm not Special Forces, but I am a veteran soldier. I am, at the very least, better than nothing."

"I seem to recall you calling us all absolutely insane," Captain Jung said to me.

"You *are* all absolutely insane," I said. "So if you're going to pull this off you're going to need all the help you can get. Also, sir," I said, turning to Crick, "remember that I lost my people on Coral. I don't feel right about sitting out this fight."

Crick looked over to Dalton. "Where are we with Aquinas?" he asked.

Dalton shrugged. "We have her on an accelerated healing regimen," he said. "It hurts like a bitch to regrow an arm this fast, but she'll be ready when we make the skip. I don't need him."

Crick turned to Jane, who was staring at me. "It's your call, Sagan," Crick said. "Hawking was your noncom. If you want him, you can have him."

"I *don't* want him," Jane said, looking directly at me as she said it. "But he's right. I'm down a man."

"Fine," Crick said. "Get him up to speed, then." He turned to me. "If Lieutenant Sagan thinks you're not going to cut it, you're getting stuffed in a shuttle. Do you get me?"

"I get you, Major," I said, staring back at Jane.

"Good," he said. "Welcome to Special Forces, Perry. You're the first realborn we've ever had in our ranks, so far as I know. Try not to fuck up, because if you do, I promise you the Rraey are going to be the least of your problems."

Jane entered my stateroom without my permission; she could do that now that she was my superior officer.

"What the fuck do you think you are doing?" she said.

"You people are down a man," I said. "I'm a man. Do the math."

"I got you on this ship because I knew you'd be put on the shuttle," Jane said. "If you were rotated back into the infantry, you'd be on one of the ships involved in the assault. If we don't take the tracking station, you know what's going to happen to those ships and everyone in them. This was the only way I knew I was going to keep you safe, and you just threw it away."

"You could have told Crick you didn't want me," I said. "You heard him. He'd be happy to kick me into a shuttle and leave me floating in Consu space until someone got around to picking me up. You didn't because you know how fucking crazy this little plan is. You know you're going to need all the help you can get. I didn't know it was *you* I'd be under, you know, Jane. If Aquinas wasn't going to be ready, I could just as easily be serving under Dalton for this mission. I didn't even know Hawking was your noncom until Crick said something about it. All I know was that if this thing is going to work, you need everyone you've got."

"Why do you care?" Jane said. "This isn't your mission. You're not one of us."

"I'm one of you right now, aren't I?" I said. "I'm on this ship. I'm here, thanks to you. And I don't have anywhere else to be. My entire company got blown up and most of my other friends are dead. And anyway, as one of *you* mentioned, we're all human. Shit, I was even grown in a lab, just like you. This body was, at least. I might as well be one of you. So now I am."

Jane flared. "You have *no* idea what it's like to be one of us," she said. "You said you wanted to know about me. What part do you want to know? Do you want to know what it's like to wake up one day, your head filled with a library full of information—everything from how to butcher a pig to how to pilot a starship—but not to know your own name? Or that you even have one? Do you want to know what it's like never to have been a child, or even to have *seen* one until you step foot on some burned-out colony and see a dead one in front of you? Maybe you'd like to hear about how the first time any of us talk to a realborn we have to keep from hitting you because you speak so slow, move so slow and *think* so fucking slow that we don't know why they even bother to enlist you.

"Or maybe you'd like to know that every single Special Forces soldier dreams up a past for themselves. We know we're the Frankenstein monster. We know we're put together from bits and pieces of the dead. We look in a mirror and we know we're seeing somebody else, and that the only reason we exist is because they *don't*—and that they are lost to us forever. So we all imagine the person they could have been. We imagine their lives, their children, their husbands and wives, and we know that *none of these things can ever be ours.*"

Jane stepped over and got right in my face. "Do you want to

know what it's like to meet the husband of the woman you used to be? To see recognition in his face but not to feel it yourself, no matter how much you want to? To know he so desperately wants to call you a name that isn't yours? To know that when he looks at you he sees decades of life—and that you know none of it. To know he'd been with you, been *inside* of you, was there holding your hand when you died, telling you that he loved you. To know he can't make you realborn, but can give you continuation, a history, an idea of who you were to help you understand who you are. Can you even imagine what it's like to want that for yourself? To keep it safe at any cost?"

Closer. Lips almost touching mine, but no hint of a kiss in them. "You lived with me ten times longer than *I've* lived with me," Jane said. "You are the keeper of me. You can't imagine what that's like for me. Because you're *not one of us*." She stepped back.

I stared as she stepped back. "You're not her," I said. "You said it to me yourself."

"Oh, Christ," Jane snapped. "I *lied*. I *am* her, and you know it. If she had lived, she'd have joined the CDF and they would have used the same goddamned DNA to make her new body as they made me with. I've got souped-up alien shit in my genes but you're not fully human anymore either, and she wouldn't be either. The human part of me is the same as what it would be in her. All I'm missing is the memory. All I'm missing is my entire other life."

Jane came back to me again, cupped my face with her hand. "I am Jane Sagan, I know that," she said. "The last six years are mine, and they're real. This is *my* life. But I'm Katherine Perry, too. I want that life back. The only way I can have it is through you. You have to stay alive, John. Without you, I lose myself again."

I reached up to her hand. "Help me stay alive," I said. "Tell me everything I need to know to do this mission well. Show me everything I need to help your platoon do its job. Help me to help you, Jane. You're right, I don't know what it's like to be you, to be one of you. But I do know I don't want to be floating around in a damned shuttle while you're getting shot at. I need you to stay alive, too. Fair enough?"

"Fair enough," she said. I took her hand and kissed it.

SEVENTEEN

This is the easy part—Jane sent to me. *Just lean into it.*

The bay doors were blown open, an explosive decompression that mirrored my previous arrival into Coral space. I was going to have to come here one time without being flung out of a cargo bay. This time, however, the bay was clear of dangerous, untethered objects; the only objects in the *Sparrowhawk*'s hold were its crew and soldiers, decked out in airtight, bulky jumpsuits. Our feet were nailed to the floor, so to speak, by electromagnetic tabs, but just as soon as the cargo bay doors were blasted away and a sufficient distance to keep from killing any of us, the tabs would cut out and we'd tumble out the door, carried away by the escaping air—the cargo bay being overpressurized to make sure there'd still be enough lift.

There was. Our toe magnets cut out, and it was like being yanked by a giant through a particularly large mouse hole. As Jane suggested, I leaned into it, and suddenly found myself tumbling into space. This was fine, since we wanted to give the appearance of sudden, unexpected exposure to the nothingness of space, just in case the Rraey were watching. I was unceremoniously bowled out the door with the rest of the Special Forces, had a sickening moment of vertigo as *out* reoriented as *down*, and *down* was two hundred klicks toward the darkened mass of Coral, the terminal of day blistering east of where we were going to end up.

My personal rotation turned me just in time to see the *Sparrowhawk* exploding in four places, the fireballs originating on the far side of the ship from me and silhouetting the ship in flame. No sound or heat, thanks to the vacuum between me and the ship, but obscene orange and yellow fireballs made up visually for the lack in other senses. Miraculously, as I turned, I saw the *Sparrowhawk* fire missiles, launching out toward a foe whose position I could not register. Somebody was still on the ship when it got hit. I rotated again, in time to see the *Sparrowhawk* crack in two as another volley of missiles hit. Whoever was in the ship was going to die in it. I hoped the missiles they launched hit home.

I was falling alone toward Coral. Other soldiers might have been near me, but it was impossible to tell; our suits were nonreflective and we were ordered on BrainPal silence until we had cleared through the upper part of Coral's atmosphere. Unless I caught a glimpse of someone occluding a star, I wouldn't know they were there. It pays to be inconspicuous when you are planning to assault a planet, especially when someone above may still be looking for you. I fell some more and watched the planet of Coral steadily eat the stars on its growing periphery.

My BrainPal chimed; it was time for shielding. I signaled assent, and from a pack on my back a stream of nanobots flowed. An electromagnetic netting of the 'bots was weaved around me, sealing me in a matte-black globe and shutting out light. Now I was truly falling in darkness. I thanked God I was not naturally claustrophobic; if I were, I might be going bugshit at this moment.

The shielding was the key to the high-orbit insertion. It protected the soldier inside from the body-charring heat generated by entering the atmosphere in two ways. First, the shielding sphere was created while the soldier was still falling through vacuum, which lessened the heat transfer unless the soldier somehow touched the skin of the shield, which was in contact with the atmosphere. To avoid this, the same electromagnetic scaffolding that 'bots constructed the shield on also pinned the soldier in the center of the sphere, clamping down on movement. It wasn't very comfortable, but neither was burning up as air molecules ripped into your flesh at high speeds.

The 'bots took the heat, used some of the energy to strengthen the electromagnetic net that isolated the soldier, and then passed off as much of the rest of the heat as possible. They'd burn up eventually, at which point another 'bot would come up through the netting to take its place. Ideally, you ran out of the need for the shield before you ran out of shield. Our allotment of 'bots was calibrated for Coral's atmosphere, with a little extra wiggle room. But you can't help being nervous.

I felt vibration as my shield began to plow through Coral's upper atmosphere; Asshole rather unhelpfully chimed in that we had begun to experience turbulence. I rattled around in my little sphere, the isolating field holding but allowing more sway than I would have liked. When the edge of a sphere can transmit a couple thousand degrees of heat directly onto your flesh, any movement toward it, no matter how small, is a cause for concern.

Down on the surface of Coral, anyone who looked up would see hundreds of meteors suddenly streaking through the night; any suspicions of the contents of these meteors would be mitigated by the knowledge that they were most likely chunks of the human spacecraft the Rraey forces had just blasted out of the sky. Hundreds of thousands of feet up, a falling soldier and a falling piece of hull look the same.

The resistance of a thickening atmosphere did its work and slowed down my sphere; several seconds after it stopped glowing from the heat, it collapsed entirely and I burst through it like a new chick launched by slingshot from its shell. The view now was not of a blank black wall of 'bots but of a darkened world, lit in just a few places by bioluminescent algae, which highlighted the languid contours of the coral reefs, and then by the harsher lights of Rraey encampments and former human settlements. We'd be heading for the second sort of lights.

BrainPal discipline up—sent Major Crick, and I was surprised; I figured he had gone down with the *Sparrowhawk*. *Platoon leaders identify; soldiers form up on platoon leaders*—

About a klick to the west of me and a few hundred meters above, Jane suddenly lit up. She had not painted herself in neon in real life; that would have been a fine way to be killed by ground forces. It was simply my BrainPal's way of showing me where she was. Around me, close in and in the distance, other soldiers began to glow; my new platoon mates, showing themselves as well. We twisted ourselves in the air and began to drift together. As we moved, the surface of Coral transformed with a topological grid overlay on which several pinpoints glowed, clustered tightly together: the tracking station and its immediate environs.

Jane began to flood her soldiers with information. Once I had joined Jane's platoon, the Special Forces soldiers stopped the courtesy of speaking to me, reverting to their usual method of BrainPal communication. If I was going to fight with them, they figured, I had to do it on their terms. The last three days had been a communication blur; when Jane said that realborn communicated at a slower speed, it was an understatement of the case. Special Forces zapped each other messages faster than I could blink. Conversations and debates would be over faster than I could grasp the first message. Most confusingly of all, Special Forces didn't limit their transmissions to text or verbal messages. They utilized the BrainPal ability to transmit emotional information to send bursts of emotion, using them like a writer uses punctuation.

Someone would tell a joke and everyone who heard it would laugh with their BrainPal, and it was like being hit with little BBs of amusement, tunneling in your skull. It gave me a headache.

But it really was a more efficient way to "speak." Jane was outlining our platoon's mission, objectives and strategy in about a tenth of the time a briefing would take a commander in the conventional CDF. This is a real bonus when you're conducting your briefing as you and your soldiers fall toward the surface of a planet at terminal velocity. Amazingly, I was able to follow the briefing almost as fast as Jane reeled it off. The secret, I found, was to stop fighting it or attempt to organize the information the way I was used to getting it, in discrete chunks of verbal speech. Just accept you're drinking from the fire hose and open wide. It also helped that I didn't talk back much.

The tracking station was located on high ground near one of the smaller human settlements that the Rraey had occupied, in a small valley closed off at the end where the station lay. The ground was originally occupied by the settlement's command center and its outlying buildings; the Rraey had set up there to take advantage of the power lines and to cannibalize the command center's computing, transmitting and other resources. The Rraey had created defensive positions on and around the command center, but real-time imaging from the site (provided by a member of Crick's command team, who had basically strapped a spy satellite onto her chest) showed that these positions were only moderately armed and staffed. The Rraey were overconfident that their technology and their spaceships would neutralize any threat.

Other platoons would take the command center, locate and secure the machines that integrated the tracking information from the satellites and prepared it for upload to the Rraey spaceships above. Our platoon's job was to take the transmission tower from which the ground signal went to the ships. If the transmission hardware was advanced Consu equipment, we were to take the tower offline and defend it against the inevitable Rraey counterattack; if it was just off-the-shelf Rraey technology, we simply got to blow it up.

Either way, the tracking station would be down and the Rraey spaceships would be flying blind, unable to track when and where our ships would appear. The tower was set away from the main command center and fairly heavily guarded relative to the rest of the area, but we had plans to thin out the herd before we even hit the ground.

Select targets — Jane sent, and an overlay of our target area zoomed up on our BrainPals. Rraey soldiers and their machines glowed in infrared; with no perceived threat, they had no heat discipline. By squads, teams and then by individual soldiers targets were selected and prepared. Whenever possible we opted to hit the Rraey and not their equipment, which we could use ourselves after the Rraey were dealt with. Guns don't kill people, the aliens behind the triggers do. With targets selected, we all drifted slightly apart from each other; all that was left to do was wait until one klick.

One klick — one thousand meters up, our remaining 'bots deployed to a maneuverable parasail, arresting the speed of our descent with a stomach-churning yank, but allowing us to bob and weave on the way down and avoid each other as we went. Our sails, like our combat wear, were camouflaged against dark and heat. Unless you knew what you were looking for, you'd never see us coming.

Take out targets — Major Crick sent, and the silence of our descent ended in the tearing rattle of Empees unloading a downpour of metal. On the ground, Rraey soldiers and personnel unexpectedly had heads and limbs blasted away from their bodies; their companions had only a fraction of a second to register what had happened before the same fate was visited on them. In my case I targeted three Rraey stationed near the transmission tower; the first two went down without a peep; the third swung its weapon out into the darkness and prepared to fire. It was of the opinion I was in front rather than above. I tapped it before it had a chance to correct that assessment. In about five seconds, every Rraey who was outside and visible was down and dead. We were still several hundred meters up when it happened.

Floodlights came on and were shot out as soon as they blazed to life. We pumped rockets into entrenchments and foxholes, splattering Rraey who were sitting in them. Rraey soldiers streaming out of the command center and encampments followed the rocket trails back up and fired; the soldiers had long since maneuvered out of the way, and were now picking off the Rraey who were firing out in the open.

I targeted a landing spot near the transmission tower and instructed Asshole to compute an evasive maneuvering path down to it. As I came in, two Rraey burst through the door of a shack next to the tower, firing up in my general direction as they ran in the direction of the command center. One I shot in the leg; it went down, screeching. The other stopped firing and ran, using the Rraey's muscular, birdlike legs to pick up distance. I signaled for Asshole to release the parasail; it dissolved as the electrostatic filaments holding it together collapsed and the 'bots transformed into inert dust. I fell the several meters to the ground, rolled, came up and sighted the rapidly receding Rraey. It was favoring a fast, straight line of escape rather than a shifting, broken run that would have made it more difficult to target. A single shot, center mass, brought it down. Behind me, the other Rraey was still screeching, and then suddenly wasn't as an abrupt burp sounded. I turned and saw Jane behind me, her Empee still angling down toward the Rraey corpse.

You're with me — she sent and signaled me toward the shack. On our way in two more Rraey came through the door, sprinting, while a third laid down fire from inside the shack. Jane dropped to the ground and returned fire while I went after the fleeing Rraey. These ones were running broken paths; I got one but the other got away, pratfalling over an embankment to do so. Meanwhile, Jane had got tired of volleying with the Rraey in the shed and shot a grenade into the shack; there was a muffled squawk and then a loud bang, followed by large chunks of Rraey flopping out of the door.

We advanced and entered the shack, which was covered with the rest of the Rraey and housed a bank of electronics. A BrainPal scan confirmed it as Rraey communication equipment; this was the operation center for the tower. Jane and I backed out and pumped rockets and grenades into the shack. It blew up pretty; the tower was now offline, although there was still the actual transmission equipment at the top of the tower to deal with.

Jane got status reports from her squad leaders; the tower and surrounding areas were taken. The Rraey never got it together after the initial targeting. Our casualties were light, with no deaths to report in the platoon. The other phases of the attack were also going well; the most intense combat coming from the command center, in which the soldiers were going from room to room, blasting the Rraey as they went. Jane sent in two squads to reinforce the command center effort, had another squad police Rraey corpses and equipment at the tower, and had another two squads create a perimeter.

And you — she said, turning to me and pointing to the tower. *Climb up there and tell me what we've got.*

I glanced up at the tower, which was your typical radio tower: About 150 meters high and not much of anything besides the metal scaffolding holding up whatever it was at the top. It was the most impressive thing about the Rraey so far. The tower hadn't been here when the Rraey had arrived, so they must have put it up almost instantly. It was just a radio tower, but on the other hand, you try putting up a radio tower in a day and see how you do. The tower had spikes forming a ladder leading up toward the top; Rraey physiology and height were close enough to humans that I could use it. Up I went.

At the top was some dangerous wind and a car-size bundle of antennae and instrumentation. I scanned it with Asshole, who compared the visual image with its library of Rraey technology. It was all Rraey, all the time. Whatever information was being piped down from the satellites was being processed down at the command center. I hoped they managed to take the command center without accidentally blowing the stuff up.

I passed along the information to Jane. She informed me that the sooner I got down from the tower, the better chance I had of not getting crushed by debris. I didn't need further convincing. As I got down, rockets launched over my head directly into the instrument package at the top of the tower. The force of the blast caused the tower's stabilizing cables to snap with a metallic *tang* that promised beheading power to any who might have been in their path. The entire tower swayed. Jane ordered the tower base struck; the rockets tore into the metal beams. The tower twisted and collapsed, groaning all the way down.

From the command center area, the sounds of combat had stopped and there was sporadic cheering; whatever Rraey there were, were now gone. I had Asshole bring up my internal chronometer. It had not been quite ninety minutes since we hurled ourselves out of the *Sparrowhawk*.

"They had no idea we were coming," I said to Jane, and was suddenly surprised at the sound of my own voice.

Jane looked at me, nodded, and then looked over to the tower.

"They didn't. That was the good news. The bad news is, now they know we're here. This was the easy part. The hard part is coming up."

She turned and started shooting commands to her platoon. We were expecting a counterattack. A big one.

"Do you want to be human again?" Jane asked me. It was the evening before our landing. We were in the mess area, picking at food.

"Again?" I said, smiling.

"You know what I mean," she said. "Back into a real human body. No artificial additives."

"Sure," I said. "I've only got eight-some-odd years left to go. Assuming I'm still alive, I'll retire and colonize."

"It means going back to being weak and slow," Jane said, with usual Special Forces tact.

"It's not *that* bad," I said. "And there are other compensations. Children, for example. Or the ability to meet others and not have to subsequently kill them because they are the alien enemies of the colonies."

"You'll get old again and die," Jane said.

"I suppose I will," I said. "That's what humans do. This"—I held up a green arm—"isn't the usual thing, you know. And as far as dying goes, in any given year of CDF life, I'm far more likely to die than if I were a colonist. Actuarially speaking, being an unmodified human colonist is the way to go."

"You're not dead yet," Jane said.

"People seem to be looking out for me," I said. "What about you? Any plans to retire and colonize?"

"Special Forces don't retire," Jane said.

"You mean you're not allowed?" I asked.

"No, we're allowed," Jane said. "Our term of service is ten

years, just like yours, although with us there's no possibility of our term lasting any less than the full ten years. We just don't retire, is all."

"Why not?" I asked.

"We don't have any experience being anything else than what we are," Jane said. "We're born, we fight, that's what we do. We're good at what we do."

"Don't you ever want to stop fighting?" I asked.

"Why?" Jane asked.

"Well, for one thing, it dramatically cuts down your chances of violent death," I said. "For another thing, it'd give you a chance to live those lives you all dream about. You know, the pasts you make up for yourselves. Us normal CDF get to have that life before we go into the service. You could have it afterward."

"I wouldn't know what to do with myself," Jane said.

"Welcome to the human race," I said. "So you're saying no Special Forces people leave the service? Ever?"

"I've known one or two," Jane admitted. "But only a couple."

"What happened to them?" I asked. "Where did they go?"

"I'm not really sure," Jane said, vaguely. Then, "Tomorrow I want you to stick by me."

"I understand," I said.

"You're still too slow," Jane said. "I don't want you to interfere with my other people."

"Thanks," I said.

"I'm sorry," Jane said. "I realize that wasn't very tactful. But you've led soldiers. You know what my concern is. I'm willing to assume the risks involved in having you around. Others shouldn't have to."

"I know," I said. "I'm not offended. And don't worry. I'll carry my own weight. I plan to retire, you know. I have to stay alive a little bit longer to do that."

"Good that you have motivations," Jane said.

"I agree," I said. "You should think about retiring yourself. As you say, it's good to have a motivation to stay alive."

"I don't want to be dead," Jane said. "It's motivation enough."

"Well," I said, "if you ever change your mind, I'll send you a postcard from wherever I retire. Come join me. We can live on a farm. Plant some chickens. Raise some corn."

Jane snorted. "You can't be serious," she said.

"Actually, I am," I said, and I realized that I was.

Jane was silent for a moment, then said, "I don't like farming."

"How would you know?" I said. "You've never done it."

"Did Kathy like to farm?" Jane said.

"Not in the least," I said. "She barely had the tolerance to keep a garden going."

"Well, there you have it, then," Jane said. "Precedent is working against me."

"Give it some thought, anyway," I said.

"Maybe I will," Jane said.

Where the hell did I put that ammo clip — Jane sent, and then the rockets hit. I threw myself down to the ground as rock from Jane's position on the outcropping showered around me. I looked up and saw Jane's hand, twitching. I started up toward her, but was held back by a spray of fire. I wheeled backward and got back behind the rock where I had been positioned.

I looked down at the team of Rraey that had blindsided us; two of them were moving slowly up the hill toward us, while a third was helping a final one load another rocket. I had no doubts where that one was headed. I flipped a grenade toward the two advancing Rraey and heard them scrambling for cover. When it went off I ignored them and took a shot at the Rraey with the rocket. It went down with a thud and triggered its rocket with an expiring twitch; the blast scorched the face of its companion Rraey, who screamed and flailed about, clutching at its eyeband. I shot it in the head. The rocket arced up and away, far from me. I didn't bother to wait to see where it landed.

The two Rraey who had been advancing on my position started to scramble back up; I launched another grenade in their general direction to keep them busy and headed to Jane. The grenade landed directly at the feet of one of the Rraey and proceeded to take those feet off; the second Rraey dove back to the ground. I launched a second grenade at that one. He didn't avoid that one fast enough.

I kneeled over Jane, who was still twitching, and saw the chunk of rock that had penetrated the side of her head. SmartBlood was rapidly clotting, but small spurts were leaking out at the edges. I spoke to Jane, but she didn't respond. I accessed her BrainPal, to erratic emotional blips of shock and pain. Her eyes scanned sightlessly. She was going to die. I clutched her hand and tried to calm the sickening rush of vertigo and déjà vu.

The counterattack had begun at dawn, not long after we took the tracking station, and it had been more than heavy; it had been ferocious. The Rraey, realizing their protection had been ripped away, had struck back hard to reclaim the tracking station. Their attack was haphazard, belying the lack of time and planning, but it was relentless. Troopship after troopship floated over the horizon, bringing more Rraey into combat.

The Special Forces soldiers used their special blend of tactics and insanity to greet the first of these troopships with teams racing to meet the ships as they landed, firing rockets and grenades into the troop bays the moment the landing doors opened. The Rraey finally added air support and troops began landing without being blown up the moment they touched down. While the bulk of our forces were defending the command center and the Consu technological prize it hid, our platoon had been roaming the periphery, harassing the Rraey and making their forward progress that much more difficult. It's why Jane and I were on the outcropping of rock, several hundred meters from the command center.

Directly below our position, another team of Rraey were beginning to pick their way toward us. It was time to move. I launched two rockets at the Rraey to stall them, then bent down and grabbed Jane in a fireman's carry. Jane moaned, but I couldn't worry about that. I spotted a boulder Jane and I had used on our way out and launched myself toward it. Behind me, the Rraey took aim. Shots whipped by; shattered rock cut at my face. I made it behind the boulder, set Jane down, pumped a grenade in the Rraey's direction. As it went off, I ran out from behind the boulder and leaped at their position, covering much of the distance in two long strides. The Rraey squawked; they didn't quite know what to do with the human launching itself directly at them. I switched my Empee to automatic fire and got them at close range before they could get themselves organized. I hurried back to Jane and accessed her BrainPal. Still there. Still alive.

The next leg of our journey was going to be difficult; about a hundred meters of open ground lay between me and where I wanted to be, a small maintenance garage. Rraey infantry lines bordered the field; a Rraey aircraft was heading in the general direction I wanted to go, looking for humans to shoot. I accessed Asshole to locate the positions of Jane's people and found three near me: two on my side of the field, thirty meters away, and another on the other side. I gave them the order to cover me, grabbed Jane again and sprinted toward the shed.

The air erupted in gunfire. Turf jumped up at me as shots buried themselves into the ground where my feet had been or would be. I was hit with a glancing blow to my left hip; my lower half torqued as pain flashed through my side. That was going to leave a bruise. I managed to keep my footing and kept running. Behind me I could hear the crumpled thump of rockets impacting on Rraey positions. The cavalry had arrived.

The Rraey airship turned to get a shot at me, then swerved to avoid the rocket launched at it from one of our soldiers. It accomplished this, but wasn't so lucky at avoiding the other two rockets bearing down on it from the other direction. The first crashed into its engine; the second into the windshield. The aircraft dipped and listed, but remained aloft long enough to get kissed by a final rocket that lodged itself in the shattered windshield and erupted into the cockpit. The aircraft collapsed into the ground with a shuddering rumble as I made it to the shed. Behind me, the Rraey who had been targeting me turned their attention to Jane's people, who were causing them far more damage than I was. I tore open the door to the shed and slid myself and Jane into the recessed repair bay inside.

In the relative calm I reassessed Jane's vitals. The wound in her head was completely caked over with SmartBlood; it was impossible to see how much damage there was or how deep the rock fragments went into her brain. Her pulse was strong but her breathing was shallow and erratic. This is where the extra oxygen-carrying capacity of SmartBlood was going to come in handy. I was no longer certain she was going to die, but I didn't know what I could do to keep her alive on my own.

I accessed Asshole for options, and one was produced: the command center had housed a small infirmary. Its accommodations were modest but featured a portable stasis chamber. It would keep Jane stable until she could make it onto one of the ships and back to Phoenix for medical attention. I recalled how Jane and the crew of the *Sparrowhawk* stuffed me into a stasis chamber after my first trip to Coral. It was time to return the favor.

A series of bullets whined through a window above me; someone had remembered I was there. Time to move again. I plotted my next sprint, to a Rraey-built trench fifty meters in front of me, now occupied by Special Forces. I let them know I was coming; they obligingly laid down suppressing fire as I ran brokenly toward them. With that I was behind Special Forces lines again. The remainder of the trip to the command center proceeded with minimal drama.

I arrived just in time for the Rraey to begin lobbing shells at the command center. They were no longer interested in taking back their tracking station; now they were intent on destroying it. I looked up at the sky. Even through the brightness of the morning sky, sparkling flashes of light glistened through the blue. The Colonial fleet had arrived.

The Rraey weren't going to take very long to demolish the command center, taking the Consu technology with it. I didn't have very much time. I ducked into the building and ran for the infirmary as everyone else was streaming out.

There was something big and complicated in the command center infirmary. It was the Consu tracking system. God only knows why the Rraey decided to house it there. But they did. As a result, the infirmary was the one room in the entire command center that wasn't all shot up; Special Forces were under orders to take the tracking system in one piece. Our boys and girls attacked the Rraey in this room with flash grenades and knives. The Rraey were still there, stab wounds and all, splayed out on the floor.

The tracking system hummed, almost contentedly, flat and

featureless, against the infirmary wall. The only sign of input/ output capability was a small monitor and an access spindle for a Rraey memory module lying haphazardly on a hospital bedside table next to the tracking system. The tracking system had no idea that in just a couple of minutes it was going to be nothing more than a bundle of broken wiring, thanks to an upcoming Rraey shell. All our work in securing the damn thing was going to go to waste.

The command center rattled. I stopped thinking about the tracking system and placed Jane gently on an infirmary bed, then looked around for the stasis chamber. I found it in an adjoining storeroom; it looked like a wheelchair encased in a half cylinder of plastic. I found two portable power sources on the shelf next to the stasis chamber; I plugged one into the chamber and read the diagnostic panel. Good for two hours. I grabbed another one. Better safe than sorry.

I wheeled the stasis chamber over to Jane as another shell hit, this one shaking the entire command center and knocking out the power. I was pushed sideways by the hit, slipped on a Rraey body and cracked my head on the wall on the way down. A flash of light pulsed behind my eyes and then an intense pain. I cursed as I righted myself, and felt a small ooze of SmartBlood from a scrape on my forehead.

The lights flicked on and off for a few seconds, and in between those few flickers Jane sent a rush of emotional information so intense I had to grab the wall to steady myself. Jane was awake; aware and in those few seconds I saw what she thought she saw. Someone else was in the room with her, looking just like her, her hands touching the sides of Jane's face as she smiled at her. Flicker, flicker, and she looked like she looked the last time I saw her. The light flickered again, came on for good, and the hallucination went away.

Jane twitched. I went over to her; her eyes were open and looking directly at me. I accessed her BrainPal; Jane was still conscious, but barely.

"Hey," I said softly, and took her hand. "You've been hit, Jane. You're okay now, but I need to put you in this stasis chamber until we can get you some help. You saved me once, remember. So we're even after this. Just hold on, okay?"

Jane gripped my hand, weakly, as if to get my attention. "I saw her," she said, whispering. "I saw Kathy. She spoke to me."

"What did she say?" I asked.

"She said," Jane said, and then drifted a little before focusing in on me again. "She said I should go farming with you."

"What did you say to that?" I asked.

"I said okay," Jane said.

"Okay," I said.

"Okay," Jane said and slipped away again. Her BrainPal feed showed erratic brain activity; I picked her up and gently as possible placed her in the stasis chamber. I gave her a kiss and turned it on. The chamber sealed and hummed; Jane's neural and physiological indices slowed to a crawl. She was ready to roll. I looked down at the wheels to navigate them around the dead Rraey I'd stepped on a few minutes before and noticed the memory module poking out of the Rraey's abdomen pouch.

The command center rattled again with a hit. Against my better judgment I reached down, grabbed the memory module, walked over to the access spindle, and slammed it in. The monitor came to life and showed a listing of files in Rraey script. I opened a file and was treated to a schematic. I closed it and opened another file. More schematics. I went back to the original listing and looked at the graphic interface to see if there was a top-level category access. There was; I accessed it and had Asshole translate what I was seeing.

What I was seeing was an owner's manual for the Consu tracking system. Schematics, operating instructions, technical settings, troubleshooting procedures. It was all there. It was the next best thing to having the system itself.

The next shell broadsided the command center, knocked me square on my ass, and sent shrapnel tearing through the infirmary. A chunk of metal made a gaping hole through the monitor I was looking at; another punched a hole through the tracking system itself. The tracking system stopped humming and began making choking sounds; I grabbed the memory module, pulled it off the spindle, grabbed the stasis chamber's handles and ran. We were a barely acceptable distance away when a final shell plowed through the command center, collapsing the building entirely.

In front of us, the Rraey were retreating; the tracking station was the least of their problems now. Overhead, dozens of descending dark points spoke of landing shuttles, filled with CDF soldiers itching to take back the planet. I was happy to let them. I wanted to get off this rock as soon as possible.

In the near distance Major Crick was conferring with some of his staff; he motioned me over. I wheeled Jane to him. He glanced down at her, and then up at me.

"They tell me you sprinted the better part of a klick with Sagan on your back, and then went into the command center when the Rraey began shelling," Crick said. "Yet I seem to recall *you* were the one who called *us* insane."

"I'm not insane, sir," I said. "I have a finely calibrated sense of acceptable risk."

"How is she?" Crick asked, nodding to Jane.

"She's stable," I said. "But she has a pretty serious head wound. We need to get her into a medical bay as soon as possible."

Crick nodded over to a landing shuttle. "That's the first transport," he said. "You'll both be on it."

"Thank you, sir," I said.

"Thank *you*, Perry," Crick said. "Sagan is one of my best officers. I'm grateful you saved her. Now, if you could have managed to save that tracking system, too, you would really have made my day. All this work defending the goddamn tracking station was for nothing."

"About that, sir," I said, and held up the memory module. "I think I have something you might find interesting."

Crick stared at the memory module, and then scowled over at me. "No one likes an overachiever, Captain," he said.

"No, sir, I guess they don't," I said, "although it's lieutenant."

"We'll just see about that," Crick said.

Jane made the first shuttle up. I was delayed quite a bit.

EIGHTEEN

I made captain. I never saw Jane again.

The first of these was the more dramatic of the two. Carrying Jane to safety on my back through several hundred meters of open battlefield, and then placing her into a stasis chamber while under fire, would have been enough to get a decent write-up in the official report of the battle. Bringing in the technical schematics for the Consu tracking system as well, as Major Crick intimated, seemed a little like piling on. But what are you going to do. I got a couple more medals out of the Second Battle of Coral, and the promotion to boot. If anybody noticed that I had gone from corporal to captain in under a month, they kept it to themselves. Well, so did I. In any event, I got my drinks bought for me for several months afterward. Of course, when you're in the CDF, all the drinks are free. But it's the thought that counts.

The Consu technical manual was shipped directly to Military Research. Harry told me later that getting to flip through it was like reading God's scribble pad. The Rraey knew how to use the tracking system but had no idea how it worked—even with the full schematic it was doubtful that they would have been able to piece together another one. They didn't have the manufacturing

capability to do it. We knew that because *we* didn't have the manufacturing capability to do it. The theory behind the machine alone
was opening up whole new branches of physics, and causing the
colonies to reassess their skip drive technology.

Harry was tapped as part of the team tasked to spin out practical applications of the technology. He was delighted with the position; Jesse complained it was making him insufferable. Harry's
old gripe about not having the math for the job was rendered im-
material, since no one else really had the math for it, either. It certainly reinforced the idea that the Consu were a race with whom
we should clearly not mess.

A few months after the Second Battle of Coral, it was rumored
that the Rraey returned to Consu space, imploring the Consu for
more technology. The Consu responded by imploding the Rraey's
ship and hurling it into the nearest black hole. This still strikes me
as overkill. But it's just a rumor.

After Coral, the CDF gave me a series of cushy assignments,
beginning with a stint touring the colonies as the CDF's latest
hero, showing the colonists how The Colonial Defense Forces Are
Fighting For YOU! I got to sit in a lot of parades and judge a lot of
cooking contests. After a few months of that I was ready to do
something else, although it was finally nice to be able to visit a
planet or two and not have to kill everyone who was there.

After my PR stint, the CDF had me ride herd on new recruit
transport ships. I was the guy who got to stand in front of a thousand old people in new bodies and tell them to have fun, and then
a week later tell them that in ten years, three-quarters of them
would be dead. This tour of duty was almost unbearably bitter-
sweet. I'd go into the dining hall on the transport ship and see
groups of new friends coalescing and bonding, the way I did with
Harry and Jesse, Alan and Maggie, Tom and Susan. I wondered
how many of them would make it. I hoped all of them would. I

knew that most of them wouldn't. After a few months of this I asked for a different assignment. Nobody said anything about it. It wasn't the sort of assignment that anyone wanted to do for a very long time.

Eventually I asked to go back into combat. It's not that I like combat, although I'm strangely good at it. It's just that in this life, I am a soldier. It was what I agreed to be and to do. I intended to give it up one day, but until then, I wanted to be on the line. I was given a company and assigned to the *Taos*. It's where I am now. It's a good ship. I command good soldiers. In this life, you can't ask for much more than that.

Never seeing Jane again is rather less dramatic. After all, there's not much to not seeing someone. Jane took the first shuttle up to the *Amarillo*; the ship's doctor there took one look at her Special Forces designation and wheeled her into the corner of the medical bay, to remain in stasis until they returned to Phoenix and she could be worked on by Special Forces medical technicians. I eventually made it back to Phoenix on the *Bakersfield*. By that time Jane was deep in the bowels of the Special Forces medical wing and unreachable by a mere mortal such as myself, even if I was a newly minted hero.

Shortly thereafter I was decorated, promoted and made to begin my barnstorming tour of the colonies. I eventually received word from Major Crick that Jane had recuperated and was reassigned, along with most of the surviving crew of the *Sparrowhawk*, to a new ship called the *Kite*. Beyond that, it did no good to try to send Jane a message. The Special Forces were the Special Forces. They were the Ghost Brigades. You're not supposed to know where they're going or what they're doing or even that they're there in front of your own face.

I know they're there, however. Whenever Special Forces soldiers see me, they ping me with their BrainPals—short little bursts of emotional information, signifying respect. I am the only real-born to have served in Special Forces, however briefly; I rescued one of their own and I snatched mission success out of the jaws of partial mission failure. I ping back, acknowledging the salute, but otherwise I outwardly say nothing to give them away. Special Forces prefer it that way. I haven't seen Jane again on Phoenix or elsewhere.

But I've heard from her. Shortly after I was assigned to the *Taos*, Asshole informed me I had a message waiting from an anonymous sender. This was new; I had never received an anonymous message via BrainPal before. I opened it. I saw a picture of a field of grain, a farmhouse in the distance and a sunrise. It could have been a sunset, but that's not the feeling that I got. It took me a second to realize the picture was supposed to be a postcard. Then I heard her voice, a voice that I knew all my life from two different women.

You once asked me where Special Forces go when we retire, and I told you that I didn't know — she sent. *But I do know. We have a place where we can go, if we like, and learn how to be human for the first time. When it's time, I think I'm going to go. I think I want you to join me. You don't have to come. But if you want to, you can. You're one of us, you know.*

I paused the message for a minute, and started it up again, when I was ready.

Part of me was once someone you loved — she sent. *I think that part of me wants to be loved by you again, and wants me to love you as well. I can't be her. I can just be me. But I think you could love me if you wanted to. I want you to. Come to me when you can. I'll be here.*

That was it.

I think back to the day I stood before my wife's grave for the final time, and turned away from it without regret, because I knew that what she was was not contained in that hole in the ground. I entered a new life and found her again, in a woman who was entirely her own person. When this life is done, I'll turn away from it without regret as well, because I know she waits for me, in another, different life.

I haven't seen her again, but I know I will. Soon. Soon enough.

ACKNOWLEDGMENTS

This novel's path to publication was filled with excitement and surprises, and along the way so many people provided help and/or encouragement that it's hard to know where to begin.

But let's begin with the people who had a hand in putting together the book you have in your hands right this instant. First and foremost, thanks to Patrick Nielsen Hayden for buying the thing and then judiciously providing the edits. Thanks also to Teresa Nielsen Hayden for her inestimable good work, sense, advice and conversation. Donato Giancola provided the cover art, which is far cooler than I could have hoped for. He rocks, as does Irene Gallo, who I hope is by now a Beach Boys fan. Everyone else at Tor: All my thanks, and I promise to learn your names by the next book.

Early on several people offered their services as "beta testers," and I offered a space in the acknowledgments in return. Stupid me, I lost the full list (it's been a couple of years), but some of the people who provided feedback include (in no particular order) Erin Rourke, Mary Anne Glazar,

Christopher McCullough, Steve Adams, Alison Becker, Lynette Millett, James Koncz, Tiffany Caron and Jeffrey Brown. There were at least this many whom I've forgotten, and whose names I can't find in my E-mail archives. I beg their forgiveness, thank them for their efforts and promise that I'll keep better records next time. I *swear*.

I am indebted to the following science fiction/fantasy writers and editors for their help and/or friendship, with the hope of returning both favors: Cory Doctorow, Robert Charles Wilson, Ken MacLeod, Justine Larbalestier, Scott Westerfeld, Charlie Stross, Naomi Kritzer, Mary Anne Mohanraj, Susan Marie Groppi, and most particularly Nick Sagan, whose family name I appropriated in the novel (a tribute to his father), and who in addition to becoming a good friend is a valued member of the Nick and John Mutual Ass-Kicking Society. Much success to my agent, Ethan Ellenberg, who now has the task of convincing people to publish this book in all sorts of different languages.

Thanks to friends and family who helped keep me from going insane. In no particular order: Deven Desai, Kevin Stampfl, Daniel Mainz, Shara Zoll, Natasha Kordus, Stephanie Lynn, Karen Meisner, Stephen Bennett, Cian Chang, Christy Gaitten, John Anderson, Rick McGinnis, Joe Rybicki, Karen and Bob Basye, Ted Rall, Shelley Skinner, Eric Zorn, Pamela Ribon (you're up!), Mykal Burns, Bill Dickson and Regan Avery. A tip of the hat to Whatever readers and By The Way readers, who have had to suffer through me blogging about the publishing experience. A kiss and love to Kristine and Athena Scalzi, who had to live through it all. Mom, Heather, Bob, Gale, Karen, Dora, Mike, Brenda, Richard, all the nieces, nephews, cousins, aunts and uncles (there's a lot). I'm forgetting people, obviously, but I don't want to overstay my welcome.

Finally: Thank you, Robert A. Heinlein, for debts that have (since these acknowledgments are placed in the back of the book) become obvious.

JOHN SCALZI
June 2004